A Place Called
TRINITY

A Place Called
TRINITY

Delia Parr

St. Martin's Griffin
New York

www.stmartins.com

Library of Congress Cataloging-in-Publication Data

Parr, Delia.
    A place called Trinity / Delia Parr.—1st ed.
        p. cm.
    ISBN 0-312-28288-5 (hc)
    ISBN 0-312-31005-6 (pbk)
    1. Midwives—Fiction. 2. Mothers and daughters—Fiction.
    3. Runaway teenagers—Fiction. 4. Pennsylvania—Fiction. I. Title.

PS3566.A7527 P56 2002
813'.54—dc21   2001048661

First St. Martin's Griffin Edition: January 2003

10 9 8 7 6 5 4 3 2 1

Dedicated to the loving memory of my sisters,
Kathy and Susan

Wish you'd stayed here . . . just a little longer.

Acknowledgments

So many have blessed me in my journey as a writer and in the creation of this book. I need to thank my sister, medical consultant, and front-line "editor," Carol Beth Hatz, R.N., and her husband, Bob, for opening their summer home on Toms River to me each year. It gave me the freedom to spend endless hours each day at the beach dreaming and writing. Thanks also to my sisters, Patricia Schmidt and Joanne Lechleidner, R.N., and my brother, John Lechleidner, for believing in me. You give true meaning to the word "family."

I also want to thank Joseph and Peg Sheehan, treasured friends who never let me doubt myself; Linda Opdyke, the world's best critiquing partner, for teaching me how to be a writer; and Jeanne Seybold, colleague and sister-by-affection, for listening, advising, and keeping me honest.

Without the enthusiasm and unwavering support of my agent, Linda Kruger, this book would not have been possible, and I will never be able to adequately acknowledge the unbelievable dedication of my editor, Jennifer Enderlin, and my St. Martin's Press "family" in New York—you are the most talented group of publishing professionals in the world. I owe you everything . . . and more.

And finally, to my children, Matt, Brett, and Elizabeth, for loving such a "crazy ole mom" and making me proud of you.

May all your days be blessed . . . and may you all know the full measure of His never ending love.

A Place Called

TRINITY

Chapter

ONE

June 1830
Western Pennsylvania

A full two weeks later than expected, the blessed moment had finally arrived.

Surrounded by a cadre of female assistants, midwife Martha Cade knelt before her patient under the watchful gaze of the soon-to-be father. She was fully satisfied, if not pleasantly surprised, at how quickly Diana Tyler's labor was proceeding. At this rate, the babe should be born before breakfast, and Martha would finally be able to head for home.

Martha's hands were steady. Her mind was focused. Her heart was starting to race. In an atmosphere charged with great expectations and high emotion, yet underlined with a respectful dose of healthy concern, her spirit trembled with anticipation. With years of experience to guide her, she knew that soon—very, very soon—she would bear witness to life's greatest miracle.

She glanced up at Captain Tyler, who held his wife on his lap. A large man, he dwarfed the collapsible birthing stool Martha carried with her for deliveries. Beads of nervous perspiration dotted his brow. His lips were set in a firm line.

When he looked back at her, she answered the unspoken questions in his gaze with a reassuring smile. Then she turned all of her attention to his wife, Diana, a young woman with fine, wide hips and a strong constitution that should make for a quick and easy delivery. Her pregnancy had proceeded perfectly, with the exception of extending well beyond the time the baby had been expected.

Martha knew better than to count on anything as certain when dealing with pregnancy and birth, but for a first-time mother-to-be like Diana, each and every additional day that passed only fueled undue concern for her, not to mention discomfort.

Normally, Martha would simply have visited Diana every few days as her confinement neared an end to reassure her that all was well. The fact that Captain Tyler and his wife lived a full fifty miles from Martha's home in Trinity had made that impossible. When Captain Tyler summoned Martha two weeks ago, expecting birth was imminent, nature surprised everyone but Martha, who always left home prepared for the unexpected.

She did not relish being so far away from home and her daughter, Victoria, now a young woman of seventeen, for so long. Martha's duties as the only midwife and healer in the area, however, carried heavy responsibilities and offered rewards, both monetary and spiritual, that often meant sacrifice—sacrifice she had been forced to make once she had been left widowed with two children to support and raise on her own.

Although burdened with the sorrows of early widowhood more than ten years ago, Martha had been blessed with a supportive family. Her son, Oliver, now lived in Boston, where he had been practicing law for the past five years. She and Victoria shared a room in her brother's tavern in Trinity, which allowed Martha to leave to attend her patients, confident her brother, James, and his wife, Lydia, would provide guidance to Victoria while Martha was away.

Freed from other concerns, Martha had been able to give her full attention to Diana these past two weeks, offering comfort and reassurance. With the birth of Diana's child now truly imminent, Martha was both excited and thrilled, and she studied her patient closely.

Damp tendrils of dark hair framed Diana's face. Her eyes were dulled from pain as she sat on her husband's lap. Martha offered her a broad smile as she lifted the woman's birthing gown and placed her hands on Diana's knees. "When the next forcing pain starts, I want you to push. Hard. One more good forcing pain should do it. This babe is in a mighty big hurry to get here," she teased.

Diana's eyes lit with surprise, and she laughed nervously. "A hurry? He's two weeks late!"

"Well, he or she is making up for lost time. So when I tell you, push. Push hard. And keep your feet flat on the floor. Nature and I will do the rest." She turned and nodded to the women on either side of her who had a firm but gentle hold on Diana's hands. "Our work is just about done, ladies."

When the forcing pain began, Diana's smile quickly disappeared. Her brows knitted together, and she clenched her teeth. Deep groans spurred Martha to action, and she rested her hands on the soft, warm flesh surrounding the birth canal.

"Push!"

Diana's groans turned into one short, shrill scream as the baby's head emerged, and Martha cradled it in the palms of her hands as more fluids emerged.

"Relax. Just relax a moment. That's a good mama. Take a breath," she urged as the pain receded and Diana closed her eyes. "Now another good, deep breath. Then one more forcing pain, and you'll have your baby."

Diana gritted her teeth and opened one eye. "You said that with the last pain."

Martha chuckled. "One more. I promise."

When Diana's body grew rigid with the next forcing pain, Martha edged a little closer and braced herself. "Push, Diana, push!"

One of the baby's shoulders emerged.

"Keep pushing!"

Once the infant slid free, safely captured by Martha's hands, Diana collapsed against her husband, panting for air, as the echoes of her cries gradually receded.

While the other women tended to Diana, Martha leaned back on her haunches and brought the spewing babe out from beneath the nightdress and laid him on her lap. "You have a son, Captain. A very lusty, healthy son," she cried, just loud enough to be heard above the baby's cries, which filled the sparsely furnished bedchamber.

With practiced skill, she made quick work of wiping the baby a bit, cut the cord, and wrapped the baby in a blanket. For several quick heartbeats, Martha gazed at the newborn, mesmerized by the true miracle she beheld, evidence of His love and His power to create life— life He entrusted to Martha to bring into the world and to this young couple to raise according to His Word.

Precious in his innocence, baby Tyler blinked repeatedly until he was finally able to open his eyes. He quieted and stared up at her, all plump and pink and so recently from heaven itself, she half expected to find wings tucked behind his back.

She stroked one side of his downy cheek and smiled at him. "A blessed welcome to the world, child," she crooned before lifting him up and placing him in his mother's anxious arms.

With tenderness and awe, Diana cradled her son against her breast while her husband gazed at his newborn child over her shoulder. His eyes misted before he turned to his wife and nuzzled the side of her face with his lips. "Thank you for my son," he whispered.

Jubilant, but exhausted, Diana leaned toward her husband and pressed her face to his before she looked down at Martha. "Thank you. For staying with me all this time. For coming so far. For helping me so much. All of you," she added as she glanced at the friends and neighbors who had gathered today to offer their assistance.

Martha watched as the newborn typically captured everyone's attention. She let the gathering of women offer congratulations and generous compliments for a few moments before she called them all back to work. As thrilling as the birth of the baby might be, Martha needed to close the loin, and Diana needed to be washed and set back to bed, where she could rest and hold her baby in greater comfort.

"Hilary, why don't you take this young man and clean him up properly while his mama and I finish up? Captain Tyler, we still need you a little longer, so don't go rushing off. I'll need those warming cloths, too, so if one of you ladies could kindly see if they're ready, we should make quick work of the rest."

Diana handed her son over to Hilary with reluctance that touched Martha's heart. Just in time. A series of forcing pains quickly expelled the afterbirth, which Martha examined closely. Satisfied all appeared to be normal, she pressed one of the warm cloths Hilary had secured against the young woman's vulva and had one of the other women hold it in place to prevent air from entering the birth canal and causing infection.

Under Martha's guidance, Captain Tyler got Diana to her feet. When the other women took over, Martha promptly dismissed him. "We'll call you back in very soon," she promised.

He squared his shoulders, keeping a close eye on his wife as well as his son. "I'd rather stay."

Martha got to her feet and wiped her hands on her birthing apron. "I'd rather you didn't. Now, if you don't mind, I still have work to do with my patient."

Rebellion flashed in his eyes.

She tilted her head back to fully lock her gaze with his and put her hands on her hips. "Now, Captain," she ordered in as firm a voice as she dared.

"There isn't a man aboard ship who would try to order me to do anything."

"We're not at sea, Captain. Childbirth is my command, not yours. Now, unless you want to prolong Diana's discomfort, I suggest you follow orders and leave the room. Please?"

He cocked one brow. "Did anyone ever tell you that you are one stubborn, headstrong woman?"

She grinned. "Quite a few," she quipped.

He grinned back at her. "I thought so. I'll be waiting right on the other side of the door." Without further argument, he left the bed-chamber, and Martha let out a sigh of relief. Handling her patients was always a far sight easier than dealing with their husbands.

When she turned her attention back to Diana, the young woman was already abed. With a sheepish grin on her face, the new mother beckoned Martha to come to her side with a weak wave of her hand. "Randolph is very protective," she offered by way of explanation.

"So am I," Martha responded. "Right now, young lady, we need to tend to a few things to make sure you're going to recover quickly so you can take care of that handsome baby of yours."

While Hilary and two of the others restored the room to order by removing the birthing cloths and stool and changing the bedclothes, Martha helped another to bathe Diana before wrapping the traditional bandages around the new mother's thighs and abdomen. She talked as they worked, if only to keep the young woman's thoughts occupied while her son had his first bath. "Does this young man have a name?"

Diana smiled. "Several. Since we couldn't agree on a name, we decided to compromise and name him for both our fathers: Henry William Alexander Lloyd Tyler."

Martha chuckled. "That's quite a big name for such a little baby. He'll grow into it, that's for sure."

As Diana covered a yawn with the back of her hand, Martha tucked the covers up to her chin before handing young Henry, who was now sound asleep, over to his mother. "You did well, Diana. Very well."

Diana nuzzled her son's head before looking up at Martha. "Will you come back next time?"

Caught off guard, Martha furrowed her brow. "Next time? You're already thinking about next time?"

A chuckle. "Of course. Having this baby was much easier than I thought, once he decided to make his appearance, of course." She yawned again and closed her eyes. "He'll need a brother or two, and several sisters," she managed before drifting off into a well-deserved sleep.

Shaking her head, Martha looked around the bed at the women who had assisted her. "I want to thank you all for your kindnesses and your help. If Diana gets her way, I have a feeling we'll all be together again in the next year or so."

A chorus of laughter. "Come on, Martha. Let's celebrate."

"I don't know about the rest of you, but I'm starving. We have lots of goodies in the other room. Let's get the groaning party started," Hilary suggested.

"If the Captain hasn't devoured all of it," another commented. "We should have told you to tell him most of it was reserved for us. He listens to you."

Another round of laughter, but clear recognition of the status Martha carried with her position—a status she clearly enjoyed.

When Martha walked over and opened the door to the bedchamber, Captain Tyler rushed in, went directly to the bed, and knelt down at his wife's side. The image of this powerful man, brought to his knees by his affection for his wife and child, inspired tears she blinked away as she led the others out.

Of all the traditions surrounding a successful birth, the groaning party afterwards was one Martha enjoyed immensely. The vast variety of foods, some prepared by the new mother during her grinding pains and others donated by neighbors, of course, was always welcome, especially the desserts.

But it was the celebration of sisterhood shared by all those in attendance that gave Martha the most satisfaction. Without the help of other women, Martha's job would be nearly impossible. Without the continued support and guidance of other women, Diana's role as a new mother would be ever more difficult. To that end, the groaning party was testimony to the bonds of womanhood that childbirth reinforced and sustained, for one generation of women after another.

Exhilarated, Martha indulged herself and filled a platter with desserts. Hilary took one look at Martha's plate, giggled, and followed

suit while the others tackled a casserole filled with sausages and potatoes.

Seated side by side together at the table in the kitchen with the
others, she and Martha nibbled on warm bread pudding and apple
tarts drenched with honey. "Will you be leaving for home today?" she
asked.

Anxious to get back home, Martha nodded, although it would take
a good two days to get back to Trinity. "It's so early in the day, I
think I will. Has anyone sent for the afternurse?"

Hilary swallowed down a generous helping of pudding before she
answered. "Mrs. Calloway should be here soon."

"Then I'll just wait to make sure she's arrived before I go."

A knock at the kitchen door interrupted the gaiety, and Martha
turned, expecting the afternurse. Instead, when one of the women
opened the door, a man she did not recognize stepped into the room.
Since he could not possibly be the afternurse, she turned her attention
back to her plate and started devouring the rest of her apple tart.

"Widow Cade?"

The man's voice sounded almost apologetic, and she said a quick
prayer that he had not come to summon her to another birthing. Not
when she was so close to going home. Feeling a tad guilty for being
selfish, she wiped her lips with a napkin, rose, and approached him.

"I'm Widow Cade."

He tipped his hat. "Jacob Rheinhold."

She cocked a brow.

He swallowed so hard, his Adam's apple bulged in his thin, narrow
neck. "I'm a peddler by trade. Heading west. Passed through Trinity
a few days back. When folks at the tavern found out I was headed
this way, they asked me to bring you this." He reached into his pocket,
pulled out a folded document, and handed it to her before he left as
abruptly as he had arrived.

More curious than concerned, and relieved he had not come to
summon her for a birthing, she unfolded the document. To her surprise, she found herself staring at a badly wrinkled broadside adver-

tising a theater troupe of some kind, replete with a list of scheduled stops at towns all the way east to New York City, including Trinity.

Why anyone might think Martha was interested in such a theater troupe defied reason, but when she turned the paper over, she read words that literally stole her breath away:

> *Dearest Martha,*
>
> *Victoria has run away with the troupe. We tried to find her, but failed. Please forgive me.*
>
> *Your brother,*
> *James*

Shock. Disbelief. Horror. They exploded with such force that they destroyed the gay celebration Martha had been enjoying within a single heartbeat. Martha's body went numb as questions raced through her mind. Victoria had run away? With a theater troupe? Impossible. Totally impossible. Victoria was a difficult young woman at times, but she could not be that irresponsible or that impetuous to just up and run away from home.

When she read James's short note again, her heart began to pound. It was true. It was true! Her daughter had run away! But when? How? Why? Dear Lord in heaven, why?

Nearing a state of total panic, she turned the broadside over and read the schedule of appearances, although her hands were shaking so badly she could scarcely make out the words. According to the broadside, the troupe had been in Trinity about a week ago. By now, the troupe itself was long gone from the local area, but the printed schedule she held in her hands was the key that would lead her to Victoria so she could bring her home.

Hilary approached her with concern etched in her features. "Is it bad news?"

Martha quickly folded the broadside and put it into her pocket. "A note . . . just a . . . note from my brother. Nothing to worry about," she murmured, too ashamed to admit to anyone here that her own daughter had been so unhappy, she had run away from home. "I'm afraid I truly must be getting along. Will you stay until Mrs. Calloway arrives?"

"Of course."

"Thank you. I'll just check Diana once more before I leave," Martha suggested. As tears formed and threatened to overflow, she hurried from the kitchen and went directly to the bedchamber. As she walked, she quickly formulated a plan of action. Rather than waste days traveling back to Trinity, she would head straight for the town where the theater troupe was scheduled to next appear, confront Victoria, and force her to come home to Trinity with her mother.

At most, finding Victoria would take a week or two, and her reward from Captain Tyler would surely cover her expenses.

By then, Martha would have complete control of her emotions. By then, Martha would be able to speak to her daughter in a civil tone of voice. By then, Lord willing, she would be ready to hear Victoria's explanation, talk some sense into that girl, and be able to forgive herself for not being at home where she belonged, especially when her daughter so obviously needed her.

Chapter
TWO

For nearly three months, Martha had battled numbing fear, anger, frustration, and despair in a quest that had taken her hundreds of miles from home. Faced with total defeat and stunned by grief after failing to find Victoria, she had had only one place left to go.

Home.

To Trinity.

Sorely tested, her faith was a bit tattered and frayed around the edges, but she kept it tucked around her broken heart to keep the pieces together. And it was her faith, along with her own determined nature, that kept her exhausted body upright in the saddle and her hands tight on the reins as she traveled the final few miles in her journey home.

She should have stopped hours ago and spent the night in York.

Instead, she had ridden on, driven by a deep yearning to bring her ill-fated journey to an end. Guided by the harvest moon overhead that filtered gentle light through the dark curtain of night, she was a solitary but familiar figure, with her split skirt lying in gentle folds across the flanks of her faithful mount, Grace.

Half draft horse and half saddle horse, the gray mare was massive and strong, but she was slow and a bit ungainly as a mount. Carrying haphazard splotches of black and white on her coat, she was a rather sorry sight, but she had stamina, a big heart, and a steady gait— qualities some attributed to her mistress, as well.

Most important to Martha, Grace never balked when Martha was called to duty. She carried Martha and her usual accoutrements—a treatment bag stocked with her simples, herbs and medicines she collected or grew herself, and a birthing stool—without complaint. "She's a true gift. In many ways," Martha murmured to herself, reminded of the many blessings she had received along with her trials.

She gave her mare an appreciative pat on the side of her neck. As they approached the final bend in the roadway that led directly into the town, the mare quickened her gait. Martha stiffened. Beneath heavy leather gloves that protected her hands, her palms began to sweat. She tightened her legs against the mare and tugged on the reins to slow their approach as memories of these past three months tumbled through her mind and a swell of self-pity threatened to consume her.

Tears stung her eyes, but she blinked them back as she relived those fateful days when she had tried to find Victoria and bring her home. The fact that Victoria had run away with that theater troupe had given Martha false hope it would be relatively easy to find her daughter. As it turned out, Martha had invariably arrived in one town a day or two after the troupe had already left for another. In the end, she had tracked the troupe all the way to New York City, but as fate would have it, she had arrived the day after they had all sailed away.

She was not sure whether or not Victoria had actually sailed off to London with the original members or had joined the group that had splintered off and sailed to Charleston. Even if Martha had known for sure which ship she should have followed, she did not have the means left to purchase her own passage.

Only then did she face the darkest, most frightening nightmare ever to shadow a mother's heart: Her young, vulnerable, seventeen-year-old daughter had disappeared, and Martha could not find her.

To compound her misery, she still could not understand why Victoria had run away, even after hours of careful rumination during sleepless nights that followed endless hours spent in the saddle during the day. Martha was able to be honest enough to admit to herself that Victoria had been increasingly discontented in Trinity. Exactly why she had chosen to leave with a theater troupe still remained a mystery, yet in and of itself, vivid testimony of the depths of Victoria's unhappiness and desperation. And Martha's failure to provide the proper guidance to her daughter.

The reality of that failure was a burden that lay so heavy on her heart, she wondered how it was able to beat at all.

Fighting to regain her composure, she choked back a sob, took a deep breath, and prayed hard for a miracle—that somehow Victoria had returned home and was waiting for her.

She tightened her hold on the reins as she battled the sin of self-pity that nibbled at her faith, and continued toward home. Soon, she heard the rushing sound of the waterfalls that anchored the town of Trinity on her right as she passed the sawmill, silent now till first light. Directly to her left, she regarded the outline of the new fence that blocked the rear exit behind the stables and wagon yard adjacent to her brother's tavern with the same regret she had when James put it up just last spring.

Preventing guests, especially transients, from leaving without paying for their accommodations by slipping out the rear yard had been necessary; unfortunately, the fence added only inconvenience for her, since she would have to use the front entrance to the property and then go all the way around to the back to reach the outside door to her room.

Given the ribald laughter than filtered from the tavern and the number of horses, mules, and wagons that filled the yard, her brother and his wife were obviously still hard at work.

Approaching Main Street, which reached a dead end directly ahead, where it met West Falls Road, she sucked in a deep breath and straightened her back. She had no doubt James and Lydia would welcome her home unconditionally. It was the rest of the community that concerned her.

When she reached the crossroad, Martha turned left. With the falls behind her now, she faced the length and breadth of Dillon's Stream, which bisected the small town of Trinity and separated the descendants of the original settlers who lived and worked along East Main Street from the newcomers whose homes and businesses lined West Main Street.

Above the falls, homesteads stretched for miles on end, scattered along and between the three creeks that joined together and dropped as one in a magnificent natural curtain of water dubbed Crying Falls long before Trinity existed. A sawmill and a gristmill lay on either side of a small pool of water that fed Dillon's Stream, which flowed into the Faded River some thirty miles to the southwest.

Save for the sounds and light emanating from Poore's Tavern, the town itself was dark and fast asleep, yet she could see the town center splayed before her mind's eye. Trinity had grown significantly since it had been founded sixty years ago, but the town had changed little in the past twenty. Because Dillon's Stream was too shallow to support any type of heavy boat or large raft, the town had little chance of developing, and in a rapidly changing world it remained an oasis where people lived much as their ancestors had done and their lives reflected the same treasured values of God, family, and community.

To her right, businesses once only a dream of the town's founder now flourished along West Main Street. Before his death, Jacob Dillon had parlayed a wilderness investment in land into a fortune through a carefully executed lottery that had eventually brought yeoman farmers and mechanics together to create a community. Those businesses now slumbered beneath a cloud-scudded sky.

Straight ahead of her down East Main Street, beyond Poore's Tavern, lay the Dillon mansions. Mayor Thomas Dillon, Jacob's son, made his home in the first and oldest mansion—a home that she would have shared with him had she accepted his marriage proposal nearly twenty-five years ago instead of John Cade's. Nestled in between the original homestead and one built a scarce twenty years ago by George Sweet for his bride, Anne Dillon, lay the simple log meetinghouse where the community gathered to worship as one each Sunday and the cemetery where they buried their dead.

Doc Beyer had his home and office farther down the road, just shy of the second covered bridge that connected the businesses and homes separated by Dillon's Stream. At the very end, near the limits of the town proper, an open-air market covered by a massive roof operated once a week on Wednesdays.

Trinity.

Home.

Her chest tightened, and her eyes filled with tears as her mind filled with images of Victoria. What drove Victoria to leave her home here? Why did she leave with a theater troupe, adding scandal to the grief Martha would suffer each and every day until Victoria returned home?

During her journey, Martha had been unable to find the answer to these questions. Now that she was home, she prayed she would find those answers, however painful they might be. She was only moments away from facing her family, her friends, and her neighbors now, when she would have to admit her failure, and she hoped they might forgive her for abandoning them so abruptly.

The greater part of her wanted to believe that the community of women, who depended on her to help treat them and their children for a host of minor ailments or to guide them through the travails of childbirth, would understand that as a mother, Martha had had no choice but to leave and try to find Victoria, even if that meant temporarily abandoning those who needed her care.

A smaller part of her knew that some would see Martha only in her role as midwife and would resent being left without a skilled and experienced midwife during illnesses or childbirth.

A small wagon pulled out from the shadows between the stable and the tavern and headed straight toward Martha, interrupting her thoughts and setting her heartbeat into double time. The hunched driver, muted by shadows, had the two horses in a near gallop, and Martha instinctively backed out of the way.

For better or for worse, she was about to meet and greet her first friend or neighbor . . . or foe.

Chapter
THREE

While wagon wheels ground to a halt, raising a cloud of choking dust, a familiar voice rang out. "Martha Fleming Cade, you're barely in time! We expected you hours ago! We need to hurry, girl. There's a babe just about ready to join this world who needs you."

With her heart pounding in her chest, Martha coughed, moistened her lips to remove the dust, and struggled to find her voice. "Aunt H-Hilda?" she stammered, amazed that her aunt-by-affection would be out so late. Aunt Hilda had been her staunchest supporter since Grandmother's death a decade ago. The last of the town's original inhabitants, Aunt Hilda carried every one of her seventy-seven years with quiet dignity and pride. Known for her uncommon good sense and straightforward manner, as well as for the thick, chalk-white braid she wore like a crown atop her head, she was also an avid beekeeper, which added an aura of eccentricity to her persona. She also brewed the best honey wine west of the Susquehanna.

There were precious few women within fifty miles who had not spent one of their lying-in periods following childbirth without Hilda Seymour as their afternurse. They sang praises about her knowledge and compassion, just as they had done when speaking of Martha's late grandmother, Sarah Poore, the first midwife to settle in Trinity.

They also lauded the healing comforts of Aunt Hilda's infamous hot tea toddy, which was laced with, of course, honey wine, a remedy that cured even the most difficult grumbling pains that inevitably followed all deliveries.

"Adelaide Finch said she'd wait and have you deliver this babe or keep it to herself till her hair turned silver. She's been suffering grinding pains since early yesterday. Her forcing pains started at supper time, and the rest of the women are with her already, so we'd best hurry."

"Adelaide Finch? Her time was nearly a month ago! She couldn't possibly still—"

"Babes always come in their own time, not ours. Besides, first babes are always hard to predict. Leastways, that's what your grandmother always said. Now, let's go before we're too late. You can tell me all about your trip and what you learned about Victoria on the way."

Without waiting for either a reply or an argument, Aunt Hilda clicked the reins and let out a sharp whistle. She passed Martha, turned the horses left, and soon had the wagon wheels clattering through the covered bridge.

Martha watched the shadow of the wagon retreat into complete darkness before her inbred sense of duty knocked her stupefaction aside, along with the irrational disappointment of learning Victoria had not miraculously returned home while Martha was away.

She spurred Grace forward to follow her aunt with all of her thoughts focused on the immediate hours ahead. Once inside the bridge, she quickly closed the gap between them. "Wait!" she cried.

Her aunt's chuckle echoed within the confines of the enclosed structure. "There's no time to waste. I've been expecting you for hours. I'm worried that young scamp of a doctor might be there already."

She paused and raised her voice over the sound of wheels clicking against wood. "*Doctor* Benjamin McMillan. He can't be a day over twenty-four, and here he comes to Trinity, Mr. University himself, ready to take over after ole Doc Beyer passed on, God rest his soul, and then some. I told that young snippersnapper I'd have him run out of town if he ever used those birthing weapons of his on any female I knew. In a proper, ladylike manner, of course," she added with a huff.

Befuddled by the old woman's rantings, and shocked to hear Doc Beyer had died during her absence, Martha held back her questions. She waited until they had passed through the bridge and were winding up West Falls Road to reach the Finch homestead, located along Candle Creek, before attempting to unravel what Aunt Hilda had said.

Eventually, Martha had the answers to most of her questions. Aunt Hilda had known to wait for Martha because earlier that day, shortly after Martha passed a tollgate and left the turnpike to travel home on back roads, Thomas Dillon had passed the very same tollgate and the gatekeeper had mentioned that Martha had recently passed by. While Martha had stopped to have lunch and take a short catnap, Thomas apparently continued straight home, a fortunate turn of events that had prevented her from sharing the last of her journey with him. As soon as he had arrived back in Trinity, he had quickly spread news of her imminent return.

She also learned there had been no word from Victoria, despite her fervent hopes otherwise. She was, however, as surprised to learn Doc Beyer had gone on to his final reward as she was to find out he had been eighty-three years old.

A physician of the old school who had learned the rudiments of his trade through apprenticeship, Doc Beyer and her grandmother had worked side by side in Trinity for nearly fifty years, each respecting the other's abilities, as well as the need for both a doctor and a midwife in Trinity and the surrounding areas.

According to Aunt Hilda, Dr. McMillan had purchased his predecessor's home and office and opened his very first practice. A bachelor, he had even kept Rosalind Andrews as his housekeeper, an arrangement that allowed Rosalind to continue living in the home as well.

Unlike Doc Beyer, who had limited his part-time practice to treating male patients, setting bones, and treating serious illnesses beyond Martha's expertise while earning additional income from farming, Dr. McMillan was an upstart straight out of medical school in Boston, and he had apparently made it very clear he intended to practice medicine full-time, treating every man, woman, and child in Trinity himself.

To do that, he would have to court the community of women there and convince them to let him handle all their medical needs. The best way to begin was to start delivering their children, relieving Martha of her role as midwife.

Unfortunately, Martha's absence these past few months had given him the very opportunity he needed. Doctors had replaced midwives in most major cities, including Boston, for nearly twenty years now. It was only a matter of time before the same happened in rural towns like Trinity as well. If that happened, Martha would lose everything: her only source of income as well as her place in the community.

She snorted at the very thought he would ever replace her and rode faster until she was alongside the wagon, instead of behind it, since she had already tolerated her own fair share of road dust on her journey home.

"There's more news," Aunt Hilda ventured, "but that can wait for now. Tell me what happened on your trip."

There was no one Martha trusted more than Aunt Hilda, and she told her all about her travels with no fear anything she said would ever be repeated. By the time they crossed Reedy Creek at a shallow point, she had nearly emptied her tale.

"What exactly did Oliver suggest you do?" Aunt Hilda asked as Martha concluded with news about her visit to her son in Boston.

Martha let out a long sigh. "He wanted me to stay with him for a spell. To 'gather my wits,' as he put it. He has a rather analytical approach to this whole sorry mess, like this is some legal issue he's trying to resolve," she admitted.

Aunt Hilda shook her head. "Oliver never did think much with his heart. That might make him a good city lawyer, but not much more. Give him time, Martha. He's still his mother's son."

Martha nodded but offered no further comment. They traveled in companionable silence for another five miles before reaching Candle Creek, and arrived at the Finch homestead less than half an hour later. Light poured an invitation from the windows of the well-lit cabin, but Martha recognized the carriage hitched near the front door as the one previously used by Doc Beyer, which did not bode well for her chances of delivering Adelaide's baby.

"We're too late," she murmured.

"Perhaps," Hilda conceded as she climbed down from the wagon while Martha dismounted and tethered Grace to the hitching post alongside the doctor's carriage. "Then again, if that babe's not yet come into this world, custom says the mother-to-be has the right to choose who helps her to deliver. Whether he likes it or not, the good Dr. McMillan best give sway to custom, unless he intends to practice somewhere else."

The door swung open before Martha could respond, and three of the watchers who had been tending to Adelaide during her grinding pains gathered together in the open doorway. Melanie Biehn and Belinda Riley, Adelaide's nearest neighbors, both wore expressions of deep concern that quickly gave way to surprise when they saw Martha. Standing behind them, Rosalind Andrews offered only a tight smile.

With relieved glances to one another, Melanie and Belinda stepped aside, forcing Rosalind to do the same to allow Martha and Aunt Hilda to enter the two-room dwelling. With a quick look around the main room, Martha was satisfied the watchers had gotten everything ready for the birth. A supply of towels and cloths warmed by the fire in the hearth. A kettle of water hissed on the cookstove, carefully watched by yet another neighbor, JoHannah Pfeifer, who returned Martha's smile with a nervous nod of her head. She ignored the assorted foods that burdened a trestle table awaiting the customary celebration following childbirth. The mood that filled the small homestead was more funereal than celebratory, and she focused all of her attention on the expectant father, Daniel Finch.

He wore a grim expression that gave life to the ditty schoolchildren had chanted while jumping rope for as long as Martha could remember:

> *Once the doctor arrives,*
> *Two never survive.*
> *Dig the hole. Etch the stone.*
> *Mama or baby got called back Home.*

Battling the fear worrying her heart, she studied the young man, who did not take his gaze from the door that led to the adjoining bedchamber. His shoulders were rigid. His stance was almost combative, as if he were ready to slay whatever demons threatened the well-being of his wife and unborn child. He flinched when the sound of deep moaning echoed from behind the closed door.

When he finally looked at Martha, his dark eyes were moist with unshed tears. When he began to speak, his voice was as steady as it was accusatory. "Dr. McMillan is here now. Your services are not—"

"My services are not the issue right now," she insisted. "How is Adelaide?"

He snorted. "I haven't been allowed near her for the past hour."

She was not surprised that the doctor had taken such preemptive control by excluding Adelaide's husband from the birthing process.

"Carrie's with Adelaide and the doctor," JoHannah offered, as if she knew Martha would take heart from knowing one of her trusted assistants was with her patient.

As if privy to the concerns of all who watched and waited for the impending arrival of the firstborn Finch, a man she assumed to be Dr. McMillan emerged from the bedchamber. Almost twenty years younger than Martha, he was uncommonly short. Although she stood an average five and a half feet, Martha was a full head taller than him. He carried a paunch around his middle large enough that, if carried by a woman, it might cause observers to suspect her teeming state would last only another few months.

Pale blue eyes and light hair accented fine, delicate features set between pudgy cheeks, but his thin lips formed a pout when quick introductions identified Martha as a midwife.

"So you're the *midwife*." If his sarcasm had been vinegar, there would have been enough for a year's supply for the entire town. "As you can see, Mrs. Finch is my patient. You're not needed here."

Unaccustomed to being publicly dismissed by anyone, even a doctor, Martha should have expected no less from this newcomer. Instead of responding to the challenge in his words, she glanced behind him into the bedchamber where a forlorn cradle sat empty in the corner.

Adelaide lay in bed, motionless. Carrie was seated by her side, gently wiping Adelaide's brow, and she gave Martha an unspoken, plaintive plea for help with a troubled gaze. Turning her attention back to Adelaide, Martha quickly noted the paleness of her face and the lines of exhaustion that etched her features, but it was the small bandage on her arm that set Martha's blood to a quick boil and quickly evaporated her reluctance to intervene.

"You bled her?" Surprised by the curtness of her own words, she charged the doctor, then stopped and clamped her lips shut before completely losing control of her temper and saying something she would later regret.

The young physician blanched. Bright splotches of red mottled his pale cheeks. Indignation flashed through his eyes. "I've been well trained to handle all aspects of the birth process for my patients, especially difficult ones," he spat.

Before Martha could fashion a reasonable retort, Aunt Hilda stepped up to him. Nearly eye-to-eye, she spoke to him quietly and calmly. "Bleeding a woman during her labor saps her strength. It doesn't help her or the baby."

The doctor sputtered, apparently flabbergasted that anyone would challenge his competency or his treatments. Aunt Hilda ignored him and turned her attention to the expectant father, who seemed paralyzed and unable to intervene. "If you want that babe of yours to enter this world and suckle at his mama's breast tonight, you'd best leave this to Martha," she suggested. "Unlike the good doctor, she knows exactly what to do because she's done it hundreds of times, not because she read some books or attended a few lectures."

At that moment, Dr. McMillan finally found his voice. "I beg your pardon! My credentials are—"

"Impeccable, I'm sure," Martha assured him. Reluctant to completely alienate the man who could very well threaten her position within the community, especially if he succeeded in convincing her neighbors he was better trained to deliver their babies than she was, she followed Aunt Hilda and kept her own contempt at bay.

As much as she wanted to intervene and take care of Adelaide, Martha knew she could not simply usurp the doctor's position.

He had been summoned first.

He had arrived first.

Like it or not, Adelaide was his patient, and until Martha was asked to intervene, she had no right to do so.

She turned to fully face Daniel, and the pained expression in his eyes made it clear he was too upset about his wife and the possibility of losing her or the babe she carried to choose between having a doctor or a midwife tend to her.

Unearthly silence filled the cabin with tension that mounted as the standoff continued . . . until Adelaide moaned and cried out for her husband. "Daniel. Daniel? Please, Daniel . . ."

He rushed past everyone to her side.

Martha moved into the bedchamber.

Dr. McMillan quickly joined her.

Daniel knelt by his wife's side and pressed a kiss to her forehead while he kept her hands folded within his own. "I'm here, love. I'm here," he assured her.

She managed a weak smile, one that broadened the moment her gaze locked with Martha's. "I knew you'd come . . . in time." She gritted her teeth as a forcing pain claimed her breath. She raised her head from the pillow, grimaced, and let out a sharp cry. When the pain subsided, she lay back down. Perspiration covered her face and damp ringlets of auburn hair splayed across her pillow.

"I don't know what to do," Daniel murmured. He stroked her cheek and pressed his forehead to hers. "Tell me what to do. Tell me who you want to help you deliver our son," he rasped as his voice cracked with emotion.

Martha tried to remain calm, but she could not keep her palms from sweating or her heart from racing. As hopeful as she was that Adelaide would want her to take over with the birthing, she also knew Dr. McMillan had spent enough time with his patient to have established some type of bond between them.

She quickly said a silent prayer, knowing full well that her future in Trinity very much depended on the answer Adelaide would give them all.

Chapter FOUR

"Help me. Will you help me, Martha? Please?"

Adelaide whimpered, then turned her tear-filled eyes from Martha to the man standing just inside the doorway. "I'm sorry, Dr. McMillan. I appreciate all you've tried to do, but . . . Martha!" she cried as she nearly doubled in pain.

Called to duty, Martha had no time to waste on relief. "I'm here to help you," she assured her.

With no time to spare, she quickly issued orders that set the rest of the womenfolk into motion. Aunt Hilda headed toward the front door to secure Martha's bag and the birthing stool while Dr. McMillan retreated back into the other room and abruptly left the cabin.

JoHannah filled a bowl with hot water and gathered up some towels. When Aunt Hilda returned, Melanie and Belinda helped to assemble the collapsible birthing stool while Martha removed her cape and bonnet and hung them on a peg by the front door.

When she heard what sounded like the doctor climbing into his carriage outside, she had second thoughts about his leaving. She opened the door and found him already seated in his carriage. The light from the cabin illuminated the scowl on his face, and she was tempted to simply wish him good riddance and close the door again.

Instead, duty to her patient took precedence over her personal feelings. She knew she had to salvage what she could from the disaster of their first encounter for Adelaide's sake, and stepped outside. "Please. You shouldn't leave. Not yet."

His scowl deepened, creating deep crevices in his fleshy cheeks. "Mrs. Finch made her choice quite clear."

"As is her right," Martha gently reminded him, loath to let her personal interests put her patient's well-being at risk. "We both know there are cases, even though they're rare, where you will be summoned to a birth that develops complications I'm not trained to handle. Until I'm sure Adelaide can be safely delivered, I'm certain Daniel and Adelaide would both feel better just knowing you are here to help should . . . should that become necessary."

She waited with bated breath for his reply. In ten years of practicing midwifery on her own, Martha had summoned Doc Beyer on occasion, usually to stitch up tears from the delivery, but she could actually count the number of those cases on her fingers. Sadly, she had attended four stillbirths. In only two cases had she lost the mother. Both times, she had summoned the doctor well ahead of time so he could perform emergency surgery and save the baby. If something did go horribly wrong tonight and Dr. McMillan went home now, he would never be able to return in time to save either Adelaide or her unborn child.

"Please stay," she repeated when the doctor failed to respond to her earlier plea.

Either mollified now or satisfied he might yet be able to establish himself as the more qualified of the two of them, he squared his shoulders, and his scowl disappeared into a smile that did not reach his eyes. "I shall wait," he pronounced, rather formally given the circumstances.

She did not waste any energy by responding to the derision that laced his words. Instead, she merely returned to the cabin, where she removed her leather gloves and stored them in her cape pocket. She used the bowl of hot water to warm her hands and wash them, and finally rinsed them with rose water before proceeding directly to the bedchamber, where her patient lay very still beneath a thin sheet.

When Daniel stood up as if to leave, Martha waved him to stay. "I expect we'll be needing your help," she said softly.

Under his watchful gaze, she laid her hand atop the sheet covering Adelaide's distended abdomen. With her brows knitted together, she carefully waited and gauged the strength of the next forcing pain and the position of the babe. When Carrie entered the room, Martha cocked her head toward her assistant. "How many hours since her groaning pains started?"

"Quite early this morning. I mean, yesterday morning. About four."

"And the forcing pains?"

"Near six hours now. After Dr. McMillan bled her, she lost her waters. That was just before you arrived."

Martha kept a reassuring smile on her face, both for Adelaide and Daniel, despite her growing concern. She had the courage and the confidence to set this birthing onto the right track. All she needed now was the confidence of her patient and her husband.

"Daniel, I'd like to be alone with Adelaide. Just for a few minutes," she added when he pursed his lips. "Then we'll need your help."

Yet another forcing pain drew a sharp cry from Adelaide's lips. When she began to twist beneath the sheets, Martha shoved all tact aside. "Now, Daniel. Leave now! Carrie, come here. You, too, Belinda. I'll need you both to help me. Aunt Hilda, please shut the door and keep everyone else out till we're done. And get that birthing stool ready!"

Like the seasoned assistants they were, the women did exactly as they had been told to do. Once the door closed, Martha took

Adelaide's hand and squeezed gently. "I know you're frightened and you're hurting something fierce, but I need you to listen carefully and do exactly as I say."

Adelaide nodded with tears streaming down her face.

Martha wiped them away and patted her cheek. "I need to turn the babe. It's going to hurt. A lot. But once I help this little one get situated right, he'll be in your arms very quickly."

"He won't die. Please promise he won't die," the girl pleaded.

"The good Lord willing, that's not going to happen," she responded. "Now, you just relax. Let me do all the work."

Her voice sounded calmer than she actually felt. She had faith in her ability to safely deliver this babe, even with Adelaide weakened by the doctor's ill-advised treatment, and quickly offered a prayer of gratitude for her catnap so she would have the strength she needed now.

While Melanie and Belinda each took a position on either side of the bed, Martha donned her birthing apron, rolled up her sleeves, lubricated her right hand and forearm, and approached her patient. After the women rolled back the sheets from the bottom of the bed and draped them just below Adelaide's ribs, Martha nodded for them to take a firm hold on the patient's bent legs.

She tugged Adelaide's nightdress up to her knees and laid her left hand atop Adelaide's abdomen. Gently, so very gently, she eased her right hand, and then her forearm, into the birth canal. "Easy. Breathe deeply. That's right," she murmured. Pleased to find the cervix fully dilated, she quickly confirmed her suspicions that the babe was in a breech position. After taking a deep breath, she nodded again to her assistants.

Talking softly and calmly, she explained what she was doing as she worked, although Adelaide was probably too distressed to be able to fully listen or understand. She never raised her voice. Even when Adelaide began screaming, Martha remained detached and calm, totally focused on turning this child.

It took every ounce of strength she possessed and called for great patience. As she worked, the memory of her grandmother, standing by her side offering encouragement, guided and sustained her, even after Adelaide swooned from the pain.

By the time Martha had finished, her entire body ached. A heavy sheen of perspiration covered her brow. Her arm was covered with bloody fluids, but her mind was already racing ahead. Her patient, roused from her swoon, lay quiet for the moment. "Well done. Well done!" she crooned. "Let's get this babe born."

While her assistants hurried to the door, Martha rinsed her hands again as well as her arm. "Set the birthing stool there. At the foot of the bed. Facing the door. Don't forget to lay the birthing sheets beneath it," she reminded them.

When she spied Daniel standing just outside the doorway, she smiled. "Come on in here. I want you to sit down on the birthing stool and brace your legs wide so Adelaide can sit on your lap and you can support her weight. Aunt Hilda, you're going to help Daniel. Sit on the bed behind him."

When they were both in position, she nodded her approval. "Daniel, lift your arms. That's right. Now Aunt Hilda can reach through. Exactly. Melanie, as soon as I tell you, fetch the warming cloths. JoHannah, make sure that water is plenty warm and ready when I need it. Carrie, you'll help me with Adelaide."

As soon as Adelaide recovered from the next forcing pain, Martha and Carrie helped her out of bed and onto the birthing stool. Once she was safely seated on her husband's lap, Aunt Hilda began to massage Adelaide's abdomen. Standing on either side of the stool, Melanie and Belinda each faced Adelaide and held one of her hands.

With the babe now in the proper position and the forcing pains less than a minute apart, Martha knew birth was imminent. She knelt down on the floor in front of Adelaide and leaned back on her haunches. She spread a warming cloth across her lap and set her bag within reach.

When the next forcing pain began, she offered spirited encouragement while she reached underneath Adelaide's nightdress and pressed the heel of her hand against the warm flesh just above the birth canal.

"This time, really push. Brace your feet against the floor and push, Adelaide. Push!"

Groaning mightily, Adelaide clenched her teeth and pushed. Her effort inspired a flush that spread across her cheeks and perspiration that dotted her forehead.

"Good. Now again. Push!" Martha felt the baby's head emerge, and her heart began to pound. "He's coming. Good. We have a fine crown of hair on this babe. Indeed we do," she crooned. "Now the shoulders. One good push . . . Yes. That's a good mama! *Good!*"

The babe slid into her waiting arms. With practiced hands, she quickly pulled the baby from beneath his mother's nightdress. She wiped the squalling newborn with the cloth on her lap, tied and cut the umbilical cord, and grinned up at the new parents. "You have a beautiful daughter," she murmured as she wrapped the baby in a soft blanket.

Daniel's eyes widened in disbelief. "A daughter?"

Adelaide chuckled. "A daughter! We have a daughter!"

As the parents discussed this obvious surprise, Martha stared at the perfectly formed babe. And in that instant, when she held that precious new life in her arms, awe nourished the famished seeds of her faith. Humbled to be the handmaiden who served the source of all life, and privileged to witness His glorious goodness, she let the tears of joy escape and flow down her cheeks.

With great reverence, she placed the baby girl into Carrie's waiting arms. Anxious to complete the birthing so that the babe could be united once again with her mama, Martha did not have to wait long before Nature herself helped to make quick work of delivering the afterbirth.

To prevent the suction of air into Adelaide's womb, which could lead to infection as well as make the grumbling pains that followed childbirth more severe, Martha pressed a warm cloth against the opening of the birth canal. Being careful to preserve the young mother's modesty, she made sure her nightdress still curtained her ministrations. "Now we need to get you into bed," she suggested.

Using Daniel's strong arms for support, Adelaide managed to get back into bed, where she collapsed onto the mattress. Martha made sure the cloth remained in place while Carrie immediately placed the babe into her mother's anxious arms.

As Martha watched the scene unfold, emotion choked her throat. The expression of pure joy on Adelaide's face added a radiance that erased the fear as well as the pain she had endured. Instead of worry, elation danced in Daniel's eyes. Then awe. The same awe that Martha had experienced only moments ago.

And then, with the same gentleness as a soft spring rain blessing a parched earth, a sense of peace descended upon the entire room.

Overwhelmed, Martha stood perfectly still, feeling both humbled and honored to bear witness to the miracle of new life. Joy opened her troubled heart and gave her a troubling new insight into all she had experienced these past few months.

Ashamed by what she now understood about herself, she had to set her feelings aside. Adelaide still needed her. She asked Daniel to leave again and reassured him he could return soon. She waited until he had left the room before making good use of a second set of warming cloths Carrie had brought to the bedchamber. With great tenderness, Martha eased a cloth between Adelaide's nightdress and laid it across her abdomen. She also wrapped warm cloths around each of Adelaide's thighs to help ease the discomfort that typically followed childbirth, and replaced the cloth covering the birth canal with a new one.

Satisfied all was now done, she removed her dirtied apron and helped Adelaide into a fresh nightdress before drawing up the covers. She fluffed the pillow under Adelaide's head and wiped her face with a fresh cloth. "You're holding one of His most precious gifts, Adelaide. Love her and keep her within your heart. Always."

Adelaide sighed, reached out, and squeezed Martha's hand. "Thank you. Thank you so much," she whispered.

Martha managed to say "You're welcome," as memories of Victoria's birth seventeen years ago threatened her composure. She cleared her throat and smiled. "Have you and Daniel picked out a name for her?"

"Thomas Adam, for both of our fathers." She giggled. "Daniel was certain we'd have a son. Glory be, there hasn't been a girl born to his family in three generations."

"Until now."

Beaming, the new father reappeared and stood in the open doorway. He hesitated, then quickly rejoined his new family. "Glory. That sounds fitting for this little angel girl. Glory Adelaide Finch," he pronounced. His gaze locked with his wife's.

She smiled. "Glory. I like that, too."

When a yawn kept her from adding anything more, Martha summoned Aunt Hilda back from the other room. "I believe this new mama could use some rest."

The elderly woman winked. "And some hot tea. It's already steeping. Carrie's going to bring some for both of us as soon as it's ready. Now, off with both of you," she insisted as she ushered Daniel and Martha to the door. "Time to celebrate. The groaning party's already started. I'll stay with Adelaide a bit till she falls asleep, then I'll join you."

She closed the bedchamber door before either of them could mount an argument.

Unlike earlier, animated chattering filled the main room of the cabin. With the exception of Rosalind and Dr. McMillan, who reportedly had left abruptly after Glory's birth when it was apparent both mother and baby were doing well, the women who had tended to Adelaide now sat around the table tackling plates filled with food prepared by the new mother during her early labor. The recent fall harvest had apparently been plentiful. Next to a platter of roasted ham, bowls of sweet peas and lush ears of corn, a mountain of boiled carrots and potatoes still remained. Cinnamon floated atop bread pudding swimming in heavy cream. A pitcher of cider kept company with a jug of honey wine, Hilda's customary contribution.

Despite the gaiety that prevailed, Martha hesitated. Now that the birthing had reached a successful conclusion, the questions about Victoria and Martha's attempt to bring her home were just waiting to be voiced.

Martha felt dizzy, like she was hanging from the blade of an emotional pendulum that kept her swinging back and forth from fear to courage, sorrow to joy, and awe to despair and back again.

"You must be starving. I know I am," Daniel admitted.

Even though her stomach was empty, the mere thought of food made Martha queasy. "You go ahead. I think I'll take in some fresh air first." She stepped outside without bothering to retrieve her cape or her bonnet.

Fall air, chilled by the night, welcomed her as she went directly to the shadows well beyond the ribbons of light pouring from the cabin windows. Driven to find a private place, she hurried around the cabin past the barn and kept going until she reached a copse of trees.

Just in time.

The dam holding back her emotions finally burst. Sobbing, she leaned her shoulder against the trunk of a tree for support. Unable to stem the tears, she stifled her sobs with the back of her hand.

Slowly, the storm ebbed. Sobs became whimpers. The flood of emotions receded, leaving her physically drained and emotionally spent.

Before she worried about facing her friends and neighbors, as well as her family, and telling them the truth about her failed attempt to bring Victoria home, she had to face herself. Honestly. And without pretense.

Chapter

FIVE

Martha faced the truth about herself and Victoria's disappearance. To deny it any longer would only keep her soul festering and her spirit in such turmoil she might never find peace or ease the pain that constantly nibbled at her gut.

Spending the coming weeks and months, possibly years, without ever knowing where Victoria was or how she fared was a difficult reality, but honesty dictated that Martha had to admit that her pride had been skewered as deeply as her heart when she learned Victoria had run off with a theater troupe.

A theater troupe!

Her entire body stiffened, and her throat tightened. The shame was nearly unbearable. Images of drunkards and scoundrels, not to mention the fallen angels who typically made up such troupes, nearly stole her breath away when she thought of her precious, innocent daughter associating with such people.

Could Victoria have chosen anything worse to do? Probably not. But then, Victoria had been her most rebellious child, locking horns with her mother almost from birth. When she was only a day old, this darling little bundle of joy had slammed her lips shut and willfully, deliberately, held her breath and turned blue to protest being set into her cradle.

The memory raised gooseflesh along the length of Martha's limbs and made her tremble.

If Grandmother Poore had not been there to force the tip of a spoon between that babe's lips and pry that little mouth open to draw in air, Victoria would have been buried before experiencing her first full day of life on this earth.

New tears escaped, and Martha brushed them away with a weak smile. Victoria still carried a small scar on her lower lip to testify to the whole affair, and Martha frequently got obedience from the child by simply saying, "Now, where did I put that spoon?"—a clear signal of who was going to be in charge.

A theater troupe!

Shame burned deeper and flamed her cheeks. Victoria could not have hurt her mother more if she had slapped her face and openly denounced the values of God, family, and community that were the cornerstone of Martha's very existence. Beyond the public scandal, which added yet another layer of shame, the personal tragedy of living, day and night, without knowing her daughter's fate within that troupe was far and beyond what Martha could endure.

Yet another layer of shame, this one of personal failure, would provide even more fodder for local gossips, and it was realizing the full scope of her situation that nearly sent Martha to her knees.

Martha had earned the respect of most women in her community and claimed friendship with many. Because of the nature of her calling as a midwife, Martha was privy to the most intimate details of her patients' lives. There were few family secrets in Trinity today not already guarded behind the mantle of her responsibility, not that folks did not try to wheedle information out of her, but she guarded carefully against even the slightest slip of the tongue.

Other secrets lay hidden in her grandmother's diary—a diary Martha continued to safeguard to this day, recording in it births, along with the rewards she received and an accounting of the debts owed to her for her services.

With the scandal surrounding Victoria's disappearance, and with Dr. McMillan's presence in Trinity, Martha's very existence as a midwife, despite Adelaide's delivery tonight, was now at risk, unleashing fears as real as those she held for her daughter. Or surpassing them?

She bowed her head and clenched her hands at her side. "Forgive me, Lord, I am a prideful, selfish woman. I don't blame Victoria, but I do—"

"Indeed!"

Startled by Aunt Hilda's voice, Martha swung away from the tree and turned about so fast she almost lost her balance. She grabbed the trunk for support.

The elderly woman helped to steady her by placing a firm hand on her shoulder. "I thought you might have wanted some time alone to pray about the miracle we just witnessed and to thank Him. Sarah always led everyone in prayer following a birth. It's a tradition you've always kept. Till now. I suppose this has something to do with Victoria."

Mortified, and quite properly rebuked, Martha was grateful for the darkness that hid the hot flush burning her cheeks. Any attempt at pretense was hopeless, especially with Aunt Hilda, who knew Martha almost better than she knew herself. "All my efforts to find Victoria were in vain. She's gone, and I don't know where else to look to find her. And now . . . now I know why," Martha offered.

Aunt Hilda patted Martha's shoulder twice before letting her hand drop away. "I'm listening. Of course, I expect it's a choker of a pill to swallow, what with Victoria gallivanting off on some wild adventure, leaving you to worry and make excuses for her when it isn't your fault why she ran off or with whom."

"Of course it's my fault. I should have been home when that theater troupe stopped overnight in Trinity, instead of being fifty miles away!"

"You were doing God's work and helping one of his creations arrive safely."

"I'm supposed to be a mother first," Martha argued, unleashing the resentment she had long harbored at being forced to choose between her roles as mother and midwife. So many times in the past, her dual roles had merged, making it hard to know where her duty to Victoria ended and her duty to her neighbors began, although she had never voiced her concerns about this to Aunt Hilda before now.

A soft sigh of understanding. "And you're angry. Victoria has disappointed you."

Hilda's words finally ignited the firestorm that had been smoldering for months. "I'm not angry. I'm ... I'm ... Yes, I'm angry! I'm very, very angry at Victoria." Martha gritted her teeth and waved her arms in frustration. Her words continued to tumble out, overwhelming her attempts to restrain them. "How could she do this to me? How could she run off and leave me to worry like this? She knew I'd follow her, yet she kept running, hiding from me, until she finally managed to completely disappear. The good Lord only knows where she got the money she needed to leave," she whimpered. "I don't know where she is. I don't know how she'll survive, if she's hungry or cold or sick or—"

"Or doing very well."

Martha paused to drag in cool air that chilled her lungs and helped extinguish some of the flames of her anger. "She had no right to run off the way she did. None. No excuse whatsoever can justify her leaving a note, a very short note, I might add, propped on top of her pillow, leaving poor James and Lydia frantic with worry."

"You're right," Aunt Hilda murmured. "She should have waited until you came home to tell you yourself. In person. Face-to-face."

"Exactly." Her feelings vindicated, Martha relaxed her stance, but only for a few heartbeats.

"Then she could have joined up with the theater troupe later."

"Yes. I mean, no!" she argued, but Aunt Hilda had opened the door to Martha's deepest disappointments and they tumbled out before Martha could stop them. "I don't approve of her associating with a . . . a theater troupe! Her place is here, in Trinity, with me, so I can continue to teach her everything Grandmother Poore taught me. One day soon, she'll be ready to be a watcher, like Melanie and Belinda. They started when they were just a little older than Victoria. Once she's married, she'll learn firsthand what childbirth entails. Then, as her children grow older, she'll have time to learn more and take over my duties. Gradually. Like I did for Grandmother."

Aunt Hilda took hold of Martha's hands and pressed them between her own. "That's your dream, Martha dear. Not Victoria's, though I agree with you that traveling with a group of no-account actors would be about my last choice for the girl. But it's not my decision to make. And it's not yours, either."

Martha clenched her teeth and briefly closed her eyes. When her heartbeat returned to normal, she swallowed hard. "I have so much I could teach her," she whispered.

"I know. Sarah felt the very same way when your mama turned her back on learning the skills she'd need to follow in *her* mother's footsteps."

"My mother? That's absurd," she protested. Orphaned before her fourth birthday when a carriage accident claimed both her parents, she had no real memory of them, only the stories Grandfather and Grandmother Poore had shared while raising Martha and her brother. "Grandmother always told me what a good midwife my mother would have been, had she lived. She told me my mother had a special talent for growing the herbs used—"

Gentle laughter interrupted her earnest protest. "Your mother, Rena, killed every living thing she ever planted. Even weeds knew better than to sprout in her garden. Sarah finally gave up and admitted growing herbs just wasn't Rena's gift."

Refusing to budge an inch, despite her shaky ground, Martha shook her head. "My mother was a wonderful watcher. Everyone says so."

"True. To a point. Rena watched over the groaning table better than anyone I ever knew. Even walked off grinding pains with those mamas, but you couldn't get that woman within twenty paces of the birthing stool when those babies were ready to enter the world. Of course, knowing her mama would have taken a hickory branch to her if she dared so much as a frown . . ."

Aunt Hilda paused. "She tried. Your mama really tried, but truth be told now, she never wanted to follow in her mama's calling. Then again, she did have a special gift of her own. Nobody made a quilt like Rena Fleming. She had a knack for teaching anyone interested how to turn the most sorry pieces of cloth into beautiful quilts. That truly was her gift, and she shared her gift by making cradle quilts. She gave one to your mama to take to every birthing, too."

Long-treasured stories about the woman who had given Martha life shattered, then reshaped themselves as Hilda's words resonated in Martha's mind. If what Aunt Hilda said was true, Martha had lost the long battle to force Victoria to fit into the mold of a family tradition because that tradition simply did not exist, at least not in an unbroken chain, as Martha had always believed.

Like it or not, she had to accept the fact that the midwife tradition would end with her.

The mantle of disappointment was so heavy her shoulders actually slumped. Her eyes filled with tears, but she felt no anger toward Grandmother for stretching and fabricating the truth for all those years. Her intentions had been good, but if Martha had known . . .

Her conscience reminded her there was no room for pretense now, either.

Even if Martha had known the truth about her own mother, she probably would not have done anything differently while raising Victoria. She still would have expected that twenty or thirty years hence, when Martha was too old and feeble to continue her work, Victoria would have been ready to take her place.

And she would have been wrong.

Once she cast aside her disappointment and bitterness, fond memories of her daughter inspired a smile. Victoria was a natural scholar, brighter by half than her older brother. She lived in a world dominated by literature and poetry. If she wasn't reading a book or a poem, she was writing her own.

"Victoria has a different gift from mine, doesn't she?".

"She does, though she doesn't quite know what to do with it." Aunt Hilda squeezed Martha's hands. "Not one of my four children's left. Only the good Lord knows for sure when Mr. Seymour will come home to me, but even after thirty years, I still wake up every morning and hope this will be the day he walks in the door. . . ."

Her voice trailed off for a moment before she cleared her throat. "Victoria's like my own. I miss her almost as much as you do, and I worry about her now, too, but you're not facing this alone. And neither am I. We both believe the good Lord is watching over that girl and we have to trust Him to protect her now, more than we ever have before. And if you have a tiny niggle of doubt He'll keep her safe, then you think back to what just happened in that cabin tonight. He didn't spare Glory a mighty tough entry into this world, but she survived because He gave you a gift, one you've embraced all these years despite the sacrifices you've had to endure, and He guided you tonight to protect that innocent babe."

Ashamed and humbled once again, Martha embraced her aunt. "I've been such a fool."

"Selfish and prideful, too," Aunt Hilda added while giving Martha a hug. "That makes you human. Faith and conviction can't cure that. They only help you to recognize your failings so you can try to overcome them. He never promised life's journey wouldn't be hard. He just promised to take the journey with you. If you'll let Him. And if you do, He'll help you see that life's troubles, as well as the joys, are all His gifts. You just need the courage to open each and every gift and be thankful for the lessons they each contain."

Martha bowed her head. She had always accepted the joys in life as His gifts, but viewing life's troubles and disappointments as gifts would be a far greater challenge—one she knew she must accept.

With renewed fervor, she stormed the heavens with silent prayers. For forgiveness. For understanding. For the strength of faith to find the gift in all that life held. In thanksgiving—for the miracle of Glory and for the miracle of Victoria, that He might protect her from all harm and bring her home to her mother's arms one day. And most of all, for the love and guidance Aunt Hilda offered to her.

When she finished, she linked her arm with Aunt Hilda's and headed back toward the cabin. "After we pray together to give thanks for Glory, I'll tell you more about what happened in New York when I tried to find Victoria."

"Just don't expect Rosalind to offer anything close to a kind word when you see her again. She's still hurting, and harboring lots of anger she'll be directing at you, too, now that you're home. You won't be alone. She's upset with most people these days."

Handed yet another challenge, Martha never lost her stride. She had known Rosalind all her life. Time and time again, their relationship had run the full gamut from adversary to close friend and everything in between. Unfortunately, when Rosalind encountered difficulties, she took her frustration out on her friends, including Martha, and alienated them instead of turning her energies to the source of her problems and enlisting the help of understanding friends. "I take it Burton hasn't returned home?"

Aunt Hilda shook her head. "Apparently, she had a letter from that husband of hers some weeks ago. She won't say where he is, but he's not coming home until Webster Cabbot drops the charges he's filed against him."

"He might have to wait till Webster dies for that to happen," Martha quipped. "He's not a man to back down from a fight, especially when he thinks he's right."

Aunt Hilda snorted. "They're arguing over a watch. *A watch!* I'm not sure I'll ever understand how either one of them would let this misunderstanding escalate into a feud, let alone formal charges that bring in the law."

Martha sighed. "For Webster, it's about honor and his sense of family, which precede friendship. The watch belonged to his grandfather. It's an heirloom," she offered, "although keeping something that valuable within full view of anyone who frequents Webster's shop is something I'll never understand. To be fair to Webster, Burton bears some responsibility here. He should have stayed to face the charges instead of running away before Sheriff Myer could arrest him. This could have all been resolved in court months ago—"

"Exactly. Instead, poor Rosalind has had to face the scandal all alone," Aunt Hilda charged.

"Poor Rosalind," Martha murmured. Dismayed that this troubling issue had not been settled during her absence, Martha knew there was nothing she could do to ease Rosalind's plight or her misery unless Rosalind opened the door to the friendship they had shared before Burton's disappearance. She did, however, realize that she and Rosalind had one thing in common: The gossipmongers in town might find it hard to decide exactly which woman's troubles deserved more discussion. "I'll try to stay clear of Rosalind for a while," she offered.

"You'll face greater challenges a bit closer to home, too," Aunt Hilda warned. She stopped in her tracks, forcing Martha to stop, too, and let out a soft sigh. "James and Lydia had an awful time keeping the tavern operating after Victoria left, especially with you gone, too. They needed help, so they hired Annabelle Swift. She's a hardworking girl, but she's only helping until Victoria gets back. I wanted you to know before you got home."

Martha clenched her jaw, shocked by the intense wave of betrayal that washed over her. For her brother to replace Victoria, even temporarily, made her absence even more of a reality—one that would pierce Martha's heart every time she saw Annabelle instead of Victoria working in the tavern.

Disappointed in her brother, as well as his wife, Martha was once again reminded of her tenuous position in their household. Too distraught to risk discussing the matter with Aunt Hilda just then, she took a deep breath and forced herself to focus only on her duties. "Let's go inside and gather the others to pray."

Chapter
SIX

Long before the sun rose to light the new day, the six women gathered together in Adelaide and Daniel's bedchamber and encircled the double bed. Adelaide cradled her sleeping daughter in the crook of her arm while Daniel stood, tall and proud, at her side. They joined their hands together to create an unbroken prayer circle. Heart-to-heart, they bowed their heads, ready to begin the tradition Trinity's first midwife had started so long ago.

From her place at the foot at the bed, Martha led them all in prayer. "O Lord, we thank You this day for Thy goodness and praise Thy name for the blessings You have bestowed upon us. We thank You for entrusting us with Thy newest creation, Glory Adelaide Finch, and we accept Thy call to love her and raise her and teach her Your Word. May the light of Your love shine always on this family, giving both Daniel and Adelaide the wisdom and courage to be good parents while Glory is in their care. Amen."

"Amen," came the chorused reply as gazes once more locked on the new mother and her babe.

Adelaide wore a dazzling smile. Propped up against a mound of pillows, she nuzzled the top of Glory's head before she turned the sleeping babe around for all to see. "She's so beautiful, and quite perfectly formed," she boasted as she unwrapped the blankets to give anxious eyes a full view. Tiny legs curled up close to a diaper covering her little bottom, and arms with clenched fists lay tight against her chest as though still confined to her mother's womb. A mop of dark ringlets capped a sweet little face still flushed from the struggle of birth.

The new mother's eyes filled with tears as she gazed around the circle of women. "Daniel and I want to thank you all for helping us," she whispered. She turned her gaze back to Martha for a moment, then looked up at her husband.

Daniel cleared his throat. "I'm especially indebted to you, Widow Cade. Thank you for keeping both of the women in my life safe."

Accustomed to receiving praise and platitudes from grateful new parents, Martha issued her traditional reply, although she could not remember when it had meant more to her. "I'm privileged to share this moment with you. With all of you," she added, addressing all the women who had helped Adelaide prepare for childbirth. "While I spend a few moments with Daniel and Adelaide, I think all of you should get some well-deserved rest. You'll have more opportunity to see Adelaide and Glory in the morning before you leave for home."

Once Aunt Hilda led the mildly protesting women out of the room, Martha went to the side of the bed and laid her hand atop her patient's abdomen. Even through the thin sheet and top blanket, she could feel nothing rigid. Adelaide complained of no pain when Martha applied gentle pressure. "Everything is proceeding perfectly normally," she informed both Adelaide and her husband. "Aunt Hilda will stay while Adelaide recovers during her lying-in period, and she'll be able to answer any questions either of you have. She'll also know if there's anything that needs my attention. I suspect that's not likely to happen," she added when concern knitted Daniel's brows together.

"Will you stay through morning?" he asked.

"Actually, with Adelaide in such good hands, I'd like to go home. I haven't seen James or Lydia yet, and I'd like to talk with them . . . about Victoria."

Adelaide clutched Glory to her chest, as if keeping her child from leaving her, too. Martha took a deep breath and used the very words she had chosen to explain Victoria's continuing absence to the other women earlier. "I pray the good Lord will watch over her and protect her until He brings her home. Until then, I'd ask for your prayers for Victoria, too," she concluded.

Adelaide worried her lower lip. "Of course. I'm so sorry. I wish there was something we could do to help more."

"I do, too," Martha whispered. "Now, I want you to get some rest, young lady. You, too," she teased Daniel when she noted the exhaustion that had slumped his shoulders. "I'll see myself out and make sure the ladies are tucked in before I go."

"I secured your bag and the birthing stool just like you told me and made sure Grace got some oats and fresh water," Daniel said quickly. He paused. "I hesitate to ask you to do anything more, but Dr. McMillan left this behind." He took the doctor's lancet out of his shirt pocket. "I won't be going to town for a while. I was wondering . . . I mean, if it isn't too much trouble, would you be able to return it to him for me tomorrow? I wouldn't want him to have to ride all the way out here, especially after what happened."

Martha wanted to see Dr. McMillan again tomorrow about as much as she might want to have a tooth pulled, but she understood how awkward it would be for Daniel to have the doctor show up on his doorstep again.

"I'll be happy to return it in the morning," she assured him, and took the lancet.

He let out a deep breath. "As for your reward . . ." He tried, but could not stifle the yawn that interrupted him.

She chuckled. "We'll take care of that in a few days when I stop back to visit Adelaide." Without giving him time to argue, Martha left the bedchamber.

In the main room of the cabin, light from a single kerosene lamp on a small table near the front door guided her past the sleeping women in their makeshift dormitory. Once she had put on both her cape and her bonnet and had extinguished the lamp, she eased her way out the door, being careful to not wake anyone. She checked to make sure Daniel had adequately secured her bag and the birthing stool, and stored the doctor's lancet in her valise. Satisfied, she untied the reins and mounted Grace. She leaned forward and patted the horse's neck before donning her leather gloves. "A girl this time," she murmured.

A snort.

"I thought so, too, but you can't tell first-time parents much of anything." She nudged the horse and turned her about. "Take me home, Grace. Take me home."

At the break of dawn, Martha led Grace into the stable behind the tavern. She made quick work of getting the horse settled into her stall at the very end of the structure, grabbed hold of the birthing stool with one hand, and carried her midwife's bag and travel bag with the other. The horses James kept for his own use in the other three stalls acknowledged her presence with little more than curious glances, although Leech, a black-and-white tomcat, offered his customary hiss from his perch on one of the horses' backs.

Leech was as nasty to humans as he was deadly to rodents, and Martha had the feeling he would eat people, too, if he were big enough to give it a try. Strangely, he preferred horses for company, and invariably jumped on the back of one of the horse to nap. Based on personal experience, she knew he was one miserable, cranky beast of an animal, and she avoided him whenever she could, although she had to admit he was one terrific hunter and kept the stable and wagon yard free of mice and snakes.

Outside, a peddler's wagon and three Conestoga wagons sat in the wagon yard. Martha gave wide skirt to the whole area for fear of waking the bulldogs the wagoneers typically used to guard their horses while they were tethered to troughs in the center of the yard. She hoped Leech would do the same. The last time he tried to take a nap on the back of one of the wagoneers' horses in the yard, one of the bulldogs ended up losing an eye, along with his pride.

She had little doubt the sleeping room on the second floor of the tavern was filled to near capacity and Lydia would appreciate an extra pair of hands to prepare breakfast as well as to start the heavier meal that would be served throughout the day.

She hurried to the outside entrance to the room James had added for her at the rear of the tavern. On her way, she glanced at the herb garden and stopped. Of the six raised beds, Lydia planted and tended only two, which provided enough herbs for both family and tavern use. The remaining four belonged to Martha to grow the simples she used as remedies for both childbirth and the minor illnesses she treated.

After three months of neglect while she was away, made worse because she had been gone during prime growing season, Martha expected to see a pitiful display of weed-choked plants too scraggly to offer anything she could salvage. Instead, healthy plants appeared to fill each bed. Pleasantly shocked, she pressed a finger to the soil. Damp and spongy. Unless it had rained recently, Lydia had watered her garden, too.

Guilt for adding to Lydia's already heavy burden of tasks tempered her joy and erased any selfish thoughts she might have entertained about trying to steal a quick nap before helping Lydia in the kitchen. She simply added yet another debt to those she already owed to her brother and his wife.

Buoyed by the unexpected gift she had found waiting for her in the herb garden, she entered her room, shut the door behind her, and latched it closed. Argentine light filtered into the room through the single window facing the wagon yard, and Martha caught and held her breath for several long heartbeats as she scanned the single chamber she and Victoria had called their home.

Straight ahead, on the wall adjoining the main tavern, a new cast-iron cookstove, which had a small surface on top to brew a warm drink, heat water for bathing, or prepare the remedies Martha used in her work, sat at rest near the door that led inside to the storeroom at the rear of the tavern. On either side of the lone window, a trunk anchored the bottom of each single cot, each covered with patchwork quilts she had inherited from her mother.

She narrowed her gaze and let out a sigh of relief when she spied the locked box containing her grandmother's diary resting on the bottom shelf of the small table separating the cots.

A narrow bench in the far opposite corner nudged a pine work-table, its scars covered in the center by a white cotton runner and a single glass vase waiting for wildflowers to add a splash of color. Near the stove, a corner cupboard, a reward her grandmother had received long ago, held only a few utensils and some cookware, since Martha and Victoria regularly took their meals in the tavern itself with James and Lydia once the last of their three daughters had married and gone to housekeeping. A fireplace on the wall facing the beds provided warmth.

A shelf directly to her right is where she stored her midwife's bag. Below the shelf, a set of brackets held the birthing stool well above the floorboards. In the corner, a water pump stood at attention next to a table holding a nest of basins and a short stack of towels. Above the table, an unframed mirror with a crack straight down the middle offered a splintered view of the room's contents, including the bare beams overhead where no herbs hung to dry.

Her heartbeat quickened for the briefest of moments, then slowed to a heavy thud. It made no sense at all, but there were parts of her—the irrational, the romantic, the child, and the dreamer—that had been hoping to find Victoria safely tucked into her bed, the way Martha had found her so many times upon returning home from a delivery. The more rational sides of her—the adult and the realist—merely accepted Victoria's absence as a sad reality.

The very sight of Victoria's empty cot brought tears to her eyes. Even though she knew it had been an impossible dream, even though

Aunt Hilda had told her Victoria was still missing and there had been no word from her, Martha had not really accepted that as reality until now, when the sight of that simple little empty bed made Victoria's disappearance finally become real, so very, very real.

"Victoria," she whispered, and struggled until she had blinked back every tear. Her mind raced in a host of directions, searching for an image of Victoria that would give her the strength and courage to endure thinking about the horrid possibilities Victoria might be enduring during her sea travel. Those thoughts would keep her sleepless if she let them.

She chose one image, with Victoria planted at the railing of a ship. The wind freed a few dark curls from beneath her bonnet and whipped at the ribbons hanging from the bow beneath her chin, raising a healthy pink glow on her cheeks. With her dark blue eyes dancing, Victoria studied the open sea, and her lips gently eased into a smile. She exuded health and happiness, an image Martha claimed, dashing all other images—shipwrecks, epidemics of shipboard diseases, and a lascivious crew, not to mention scalawag traveling companions—to the netherworld where they belonged.

After storing away her midwife's bag and the birthing stool, she placed her travel bag and gloves on top of the trunk at the foot of her cot. She hung her bonnet and cape on wooden pegs on the wall. Working quickly, she took a fresh gown from the trunk, changed, and then pumped a basin of water so she could wash.

She chanced a look into the mirror, grimaced, and unpinned her hair. Several quick brush strokes were all she needed to clear the tangles. She twisted her hair into a knot and pinned it at the nape of her neck. When she glanced back at her image in the mirror, she studied the stranger looking back at her. Gray hair at each temple now streaked gently through her auburn hair. A frightening number of new lines etched the corners of her dark brown eyes. The generous number of freckles that were sprinkled across the bridge of her nose and spilled down her cheeks were darker, her naturally pale skin had tanned, and the deep dimples in her cheeks now appeared to be bottomless caverns.

She leaned closer to the mirror, tilted her head to catch more of the light, and sighed, but there was nothing she could do now to prevent wrinkles from forming on her sun-drenched face. "And I'm getting gray now, too. I suppose I'll look like Grace before long."

Dismayed to find herself preoccupied with her appearance, she looked herself straight in the eye, squared her shoulders, pursed her lips, and turned away from the mirror.

Met by sounds emanating from the storeroom, she hurried to the connecting door, threw the bolt, and opened the door.

James turned around so fast he nearly dropped the cask of rum in his arms. "Martha! Land sakes, you just took five years off my life!" he complained, but the tender look in his dark eyes gentled his reprimand. Although they shared the same coloring, they were a contrast in shapes, even given their gender. Martha was near average in height and carried enough weight to have the abundant curves most men admired. James was overly tall and decidedly angular, to the extent he carried his childhood nickname, Stick, even to this day.

"I'm sorry," she gushed. "I didn't mean to startle you. I thought you knew I was back."

He sat the cask down on the floor, brushed his hands off on his overalls, and pulled her into a crushing embrace. "Dillon thought you'd have been here long before him. Once Aunt Hilda left and you didn't come home during the night, I figured you met up with her at some point and wound up at the Finches'."

She squeezed him back before breaking free. "Indeed. I got there just in time to help Glory Adelaide Finch arrive safe and sound. Her mama's doing just fine, too," she added, and made a mental note to add this most recent birth to her diary.

He placed one of his hands on her shoulder. "But what about you? How are you, Martha?"

She reached across her chest to cover his hand with her own. "I'll be fine. I'm just . . . disappointed I couldn't bring Victoria home," she murmured, and quickly shared some of the details of her ill-fated travels.

His eyes deepened, changing from a gentle shade of brown to

almost black. "I should have stopped her. Somehow, I should have known she might run away. I should have paid closer attention to her that night. Maybe if I had—"

"You can't blame yourself. The good Lord knows I've learned that lesson over the past few months. Victoria made her choice. As hurtful and as reckless as it was, she has to bear responsibility for what she's done. All we can do is pray she'll be safe and come home soon."

She paused and took a deep breath. "I know it hasn't been easy for you or for Lydia. Aunt Hilda told me you have someone here to help you," she murmured, still hurt by his decision to hire a replacement for Victoria, yet aware now it had been necessary once she noted the lines of exhaustion that lined his narrow forehead.

His gaze grew more troubled. "It's not that we don't think Victoria will be back soon or that we don't want her back—"

"I know. You did the right thing to hire Annabelle," she admitted, seeing her disappointment now as pure selfishness.

"You're not cross with us?"

She patted his hand. "I'm not cross. You and Lydia welcomed me and my children into your home for too long for me to ever be cross with you. Besides, you're my big brother. We're family," she teased. Her heart swelled when relief filled his eyes and brought a smile to his lips.

He nodded and swallowed a visible lump in his throat. "Let's see about getting breakfast ready. Lydia's anxious to see you. And there's lots of news here at home. You're . . . you're not going to like some of it," he warned as he led her out of the storeroom.

She followed him into the kitchen without comment and found Annabelle kneading bread at the kitchen table with her sister-in-law. Martha was grateful Aunt Hilda had warned her in advance and twice as grateful she had been able to purge her selfish feelings before this moment.

Lydia looked up and dropped a mound of dough she had been working to the table. "Martha!" she cried. She wiped her hands on her apron as she rushed straight over to embrace her. "It's so good to have you home, but I'm so sorry Victoria isn't with you," she gushed.

She set Martha back, took a good look at her, and frowned. "Just as I feared. You've gotten too much sun again. After breakfast, we'll see about getting some milk to bathe your face."

Martha laughed. "We're going to need gallons this time, I'm afraid." She looked past Lydia to catch Annabelle's gaze and noted how Lydia nervously twisted the hem of her apron with her fingers.

The girl blushed and dropped her gaze, along with the dough she had been kneading. Her hands began to tremble. "Good morning. Welcome home," she murmured.

Touched, Martha smiled. "Aunt Hilda tells me you're doing a fine job here at the tavern."

When Annabelle looked up, her eyes were open wide with distrust. "I'm only helping till Victoria comes home."

"I know," Martha assured her. "We're all blessed to have you here." Her words were truly heartfelt and her smile was genuine. Praise God. She rolled up her sleeves and went directly to the pump to wash her hands. She looked over her shoulder again and smiled. "I'll help with the bread and let you all tell me what's been happening in Trinity while I've been gone," she suggested, curious about James's warning that some of the news might not be easy to hear.

Chapter
SEVEN

Martha walked into the kitchen later that day, glanced around, took a good whiff, and smiled. At least some things had not changed.

A huge kettle of mutton stew simmered on the hearth. A parade of fresh loaves of bread cooled on wooden racks, while apple pies laced with cinnamon and butter baking in the oven created even more tantalizing aromas that had begun to spread throughout the tavern.

In the lull between the departure of last night's guests and new arrivals, including townspeople anxious for a hearty meal, James was outside tending to the wagon yard and stables while Annabelle helped Lydia tidy the second-floor sleeping dormitory. Martha had used the time she had to herself, now that Annabelle was there, to bathe and change into a fresh gown before trying the milk remedy for her face.

When she checked her complexion in the mirror, she did not see any change at all and decided the milk should be put to far better use. She washed the empty bowl and rinsed out the cloth she had used before storing them both away and returning to her room. Feeling refreshed, but still weary, she sat down at the worktable in her room. She added two new entries to her diary, and in the process, felt a familiar sense of order return to her life, a necessity since nothing much else in Trinity had stayed the same:

15 June	*A son for Captain Tyler. Received $3 reward.*
10 September	*Delivered a girl to Mr. Finch and wife. Left her doing cleverly. Debt $2.*

She was satisfied she still had enough room on the last line to record her reward when it was paid, but as an afterthought, she added one additional line to the entry:

Met the new doctor, Benjamin McMillan.

Gazing at her two entries, she swallowed hard. There was nothing she could do now to change all she had failed to do between the birth of Captain Tyler's son and the arrival of Glory Finch. There was nothing she could do about the three-month gap between entries, either. She had been faithful to her promise to her grandmother and had kept a diary of her work for the past ten years. She had never had a lapse of more than a few days. Until now.

She would not find a three-month gap in her grandmother's diary, either. That diary was actually a collection of papers kept in chronological order, as opposed to the bound book Martha used. Someday, perhaps, Grandmother's papers and Martha's diary would become part of the official town records since they contained accounts of all the births in Trinity since its founding in 1770.

The chain linking past to present for all those who lived in Trinity now, as well as for future generations, had been broken. Disheartened, she set her diary aside.

She was far beyond exhaustion at this juncture, but pent-up nervous energy would never let her sleep until she got rid of it. Rather than waste the energy, she put on her old canvas apron, garden gloves, and a wide-brimmed straw hat. She slipped her hand into one of the two wide pockets lining the front of the apron, felt the old pair of scissors, and went outside to her herb garden.

With the smell and feel of autumn in the air now, she needed to dry enough herbs to last until next summer. The first frost was probably several weeks away, but she never knew when duty might call her away or for how long. Touched by the full light of day, however, her herb garden looked far less bountiful than it had earlier that morning.

In the first bed of herbs, the wormwood had grown to nearly three feet high this year, although some kind of insect had attacked the silver-green leaves on many of the plants with a vengeance. Out of the entire planting, she barely had enough to line the bottom of her basket.

Battling for dominance in the same bed, hyssop, with purple-flowered spikes, added grace and color but had apparently not held the same appeal to the bugs that had eaten the wormwood. She cut several dozen stalks, especially pleased with the size of the leaves this season. She turned her attention next to a graceful but sparse display of Lady's Thumb. Clusters of small pink flowers lined the reddish stems, but at least half of the plants had been eaten clear down to the roots. She added a single layer to her basket and made a mental note to treat the soil before winter set in.

She slipped the scissors back into her apron pocket, got back to her feet, and slipped the basket onto her arm. When she turned to go back to her room, she saw the mayor, Thomas Dillon, riding past the rear fence with Sheriff Myer.

Her heart leaped in her chest. Instinctively. Before her mind could control the affection for Thomas she thought she had buried long ago.

She rubbed her brow with the back of her free hand and shook her head. She must be truly exhausted to have let that happen.

She held very still while her heart continued to race. It was probably too much to hope the men would not see her, but she hoped for just that. With any kind of luck, Thomas would be too engrossed in his conversation with the sheriff to take any notice of her. For several very long moments, she had the opportunity to observe him as he rode by.

Memories washed over her—memories made more vivid now that he was no longer married. Following his wife's death over a year ago, Thomas had become the most eligible widower between Clarion, in the west, and Sunrise, some thirty miles to the east. Remarkably fit at forty-five, he was not only the wealthiest man in Trinity, but probably also the most handsome, too. He topped six feet by four inches, had a thick head of black hair without a single touch of gray, and could sweet-talk a woman like no other man she had ever met.

Another huge wave of emotion washed away the past twenty-five years, sweeping her back to a time when they both were young and filled with the optimism of the future that lay ahead, their untested hearts vulnerable to a passion that was consuming. So consuming Martha almost accepted his proposal of marriage before she realized making her life with Thomas, a man also destined to play a leadership role in their community, would leave no room for anything else in her life.

Her sense of duty to her grandmother and her future as a midwife had prevailed.

Her marriage to John Cade the following year was not based on romantic passion but on mutual respect that grew, over the years, into an affection they shared that was both companionate and satisfying. It was a marriage in which Martha also found unyielding support for her work with Grandmother Poore.

Eventually, Thomas had married, too, and from all accounts, his marriage to Sally Moore had been a good one.

But John was gone now, and Martha still missed him. Ten years of widowhood had softened the blow of his untimely death as only one of many victims of an epidemic that had claimed too many of Trinity's citizens. With his death, she had lost her safe haven, and she had rebuilt her life the only way she knew how—by focusing her love on her children and her energies on her calling.

Sally Dillon was gone now, too. With Thomas's mourning period nearly over, Martha's heart beat a little bit faster when he was near, opening the window to dreams that belonged to the past.

"Older is not necessarily wiser," she grumbled as her heartbeat continued to race. Although she knew the barriers that separated them now were just as real as they had been twenty-five years ago, her heart refused to listen and beat even faster, demanding her attention and forcing her to face her feelings for Thomas again.

She held her breath until the two men passed by on East Falls Road. Miraculously, neither man had taken any notice of her. She kept her place for several minutes after they disappeared from view, and waited until her heartbeat returned to normal. With pure strength of will, she closed the window in her heart and concentrated all of her efforts on reclaiming the path she had chosen for her life so long ago.

With sure steps, she returned to her room. After removing her hat and gloves, she spread the herbs on the worktable and inhaled, enjoying the blend of distinctive aromas that began to fill her chamber and steadied her resolve to put Thomas out of her mind as well as her heart.

She worked efficiently but carefully, loosely tying thin twine to the stems and stalks before securing a ladder from the storeroom and hanging her harvest from the overhead beams. When she was finished and had restored the room to order again, the fragrant and colorful canopy overhead also restored her spirit.

Her work had used up all her nervous energy, and her body now demanded rest. She laid down on her cot and savored a long view of her herbs overhead, but her heart and mind refused to quiet and find peace. Worry for Victoria inspired a fervent prayer before she replayed snippets of her earlier conversations with Lydia and Annabelle in her mind.

Martha had spent most of their time together describing her recent travels and the arrival of the Finch baby. Annabelle listened rather than offered much by way of town news. Lydia did tell her about the new sidewalk being constructed on West Main Street and the planned construction of a new meetinghouse, but little else, since she appeared to be obsessed with providing all the details surrounding the death of Doc Beyer and the arrival of Dr. McMillan.

As tired as she was, Martha's thoughts kept leading her straight back to Rosalind. Since she still had to return the doctor's lancet, there was no question she would see the woman again very soon.

Rather than prolonging the inevitable or letting her mind exaggerate the problem, Martha prayed for patience and understanding while she freshened up. Before she left her room, she rewrapped the lancet in cloth, slipped it into her reticule, and tried to not think about the irony that she was about to return a weapon to one of her opponents. En route, she would have an opportunity to see some of the changes Lydia had described before a rush of patrons demanding breakfast had interrupted their conversation.

East Main Street had a fresh bed of cinders, thank goodness, but little traffic even at midday, and Martha walked down the middle of the street under a clear blue sky and gentle sun.

On the opposite side of Dillon's Stream, several wagons and carriages rested outside the row of homes and businesses on West Main Street where workers continued to cut and hammer the new planked sidewalk into place, exactly as Lydia had described. Six or seven women with young children in tow had gathered outside the general store, too preoccupied to pay any attention to Martha as she strode toward her destination.

Normally, she would use the covered bridge at the other end of town and cross over to visit with the other women and talk to the children, most of whom she had helped to deliver. Today, however, she had a mission that kept her focused only on the task at hand.

The farther she walked, the more the activity at the sawmill and gristmill behind her receded into muted testimony that almost half the workday had already been spent. She had to hurry if she expected to return and help Lydia and Annabelle before the mill workers broke for their midday meal or wagons en route to Clarion arrived to fill the tavern to near capacity.

She quickened her steps as she passed the mayor's home and once more blocked out any thoughts of Thomas, but she rocked to a halt when she reached the site where the meetinghouse had always stood. Even though Lydia had tried to warn her, she was still unprepared for what she beheld with her own eyes. Only the foundation remained of the log structure where generations had gathered to worship as a community of believers each Sunday morning. She could see clear through to the cemetery, once hidden by the meetinghouse, and rows of tombstones weathered by time paid silent homage to so many loved ones who rested beneath them.

She shook her head and felt her heart constrict with grief for the loss of the familiar meetinghouse, but she also understood the need for a larger building. According to James, who had attended the elders' meeting in July, when the final decision had been made, the old meetinghouse had been removed from its foundation and rolled to the far end of East Main Street, next to the market, where it sat waiting to be converted into a new schoolhouse.

Construction of the new meetinghouse, planned as a grand brick church with a parsonage alongside, had been delayed because the builder from Clarion had taken ill and died, leaving the elders no choice but to find a new builder. Unfortunately, he was not able to start work until spring. In the meantime, Sunday meeting would be held in the old meetinghouse, which would also be used as a town meeting place while the debate about where to build a permanent town hall continued.

When she glimpsed the familiar figure of a large man making his way through the woods behind the cemetery, her heart leaped from despair to hope. Of all the things and people she knew and loved in Trinity, Samuel Meeks was a man on whom she could depend to be a constant, however odd others might find that to be if they ever found out she had become friends with the town's infamous hermit nearly a year ago.

Known as much for his formidable size and salty vocabulary as for the mystery surrounding his past, Samuel was a hairy bear of a man with thick dark hair that covered his head and his arms. If his size alone did not frighten you, then the tattoo on his left cheek certainly would—as would the tatoos on both of his forearms, although no one in Trinity had ever seen more than his face.

For most people, his face was more than enough. The tattoo on his cheek was not colored with any dye, but had been created by a series of raised scars that must have been incredibly painful to endure while the image of the sea serpent they formed had been created.

A long-retired seaman now nearing seventy, he had moved to Trinity ten years ago and lived in an isolated cabin deep in the woods on the outskirts of town. Martha had finally met him only last year and had tended to him simply because he refused to see a doctor or admit that his clouding vision might be a prelude to total blindness.

Hoping she might be able to let him know she had finally returned to Trinity, she gathered up her skirts and hurried past the foundation of the meetinghouse, the charred remains of an old oak tree, and through the cemetery. By the time she entered the woods, however, Samuel had disappeared. "Samuel? It's Martha," she cried as she scanned the area. His cabin lay hidden in the woods several hundred yards ahead, and she was reluctant to pursue him that far without being certain he had been heading for home.

"No need to yell. I'm right here."

Startled, she swung around and found him leaning against the trunk of a large tree. He had a string of fish in one hand and a crude fishing pole in the other. "Heard you were back. Heard 'bout Victoria, too."

She swallowed hard. She was amazed at how much this virtual recluse knew about the townspeople he avoided. "I was on my way to see Dr. McMillan when I saw you. How's your vision?"

He held up his catch. "Good enough to get me some breakfast."

"That's not what I meant," she countered. "Have you seen any improvement after using the eyewash?"

He pursed his lips. "Can't say it did much 'cept take up a lot of my time."

She let out a sigh. Apparently, the goldenseal she had left with him had not been effective, and it was hard not to be disappointed. With Doc Beyer gone now, she had no one to turn to for other ideas, and she had exhausted her usual remedies. She doubted if Samuel would even consider talking with Dr. McMillan. "I'm sorry. I really thought it would help. Let me see if I can figure out something else."

His eyes flashed with hope he quickly extinguished with the brusque manner he usually used to cover up his fears about facing possible blindness. "Got work to do. Don't go worryin' yourself 'bout it. Nothing worse than a naggin' woman," he grumbled. He pulled back from the trunk of the tree and walked past her, paused, and turned around to face her again. "Stop by in a week or two. If you have a mind for it," he murmured before he turned and headed toward home.

She watched him until the woods closed around his figure. Reassured by his offer to have her visit at his cabin, she welcomed the opportunity to renew and restore their friendship as much as the chance to truly find a simple or any other remedy that would cure his vision once and for all.

With a lighter heart, she backtracked and continued on her way down East Main Street, which was virtually deserted. She was grateful Market Day was tomorrow, instead of today. On Market Day the town would literally swell with families from the outlying areas who came to trade or sell their wares and purchase their needs before returning to the farms and homesteads that surrounded the center of town.

She reached the home and office where Doc Beyer had lived and worked, and stopped at the end of the stone walkway that led to the front door. A new sign with Dr. McMillan's name now hung from the post at the street edge of the front yard, replacing the weathered, paint-chipped sign that had hung there for over fifty years.

The house itself looked different, too. A fresh coat of white paint brightened the plaster that covered the fieldstone underneath. The single-wide shutters on the two windows to the left of the front door were open. The door itself, once natural wood, had been painted dark brown, and a brass knocker now adorned the center of the door. Directly overhead, the stone lintel still carried the date, 1770, and the builder's initials, MLL, a gentle reminder that this house had been one of the first constructed in town.

A steep, slanting roof topped the three-story home, its slate shingles reflecting strong sunlight. Old shrubs of buttonbush and wild hydrangeas hugged either side of the walkway as lush testimony to the woman Doc Beyer had married and buried many years ago. Martha had missed their flowers this last summer, but she was more interested in the leaves and bark. Upon close inspection, she saw that the foliage was healthy, yet Doc Beyer's passing and Dr. McMillan's purchase of the property meant she no longer had permission to gather the bark and leaves from the buttonbush and wild hydrangeas.

Now was probably not the time to broach the subject.

Her hand was only inches from the knocker when the door opened. Rosalind blocked Martha's entry and kept her hand on the frame of the door with her face and figure kissed by the full light of day.

For one very long heartbeat, Martha studied the woman's features. Deep valleys like those between her brows also appeared on either side of her face like elongated teardrops made of acid that had permanently etched her skin. The corners of Rosalind's lips were turned downward in a permanent frown, but it was the bitterness in her eyes and the pallor on her face that pierced Martha's heart.

In the rush of things at the Finch household, Martha had not noticed the changes in Rosalind's appearance, although the artificial light in the cabin had certainly been more forgiving than natural sunlight. It was also possible that after an absence of several months,

Martha simply had the opportunity to see Rosalind now with a fresh eye.

If ever Martha needed proof that a hardened heart drained not only the spirit but also the physical body, she had only to look at Rosalind to see how bitterness had marred Rosalind's once-lovely countenance. Looking at Rosalind as she appeared now also gave Martha a chance to see how she herself might look if she did not accept the troubles life had to offer as anything less than a gift meant to be opened and treasured for the lessons it contained.

She offered a genuine smile, but remained standing in place, all the while praying Rosalind might be willing to resume their friend-ship. "It's a splendid morning, isn't it?"

"Dr. McMillan is resting this morning. He had a very late night last night, as you well know. You'll have to come back later," she snapped, and started to close the door.

Martha took a step forward so that her shoulder was even with the jam of the door, effectively forcing Rosalind to keep the door open. "I don't mean to disturb him, but he left one of his instruments behind last night. I wanted to return it to him so he wouldn't have to go all the way back to the Finch homestead to retrieve it."

"How kind of you," the housekeeper quipped, as if unleashing her frustration over Burton's situation at Martha might make the problem disappear.

Martha ignored the nasty tone in Rosalind's voice. She simply opened her reticule, retrieved the wrapped lancet, and held it out to the other woman. "If you'll give this to Dr. McMillan for me, I can be on my way."

"Widow Cade?" The doctor's voice sounded very close, and he came into view once Rosalind stepped aside without taking the lancet and swung the door wide open.

With his frock coat sorely rumpled and a day's growth of stubble on his face, he looked like he had fallen asleep fully dressed after returning from the Finch homestead and only just awakened.

"I'm sorry. I didn't mean to disturb you," Martha offered as she entered the kitchen, typically the first room in homes this old. Rosalind presented her back and returned to a bowl and a pile of peas she apparently had been shelling when Martha interrupted her.

"I only wanted to return your lancet. You left it behind last night." She handed him the instrument. "It's a long ride. I thought I might save you the trouble."

He took hold of the lancet, and the wariness in his gaze softened to appreciation. "Thank you. I trust Mrs. Finch is doing well?"

"Very cleverly. The babe also. A girl."

He nodded, turning the lancet over and over in his hand. His brows knitted together as if he were mentally reviewing all he had done to aid Adelaide's labor before Martha arrived, trying to figure out what he could have done differently so that he could have delivered the baby instead of Martha.

The genuine concern she detected in his gaze earned him her respect, although she did not condone what he had done by bleeding a woman in labor. Nor had she altered her opinion that doctors in general—and this doctor in particular—had much to learn about treating and safely delivering a teeming woman. He was also, she noted, young enough to be her son, and her maternal instincts softened her attitude toward him.

"May I offer you some refreshment? Coffee? Tea?" he asked. He gave her a sheepish grin that only made him look younger. "I'm afraid I haven't changed or shaved since yesterday. It was so late when I returned—"

"I understand completely," she insisted. "A cup of tea would be most welcome, although perhaps you'd rather make it another time."

"One cup of tea. And some coffee, Mrs. Andrews. We'll take it in my office," he suggested, and led Martha to the room directly to their left without waiting for her to answer him.

She entered the room and quickly determined that he had not changed or added much since taking over Doc Beyer's practice, although she had to admit he was a far sight neater than his predecessor. Straight ahead, a stack of books and pamphlets lay neatly on the corner of his desk. The cabinets flush against the wall on either side of the desk looked familiar. One was filled with instruments; the other contained bottles of medicines and other supplies. A door on the far right wall that led to a treatment room was closed, but Martha suspected the room remained the same, along with the second treatment room that lay beyond it.

While he took a moment to return his lancet to its proper place in one of the cabinets, she took a seat in one of the two wooden chairs in front of his desk. Framed diplomas and certificates hung on the wall directly in front of her. Unlike Doc Beyer, who had served only an apprenticeship under a practicing physician before starting his own practice here in Trinity, Dr. McMillan was apparently university trained, both here in the United States and abroad, just as Aunt Hilda had claimed.

She could not read the documents without getting closer to them to determine exactly where he had received his education, and she had no intention of being rude enough to inquire.

He joined her and took his own seat, folded his hands atop his desk, and smiled. "I understand you worked with Dr. Beyer for many years," he prompted.

"And my grandmother before me."

He narrowed his gaze. "I've been told she was also a midwife."

She smiled. "The first here in Trinity."

"Then you're following family tradition, just like I am. All the McMillan men in the past four generations have practiced medicine, although I'm the first to venture this far west."

"You're from New York?"

"Born and bred. My father still practices there with my brother. My grandfather retired many years ago, but he knew Dr. Beyer. That's how I came to settle here after he died." He paused to clear his throat. "In any event, I'm looking forward to serving the people here, and I'm grateful that Mrs. Andrews agreed to remain as housekeeper."

Martha nodded. Rosalind and Burton Andrews had moved in with her uncle, Doc Beyer, after his wife died nearly twenty years ago. In addition to working at the sawmill, Burt handled routine maintenance while Rosalind kept house, which included keeping the doctor's office and treatment rooms spotlessly clean.

The house was certainly large enough to accommodate everyone. Doc Beyer had had his own private rooms on the second floor while the Andrews had claimed the third floor for themselves and their only child, Charlotte. Whether or not this arrangement would continue, she supposed, depended on how long Burton Andrews decided to remain in self-imposed exile.

Rosalind entered with a tray and had scarcely placed it atop the doctor's desk when the front door banged open and a man charged into the doctor's office.

Breathing hard, he stopped to draw in a deep breath before rattling off a plea. "Doc. You gotta come to the sawmill. Quick. Charlie Greywald's got his hand caught in a saw. He's hurt real bad. Real bad. They've been tryin' to get his hand free, but——"

Dr. McMillan leaped to his feet, grabbed his medical bag, and called back over his shoulder as he followed the man out of the room. "I'm sorry. We'll talk again. Soon," he promised, and promptly disappeared.

Martha bowed her head and said a prayer for Charlie Greywald. When she looked up, Rosalind was standing in front of her holding on to the side of the desk with her lips set in a firm line. "I'm afraid you'll have to leave now."

"I could help you," Martha offered. "Maybe we could talk."

Rosalind's gaze hardened. "I don't need any help, and I don't have time for idle gossip."

Martha flinched. "I didn't intend to gossip. I only wanted you to know how badly I feel that Burton still hasn't come home. I know how hard it is for you," she murmured.

"Do you?" Her eyes glistened. "How could you possibly know what it's like to have a husband who runs off when he's wrongly charged with a crime, leaving me behind to defend him to friends and neighbors who are all convinced he's guilty of stealing that watch? I can't go to the general store or the confectionery without people staring at me or hearing them whisper behind my back."

"Not everyone believes——"

"Oh, please spare me your misplaced sympathy and your insufferable optimism!" she cried. "I'm not deaf, any more than I'm blind or stupid. And neither are you. I hope you're stronger than I am, because you'll need to be, now that you've come home without your daughter."

She nodded. "The only good thing about having you home is that maybe, just maybe, the gossipmongers will leave me in peace now and focus on you and Victoria instead of me and my husband. At least Charlotte will be spared any more shame, which is far less than you can expect for your own daughter. Now, if you'll excuse me, I have a room to get ready for the doctor's patient," she snapped, and marched off to the adjoining treatment room.

Martha flinched. Her cheeks stung as if she had been slapped. She stared at the doorway through which Rosalind had disappeared and debated whether or not she should follow Rosalind to confront her or run home.

Chapter

EIGHT

Martha gripped her reticule with both hands and clamped her knees together. The greater part of her wanted to storm into the next room and throttle Rosalind until her bones ached and her bitter heart snapped in half. Maybe then she would be willing to listen, to understand that she was not alone, that she was not responsible for what her husband had done.

Martha's conscience, if not her faith, reminded her that there was nothing she could do for Rosalind unless the woman opened her own heart. At one time, they had been friends. Close friends. It hurt deeply to be rejected, but it hurt more to feel utterly helpless and to stand by, watching her former friend become so bitter.

When she stood up, her legs were shaking. She squared her shoulders, and her steps grew steadier as she passed through to the kitchen and out the front door. She forced herself not to run all the way home, but the echo of Rosalind's bitter words did not fade. Frightened by the depth of her own emotions, Martha slipped into her room and closed the door behind her.

She collapsed back against the door and stifled deep sobs with a clenched fist. Oh, how she hurt. So deeply her chest ached with the struggle to keep her heart from bursting. So completely her mind could fashion not a single thought. She could only feel and react, completely defenseless as anger, resentment, and fear fought bitterly against hope, trust, and faith on the battleground of her soul.

The skirmish was fierce but quick.

As her sobs eased into gentle whimpers, she was as weak as a newborn babe. A glance at the mirror startled her, and she let her shoulders slump. "I feel ninety, and I look ninety," she groaned. She quickly removed her bonnet and set her reticule on the table.

After she moistened a facecloth in cold water, she wiped the tears from her face. She rinsed the cloth, folded it into a long rectangle, and pressed it across the bridge of her nose and both eyes. Each time the cloth warmed, she repeated the process and then checked her progress in the mirror.

After half a dozen tries, she gave up and accepted the puffiness around her eyes and the red streaks that remained. She leaned closer to the mirror and brushed damp hair away from her face. "I was right before. I do look ninety," she grumbled.

She ignored the traitorous streaks of gray at her temples, traced the lines at the outer corners of her eyes with her fingertips, and caressed the sun-kissed flesh on her cheeks. Still firm. But those blasted dimples still looked ridiculous on a woman her age. She studied, really studied, her features, searching for an answer as to why she appeared to have aged so much in the course of only three months.

The answer stared back at her from the depths of her dark brown eyes. Once sparkling and filled with the joy of life, her eyes were now opaque and listless, dulled by the pain of loss and failure, and there was no way the light of her spirit could shine through.

Unless she was wrong. Unless her spirit itself had dulled, devoid of hope, lacking faith strong enough to rebound from Rosalind's verbal attack.

"Not lack of faith," she whispered. "I have faith, but I'm only human. I'm—"

A harsh pounding at her door interrupted her slide into self-pity. She flinched and whirled about. She managed to open the door before her bear of a caller broke it down.

To her surprise, Byron Shaw stood just outside her door holding what appeared to be a large box wrapped in canvas that was secured by twine. Two squat barrels rested on the ground next to his feet. When he grimaced, she realized she must have a mighty frown on her face.

"Sorry," he blurted, and the rest of his words tumbled out in a rush, as if he believed that if he talked quickly enough she might forgive him. "Had to use one of my feet to knock. Sam Ward told me you passed the tollgate late yesterday afternoon." He blushed. "Actually, his son Aaron told me," he admitted.

She nodded. The Shaw and Ward homesteads shared a common boundary, which explained how quickly news of her arrival back home had spread.

"I wanted to settle my debt with you, so I left at first light. Didn't have a chance before, what with . . . with all that happened."

His pale cheeks flamed. "Me and Libby are right sorry about Victoria. We're both praying hard she'll come back home soon," he managed, before pausing to draw in a long breath.

"I thank you. For your prayers," she murmured as memories flooded her mind, sweeping her back to June, when she had delivered the newest baby Shaw and left late the following day to tend to Captain Tyler's wife, a call to duty that had kept her fifty miles away when the theater troupe came through Trinity and left with her precious daughter.

"Come in. Please," she urged, eager to dispel her painful memories with more heartening news about Libby Shaw and her new son, who had joined three female siblings.

When she stepped aside, he carried his oversized package into the room, looked around for a moment, set it atop the trunk at the foot of Victoria's bed, and put his hat on top of it.

She tried not to let her imagination conjure up anything too bizarre in terms of what he had made for her. His reputation as a fledgling inventor was well-known, and his attempts to fashion any number of household aids had fueled many a humorous anecdote told by patrons over pints of rum at the tavern. Whatever it was, it squeaked, inspiring visions of some kind of contraption sorely in need of oiling.

Without offering any explanation, he walked back outside and hoisted one of the barrels to his shoulder. "Pickles. We had a good crop this year. Libby's been busy in the kitchen," he added.

"Let's put that in the storeroom. This way." She crossed the room and opened the connecting door.

He followed, set the barrel down, and within moments had the second barrel on top of the first. While he performed his task, he assured her that Libby had completely recovered and baby Joshua was growing bigger every day.

"Libby said to tell you the pickles need to soak a few more weeks before they'll be at full flavor."

"I'll be sure to tell Lydia."

He grinned. "Good. Now I've got somethin' else to show you. Somethin' really special for you," he teased, and walked back into her room.

She followed him, and her curiosity grew stronger with every step she took. Certainly the barrels of pickles were more than enough to settle his debt for her services as a midwife, but it was not uncommon for fathers celebrating a firstborn son to offer her extra, especially when there had been an exceptionally good harvest. She promised herself that no matter what he had made for her, she absolutely must reward his efforts with a smile that most definitely could *not* erupt into laughter.

He set his hat aside. Almost tenderly, he loosened the twine and began to peel away the canvas covering. He blocked most of her view, and while he worked, the contraption inside squeaked again and sounded like it was moving around, although the box itself appeared to be stable as it rested on top of the trunk.

She half held her breath when he stepped aside, but when he waved his arm with a flourish and her gaze settled on his invention, she caught her breath completely and held it.

Instead of a box, she saw a wooden cage that was exquisitely detailed. Inside, peering back at her was something no man could ever create. Awed, she let her breath out slowly and approached the most unique reward she had ever received.

Her fingers trembled when she ran them over the contours of the vertical band of carved spokes. The round cage stood nearly three feet tall. There was a sturdy latch on the tiny door. Inside the cage, there were three perches, each at a different height, and a haphazard collection of twigs and cloth filled one corner.

Unable to speak with emotion choking her throat, she peered inside and stared at the creature cowering in the corner. Small and yellow, the warbler stared back at her. He fluffed his feathers, distorting the chestnut streaks on his chest, and snapped his beak up and down while issuing a squeaky protest. When he flapped his wings, one hung at his side, twisted in a most unnatural position. Saddened by his plight, she did feel relieved. She did not like to see wild animals restrained for the selfish enjoyment of the folks who fancied having an unusual pet.

Byron poked a finger through the wooden bars and petted the bird's head until he quieted. "Libby and the girls found him in August when they were picking berries, and brought him home. Poor fella. With that busted wing healed the wrong way, he'll never be able to fly again. He keeps tryin', but it's pitiful. He won't be able to migrate south with the few songbirds that are left, either."

"No, I don't believe he would," she admitted.

"If we set him free, he'll either die from the cold that's comin' or starve to death, if he even lasts that long. He can sing, though. We thought . . . well, knowin' how good you are with treatin' all kinds of folks, we thought you might be able to take care of him. He's very tame, and he's good company, too."

Martha could not take her eyes off the bird. "He's the sweetest reward I've ever received. Ever," she repeated. "And the cage, well, it's simply grand. You're a talented man. I'll treasure it always."

Byron smiled. "Thank you, ma'am." He cleared his throat and pointed at the bird. "He'll need a name."

"Oh? What did the children call him?"

He chuckled. "Elsa and Kate called him Bird. Pamela, she's two now, she just called him Mine."

Now Martha chuckled. "Well now, I suppose he wouldn't mind having another name. I'll have to think about it, though."

"Yes, ma'am. I—I best be headin' home. Oh, I almost forgot." He pulled a pair of miniature wooden bowls out of his pocket and handed them to her. "Fill one with water; the other one is for his food. He's partial to berries, of course, but he'll snap up as many insects as you can find in your herb garden. I'm not sure what he'll eat all winter—"

"I have plenty of seeds," she assured him, even though she had no firm idea in mind about what to do with the creature when she was called away for several days or more. "Tell Libby I'll stop by soon. And hug all four of those babies for me."

He plopped his hat back on his head and grinned. "Yes, ma'am. We'll be lookin' forward to your visit."

After he left, she peered into the cage again. "Well, Bird, we'll have to see about that name, but not till I help Lydia and Annabelle with dinner. When you trust me enough, I'll take a closer look at that wing, too, and see if something can't be done to set it right."

She filled one of the bowls with water and set it into the cage. She tucked the second bowl into her apron pocket. Humming softly, she checked her image in the mirror. She looked the same. Almost. Except for just the barest hint of a smile glowing in her eyes.

While Annabelle served the patrons, Martha filled and refilled trenchers with mutton stew and kept the fire steady. Lydia sliced the bread and pies fast enough to keep the patrons content and refilled other supplies from the storeroom while James dispensed the spirits and added coins to the till when patrons had had their fill.

Spirited speculation today centered on the fate of poor Charlie Greywald. According to the latest rumor, Charlie's hand had been freed and he had been taken to Dr. McMillan's office, where his mangled hand was about to be amputated. It sounded logical, but so had the other rumors that had filtered in through the dinner hour. At one point, patrons argued Charlie had bled to death, had recovered after receiving ten stitches, or still remained at the sawmill with the saw embedded in his hand. And this from men all at the same table!

Even if Martha had listened with half an ear, she could not have missed one universal factor common to all accounts. Apparently, Dr. McMillan was handling both himself and the situation well, earning the respect of all those who had come to the tavern that day.

The tragic event at the sawmill had drawn quite a crowd of spectators, so the normal lull between dinner and supper had never materialized. The arrival of six wagons filled with folks headed west would have drained the kettle dry, but Lydia had had enough foresight to start another kettle of stew earlier. All the pies were gone, and Lydia had to slice the bread thinner to make it stretch to meet demand.

By eight o'clock at night, Annabelle had been sent home. There was no room in the wagon yard for more than a mouse. The sleeping dormitory upstairs was filled to capacity with four to a bed. In the main room of the tavern, James continued to serve the half a dozen patrons still nibbling on the day's gossip over pints of their favorite spirits while Lydia and Martha finished clearing up the last of the day's clutter in the kitchen.

While she worked, Martha studied her sister-in-law. Nearly fifty, Lydia had little meat on her bones, which made her seem even taller. Gray mixed with the black in her hair to such an extent now that there was twice as much salt as pepper, accentuating the new wrinkles on her brow. Her complexion, however, was as clear and flawless as it had been when she was a young bride, nearly thirty years ago, and her eyes still shined with love when she gazed at her husband.

Martha could not have chosen a better companion or helpmate for her brother, which only added to the burden of guilt she already carried. "I truly do apologize for being gone so long," she murmured, and plunged the last of the dirty trenchers into a pan of soapy water. "I know it's been hard for you and James to handle the work at the tavern, even with Annabelle's help."

Lydia dried the trencher Martha handed to her. "It was easier when I was younger. That I'll admit." She added the trencher to the stack of clean ones on the table and covered a yawn with the back of her hand. "I can't remember ever being so tired."

Martha caught the yawn and returned it.

Lydia chuckled. "I'm so tired I can't get my eyes to see straight. Can't hear right, either."

"You can't hear right?"

"That's what I said, and if you repeat what I'm going to tell you to James, I'll deny it. Every word."

Intrigued, Martha dried her hands on a towel. "Spit it out, Lydia. What is it you can't hear?"

"It's not what I can't hear. It's what I do hear . . . or heard all afternoon. Every time I went back into the storeroom, I thought I heard a warbler singing his heart out, and we both know most of the songbirds already flew south. Anyway, he sounded like he was close enough to be right in your room, which is a ridiculous notion—"

"Bird! I forgot all about Bird!" Martha cried. She pulled the miniature bowl out of her pocket, scanned the room for something, anything, he might eat, but the heavy crowd of patrons had consumed everything.

Almost.

She used a spoon to poke at the contents of a pail where they had scraped the remnants of meals from each trencher. She scooped out a crust of bread, scraped off the gravy, and tore the crust into tiny bits that fit into the bowl. "Your hearing is just fine," she assured Lydia, who was watching her with concern. "Just fine. Follow me."

Lydia followed close enough behind Martha to be her shadow. They moved from the kitchen and through the storeroom. When

Martha opened the door, a shaft of light spilled into her chamber and provided just enough light for her to guide her sister-in-law to the cage. "Byron Shaw stopped today with my reward and gave me Bird, along with two barrels of pickles he put into the storeroom."

Lydia peered inside. "What bird? I don't see a bird."

Martha stooped down and looked inside, too, but Lydia was right. The cage was indeed empty. Oddly, the door to the cage hung wide open, and it appeared that the twigs and bits of cloth in the corner had been rearranged. Bird was nowhere to be seen.

"Now, how on earth did he manage that?" Martha wondered aloud. Half afraid he might lay hurt and injured somewhere in the room, she stepped cautiously as she made her way to the table. She lit a kerosene lamp to chase away the shadows, but when she looked around, she stifled a cry of surprise when she spied him.

Bird was fast, fast asleep in a nest of sorts that lay on top of the pillow on Victoria's cot. She should put him right back into his cage. She just did not have the heart to do it.

Chapter
NINE

Market Day always drew a lot of people to town and lured most residents out of their homes, but the crowd of people today was as remarkable as the unusually warm weather. Quite spirited, too, given the volume of animated conversation and laughter that filtered from around the bend in the roadway ahead.

With a basket swinging from each hand, Martha held her head high and her spine stiff as she walked. She dreaded the next hour, when she would face many of her friends and neighbors again for the first time, although fielding their questions about Victoria now would be a far sight better than letting gossip continue to fester. She had no desire today to see Rosalind, either.

Martha kept her gaze downcast until she passed the doctor's home and the covered bridge at the far end of town, and prayed for the courage and fortitude to keep a smile on her face regardless of what happened this morning.

"Martha! Martha Cade!"

Good omen.

She recognized the two voices calling out from behind her and turned to greet the Lynn spinsters. Wearing long white aprons, Fern and Ivy waddled toward her like a pair of plump Christmas geese running to escape the ax. By the time they reached Martha, their cheeks were flushed the color of overripe cherries and they were panting.

"We saw . . . you. From . . . from the shop," Fern managed while fanning her face with one hand and balancing a cloth-covered plate with the other.

Ivy mopped her brow. "You always did have a quick stride." She gave Martha a hug and patted her back. "How are you, dearie? We've been so worried about you."

With her arms literally pinned at her sides, Martha could not return the hug and relaxed in her friend's embrace. "I'll be fine. Truly."

"Of course you will," Ivy assured her. "You don't have to tell us anything more than that, but we're here if you need a friendly ear or a shoulder to cry upon." She stepped aside, took the plate from Fern, and let her have a turn.

Another hug, just as powerful and just as welcome. "We've brought you some treats. Fresh from the oven," Ivy explained as she set the plate into one of Martha's baskets. "We took some to Patience Greywald earlier. Poor Charlie. He's going to be out of work for several months, you know. Thank Providence, he's not going to lose his hand. Nothing eases a troubled body or heart better than chocolate tarts."

Fern nodded her head. "Or oatmeal cookies. We made some of each for you, too. Now, make sure you eat every bite."

The smell that wafted up from the basket was heavenly, even decadent, and Martha offered a prayer of thanksgiving for her two friends along with one for Charlie Greywald.

She smiled. "I'll savor every one."

Judging by their ample girth, they had practiced what they preached for many years before opening the confectionery they operated from their home on West Main Street. She suspected each sister had known heartbreak, but Martha made no attempt to pry, even in the name of friendship, unlike gossipmongers who had been trying to learn about the sisters' pasts from the moment they had arrived four years ago. As sweet as the amazing pastries they baked, and just as generous to those in need, there was not a malicious bone in either of their bodies.

"Were you going to the market today? I'd be grateful for your company," Martha suggested.

Ivy's blue eyes twinkled. "We've already been there and back, but we wouldn't mind getting another look."

Fern blushed. "Just one more peek. Before they take it down."

Martha cocked her head and knitted her brows together. "Get a look at what? Take what down?"

Two pairs of blue eyes flashed with disbelief before Fern merely turned Martha about and led her down the road to the bend, where they had a full view of the crowd as well as the market itself. "There. Look up. No, all the way up. To the market roof."

As curious as she was confused, Martha raised her gaze above the throng of people. Her eyes widened. Her mouth dropped open. She blinked several times, but the unbelievable image of a full-sized carriage straddling the center peak of the roof remained. While she watched, several men with coils of rope climbed up a ladder, and she assumed they were going to attempt to get the carriage down.

In spite of herself, she laughed out loud at the outrageously clever prank. The sisters joined in, and Martha laughed until her sides ached and her conscience reminded her this was no laughing matter. Guilt quickly sobered her demeanor, and she realized now why the crowd was so unusually large. "What on earth is that carriage doing up there? Whose carriage is it, do you know?"

Fern shrugged her shoulders. "Can't say for sure how it got there or why, but Dr. McMillan isn't too pleased. Downright snippy, I heard, barking orders to have his carriage brought down. He even offered a reward—"

"To catch the culprits," Ivy interjected. "I overheard some of the menfolk. Apparently, there must have been more than one prankster who worked through the night. Had to be, since they had to take the carriage apart and haul each piece up to the roof before they reassembled it. Well, almost all of it," she explained, and pointed to the market roof again. "See? There's a wheel missing."

"And the carriage top," Fern added. "Guess the sun came up before they finished. They got clean away, too, but most folks are already blaming the academy boys."

Martha shook her head. Either she was losing her hearing or she had laughed her brain silly. "Did you say academy boys? Lydia didn't mention anything about an academy opening here in Trinity."

Fern and Ivy looked at one another and then back at Martha before Fern offered an explanation. "The boys they suspect are from the Hampton Academy. It's a sort of boarding school, I suppose. It opened up while you were gone. Late August, I believe," Fern explained.

Ivy shook her head. "No. It was early August. Remember? We'd just finished using the last of our skyberries when the Reverend Mr. Hampton and his wife arrived with half a dozen young snippersnappers in tow. Bought every last sticky bun we had that day." She wrinkled her brows and shook her head again. "For the life of me, I can't remember that poor woman's name."

"Olympia," Fern prompted. "You remember the old Rhule homestead, Martha. It's right above the falls on Reedy Creek."

She remembered it well, along with the entire Rhule family of five who lay buried in the cemetery behind the meetinghouse, victims of the same epidemic that had claimed her beloved husband, John. Still, she could not make the connection between a minister, a boys' academy, and the homestead abandoned so long ago.

Ivy patted Martha's arm as if to ease the quizzical expression from her face. "I thought it odd, too, but it's true. Reverend and Mrs. Hampton brought those boys out here and settled on the Rhule place.

Fixed it up the best they could for now, so I heard. I also heard they've got a big order in at the sawmill to make the house bigger. They're going to do it themselves in the spring and work the farm again, too."

Martha still found the concept confusing. "But why would anyone of means send a son to an academy that's nothing more than a farm?"

Now Fern sniffed. "They're not from people of means. They're all orphans. Every last one of them. Reverend Hampton plucked them off the streets of New York City after he got the call to minister to these poor lost souls. He's got a mighty task ahead of him, and folks are none too pleased to have the likes of those street urchins running about."

It was completely out of character for either Fern or Ivy to be so set against anyone, let alone a group of orphans, but the women were as prejudiced against any semblance of city life invading the town as everyone else in Trinity. Martha's own low opinion about life in the cities had only solidified during her journey, although she could not harbor any ill feelings toward children who had no control of their own fate.

Martha nodded now that it had all been explained to her. "Do you really think the academy boys are responsible for this prank? Is there any proof?" she asked, as her mind attempted to create a list of suspects who lived right in town.

"It doesn't matter much what we think," Fern quipped. "The blame's been set in folks' minds. Mayor Dillon already left. He rode out to see Reverend Hampton. Come along, let's go to the market. Maybe we'll be able to learn more about it while you get what you need."

While Martha could not condone any prank which would put someone who needed medical help during the night at risk, she did have to credit those responsible for having both the skill and the daring to carry it out. She also knew her venture into the marketplace today would invite far less interest now. There was nothing like an unhealthy dose of new gossip to replace the old. She also knew her day of reckoning had merely been postponed, and she recognized her

debt to poor Dr. McMillan and the academy boys. At least no reasonable soul could blame her for antagonizing the doctor with this prank,
but she feared there were enough unreasonable folks in town who
might try.

"Welcome to Trinity, Dr. McMillan and Reverend Hampton," she
whispered, and made a mental note to say an extra prayer for forgiveness tonight for taking even the smallest comfort from someone
else's suffering or misfortune.

In midafternoon, bright sunshine warmed the day even more. Already
blessed, Martha also had the rest of the day to herself since Lydia had
Annabelle to help her with supper. After changing into a riding skirt,
she checked to make sure the door to the birdcage was latched tight
and nodded with approval when she noticed the food bowl she had
filled earlier with seeds was nearly empty. She smiled and tapped the
top of the cage. "Good, Bird. Now, stay put," she warned, and dismissed any notion Bird might escape again as ludicrous. "I'm still
working on that name," she added, and promised herself she would
think of something better than Bird very soon.

When she went outside and passed her herb gardens, she made
another promise to cut more herbs tonight before nightfall and went
directly to the stable. Once she was inside, she had to stand still and
wait a moment until her eyes adjusted to the dim light. When they
did, she walked directly to Grace's stall at the far end.

Grace greeted her by stomping her front foot and greedily accepted
the apple Martha offered to her. "You need an outing today, too, don't
you?" she crooned, and scratched behind the mare's ears until the
entire apple had been chomped to bits and swallowed.

Martha had her hand on the latch at the end of the rope that kept
Grace in her stall when she heard the distinctive sound of hissing,
then a cry that came from directly overhead. More hissing. Then,
"Damn whoreson! You bit me!"

She ran as fast as she could to get to the ladder that led to the half-loft overhead. She was only two steps up the ladder when a hissing, spitting, black-and-white ball of fur flew from the loft and miraculously landed on all four feet on the floor below.

She let out a sigh when Leech shook himself and turned to stare at her as if daring her to comment.

She could not resist. "That was your fourteenth life, unless I've missed a few."

Leech hissed at her, eyed the ladder, and promptly turned his back and walked out of the stable.

Overhead, a shuffle of feet continued, then abruptly stopped.

She was anxious about what she might find in the loft, but she was fairly certain the soft steps belonged to a child, possibly one of the academy boys, since the youngsters in town knew better than to invade Leech's territory. She turned her attention back to the ladder and climbed up until she had a clear view of the entire loft. Actually, nothing seemed amiss. Bales of hay that ran the length of the loft were lined up end-to-end against the outer wall to her left. Bags of feed grains for the horses were stacked to her right, leaving a narrow aisle between them.

"I hope I don't have to come all the way into the loft to get you, but I will," she warned.

No response.

"You'd be well advised to show yourself, young man. Right now."

Again, no response.

She smacked the side of the ladder with the palm of her hand. "I said *now*!" she ordered, using the same tone of voice she had always used to intimidate Oliver into obedience whenever she had been frustrated by his behavior.

That did not evoke a response, either.

Mumbling and grumbling to herself, she climbed up the rest of the ladder and onto the floor of the loft. She hunched her shoulders to keep from hitting her head on the overhead beams. She searched her way down the aisle while keeping part of her gaze on the ladder and the rest on her task.

She found the source of the footsteps at the very end, crouched behind a bale of hay.

"Cornered," she announced, and plopped down onto the bale of hay to keep him from escaping.

A bundle of sheer defiance in the guise of a young boy she did not recognize glared back at her, issuing a challenge she hoped she was ready to meet.

Chapter
TEN

Martha studied the slight boy who sat with his back against the wall with his lips parted, his teeth bared as if he was about to snarl. His clothes were well-worn and a bit overlarge for his small frame. A tear in his trousers revealed a nasty set of scrapes and bruises on one of his knees.

No more than seven or eight years old, he had telltale streaks from tears that had cut a wide swath through the dirt on his cheeks. His deep hazel eyes, topped by sandy brown brows that matched the mop of unruly hair on his head, flashed with a feral intensity that cut straight through her soul.

When she reached out to touch him and reassure him she meant him no harm, he flinched and pulled back out of reach. "Didn't steal nothin' but a place in the hay," he spat. "Ain't botherin' nobody, either."

She laid her hand on her lap. "It sure sounded to me like you bothered Leech, not that he's much for socializing with folks. He prefers horses." The boy cocked his head and sniffled in a vain attempt to stop his nose from running.

"The cat. His name is Leech," she explained.

His eyes widened. His gaze snapped. "Bloody bastard! He *bit* me!" he complained, and held up his hand.

Sure enough, he had a nasty bite on the tender web of flesh between his thumb and forefinger. While sympathetic to the pain he must be feeling, she frowned at his rough language. Her suspicion he might be from the academy seemed more than likely, unless there were other newcomers she had yet to meet. In either case, she could not tolerate this boy's language or surly attitude. "Your language is atrocious, sinful, and unacceptable, young man."

He glared at her.

She glared back and quickly found herself taken by the notion that this young boy was just a younger, smaller version of the crusty old seaman she had befriended. Just as she had done with Samuel when they first met, she had tried vinegar and failed. Time for sugar. And time to put Aunt Hilda's concept of gifts into practice again.

She softened her gaze and rolled up the sleeve to her gown all the way to the elbow. She pointed to the thin white scar that ran from her wrist halfway up her forearm. "You're not the only one Leech has attacked. That scar is my gift from Leech. Fortunately, yours will be much smaller."

He snorted. "A scar's no gift."

"I didn't think so, either," she admitted. "Not at first. But I do see it as a gift now because I've learned gifts contain all sorts of things. Some we like. Some we don't."

He rolled his eyes.

"Leech is one nasty cat, as far as I'm concerned, but I must give him credit," she continued. "He keeps the stable and wagon yard free from snakes and mice. He's got work to do, and he does it well. That's his gift to all of us. Every time I see my scar, I'm reminded that he's not supposed to be a pet. That's the gift he gave to me."

He rolled his eyes again.

She dug in her heels. She had not been outwitted or outmaneuvered by a child for at least a few months, and she was not ready to repeat the experience, especially with this boy. "I'm Widow Cade. I live here at my brother's tavern with him and his wife. That big spotted horse below is my mare, Grace."

He sniffled and wiped his nose with the cuff of his sleeve. "You can call me Boy."

"Boy?"

He narrowed his gaze. "That's my name. Boy."

She nodded and decided to wait until he trusted her more before pressing him to get his real name.

"I was just about to go for a ride, Boy. I can take you home if you like," she suggested.

His eyes widened and filled with tears he battled back before they could course down his cheeks. "I can't go back there yet."

"Are you waiting for someone?"

Two monstrous tears managed to escape when he shook his head.

"Then you're hiding from everyone here."

"I was hiding real good, till that blasted cat bit me. But just till nightfall. P. J. said I couldn't tell—" He snapped his mouth shut and clenched his jaw, as if he realized he had already said too much.

"You're sworn to secrecy, I suppose."

He nodded.

"A man's word should count for something," she admitted. She pointed to his bleeding hand. "Leech has very sharp teeth. I bet that hurts like the dickens."

His bottom lip trembled.

She pressed her case. "I could put some salve on it to take out the sting. I could clean up your knee, too. Then when you leave after dark, you'd be stronger and feeling better."

He straightened his shoulders and tilted up his chin. "It don't hurt that much."

She wanted to take him into her arms and hold him tight, long enough to melt the armor of false bravado and mistrust he wore and comfort the frightened little boy inside. She knew that was exactly what she could not do, not if she ever hoped to earn his trust.

She glanced out the window. There were still several good hours of sunlight left, which gave her plenty of time to convince him he should let her take him home.

If he refused, she would have to assert her authority as his elder and insist. There was no way she would let that boy traipse home in the dark, yet she knew from experience it would serve the boy better to let him reach that conclusion on his own. There was more than a little part of her that felt guilty for not alerting someone or taking him back right away. Given the strong feeling in town against the academy boys, both she and the boy would be better off if they traveled at night and avoided meeting anyone from town. If he even suspected she might alert someone else to his presence here, he might run off to somewhere other than home, which led her right back to following her intuition and giving him a little time.

She prayed for patience, stood up, and rearranged her skirts. "You rest up here a while. Instead of going for a ride now, I think I'll wait till later. I have some herbs I need to harvest. If you change your mind about letting me tend to your cuts and scrapes, you'll find me in the herb garden between here and the tavern. If I'm not there, that means I finished and went to my room. It's the one jutting off the rear of the tavern. I'll tie back the curtain on the window so you can look inside and see me," she murmured before turning away from him and walking back toward the ladder.

She had only taken a few steps when he called out to her. "You won't get someone to make me go home right now?"

She turned and looked back at him over her shoulder. "Since you didn't tell me your name or where you live, that might be hard to do. Right now, maybe you should do some thinking about the people who are worried about you. I'll bring you some supper later."

Mistrust darkened his eyes. "You won't tell anyone I'm here?"

"You have my word, but I must have your word you won't leave until dark and we've had another chance to talk and decide what's best for you to do."

"How do I know you're not lyin'? That you won't send for the sheriff or Reverend Hampton?"

She caught the smile of relief that he had unwittingly given her a clue to his identity and affirmed her suspicion he was, indeed, one of the academy boys. "You have my word, young man. That should count for something."

He worried his bottom lip. "I'll stay. Just till dark."

She nodded and made her way back to the ladder. She was halfway down when she heard his voice speak in a loud whisper. "I sure do like corn bread with lots of honey for supper. If you got any."

"I'll see what I can do." She chuckled all the way to the bottom of the ladder. The way to a young boy's trust, if not his heart, was apparently still through his stomach. Given the size of the little waif, with his pitifully thin face and limbs, no one had tried to earn either his trust or his heart for a very long time.

There was still no sign of the boy.

Martha prolonged her work in the herb garden as long as she could, hoping against hope he might come to her for help. After two hours of picking the best of the herbs, pruning away those damaged by insects, and gathering seeds for Bird, while keeping one eye on the stable door to make sure the boy did not run off, she had no choice but to retire to her room and wait for him there.

Once inside, she placed the baskets on her worktable and stored away her garden gloves. She refilled the seed bowl for Bird, who eyed her warily from his nest in the corner of the cage. One quick glance around the floor of his cage told her she had better clean it out while she had the door open. While she worked, she realized she really had not given the animal's name much thought.

She sighed. She had a bird in a cage named Bird and a boy in the stable loft named Boy. Both had been severely wounded, one in body, the other in spirit. Both were completely dependent on her right now, although Boy would probably argue that point. She carefully latched the cage door when she finished and took some comfort that at least Bird was easy to control. "That should keep you in for the night," she teased.

He cocked his head and ruffled his feathers.

She chuckled. "Go ahead. Try. You can't get out and sleep on Victoria's cot again tonight, so accept it. You have a perfectly fine nest right where you are."

Humming softly, she spread out the comfrey from the first basket. Her hands halted in midair when a thought suddenly interrupted her work. "The curtain! I forgot!" She hurried to the window and tied back the curtain. She glanced outside and surveyed the rear of the property. The door to the stable was still closed. There were several wagons, including a Conestoga, in the yard now, and a lone bulldog stood guard near the horses tethered together at the trough.

There was no sign of the boy.

"Guide him, Lord. Help him to trust me," she whispered, and returned to her work.

She positioned her chair at the end of the table to give her a view through the window while she worked. She bundled and tied the rest of the comfrey and finished off every one of the sweet treats Fern and Ivy had given her that morning.

The combination of work and sweets helped to mitigate the sense of total frustration she had experienced since coming home. Unable to resolve her daughter's disappearance or Rosalind's troubles or her feelings for Thomas, to come to terms with the impact Dr. McMillan's presence might have on her calling, or to help Samuel Meeks, she faced the challenge the boy in the stable presented with renewed energy and hope.

In truth, the boy had a real chance for a good future, assuming she could convince him to return to the academy and let Reverend

Hampton provide the guidance the child so sorely needed. Of all the people in Trinity whose needs lay heavy on her heart, only Samuel Meeks seemed to face a future bleaker than this boy's.

If she did not find a remedy for Samuel's failing vision and he did become blind, she had no idea how he would survive. As adept as he had become in making the transition from life at sea to life here in an isolated cabin, Samuel had not endeared himself to the community—a community that would be his only source of help if he faced the future in total blindness. Stymied for the present in her efforts to help Samuel, she rallied all of her energies to help the boy.

When she paused to stretch the muscles in her neck and looked down, she found that the contents of the baskets of dill and horehound had been emptied and prepared for hanging as well.

But still no boy appeared.

She retrieved the ladder she needed from the storeroom and set it into place with the top of the ladder leaning against a crossbeam in the middle of the room. She wiped her brow with the hem of her apron. "Either that ladder is getting heavier or I'm getting far too old to haul it around all the time," she grumbled, but she found a great deal of satisfaction in doing physical work. In truth, she had only to ask her brother for help. He would gladly have set the ladder into place for her, but she was as independent as she was determined to make her own way in this world.

Grateful to have the worst of her task done, she grabbed three bundles of comfrey. After climbing up the ladder, she hung one bundle, then the second. When she stretched a bit too far to hang the third, she lost her balance, dropped the last bundle, and grabbed the ladder with both hands. With her heart pounding, she looked down and saw the third bundle lying in a heap on the floor. She pressed her forehead to a rung on the ladder and waited for her heartbeat to return to normal, then climbed back down.

With her feet now on firm ground, she bent down to retrieve the bundle she had dropped and heard a loud racket in the rear yard. Horses whinnied. A dog barked. Again and again; the sound of the dog's frenzied charge around the wagon yard was all too familiar. She half expected to hear the dog yelp if he had the misfortune to corner Leech when a mighty pounding at her door interrupted her thoughts.

She whirled about, only to see the door hurl open and bang against the wall. A whirlwind of fury and fear charged inside, grabbed hold of the door, and slammed it closed.

Apparently just in time. A loud thud on the outside of the door was followed by a vicious, barking harangue that lasted for several minutes before the bulldog finally quieted in defeat.

She grinned, in spite of herself, but the look in Boy's eyes told her she was going to need divine intervention now more than ever to win his trust.

Chapter
ELEVEN

The boy pressed his back to the door and fought to catch his breath. When he did, he glared at her. "Cudda warned me about the damn dog," he spat.

"I'm sorry. I forgot."

"You musta heard him barkin' and tryin' to take a chunk outta my leg. You cudda tried to stop him—"

"I really thought he was chasing Leech."

"Do I look like a cat?"

She cringed and accepted the guilt she deserved from his reprimand. She should have warned him about the dog in the yard or checked sooner to see if he needed help, although she could not condone the lack of respect he showed to her. She saved her own reprimand for later.

"He was only trying to protect the horses. That's his job. Unfortunately, he doesn't know how Leech loves horses."

He waved one of his arms in the air. "Stupid dog. I hate dogs. Cats, too. Matter of fact, there ain't one damn animal worth nothin', 'cept for horses. Too bad they're so dumb."

She held back an immediate retort. The boy had probably known a fair share of both street dogs and cats, and she tried not to think about the other critters, like rats, he had encountered on the streets of New York City. Out of loyalty to her mare, however, she felt obliged to speak up. "Grace isn't dumb."

He shrugged his shoulders. "I saw her in the stable. She's the ugliest one there. Might be the ugliest horse I ever saw."

She almost bit her tongue holding back a reprimand. "I happen to agree with you," she admitted, "but you might have put it a kinder way. Grace might be the ugliest horse in these parts, but her beauty lies beneath her coat. In her spirit. Where true beauty lies."

He looked at her like she had grown an extra ear in the middle of her forehead. "Horses don't have spirits."

"Of course they do. All creatures do, once you get to know them. Grace has a very loyal spirit. She never lets me down," she countered.

The boy inched into the room and pointed to the cage. "What's in there?"

She raised a brow. "A bird. I'm taking care of him because he broke his wing and it didn't heal properly, so he can't fly."

While he approached the cage, she went to the window and dropped the curtain back into place.

He peered into the cage. "What's his name?"

She drew in a long breath. She was reluctant to give the boy any advantage, but knew he would not let the opportunity pass when he discovered the bird's name, or lack of one. "His name is Bird."

"Just Bird?"

She nodded.

He grinned.

She took a deep breath and walked away. She got several bundles of herbs and returned to the ladder. She talked to the boy while she passed back and forth across the room, trying to change the course of their conversation. "Sometimes I like to ride for pleasure or to keep Grace exercised, but most of the time I ride because someone needs me. I'm a midwife and a healer. I help babies to get born and I help sick mamas and their children to get better," she explained. "Come here. Hold these for me."

He eyed her warily as he approached her.

"See these?" she asked as she passed the bundles to him once he was close enough. "These are healing herbs I use to make teas or ointments or poultices. I have to hang them up to dry so I have enough simples to last until next summer."

He stiffened, but cradled the herbs in his arms.

She took several bundles, climbed up the ladder, hung them up, and returned for more. Four trips later, all the bundles had been hung up to dry, including the ones on her worktable. When she carried the ladder toward the storeroom, he backed toward the door that led outside.

"I have to stow the ladder away," she explained. "There's a storeroom on the other side of this door that leads to the tavern. If you stand here, in the corner, no one will be able to see you when I open the door. Sometimes they need to get something from the storeroom," she added to ease the mistrust that still stared back at her.

He edged around the perimeter of the room and into the corner. She balanced the ladder with one hand, opened the connecting door with the other, and quickly had the ladder back in its place. Before she could reenter her room, Lydia poked her head into the storeroom.

"James and I are ready for supper. Shall I have Annabelle bring you some or do you want to join us?"

"I think I'll have my supper in my room. I still have some unpacking to do, and I think I'll take Grace out for a ride later. I'm not sure at what point I'll have time to eat."

Lydia smiled. "Then I'll have Annabelle bring your platter to you now before I send her home."

"I'm . . . well, I'm actually rather hungry after working out in the garden all afternoon," she lied. After eating a chocolate tart and half a dozen cookies, she had no appetite at all, but she had a feeling the boy was truly hungry.

"Extra helpings it is."

Martha hesitated. "With some corn bread and honey, too. If you have it to spare. I didn't have a truly good hunk of corn bread all the while I was gone. Not like yours."

Another smile. "I'm sure there's plenty. I'll tell Annabelle," she offered, and returned to the kitchen.

As soon as Lydia left, Martha shut the door to her room. When Boy's stomach rumbled, she captured his gaze and held it. "I suppose you want supper. Is that why you came to my room?"

He nodded and dropped his gaze. "You got somethin' for my hand? Blasted cat must have bayonets for teeth. Sliced into my hand real deep," he murmured, "not that I can't do with the pain. It's just . . . well, when I get home I don't wanna be botherin' Miz Hampton. She gets all weepy and . . . and she don't always know what to do."

"You stay put for now. Annabelle is a young lady who helps in the tavern. She's going to bring us supper, which means I'm going to have to open the door again. While we're waiting for her, I'll get everything ready to take care of your hand. And your knee, too."

He did not move a muscle and kept his body braced in the corner, ready to sprint away at the first sign she might not be telling him the truth.

She went directly to the corner cupboard for a small bowl and filled it with fresh water from the pump. After gathering up several fresh cloths, strips of cotton to use for bandages, and the smartweed ointment to take the sting out of his wounds, she put everything at one end of the table.

She answered the knock on the adjoining door and greeted Annabelle with a smile that broadened when she saw that the platter was nearly overflowing with food. Three thick squares of corn bread on one side balanced an enormous mound of boiled potatoes and peas swimming in cream. "You surely are a blessing, child," she murmured as she took the platter. "Goodness gracious, this smells delicious."

Annabelle winked, turned about, and retrieved yet another plate she placed in Martha's free hand. "Mrs. Fleming let me make baked apples. Just for the family. I hope you like them. It's my mother's special recipe."

Martha's mouth actually watered the moment she smelled the two plump apples nearly drowning in a dark sauce that smelled of cinnamon, cloves, and lots of butter—just what she needed to win the boy's heart.

"I'm afraid both of them will quickly disappear," she admitted. "Thank you. And don't bother yourself about coming back for the dishes. I'll wash them up here and return them in the morning."

Annabelle grinned. "Yes, ma'am." She reached around Martha as soon as she stepped back and closed the door.

With both hands full, Martha glanced at Boy, whose eyes were wide with hungry approval. "I suppose you want to eat first."

He swallowed hard and nodded.

"I'll set our places at the table. You get yourself to that pump over there and wash your hands. Your face, too."

He scowled, but headed to the pump.

Martha set the food on the table at the end opposite her remedies. After securing crocks of butter and honey, along with an extra plate and utensils from the cupboard, she set them onto the table as well before she poured two mugs of cider. He met her at the table, and she pointed to a chair. "Sit."

When he plopped onto the seat, he was careful to keep his one leg extended to accommodate his scraped knee.

She sat down at the end of the table next to him, ladled a small serving of supper onto the extra plate, and laid a single piece of corn bread alongside it for herself. She placed the original platter in front of him, but his gaze was glued to the baked apples. She hesitated, then offered him a baked apple before taking a generous spoonful of her own.

She closed her eyes briefly and chewed slowly to savor the warm, delicious concoction. "I do love baked apples," she whispered.

His quizzical expression was almost humorous. "Don't you eat your supper first? Miz Hampton would box my ears if I touched my dessert first."

She paused, held a spoonful of apple halfway to her mouth for a moment, then devoured another bite. "Mrs. Hampton is right, actually, but the way I see it, everything I eat for supper is going to end up in the same place anyway. I just don't think it matters if I eat my meal first or my dessert. I don't make a habit of it, but every once in a while, when I feel like doing something . . . something a little bit bad, I treat myself to dessert first. You won't tell anyone, will you?"

A smile. Tentative. But a smile. "No, ma'am."

"Good. You go ahead. Try it," she urged.

He plowed through that entire apple before she could get half of hers down, and began to attack the main meal with a vengeance.

He had the worst table manners she had ever had the misfortune to witness. He ate with both elbows on the table and chewed with his mouth open. He never bothered once to wipe away the food that collected in the corners of his mouth, but when he gulped down the entire mug of cider in one long, very loud gulp, she could not keep silent a moment longer.

"Elbows off the table," she cautioned. "And slow down! You're shoveling that in so fast you're going to end up with a stomachache."

He dropped one elbow and laid his injured hand on his lap. "It's good."

"Obviously. Now the other elbow."

He belched and lowered his other arm before finishing the rest of his meal.

She shook her head. Poor Mrs. Hampton. If she had half a dozen boys like this one, she certainly had a long, difficult road ahead. When the boy eyed her chunk of corn bread, she raised a brow. "You couldn't possibly have room for more."

He belched. "Do now."

Lord, give me patience.

She handed him the corn bread and watched as he smothered it with honey before polishing it all off in four big bites.

"Best . . . corn bread . . . I ever had," he explained while chewing and nodding his head.

"Please wait to talk until you've finished chewing."

He rolled his eyes. Again.

"Someday your eyes might just roll right back into your head and stay there," she warned. "Now that you're finished, I'll see to that bite on your hand and your scraped knee."

When he opened his mouth as if to argue, she silenced him by holding up her hand. "Not one word. Unless it's your name."

He snapped his mouth shut and never uttered a single sound as she tended to his injuries, even when she had to work out the dirt and cinders embedded in his knee. By the time she had both his hand and his knee bandaged, she had no doubt he was one tough little scrapper, especially when she considered his age. She did not need to know any details about his life on the street. She had seen enough in her recent travels to know he had faced horrors as a street orphan no one, especially an innocent child, should ever face.

Images of Victoria, off alone without family or friends to protect her while she traipsed around with that theater troupe, made her shiver. She might not be able to help her daughter, but she could help this boy and pray someone else might do the same for Victoria if she needed help.

The savvy little urchin, however, presented quite a challenge—one she decided to meet right now before he got too sure of himself. "Your knee will be stiff for a few days," she announced as she tied the bandage into place. "You owe me twenty-five cents. Cash or in kind. The supper is another ten cents, which brings your debt to thirty-five cents."

His eyes flashed. "You expect me . . . to pay you?"

"Of course."

He narrowed his gaze and skewed his mouth. "You invited me to supper. I didn't ask for it. Shouldn't have to pay for it, neither."

"Hmmm. You're right. That's still twenty-five cents for patching you up," she argued. Before he could issue a retort, she rose from her seat, secured her diary, and carried it back to the table, where she entered his debt.

He watched her and shrugged his shoulders. "I got no money. I'm just a boy. Where'd you think I'd get any money?"

"A man's got to earn his place in this world, as well as the next. Cash or kind," she repeated. "That means if you don't have the coin, you can give me something of equal value."

He started to roll his eyes.

She frowned.

He stopped and looked directly at her. "Like what? I got nothin' to give you."

"Sure you do," she insisted. "Once you're all healed up, you can sweep the floor for me, or weed the garden, or clean out Grace's stall."

He squared his shoulders. "I'm not goin' outside anywhere near that dog. Leech, neither."

"Then you can sweep the floor."

"That's woman's work! I ain't sweepin' no floor." His gaze brightened. "I already helped you hang them herbs. That should settle it."

She shook her head. "You were being polite."

"Didn't give me a choice now, did you? Just plopped them bundles into my arms without even askin' if I wanted to help."

"Five cents. That's all that little bit of work was worth."

"Twenty."

"Six."

"Fifteen."

"Eight. That's my final offer," she snapped.

He snorted. "Eight."

She bowed her head to hide her smile and noted the amount in her diary. "You still owe me seventeen cents, and you can pay me by doing one thing. It's so easy, you won't even have to get out of your chair."

He eyed her warily. "One thing. For seventeen cents. And I won't have to get up?"

She nodded.

He fidgeted in his seat. "Your word?"

"Given."

He swallowed hard. "What do I have to do?"

"Tell me your name," she murmured. She caught her breath and held it while she waited for him to answer.

His eyes darkened. A flush spread across his cheeks. His hands tightened into fists. "I told you my name. It's Boy. Just Boy."

"That's not a name and you know it."

"Bird's not a name, either," he argued.

"He's not a little boy like you are. Animals don't have to have names. People do."

"It's my *name*," he screamed, as if she had ignited something deep inside of him that had been smoldering for a very long time. Without warning, without any rational explanation, he unleashed a diatribe of bitter, angry words that spilled out of his mouth. "My papa called me Boy. He did! He'd say, 'Boy, get me my strap. Boy, get me my whiskey. Boy, get outta my sight. Boy, you're stupid. Good-for-nothing. Dumb. You're dumb, Boy!'" he repeated, over and over, until the tough little street urchin dissolved into a weeping child with a little heart that had suffered far too many hurts.

Martha knelt by his side and cradled his head against her bosom while tremors racked his body and tears washed the bitterness and shame from his heart. She held him, still, long after he had quieted and lay limp in her embrace. She caressed his brow and wiped the tears from his cheeks. His eyes remained closed. His breathing returned to normal, then slowed, as if he had fallen asleep.

Very gently, she lifted him into her arms and carried him to Victoria's cot. When she laid him down, he stirred and looked up at her with swollen, red-streaked eyes. "You feel like my mama did. Then she died."

He struggled, but lost the battle to keep his eyes open. Before he fell asleep, he managed to whisper the answer she had been waiting to hear.

"My Mama used to call me Will."

"You sleep, darlin' Will. Just sleep," she crooned as she tugged the quilt around his little body. When she finished, she dropped to her knees and bowed her head in prayer before she tidied the room.

She pulled the curtain aside and glanced at the twilight with a satisfied smile. As soon as it grew dark enough, she would take him home, very certain he would proffer no argument about having an escort.

Chapter
TWELVE

The tough little street urchin was back in full form the moment Will woke up.

Martha should have known better than to hope otherwise. Short of dying, there were no certainties in this world. She had only to glance at this young boy to know that for a fact. She was not quite sure why this little *gift* had been dropped in her lap via the loft, or exactly what kind of gift he actually would turn out to be, but she was darned determined to unwrap him.

She locked her gaze with his and tried to stare him down. Inside Boy, that tough, independent street urchin who scraped his way to survive by trusting no one, there was a little orphan boy named Will who was desperate for love and affection and the comfort of strong arms to protect him from a cruel and dangerous world. She could only imagine how difficult it must be for him to constantly battle between being one boy or the other, yet she dared to hope and pray Will would one day be strong enough to trust and love again.

And for the patience to be there when he did.

"It's time to go," she insisted. Again.

"Ain't no way I'm ridin' that ugly ole horse. I'm walkin'. By myself," he repeated, fifty pounds of pure defiance with unruly hair and a tongue sharp enough to whittle wood.

Her patience finally snapped. "We'll have to ride together. I'm too old to walk that far. Grace is right outside, saddled and ready to go."

"Then unsaddle her. You ain't goin' with me."

"You mind your tongue and your manners, young man," she warned.

He snorted. "You ain't my mama and you ain't tellin' me what to do," he countered before he charged out the door as fast as his bad knee could carry him. He headed out through the rear yard, where darkness quickly claimed his little form.

"Be careful of the dogs," she warned in as loud a whisper as she dared.

His lopsided footsteps hesitated, then kept going.

Mumbling to herself about how far she had fallen to try to frighten him into coming with her, she mounted Grace and nudged her forward since she could not follow the boy without running into that dratted new fence.

By the time she made her way out past the main entrance to the tavern, down East Main Street, and onto East Falls Road, her eyes had completely adjusted to the dark and she had a firmer grip on her temper. Fortunately, there was just enough moonlight to guide her. Just as fortunately, Will's scraped knee slowed him down enough that she easily caught up with him. Since she had not had enough foresight to bring a rope with her to hog-tie the boy to the saddle, she had to settle for outwitting him.

He looked back over his shoulder and snorted. "Go away. I don't need you to take me home."

"Will? Is that you?"

"Of course it's me," he grumbled, almost as if he was upset she had not recognized him.

"I wasn't sure. I thought you'd be long gone by now."

He turned his attention back to the road ahead. "I'm goin' fast as I can. What're you doin' here? I told you not to come with me, didn't I?"

"I thought I might just take a ride since Grace was already saddled."

"Take another road," he suggested.

"I like this one."

No response.

She followed him for about a quarter of a mile in total silence, save for the sound of Grace's hooves hitting hard dirt and his beleaguered footsteps. When he left the road and entered the woods, she did the same and smiled. There was not a shortcut within ten miles she had not used herself, and she was actually surprised he knew about this one.

Although the ground grew steeper here than if they had stayed on the main road, the shortcut that led to Reedy Creek was faster. Better still, there was not an obstacle along the way that would prevent Grace from following the boy, although there were plenty of paths that branched out and could confuse someone not familiar with the right route.

Like a young boy new to the area.

The stands of trees shut out much of the moonlight. Will would find that more of a deterrent than Grace, which meant Martha could simply relax in the saddle and wait for him to grow tired and ask for help.

He walked nearly a mile into the woods before he stopped and turned around to face her. She could see nothing more than a muted shape. He had squared his shoulders, ready to launch another round of verbal bantering. "You're follerin' me," he spat.

"Yes, I am."

"Don't."

"Why not?"

He limped his way back toward her and stopped just out of arm's reach. He was close enough now, though, that she could see his features clearly. Eyes flashing with indignation, he tilted up his chin. "I don't need you. I can get back by myself."

"You still have three or four miles to go."

"I'll get there."

"I'm sure you will. Along the way, you might consider what you're going to tell Reverend Hampton and his wife that would explain where you've been and why you've been gone so long."

He flinched, turned around, and started walking again. "I got lost in the woods. That's all. And you can't say nothin' different, 'case you're thinkin' about it. Gave your word you wouldn't tell nobody I was in the stable."

"Yes, I did," she agreed.

"So go home."

"After my ride. By the way, before you get home, you'd better take off those bandages. Unless you want to explain how you got them."

"I'm not dumb," he spat as he veered down a path to the left. "Not like that ugly ole horse of yours."

Give me patience, Lord. Patience.

"I wouldn't go that way. Stay on the main path, unless you want to—"

"I know the right way," he argued, and continued down the same narrow path anyway. "You're just tryin' to get me confused, hopin' I'll tucker out and give in. I won't."

"Suit yourself. I didn't realize you wanted to climb up all those rocks to get home. With your bad knee, that is."

He halted.

She took a deep breath. "This path leads down to the pond and Crying Falls. They're not very high, but they are dangerous. You can still get home this way, but you'll have to climb up a steep incline covered with rocks and boulders when the path ends. You're a strong boy, though. You'll do fine, but Grace isn't up to that."

She paused, but thought better of telling him that this narrow path would meet up again with the main one they had just left.

He started walking forward again. "Good. Then you'll have to turn back."

She followed him all the way to the pond and around it until the path came to an abrupt end at the base of the steep incline she had warned him about. The rushing, tumbling waters of the falls nearby broke the eerie silence as he studied the terrain before he turned around and walked back to her.

He tried to grin, but only made it halfway between hope and dismay. His gaze kept shifting back and forth between the rocks and boulders ahead waiting to challenge him and the stubborn woman in front of him now. "Guess you'll be headin' back now."

She nodded. "I think I'll let Grace drink at the pond a bit, then we'll go back to the main path and ride a while. You could come back with me, in case you think I'll get lost," she offered, giving him a chance to change his mind without losing face.

"This way's faster for me," he countered before he turned and started up the incline.

She watched him climb until the shadows claimed him and distance muted the struggle of his efforts. She even waited just a little longer, just in case he decided to turn back or cried out for help. When she was certain he would do neither, she retraced her way back along the path and followed the main shortcut until she was at the top of the incline.

With no sign of Will, she rode ahead a good half of a mile before turning back. She remained astride and strained to listen for signs that he might be still climbing his way up. Seconds stretched into anxious minutes. Her heart began to pound.

Where was that child?

"Bloody, wretched rock!" His voice echoed close by, followed by the sound of falling rock. "There. That'll teach ya!"

She grinned, dismounted, tethered Grace to a nearby tree, and sat down on an old stump a few feet away from the top of the incline.

She waited and said a silent prayer he would not tumble back down.

When he finally clawed his way to the top, he lay facedown on the ground not ten feet away from her. He was panting heavily, but otherwise appeared to be none the worse for his efforts, although it was too dark to tell for sure.

She held silent and very still for fear she might frighten him.

He rolled to his side, looked directly at her, and glared. "What happened? That dumb horse of yours get you lost?"

She chuckled. "No. We went back to the shortcut and wound up here. Turns out it was faster. Easier, too," she added when he stood up.

His clothes were thoroughly disheveled, and it would take a woman with a lot of skill to mend those trousers now. Miraculously, the bandage on his knee looked intact, but strips of tattered cotton hung from his hand. He tore them off and started toward the path ahead with a heavier limp than earlier.

She let him pass her by. When he continued on his way without looking back at her, she untethered Grace and led her by the reins until she caught up with him. She walked alongside of him and slackened her hold on the reins so Grace was behind them. "You still have another few miles to go. You're still welcome to ride Grace with me."

He snorted. "I ain't ridin' that old horse or any other horse till I got my own."

"I'm surprised you want a horse at all since you think all horses are dumb." She looked back over her shoulder to her mare. "He didn't mean you, of course."

"A man's gotta have a horse to ride or plow or pull a wagon. I said they were useful. Just so happens they're also dumb. Not much a man can do about that."

Before Martha could respond, Grace gave Will a nudge right in the middle of his back. He spun around and went face-to-face with the horse. "Hey! What're you doin', you mangy, ugly—"

The mare nudged him in the chest.

"That's enough from both of you," Martha warned, and tightened her hold on the reins to keep Grace under control. She patted the mare's face, but kept her gaze focused on Will. "You hurt her feelings, and she let you know it, didn't she? Next time, mind your tongue as well as your manners."

"She tried to bite me, and all you're worried 'bout are my manners?"

"If Grace wanted to bite you, which I doubt, she would. Good and proper, too. Several months back, Debra Collins found that out for herself."

He inched back from the horse. "What'd . . . what'd she do?"

"I gave Debra a carrot to give to Grace. Debra thought it would be more fun to tease her. I tried to warn her, but that girl just wouldn't stop. Next thing, Grace had the carrot and all four of Debra's fingers clamped between her teeth."

He stepped back a little farther and clenched his fingers into tight fists. "The horse ate her fingers?"

Martha chuckled. "No, Grace just held on to them for a bit. She never even broke the skin, but I doubt Debra will ever tease Grace or any other animal again soon. I'm sure if you apologize to Grace for calling her dumb and ugly, she'll leave you be."

"You made that up," he charged. "I ain't apologizin' to no horse."

Grace stomped her foot, whinnied, and tugged at the reins.

He flinched, but held his ground.

Martha shrugged her shoulders. "Have it your way, then. I should probably warn you Grace is just as stubborn as you are. Might make for a longer walk home since you'll have to keep well ahead of her. I'm not sure I can hold her back when I'm walking. Now, if I rode, I surely would, and if you rode behind me, Grace couldn't do much about that. At least it would give you both time to settle down a bit."

"She'd throw me right quick!"

"Not if I'm riding her, too," she countered. She mounted Grace and patted the saddle behind her. "I've got her steady now," she assured him. "Climb up."

He hesitated, but limped toward her by circling around to avoid the horse's head. After a few awkward attempts, he finally managed to get his foot into the stirrup. Martha grabbed hold of his puny arm and helped to hoist him up behind her. He was barely astride when he grabbed her shoulders. Hard.

"Put your arms around my waist or we'll both fall off if Grace stumbles. That's it. Now, hold on. We'll go slow and easy and let Grace lead us," she suggested as she nudged the mare with her knees. "Horses see better in the dark than we do."

"Like I said, they're useful. At times," he murmured. His grip around her waist tightened as they started off. His body was stiff. The farther they rode, however, the more he relaxed. When he laid his head against her back, she smiled, but kept her hands steady on the reins and her comments to herself to let him sleep.

As she rode, the sky grew cloudy, and the temperature began to drop. There would be rain before morning. She could feel it in the air. They passed several farms before the old Rhule homestead finally came into view some fifty yards up the road. She brought Grace to a halt. The boy stirred, then settled back against her while she studied the old house Will and the other boys now called home.

Memories both joyful and sorrowful quickly surfaced. Bertram and Zena Rhule had come to Trinity just before Grandmother Poore retired from her calling, so she had delivered their first child. Martha had been there, too, and delivered the next two children herself. She had watched them grow. She had tended to them when they got sick. She had prayed with them at Sunday meeting.

And she had helped to prepare them all for burial, as united in death as they had been in life.

Long abandoned, the single-story dwelling now blazed with light that silently spoke of new life, of a new beginning here for Will and boys like him. She had no idea what Reverend Hampton and his wife looked like, but she knew their spirits. Anyone who would devote their lives and resources and energies to care for orphaned boys deserved admiration and respect, along with an abundant dose of help and understanding.

The journey to redemption in body and soul for these boys would be difficult, and Martha pledged at this very moment to do what she could to ease the way. Perhaps that was what the gift of Will had been—an invitation to take part in their journey.

She nudged Grace forward. "Will? It's time to wake up. Will?"

He stirred and leaned back from her, but his hold around her waist tightened the closer they got to the house. She had to pry his hands apart to dismount, and tethered Grace to a hitching post near the door before she reached up to the boy.

His gaze was still sleepy, but fear found ample room to enter. He immediately masked it with that false, brittle bravado she had come to expect. "I don't need no help," he insisted, and stiffened when she steadied him anyway during his awkward dismount.

"Is there anything you want to say to Grace before you go inside?"

He straightened his shoulders and sniffed at the mare. "Guess she ain't too dumb if she found this ole place. She's still ugly, though," he added.

Fully ready to reprimand Will for hedging his apology with another taunt, Martha was interrupted when the front door suddenly opened, spilling light outside that was blocked only by the couple standing there.

Martha stared openly, mesmerized by the surprising images that stared back at her. She took a deep breath, set her disbelief aside, and waited to see how this unusual set of guardians would welcome Will home.

Chapter
THIRTEEN

The two people standing in the doorway could not be Reverend Hampton and his wife. Impossible. Absolutely impossible. They were old enough to be grandparents, not guardians for a group of orphans!

As best as Martha could judge, the woman was nearly sixty, with a thin braid of red hair tinged with gray that hung over her shoulder and fell to her waist. Neither fat nor thin, she stood at average height and might have been considered quite ordinary. Until you looked into her eyes. Pale, pale green, they were simply remarkable in color and were so large they nearly overwhelmed her features.

The woman's companion, a portly man of approximately the same age, watched her with a guarded but warm expression on his face. He had a full, milk-white beard, but not a hair on top of his head.

"My dear boy!" The woman rushed forward to enfold Will in her embrace. "We were so worried about you," she crooned before dissolving into a fit of weeping.

Will held himself as stiff as one of the rocks he had just climbed. When he finally struggled free, the man's expression turned into a stone mask that brooked no argument. "We're thankful you found your way home," he murmured to the boy. "For now, I think it's best if you get right to bed. We'll discuss your misadventure in the morning."

Will lowered his head and kicked at the ground with the toe of his shoe.

"Speak up, boy."

"Yes sir."

"I'll tuck you in. Poor lad. What a fright you must have had all day," the woman crooned as she led Will into the house.

When the man cocked his head and looked at her with upraised brows, Martha smiled. "I'm Widow Cade. Martha Cade."

He extended his hand, and she found his grip quite strong for a man his age.

"The midwife. Of course! I'm Reverend Hampton. Thank you for bringing Boy home."

She nodded, but found it odd that he referred to Will as Boy. "I'd like to have brought him home sooner, but . . ." She paused, unsure exactly how much she should tell the man.

He chuckled. "I quite understand. Boy has a quick mind and an even quicker tongue, along with an unusually independent nature. I'm just glad he's home safe. Please come in. My wife, Olympia, should be able to join us shortly."

Martha stepped into the single-story dwelling, where a low fire burned in the hearth and a pair of kerosene lamps on the mantel provided ample light. With a quick glance around, she realized the interior had changed little from what she remembered. Straight ahead, the large kitchen ran the full depth of the house. To her left, there had been two bedrooms, but the door had been closed and blocked any view she might have had of them.

The minister waved his arm and pointed to the rough planked table with benches along all four sides that sat in front of the hearth in the middle of the room. "Won't you have a seat? Until we enlarge the house and have a parlor, I'm afraid this is the best I can offer you."

"This will be fine," she assured him, and removed her gloves and laid them on her lap as she sat down on the bench facing the fire.

He took a seat at the head of the table facing the front door and gazed at her gently. "I hadn't heard you were back home. How is your daughter?" He tugged on the end of his beard and shook his head. "I'm sorry. I can't seem to recall her name."

Martha drew in a deep breath. "Victoria. I . . . I pray she's well. As hard as I tried, I never did find her to bring her home," she admitted.

Try as she might, she found no censure in his dark eyes, only compassion and understanding.

"She'll come home. Until she does, Olympia and I will keep her in our prayers. And you, as well."

Gratitude tightened around the ache in her heart. "Thank you," she whispered. She cleared her throat, anxious to turn the subject away from her own troubles. "You seem to have taken on quite a task," she suggested, also curious as to why he had not pressed her for details about Will and her return home with him.

He chuckled. "The Lord calls us. Whether or not we answer is up to us, isn't it?"

"Yes, that's true, but—"

"But what in heaven's name is an old retired goat of a minister doing with a crew of recalcitrant orphans clear out in the middle of God's good country?"

She blushed.

He laughed out loud. "You're not the first one to be surprised. I could hardly believe it myself, but Olympia was quick to remind me that my ministry never did require a church. After thirty years as a prison chaplain, I was ready for a small cottage near a fine lake. I do love to fish."

He paused and let out a small sigh. "Seems the good Lord had other ideas. Some years ago, one of the inmates I ministered to told me he had grown up as an orphan. After his release, he wrote to me from time to time. Made a little fortune for himself in New York City, as it turned out. When he died last year, he left his entire estate to be used to establish an academy in the countryside for orphan boys, provided I would agree to act as the boys' guardian and run the academy."

"With six orphans under your care," she offered.

"Actually, we have seven now that Boy is back. We left the city with ten. Unfortunately, we lost a few on the way."

"Lost a few?" Had the children taken ill and died or had they truly run away and gotten lost? In either case, he seemed to regard their loss rather callously, something that did not bode well for Will or any of the others.

His expression sobered. "Three ran off. One left when we were only a day's journey out of the city, and another disappeared three days later. The last one left us just east of Lancaster." He shook his head. "I knew I couldn't force any of them to remain with us, so I set the conditions before we left for Trinity. Each of the boys is free to stay or go. They make the choice, and they know they're always welcome to come back if they do leave, as long as they agree to follow the rules while they're here."

"But they're only children," she argued, making a deliberate attempt to keep her voice even and nonjudgmental. As pious as the minister appeared to be, his attitude toward the children was too callous for her to accept his views as valid. "They can't just come and go at will. They need supervision. They need guidance and protection."

"They do," he countered, but he made no attempt to explain how he could allow children to simply leave of their own accord to wander about the countryside on their own without either the guidance or protection he was required to provide as their guardian. "I'm grateful to you for helping one of our boys to come home. I hope the experience didn't harden you against what we're trying to do."

His troubled gaze suggested that his experiences with neighbors and townspeople had not been all positive. Despite her reservations about his attitude toward the boys, she did not want to make his mission here more difficult. "Not at all," she assured him, and quickly recounted the events that had begun with finding Will in the loft and ended with her bringing him home.

He listened, nodding from time to time, but never interrupted her. When she finished, he cocked his head. "You call him Will?"

She nodded. "Yes. He told me that was his name."

He shook his head. "He's never told us his name. Not even the other boys know it. He must be especially fond of you."

She let out a chuckle. "Hardly. He seems to make a very strong effort to insult me and even my horse—"

"Because he's not sure he can trust himself to let someone else care."

"I . . . yes . . . I think you might be right. At least you know his name now, and you can call him Will instead of Boy."

He narrowed his gaze, thought for a moment, and shook his head. "I don't think that would be wise. At least for now. He might take your telling us as some sort of betrayal of his trust. He'll tell us himself when he's ready."

On the one hand, Martha could not quite believe he could be that patient, that understanding, especially when working with children like these. On the other, she simply could not accept that he could just dismiss those children who had run away. Given his status as a man of the cloth and his experience counseling prisoners, however, she dismissed her concerns and focused on the sacrifices he was making to help Will and the others at the academy. "It's very complicated, isn't it? He's only a child—barely eight, I'd venture—yet he acts so . . . so old at times."

"He's closer to six or seven, as far as we've been able to determine. We think he's been on the streets for better than four years."

"Which explains . . . everything," she whispered. "He's still only a child."

"He is, but Boy and the others aren't like the children you know, with parents and neighbors to teach them to walk the path of righteousness. Two of these children came from orphanages too awful to describe. The rest, like Boy, have been on their own, struggling to survive in the streets, for years. They've been deeply hurt, either abandoned by parents who set them loose because they couldn't or wouldn't care for them or orphaned, with no one willing to take them in. They're scorned by righteous people, even feared, because these boys travel in packs like wolves, scavenging a bit of garbage to eat or a place to sleep out of the cold or rain. The older ones are pickpockets and thieves who swear better than the hardest inmates I've ever met, and some can con you out of your money without a twinge of conscience."

He paused to catch his breath. When he spoke again, his voice was just above a whisper. "But they are all His children. Just like the rest of us, each of them must choose to be saved. That's all I'm trying to do—to give them a choice between the life they had before and a future life filled with purpose. To get them to accept our help or to struggle on their own until they do."

He made perfect sense, especially given his description of the boys' backgrounds and her encounter with Will. She found the call he had answered to be so formidable, and the opportunities for failure to be so endless, that any reservations she had about Reverend Hampton now appeared to be very petty. "If there's anything I can do for you both or the boys, just send for me. I have a room at the tavern," she offered.

His eyes softened into twin pools of gratitude. "They tell me you have a healing hand, a generous heart, and abide no hint of gossip." Suddenly, his demeanor changed and his eyes began to twinkle mischievously. "Mayor Dillon left several hours ago. Unfortunately, we were able to confirm his suspicions that our boys were involved in that prank. I don't think they suffered anything worse than some scrapes and bruises for their efforts during the night, but under the circumstances, I didn't think Dr. McMillan would welcome taking a look at them."

"You might be right to keep the doctor away for a few days . . . until . . . until he calms down and the gossipmongers find something else to amuse them. Did the boys actually target the doctor with their prank?"

He nodded. "Dr. McMillan called on us shortly after we arrived. Unfortunately, our boys weren't quite what he expected. Several weeks later, when we were in town one day, two of the boys overheard the doctor make remarks they perceived as disparaging, so they retaliated. I hate to impose, but I wonder if you would mind taking a look at them? I know Olympia would sleep better tonight if you could make sure they'll be all right. We've never been blessed with children of our own, so she hasn't had much experience with them."

"I didn't bring my bag of simples, but I'll be glad to look them over . . . if you think they'll let me. Will wasn't too keen on the idea at first."

He nodded. "To Boy and the others, being hurt and asking for help means being vulnerable or weak, a sure way to invite disaster on the streets. After what happened at the market today and the mayor's visit, the boys are waiting to hear their punishment announced in the morning. They're not likely to protest anything I tell them to do tonight, especially if they think it might soften the blow tomorrow, so to speak."

"Will it?" she asked as she put her gloves on top of the table and let him lead her to the door to the sleeping rooms.

He grinned. "Not in the least. For tonight, they were sent to bed without supper even though only four, plus Boy, actually participated in the prank. They're all waiting to hear their punishment tomorrow. I've learned not to be too quick to dish out punishment. It helps me to think straight, after I've prayed on it, of course. Besides, it doesn't hurt to let the boys stew a bit."

She leaned toward him and lowered her voice. "If only some were involved, why are the others going to be punished, too?" she asked, curious to understand his reasoning.

"They might not have participated, but they knew what the others were all about. They'll share in the punishment tomorrow as well. But don't worry. I've already told Mayor Dillon what I have in mind."

"So far," he added as he reached to open the door, "what they can conjure up in their vivid imaginations tends to be far worse than what I've decided they must do tomorrow to make amends to Dr. McMillan. They can always leave in the morning, instead, but that hasn't happened in the past and I don't think it will happen tomorrow, either. You might want to be at the market tomorrow morning about eight and see for yourself."

Before she could answer or warn him that bringing all of those boys into town might only add more fuel to the simmering resentment against them, he opened the door and waved her inside. "They're all yours. I'll just introduce you first."

Not quite certain she was up to handling six boys as difficult or challenging as Will, Martha was unable to resist the minster's charming ability to set her at ease. She walked into the room and waited while he lit several candles on a table just inside the door and they sputtered to life. Added to the brighter light spilling into the room through the doorway, the candlelight gave her a good view of the small chamber.

All the boys except Will had burrowed under their blankets. Four were lying on the floor on top of corn husk mattresses that were lined up side by side along the far wall with scarcely walking room between them. Two boys slept on the floor to her left. Will was curled up on the floor in the right corner with Mrs. Hampton sitting in a chair at the head of his mattress.

The woman put a finger to her lips. "He's almost asleep," she whispered as she rose to meet her husband and their guest.

After a quick introduction, Reverend Hampton clapped his hands several times and glanced around the room. "Sit up, boys. I know you're all awake so don't bother trying to convince us otherwise. Hurry now. Sit straight up. Widow Cade is here to see to your injuries, such as they are, and to make sure you're fit for tomorrow."

Martha braced herself for an onslaught of snarls and wicked looks by setting a smile to her lips. The two boys to her left sat up first and looked at her with the same distrust she had seen so often in Will's eyes, but no snarl.

They were a study in contrasts, to say the least. The boy closest to the wall had a small frame like Will, but had straight fair hair and a sprinkle of freckles across the bridge of his nose. The other glared at her with frosty blue eyes below dark brows the same color as the curls on his head, and he was very plump.

The minister pointed to each of them, starting with the first. "This is Samuel, and Curtis."

They frowned, but held their gazes steady.

"Over here," he continued as he moved to the mattresses along the far wall, "we have Wesley, Peter Jacob, better known as P. J., Joseph, and Adam."

Since P. J. was the one boy Will had mentioned, she focused her attention on him after giving the others a cursory look. By far the biggest, and probably the oldest, P. J. appeared to be about twelve. Judging by his size now, he would probably top six feet by several inches when he reached full manhood. He had dark eyes and hair and olive skin, and she could almost see the chip he carried on his shoulder.

Despite his scowl, she kept her smile intact, even though her heart trembled at the sight of all these poor boys, and offered a quick prayer for each of them.

"You know Boy, of course," the minister concluded.

She waited, hoping to meet Will's gaze, but he kept his eyes downcast and only acknowledged her with a curt nod.

"Olympia, dear, why don't you stay here with the boys. I'll take them out to the kitchen one at a time to see Widow Cade. The light will be better there, don't you think?" he asked, directing his question to Martha.

"Yes, but I'd like to wash up first. Then we'll have a look," she suggested. Then she turned about and left the room. She waited until she was back in the kitchen before she let out a long sigh of worry about what morning would bring. With luck and a good bit of assistance from above, all seven boys would appear in a town filled with lots of folks who were already convinced the boys did not belong there. If less than seven showed up, only God knew what the townspeople would do if they found out one or several had balked at their punishment and were running loose in the countryside.

Chapter

FOURTEEN

The drizzle started just before Martha got home from the academy. By dawn, the rain was steady, promising a gray day that would be chill and dreary. Not a good omen, but perhaps a valuable gift since the weather might keep most folks indoors when Reverend Hampton arrived with his charges. After talking with him last night and meeting all six of the other boys, she knew he would not let foul weather eclipse whatever plans he had for the boys' punishment.

At precisely seven o'clock, according to the watch she usually carried to time birthing pains, Martha peeked out from the covered bridge and scanned up and down West Main Street. Not a wagon or shopper in sight. None of the workmen were extending the planked sidewalk today, either, but the distant sound of both mills at the far end of town told her their day's work continued unaffected by the weather.

She waited, hoping for a lull in the rain, but after searching the overcast sky, she realized a lull might be long in coming. She tightened her grip on the covered baskets she held in each hand, bowed her head, and took a deep breath before she made a mad dash for the confectionery. With one basket nearly full and the other empty, she felt a bit lopsided and nearly lost her footing twice, along with her balance, when she tried to avoid puddles at the last minute.

When she reached the confectionery, she charged toward the door and huddled under the overhang of the roof. Her cape was drenched. The hem of her gown was coated with mud, and her shoes were soaked clear through. Breathing heavily, she shook herself to get rid of the water still dripping from her cape. In the process, her hood dropped back and settled into a crumpled, soggy mass of fabric at the nape of her neck, and unleashed a trickle of cold water that ran down her back and left gooseflesh in its wake.

Oddly exhilarated, she set down the full basket to open the door and stepped into the vestibule the Lynn sisters had had built several years ago. In the next heartbeat, she grabbed the empty basket with her full hand, yanked it inside, and closed the door with a hearty swing of her hip.

She managed to get the door shut before the echo of the bell overhead stopped tinkling. Greeted by a steady warmth and smells beyond delicious, she ventured to the doorway of the room on her right and peeked inside. Her mouth began to water immediately.

The sisters had prepared so much today she could barely see the yellow gingham cloths topping the tables that skirted the perimeter of the former parlor. The aroma of freshly baked bread filled the room where loaves nestled together in long rows, overwhelming the top of one table.

The sundry cookies, tarts, pies, and other pastries on the other tables were even more tempting and added a sweet smell to the air. You did not have to check a calendar, consult a farmer's almanac, or gauge the temperature to know what fruits were in season. One whiff of the air and a glance around this room were all you needed.

Today, the cloistered aroma of cinnamon and nutmeg that laced the distinctive fragrance of apples proved fall had arrived. Apples peeked through the center of deep-dish pies, oozed from the ends of sugar-crusted tarts and strudels, and lay in soft puddles atop bread pudding.

On the table in the center of the room, a small wooden box used to collect rewards from customers lay next to a roll of brown wrapping paper and several balls of string and a single pencil.

None of the prices had changed for as long as Martha could remember, so there was no need to post them. More often than not, so the sisters believed, folks were generally honest, so they just picked out what they wanted and dropped their coins into the box or tore off a piece of brown paper and scribbled down what they would bring to the kitchen door at the rear of the building as payment in kind when they returned pie plates or other baking dishes.

The sisters, as everyone knew, were too kindhearted to turn anyone away empty-handed for lack of coin or something for barter, so the system worked well for all concerned, except for Wesley Sweet, who operated the general store. He had inherited his grandfather's talent for business and turning a coin, and had a keener eye when it came to balancing his accounts but none of his ancestor's compassion or kindness toward folks in need.

With no sign of Fern or Ivy, Martha turned about and headed for the other door. She cringed, but she couldn't stop her shoes from squeaking and squishing as she walked any more than she could keep the water from dripping from her cape and pooling on the wooden floor.

Inside the second room, tins of hard biscuits, crackers, and pretzels vied for space on a table along the front. Directly ahead, beyond another wrapping table in the center of the room, lay day-old baked goods. Today's offerings, only two loaves of bread and a tray of oatmeal cookies, waited to be claimed for half the price of yesterday.

Still no sign of Fern or Ivy, but Martha knew exactly where to look for them now. She set her baskets down and wriggled her toes to try to get them warmer before heading directly to the kitchen, which was located just beyond a door in the vestibule. A second closed door in the vestibule hid a staircase leading to the living quarters on the second floor, which was private. She knocked and poked her head inside, took one look at the sisters tugging an unsightly pink wad of taffy between them, and grinned.

"Having some trouble?" she teased.

With her face flushed the same color as the taffy, Fern looked up and promptly tossed her end to her sister. "That's the sorriest mess I've ever created," she groaned. "Mornin', Martha."

Ivy held the sticky mound at arm's length, glanced at Martha, and made a visible effort not to grimace when she nodded welcome. "It's not a mess, is it, Martha? It's . . . it's . . ."

"A mess. And a disaster headed straight for the trash pit," Fern countered. She slumped her shoulders as she wiped her hands on a wet cloth. "I let it sit too long," she explained while holding Martha's gaze. "Are you heading over to the market?"

Martha raised a brow. "You know about that?"

Ivy plopped the disaster onto the table. "Mayor Dillon stopped by late last night. He didn't tell us much. Just said to come to the market at eight if we wanted to see those boys held accountable for putting Dr. McMillan's carriage on top of the market roof. From what he said, I gather most folks are going, which is why we spent most of the night baking extra goodies."

Fern sighed, her forehead lined with exhaustion. "Baking and try-ing to make taffy at the same time was a mistake. You were right, Ivy. I should have waited until we finished baking to start on this," she admitted after she gave the gob of taffy a good poke.

"It's probably not a total waste," Martha suggested as she ventured into the room.

Fern snorted. "That taffy is getting as hard as a rock as we speak. We can't salvage it, and we can't even give it away to anyone because it's bound to break their teeth. A pure waste of good ingredients, too. Lord forgive me."

Prompted to test the perception of all things, even disasters, as gifts, Martha tried not to think of the sugary confection as taffy but as something else. She offered the distraught woman an encouraging smile. "What if no one knows it was supposed to be taffy? What if you stretch it as thin as you can, cut it into really small pieces, and sell it as . . . as hard candy. It probably tastes good enough, and people wouldn't be tempted to chew it," she added.

When their disbelieving expressions did not brighten, she tugged off a small piece of the taffy and popped it into her mouth. She held it between the roof of her mouth and her tongue, closed her eyes briefly, and sighed. "Sweet. Wondrously sweet. And refreshing, too. Is that apple I taste?"

Ivy nodded. "That was my idea. Just to try something different."

"And I ruined it for you," Fern whined. "Wasted a jug of Hilda Seymour's honey and half a basket of apples, too. At least we didn't waste time peeling them first."

"Well, I think the taste is delicious. Actually, it's very soothing to the throat. If you did cut it into little pieces, it would be like . . . like lozenges. Folks can always use something like this with winter coming on. You know how cold it can get and how it hurts to breathe when you're outside for any bit of time."

Fern raised a brow. "Like Harper's Lozenges at the general store?"

"Exactly. You can call them . . . let's see . . ."

Ivy's face lit up. "Lynn's Little Lozenges. We could even make more, if folks like them. You know how strict young Sweet is with his books. He always gives credit to you in the end, but he slices off a layer of a person's pride before he does. Poor folks can't help getting sick or suffering from the cold. We could have the lozenges here for anyone who needs them, whether or not they're able to pay."

"We could set plates of them in the confectionery with a sign telling folks they were free, as long as they came back and gave us their honest opinion," Fern suggested, breathing more life into Martha's idea. "Truth be told, we probably have enough already to supply every man, woman, and child from here to Clarion and back again for the entire winter." She offered Martha a sheepish look as she pointed to several bowls on a side table. "That's more taffy."

Martha laughed in spite of herself. With the mood suddenly filled with hope instead of despair, she had to admit that Aunt Hilda might really be right. Even if the sisters' plans for the taffy-turned-lozenges ultimately fizzled, they would find some satisfaction in their efforts. "You two start rolling this all out so I can help you cut it into lozenges. We'll try several different sizes until you decide which is best."

She paused and checked her watch. "I don't have much time, but while we work, I'd like to tell you what I learned about the academy last night before I head off to the market."

Martha left the confectionery alone at a quarter to eight. The rain had reverted back to a cold drizzle that covered the town like a blanket of fog, but the atmosphere in the confectionery was bubbling with warmth and excitement. Both of her baskets now were nearly over-flowing, thanks to a generous donation from the sisters.

With her spirit heartened by having Fern and Ivy as her allies in her plans to support Reverend Hampton's endeavor, she crossed back to the other side of Dillon's Stream. When the rain began to fall in heavy sheets again, she waited just inside the covered bridge to protect her cargo as well as herself. If she tried to get to the market around the bend in this downpour, she would be drenched to the skin before she took as few as four steps.

From behind, she could hear the sounds of horses and wagons traveling down West Main Street as the town stirred to life. By look-ing ahead, she had a clear view of Dr. McMillan's home, although the rain made it nearly impossible to see the sign out front, let alone read it.

She watched with curious fascination as several people arrived, knocked on the doctor's door, and were ushered inside. Stanley Pitt, the owner of the gristmill, arrived first, followed by Sheriff Myer and Reverend Welsh, who had apparently returned from Clarion. Each time the door opened, she got a glimpse of Rosalind. So far, Dr. McMillan remained out of view, although she distinctly heard his voice at least twice.

Surprisingly, none of the callers remained in the house for more than five minutes, which made her wonder whether Dr. McMillan was going to attend the event. She rechecked her watch. Eight o'clock. She scanned up and down East Main Street. No sign of any activity yet, let alone Reverend Hampton or the boys, but the rain might have slowed them down a bit.

The sound of wagon wheels clicking on the bridge behind her inspired her to turn around, but she was completely unprepared for the parade of wagons that appeared to be waiting to enter the covered bridge at the opposite end. Convinced she must be mistaken, she went back to the opening at her end of the bridge and peered down West Main Street. Sure enough, there was a line of wagons approaching that extended halfway down the street!

With the sound of the wagons already on the bridge growing louder and closer, she instinctively nudged her baskets closer to the wall and put her back against it, although the canvas bag kept her from getting as close as she would have liked.

One by one, the wagons entered the bridge, approached her, and finally began to pass her by. Abner Sparks and his family led the brigade, the second bad omen for the day. He waved at her. "You lookin' for a ride? Got some room in the back."

She waved back, but shook her head. "No, thank you. Where's everyone going?" she asked, half hoping there was some other event that had lured half the town out on such a miserable day.

"The market," his wife chimed in her singsongy whine. Her face crinkled into a scowl. "Those boys need to find out we won't tolerate the likes of them here," she spat. She tightened her hold on her two dour-faced sons, sitting on either side of her.

Fortunately, the wagon never halted and passed by before Martha could think of an appropriate response, but as the rest of the wagons passed by and she greeted the others, she found Priscilla Sparks's attitude to be the most prevalent.

Trying hard to keep the few more understanding folks in mind, she decided to follow the last wagon. She stooped to pick up her baskets and barely had a grip on them when a pair of strong hands snatched them away from her. Startled, she stood up, only to find herself nearly cornered with her back to the wall of the bridge. A very masculine body blocked her way forward and a pair of familiar gray eyes glistened with amusement.

With her heart pounding, she clapped her hand to her chest. "Mayor Dillon! You frightened me half to death!"

His dazzling smile slipped into a frown. "*Mayor* Dillon? You used to call me Thomas," he murmured while hefting each basket to get a firmer grip.

He was close. Too close.

She sidestepped to put several feet between them. "You used to be more of a gentleman," she charged. "What . . . what are you doing here?"

His frown deepened. "I was just leaving Dr. McMillan's when I noticed you standing inside the bridge. I thought I might be able to help you carry these," he offered while lifting the baskets. "I'm sorry. I didn't mean to startle you. Forgive me. My intention was to be helpful. Truly," he added, as if he might be able to talk away the disbelief she knew etched her features.

Reminded of how persuasive and charming he could be, she sniffed. "I can handle everything quite nicely."

He ignored her comment, offered her his arm, and chuckled. "You're as stubborn and petulant as ever. Since I've got both baskets, you'll have to carry the umbrella. Now, take my arm. The roadway is very slippery."

She spied the umbrella leaning up against the wall just inside the bridge. When she hesitated, he swung one of the baskets toward the umbrella. "We've got to hurry if we're going to get to the market in time. While we walk, you can tell me all about your trip. I'm sorry Victoria didn't come home with you."

This time his smile was sincere.

Still, she peeked around him, studied the roadway where mud was oozing up from below the cinders, and retrieved the umbrella. She had to hold it very high to accommodate his height and reluctantly took his arm.

Appearing at the market with Thomas as her escort was bound to unleash a round of gossip. More gossip. That was why she was weak in the knees and why her stomach was flip-flopping and why shivers raced down her spine. Certainly not because she cared a whit about the feel of his arm beneath her fingertips, offering strength and support, or the sound of his laughter that still echoed in her mind, or the sense of being safe and protected when he was so near.

Certainly . . . not.

Chapter

FIFTEEN

Beneath the very roof that had provided a showcase for yesterday's prank, seven somber boys stood shoulder-to-shoulder in front of a jury of the town's leading citizens and faced a crowd of townspeople that seemed unnaturally quiet.

Perhaps, Martha mused, the rainy weather had dampened the embers of their discontent. Curious glances and murmurs rippled through the audience when she entered the market with their mayor, much as she had anticipated. Most, she hoped, expressed excitement and relief that the public renunciation of the prank and the boys' punishment was close at hand, but she had lived in this town for too long not to know many of the whispers duly noted that the recently returned Widow Cade had been escorted to the event by widower Thomas Dillon.

While Thomas briefly conferred with the other men, she caught Olympia Hampton's worried gaze as she stood at the opposite end of their line and offered a smile of encouragement.

The smile she received in return was tenuous, and her stomach began to churn with worry. She did not know exactly how the boys would be punished any more than she could predict the townspeople's reaction to that punishment, but she trusted Thomas to be as fair and evenhanded today as he had proven to be all the years she had known him.

She could only pray the rest of the folks would be swayed by his hard-won reputation as well and begin to accept the academy. If not, Reverend Hampton might very well have to abandon his efforts here and move elsewhere to continue his ministry. In either case, Dr. McMillan's pride would have been properly avenged; in fact, he would probably find that the prank itself had opened more than a few doors of folks who wanted to rehash the whole scenario with him, creating a bond between them that would further his standing in the community as well as his career.

How the doctor handled himself today would also provide a glimpse of his character for all of them, and she was probably as anxious as the boys in front of her to have this unusual event begin.

Lost to her myriad concerns, she was startled when Thomas called the increasingly restless crowd to order.

"My friends and neighbors, I'm grateful to all of you for venturing out on such a miserable day."

Nods and a few grumbles.

He smiled. "Reverend Hampton asked for a moment of your time before we hear from the boys involved in yesterday's prank."

Without waiting for any further introduction, Reverend Hampton stepped forward, closed the distance between himself and his charges, and stood directly behind the two boys in the center.

From where she stood, Martha had a side view of his face. His expression softened from stern to repentant. "We haven't met many of you until today, and I'm deeply sorrowed that this occasion has brought us together. The boys' prank was meant as that—a childish prank—but I believe they now understand how they put all of you in danger by having made it difficult, if not impossible, for Dr. Mc-Millan to have responded to a call for help should any one of you have taken ill during the night. They were also disrespectful to a man who has come to their community to help others, not be subjected to ridicule."

He paused and scanned the crowd. "As guardian and teacher for the boys you see in front of me, I hold myself responsible for their misadventure yesterday, but when the good Lord called me to this task, I knew the journey would be as trying as it would be rewarding, a reality perhaps you can understand as you raise your own children."

A few understanding glances. Only a few.

He shook his head. "Pride can be a terrible, sinful curse. Each time we succeed in any of our endeavors, we unwittingly open the doors to our souls, and before we know it, pride slips in and convinces us we are men of righteousness and distinction. We are quick to judge others when they stumble and fall. We judge them as sinners who need God's grace and forgiveness, so we give them ours because we don't need either. Or so we think . . . until we stumble and fall our-selves. Once glorious and boastful, we're embarrassed and shamed because our pride is pricked and our reputation tainted."

He bowed his head for a moment, then gazed once again at the crowd. "I stand before you, my dear brothers and sisters in faith, both embarrassed and ashamed by my boys' behavior. My reputation as a man, as well as a man of the cloth, is duly stained. I ask for your understanding . . . and your forgiveness . . . along with your prayers that I might be given the grace to be a better teacher to these boys and that I might guide them on the path of righteousness as I continue to answer His call and serve Him through these boys—His creations, His joy, and His beloved."

Martha watched as men and women turned to one another. Their murmurs grew to heated whispers, but no one openly challenged the minister's message.

Touched by the man's eloquence, Martha glanced beyond the gath-ering at the gentle rain now falling, at the horses and wagons that surrounded them, at the familiar market itself. Somehow, Reverend Hampton had turned their ordinary market into a church without walls, a speech of apology into a sermon, and a gathering of discontented townspeople into a congregation.

And it wasn't even meeting day.

He had a true gift for preaching, a gift that easily could have been misused had it been given to a man with chicanery or evil in his heart instead of faith and goodness.

"If you please. If you please," he repeated, and eventually silenced the crowd by waving his hands up and down. "The boys have something to say to you all—and to Dr. McMillan, of course."

Given the boys' ages, which ranged from eight to about twelve, not a few expressions in the crowd filled with a combination of doubt and wonder. That mere boys could have taken the carriage apart, hauled it to the roof, and reassembled it amazed almost everyone in town. It was a task some of the able-bodied men present would find too great a challenge. The boys' accounting, however, soon erased all doubt and further enhanced their reputation as street urchins capable of almost anything.

Reverend Hampton tapped the tallest boy on the shoulder. The boy, whom she recognized to be P. J., took two steps forward and straightened his shoulders.

Martha could not see the boy's face at all and strained forward. She expected a rather meek apology, but when he spoke, his voice rang sure and clear.

"My name is Peter Jacob Yates. P. J. The prank was all my idea, and I'm very sorry. I won't do nothin' like that again." He turned, marched stiffly to Dr. McMillan, and extended his hand.

Now that Martha had a full view of his face, she could see his expression was properly remorseful.

"I apologize, sir."

Dr. McMillan shook the boy's hand and nodded. "Accepted."

When P. J. returned to his place in line, Reverend Hampton tapped another boy, who followed P. J.'s lead, and then another boy, until a full accounting had been made describing each boy's role in the affair.

Not a single boy had been spared, including Will, who had held the ladder and confessed last. When he turned from Dr. McMillan and locked his gaze with Martha's, she smiled approvingly, although she detected a glimmer of devilment in his eyes that his punishment today had not extinguished.

With all the confessions now given, the mood of the crowd had changed. The hardened expressions, filled with fear and scorn on some faces, told Martha the minister had been right. Some people would never accept these boys. But most of the people in the gathering appeared to be impressed by the boys' demeanor and their willingness to confess to their role in the prank before them all.

Until the minister changed the atmosphere once again. At his whispered command, the boys took to the crowd. They introduced themselves again and apologized, individually, to every adult member in the audience. The minister followed suit, shaking hands with the men and women and giving every child present a pat on the head.

Before her very eyes, the somber event that had come to resemble Sunday meeting became as animated as a revival. The atmosphere was charged with energy—positive energy that renewed her faith in humankind in general and in her friends and neighbors in particular.

When the boys finished and returned to their places, Reverend Hampton once again stood behind them. The townspeople edged closer, and Thomas nodded to the doctor.

Dr. McMillan stepped forward. He kept his back as straight as a broom handle and his expression sober. The only visible sign he was unnerved was the line of perspiration dotting his forehead and the opening and closing of his fists.

As he began to speak, a young boy Martha thought might be Jeremy Farnsworth rushed up to Thomas. The mayor leaned down, listened to what the lad had to say, and followed him outside. Unfortunately, with Dr. McMillan speaking, she was not able to hear what Jeremy had said.

"... and now, as you all witnessed, the boys have confessed and apologized to all of you and to me." He mopped his brow. "Their punishment should be fair and equal to the distress and inconvenience they have caused."

Martha's heart began to pound as she contemplated what further punishment, beyond the humiliation of a public confession and apology, might be given. More particularly, she worried Dr. McMillan might actually want to use a strap or a paddle to give each of the boys a solid whipping. Some members of the crowd clearly anticipated the same, judging by the gleam she saw in some men's eyes and the number of children who edged closer to their mothers' sides and clung to their hands or their skirts. Others frowned, clearly satisfied with the punishment already given.

"I've discussed the boys' punishment with most of the good people standing behind me. I'm a man dedicated to easing pain and suffering, not deliberately inflicting it." He clenched his fists and held them against the sides of his trousers. "I've agreed . . . that is, I've decided that to have the boys apologize, as they've already done, and reassemble the carriage, in full view of everyone here, would be . . . will be satisfactory punishment, provided they keep their word never to cause such trouble again."

He nodded over his shoulder. "We'll all be staying to watch, and I invite you to do the same."

Like a sun slowly struggling through stubborn clouds, the applause began with several women, then spread, becoming loud enough to overwhelm a mere whisper of jeers and taunts directed at the boys.

With no physical punishment to be delivered, relief washed over her, and Martha realized how stiff she had been holding herself.

Reverend Hampton stood on the sidelines while P. J. barked orders to the other boys. The audience chatted and watched with both awe and amusement as the boys struggled with the frame of the carriage and the sundry parts. Some of the parts were either too bulky or too heavy for some of the boys, but Reverend Hampton did not lend a hand. Harold Givens, a gunsmith with several sons of his own, stepped from the crowd to give the boys a hand. His neighbor, Lars Hoffbrauer, quickly joined them, inspiring a number of men, along with their sons, to do the same.

Before long, the carriage came to life, and the air fairly rippled with the sounds of laughter and good cheer, a transformation just short of miraculous. Awed, Martha picked up the baskets Thomas had carried for her and worked her way behind the assembled dignitaries to reach Olympia Hampton.

"Just a little something for your larder," she explained as she handed over the first basket. "My rewards are always unpredictable. Since we have more than we need right now, even for the tavern, I thought . . . well, it's sinful to waste."

She held out the second basket, which was much lighter. "Sweet breads from the confectionery. Fern and Ivy wanted you to know . . ." She paused, reluctant to speak for them. "They're hoping you'll stop to see them the next time you come to town."

The older woman's eyes filled with tears. "I can't tell you much I . . . we appreciate your kindness last night, Widow Cade, and now this . . ."

Martha pressed Olympia's hand around the basket handle. "Please. If we're going to be friends, you should call me Martha."

"Friends," she murmured. "Then you must call me Olympia." She glanced at the center of the market, where townspeople worked alongside her husband and her charges. "We'll never forget what happened here today. I doubt the boys will, either."

Before Martha could respond, Thomas joined them. Given the jovial atmosphere, his expression was oddly sober. "I'm sorry to interrupt."

"Not at all," Olympia murmured.

He looked directly at Martha. "Daniel Finch came looking for you. Mrs. Seymour sent him. Adelaide seems to be having some difficulties. He wanted to know if you would come to see her."

Martha's heart began to race as fast as her mind could conjure up a number of problems serious enough to call her back to her patient. "Of course. If you'll excuse me, Olympia, I need to get back to the tavern to get my bag."

Thomas shook his head. "No need. I knew you'd want to leave right away so I sent Daniel to the tavern to collect it. It's already in my buggy, which is just outside. Daniel's already left for home."

Her heart skipped a beat. "Your buggy?"

"It's pouring rain," he argued as he guided her past the rest of the men to his buggy.

Martha locked her knees together and braced her feet. Independence stiffened her spine. "I don't need a buggy to get to my patients. I have Grace and a perfectly fine cape to keep me dry."

He lifted the mud-splattered hem of her gown and wrung it out. "That's not dry, is it? And even if it were, it would be soaked before you got to Falls Road. By the time you got to Adelaide, you'd be sopping wet and chilled to the bone, which wouldn't help your patient, now, would it?"

"No," she admitted. "It wouldn't, but I've managed to travel in worse weather on my own for nearly ten years now. I don't need your help, Thomas. Truly."

His gaze softened. "No, you don't, but I . . . I need to give it. Truly."

She stared into his eyes and found no hint of guile, only sincerity and an earnestness that nudged the window in her heart open again. Beyond the promise of passion that beckoned in his eyes, she saw the buds of mutual need and respect that had never been there before. She saw him now not as a youthful, inexperienced man, but a man tempered by life, a man whose body and spirit had grown in both faith and character. A man who could come dangerously close to forcing her to confront her true feelings for him—if she did not carefully guard herself against his charm.

Both frightened and challenged by the man he had become, she climbed into the buggy, more determined than ever to keep a tight rein on her thoughts as well as her heart.

Chapter

SIXTEEN

T he buggy's wheels crunched over the rain-slicked cinders in the roadway and rocked its way toward the Finch homestead. The smell of damp wool emanating from Martha's cape was near suffocating, and Martha loosened the neck of her cape. The roof overhead protected them from the bulk of the rain. Fortunately, the rain fell straight and there was no wind to blow it at them, and the open sides of the buggy did allow for fresh, if moist, air.

Being in a buggy, sitting side by side with Thomas Dillon, was just about the last place Martha had ever expected to find herself today. Given all that had happened at the market earlier, however, the day was turning almost surreal.

"You might want to remove your cape, at least until we get there," Thomas suggested.

She tugged her cape closed again and tightened her grip on her bag, which was resting on her lap. "I'm fine. Did Daniel say what's wrong with Adelaide? Aunt Hilda wouldn't send for me, especially in this weather, unless something was truly amiss. Both Adelaide and the babe were doing cleverly when I left," she murmured, trying to think of something she might have missed as a portent of future difficulty she might have prevented.

"Whatever has developed, I'm sure you'll be able to help."

She nodded. "I pray you're right."

As though he sensed Martha's worry, he smiled and changed the subject. "We almost met the other day at the tollgate. I was beginning to worry when you hadn't arrived back in Trinity before me."

Fiercely independent, she hesitated to respond or to admit that the idea that someone might worry about her was oddly comforting. No one had worried about her for a very long time. John, rest his soul, had been gone for so long she could scarcely recall having him worry about her. She lived with James and Lydia, of course, but they were also too busy raising their three girls and running the tavern to worry overmuch about Martha. Now that their three girls were all married with children of their own, James and Lydia were quite accustomed to having Martha appear or disappear without notice.

Victoria never appeared to worry; in fact, Martha had the distinct impression the girl welcomed Martha's frequent absences as a respite from the inevitable clash of wills that had become the hallmark of their relationship.

Hearing Thomas say he had been worried about her was a novel experience. Encouraging him to worry, however, implied reconnecting something between them she had severed long ago. Anxious to dispel any thought that she might want to rekindle emotions she had battled through before, she met his gaze and held it. "There was no need to worry. No need at all . . . I hope you're not implying Grace is anything but a steady, reliable mount," she ventured, steering the conversation to safer ground.

He chuckled. "I wouldn't dream of it. She's a tough old girl, I'll grant you that. But she did take you on a very long journey. Even the best horse loses a shoe or stumbles on a rock from time to time. Or just plain gets tuckered out, especially after traipsing through the countryside for how long now? Ten years?"

"About that," Martha admitted, although she suspected he was concerned more about her than her horse, which only made her feel more uncomfortable. "We do get to rest in between calls."

"Not always," he countered. "Seems to me I could name more than one occasion when you literally rode Grace from one house to another for several weeks."

"And never once failed to make it home safe and sound. Eventually."

"No. Never once," he murmured. His gaze grew anxious and troubled, and he glanced out his side of the buggy. "The rain's letting up." His voice caught, and he cleared his throat.

A belated flash of insight inspired a blush that burned her cheeks, along with the sin of selfishness that now tainted her soul. Memories of the riding accident that had claimed his wife surfaced, and Martha laid her hand on top of his, finding them cold and stiff.

"You miss her terribly, don't you?"

He enfolded her hands within one of his own, but kept his gaze on the roadway ahead. The mask of the confident, outgoing widower he wore slipped away, revealing a vulnerable man grieving the loss of his wife while the single women in the world around him hustled to be the first in line when he chose a new one.

"I should have been there. I should have insisted she take the buggy. It was such a *stupid* accident," he whispered. "This past year I've laid in bed some nights and wondered if I'd have the strength to make it through another day without her. It's getting easier, but now . . ."

He paused and squeezed her hand. "She's fading away, Martha. I have to struggle to recall her face or the sound of her voice. What kind of man does that make me? I shared her life and her bed for nineteen years. We had four children together. Now she's buried next to two of our babes, and I can't even remember the feel of her anymore."

Compassion filled her spirit. She had gone through the same troubling experience after losing John. She had learned over the years, however, that the passing of time was a gift, both wondrous and painful. Time might have muted her memories, but it had also eased the pain of loss and had allowed her shattered heart to heal. Would the same thing happen if Victoria never came home? She shuddered.

"There's nothing wrong with you," she assured him. "Time lets the past slip away from all but your heart. She'll always be there. And in your children, too."

When he shrugged his shoulders, she continued. "Harry has his mother's smile, doesn't he? And Eleanor. She might have your smile, but she has her mother's infallible good humor and grace. I know Harry can't come home during the school term, but Eleanor's only living in Clarion now. Have her come home for a visit. Eva Clark certainly wouldn't object to having a guest to care for."

Upon hearing his housekeeper's name, he smiled. "She says the same thing at least twice a week: 'Invite Eleanor home for a spell.' And I always give her the same reply: 'I'll think it over.' "

Briefly, he turned his gaze from the roadway, captured Martha's, and held it. "Truth be told, Martha, Eleanor is teeming again. After losing the first two, she's frightened the same thing will happen again. The doctor confined her to bed for this one. She doesn't want anyone to know about this," he added.

"You mean Anne."

He nodded. "My sister, dear heart that she is, is apt to leave the capital, head straight to Clarion, and park herself in Eleanor's bed-chamber for the next five or six months."

In spite of herself, Martha groaned. Anne Sweet, ten years older than Thomas, had a heart as pure as the driven snow, but she had a reputation as an incurable chitchat. She could talk nonstop for hours, seemingly without stopping to draw a breath. Well-intentioned, she never stopped long enough to think she might be saying something that could be painful to the very person she was attempting to cheer.

"In her last letter, Eleanor made me promise not to tell anyone, especially Anne. Except for you, of course."

"I'll keep this in strictest confidence."

He smiled. "I trusted you would. Actually . . . when you're rested from your last trip, I was wondering . . . that is . . . Eleanor asked me if you could go to Clarion and talk to her. Reassure her this time she might carry her babe."

"I'll leave once I'm certain Adelaide is mending properly," she assured him, although traveling such a distance so soon was about as appealing as the dismal weather that surrounded her. Going to Clarion, however, would allow her to replenish her dwindling supply of simples, which she usually purchased from Doc Beyer, at the large apothecary there. She would also have the opportunity to pursue a new remedy for Samuel, one that might fully restore his vision.

Relief flooded Thomas's features, and he leaned back against the seat.

She withdrew her hand, finding herself in an awkward, thoroughly embarrassed state. The interest she had perceived Thomas felt for her was not a personal one. He was concerned about his daughter and needed Martha's skills as a healer, a reality she found only deepened her sense of shame at believing he might have wanted more.

While he toyed with the reins to guide the horses around a rather large hole in the road, she quickly dismissed any notion that her foolish perceptions about him earlier had stemmed from her own interest in him. She had loved him once with all her heart, but wisely chose another when she married John Cade.

"Naturally, I'd take care of all your expenses. Micah is still young and struggling with his law practice," he explained.

She expected Thomas might. Although Eleanor had married equal to her station, Martha also knew a husband with a good family name, excellent education, and a solid future in his father's law firm did not make the early years free from financial worry. "I'll keep a record and give it to you when I return."

He moistened his lips. "I can give you funds before you leave and put my buggy at your disposal, as well."

She shook her head. "That might prove awkward to explain. For both of us," she advised, fully aware of the double entendre of her words.

"What will you tell James and Lydia?"

She shrugged her shoulders. "I usually just leave a note for them if I have to leave in the middle of the night. I'll do that and simply write that I've gone to Clarion to purchase some of the remedies I used to buy from Doc Beyer. In the meantime, you can write to Eleanor and tell her to expect me." She chuckled. "With the mail delivery as slow as it is, I'll probably get there ahead of the letter, but try anyway."

"First thing in the morning," he promised. He sat up straighter, then turned toward her. "Now that I've got that out of the way, why don't you tell me what happened after you left New York to see Oliver in Boston?"

By the time they reached the Finch homestead, Martha had shared most of the details of her brief visit with her son, Oliver, who practiced law in Boston. Daniel opened the door before the buggy had rolled to a complete stop. Relief flooded his features. "Thank you for coming," he called.

Martha disembarked and followed him into the cabin while Thomas secured the horse. Any curiosity she had about the difference between the man she had loved twenty-five years ago and the man Thomas had become took a back seat to duty the moment she entered the bedchamber.

Adelaide lay abed, her face pale as she slept. Aunt Hilda rose and greeted Martha with a relieved look before shutting the door to keep the menfolk out. "I'm mighty glad you came so quickly. I wasn't sure Daniel would find you at home."

Martha removed her cape and tossed it onto the chair at the side of the bed where Aunt Hilda had been sitting. "I was at the market, actually, but I'll save that tale for later," she murmured while peeking into the cradle at the foot of the bed. Glory was fast asleep, too, with her cheeks still plump and rosy. Satisfied all was well with the babe, she approached Adelaide and laid a hand on her brow.

"No fever. What's wrong that's got you so worried?"

"She's bleeding heavily. Too heavily, I think. I didn't want to alarm Daniel or Adelaide, for that matter, but I . . . well, I'll feel better if you took a look." She led Martha to the table in the corner of the room where she had stored the cloths Adelaide had been using.

Martha counted them and inspected all four. "The blood is bright and clear, and I don't see any sign of infection. There certainly appears to be more than normal, though."

"And those are just from this morning. I already washed yesterday's."

Concerned, but not yet alarmed, Martha cocked her head. "How many did she use all told since the birth?"

"Seven or eight, not counting what's on the table, but they weren't anywhere as saturated as those. Poor darlin'. She's getting paler by the hour and getting weaker."

"Well, let's see if we can't get this mama feeling better. It was a difficult birth, so I'm not too concerned. I have some sawbrier root in my bag. We'll let her rest while we brew some tea. I'll stay to make sure this is all she needs and show you how to make more. It won't hurt to let her use the tea for a few more days."

Aunt Hilda let out a sigh. "I knew you'd have something to help."

Martha gave her a reassuring hug. "We need to get the water good and hot," she suggested, but kept her own counsel about what might need to happen if the herbal tea did not stem the bleeding. She usually reserved the sawbrier root to help dispel the afterbirth, but she had used it once before to stem a heavy flow.

At the moment, she was also worried about what Aunt Hilda would say when she found Thomas Dillon waiting for them with Daniel.

Chapter
SEVENTEEN

When Martha opened the bedchamber door, Daniel was standing there with his eyes glazed. He looked like he had been staring at the door, willing it to open.

He took one look at her and his eyes simmered with worry and hope. "Is Adelaide going to—"

"Sh-h-h," she whispered, noting that Thomas stood by the hearth warming his hands. "She'll be fine in no time."

Daniel backed up as she inched forward until Aunt Hilda closed the door behind them. "Why don't you add some wood to the cook-stove? We need to heat some water for tea as quickly as we can."

His gaze darted back and forth from the bedchamber door to the kitchen and back again. "Wood for the stove," he murmured. "Anything else? There must be something else I can do. I can't just stand idly by—"

"Maybe you should sit with Adelaide and call us if she wakes up," Aunt Hilda suggested as she stepped around them. Her eyes widened when she saw Thomas, who acknowledged her with a broad smile. "I see Thomas is here. He'll take care of loading the wood, won't you, Thomas?"

Her voice reflected no surprise or wonder, as if finding Thomas there was not unusual.

"Certainly." He looked around and walked directly to the wood stacked in the front corner of the cabin.

"Go on, Daniel," Martha urged. "Be sure to let us know the moment she wakes up."

Without further prompting, Daniel slipped past both women and into the room, and Martha averted her gaze from Aunt Hilda's as she went directly to the table and opened her bag.

Aunt Hilda busied herself by pumping water into a large kettle. "What brings you all the way out here, Thomas?"

He stopped in his tracks, adjusted the logs in his arms, and nodded toward Martha. "Just trying to protect Martha from herself. It's been quite a downpour, so when Daniel showed up at the market looking for her, I insisted we use my buggy. We can't have her taking sick now that she's finally home, can we?"

The older woman chuckled. "Martha's got the constitution of a plow horse. It's going to take more than a little rain to put her in a sickbed."

Martha cringed. A plow horse? She might be middle-aged, but she was still a woman! The image of a plow horse was not exactly the one she might have picked for herself. She much preferred the image of a sturdy chestnut tree, with firm roots and graceful limbs, that came to mind, along with a self-conscious awareness she was being vain. "Thank you for the compliment. I think," she grumbled.

"I meant it as one," Aunt Hilda insisted as she set the kettle on the cookstove. "Did you say you were at the market? Today?" she asked as Thomas finished loading wood into the cookstove and closed the door.

While Thomas explained all about the prank she had missed seeing while tending to Adelaide, his visit to the academy, and the public confessions and punishment that continued even as they spoke, Martha retrieved the sawbrier root and proceeded to snap it into smaller pieces.

"There are still places in the fence to be mended," he commented as he stood up and brushed his hands against his trousers, "but I think the boys handled themselves very well. Reverend Hampton really won most people over. He's quite a preacher, for a man who hasn't taken to the pulpit for most of his ministry."

Aunt Hilda cocked her head. "What kind of minister doesn't use the pulpit?"

"He worked with inmates at several prisons. Lemon Hill in New York was his last one, I believe," Martha interjected, annoyed by the thin layer of skepticism that laced Thomas's opinion of the minister. The moment she blurted out her words, she realized what she had done. When she looked directly at Aunt Hilda and Thomas, a blush warmed her cheeks. She really had no intention of telling anyone about her visit to the academy last night, but she had no choice now. Not with both of them looking at her with quizzical expressions on their faces.

Aunt Hilda broke the awkward silence first. "He worked as a chaplain in a prison? How'd you learn about that? The man's been rather mum about his former life, at least on his few visits to town when folks had a chance to talk with him."

Thomas narrowed his gaze and spoke up before Martha had a chance to say a word. "You went out there. To the academy, didn't you? I thought I detected an unusual sense of familiarity when you were talking with his wife."

She nodded, but once again, before she could fashion an accounting of her visit that would not betray any confidences, especially where Will was concerned, Thomas's face lit up. He paused as if he were mentally replaying the morning's event in his mind. "There *were* seven boys at the market, not six. The missing boy! You found him and took him home."

Drat. The man really could read her mind! "Well . . . I . . . yes, as a matter of fact, I did find the boy. To be more precise, Leech did, when the boy decided to hide in the stable loft. The other boys had left him behind after he fell and hurt his knee. I managed to patch him up, but I didn't take him home. I followed him. More or less. He's only eight or so, but he wears the armor of a knight who's seen a lifetime of misery that's been squashed into a few years. If the other boys are like him, Reverend Hampton has a plate that's overflowing. He needs all of us to help," she suggested.

A seasoned realist, Thomas approached the fire in the hearth and leaned his shoulder against the mantel.

"Notwithstanding yesterday's prank and today's events at the market, the academy makes people . . . They're uncomfortable, even uneasy. Most of them, except for Dr. McMillan, would have accepted that prank as uncommonly clever, had a hearty laugh, and dismissed it. Unfortunately, since Reverend Hampton arrived with his charges in tow, people have been quick to set blame on those boys' shoulders for 'most anything that goes wrong. Just last week, George Rottham up on Candle Creek summoned the sheriff because his hens stopped laying eggs."

Aunt Hilda snorted. "The sheriff can't do much about that."

"No," he countered, "but it turned out George finally realized the hens were fine. He caught sight of someone, a boy, hightailing it off the property with the eggs. He only saw the boy from behind, but he laid the blame on one of Reverend Hampton's charges."

He raised his hand to silence Martha when she started to protest. "Before that, Amos Wilkes found two sacks of grain missing from his barn. One day, Simeon Brooks's sow had eight piglets ready to be weaned; the next day, she had four."

Martha sighed. "And they all blame the academy boys."

"Exactly. No one has any proof, of course, but word is starting to spread back to town, and suspicions can take on a life of their own."

Martha lowered her gaze and toyed with several pieces of the root.

She wanted to argue that neither Reverend Hampton nor his wife would condone pilfering eggs or grain or even piglets. The boys themselves had learned to steal when they lived on the streets to survive, but their basic needs for food, shelter, and clothing were being met now, albeit with conditions.

Pulling a prank on Dr. McMillan to even a slight fit these boys' natures. Stealing unnecessarily did not, but Martha knew better than to proffer any argument against what Thomas said without proof of her own. People would not stop to think the issue through. They would react instinctively, and the academy boys would become scapegoats because the root of the question was more painful: Who, in their own community, had become a thief?

She shuddered and refused to even contemplate the answer for fear of unjustly putting someone's name on the list—a list she might be able to compile better than anyone else in the community. No one, not the mayor or the sheriff or Wesley Sweet at the general store, knew the faults or needs of the people in Trinity better than Martha. As a midwife and healer, she had visited or lived in their homes when they were the most vulnerable, unable to conceal the depths of their characters, for good or for bad, or the state of their worldly existence, whether bountiful or desperate.

She had earned their trust and goodwill, if not their rewards, by keeping her own counsel about all she saw and heard and refraining from gossip, even when she might have used the knowledge she had about people for their benefit. It was no easy task to be always on guard or to stay neutral, but with Grandmother Poore's example as her guidepost, she knew it was the only path she could follow—if she wanted to use her skills to serve her friends and neighbors.

A troubling notion that Thomas might ask her to help narrow the search for the real culprit or culprits made her hands tremble, and she tried to focus only on the work she needed to do now. She dropped a small piece of root into a mug and carried it with her to the kettle on the stove.

Thomas took her silence as an opportunity to continue. "People live and work and raise their families here in Trinity because they choose to. They're good, honest folks. Most of them, anyway. They don't like change, and they surely don't want the sins of the city staining their community. Frankly speaking, bringing those boys here, however well-intentioned, invites a kind of self-righteousness and even snobbery. Now, it's all well and good for Reverend Hampton to speak in platitudes and to tweak people's consciences, but the truth of the matter is this: If we don't find out who's responsible for the thefts, and they continue, I don't think there's much of a future here for the academy."

Aunt Hilda let out a long sigh. "That would be sinful and down-right wrong, but you shouldn't be too quick to think the worst of folks, Thomas. Show a little faith. We may not live in Paradise yet, but we've got ourselves a good place here in Trinity, with good people who have good values based on faith and trust in God as well as one another. From what you've told me, most of the townspeople at the market today seemed to accept the boys' confessions and apologies."

Thomas pulled away from the mantel and flexed his shoulders. "For the most part, they did," he agreed, although he appeared to be less convinced than Martha.

"That's precisely my point," the older woman countered. "When it comes to being fair, folks just need a good opportunity, and it sounds like you and Reverend Hampton gave them that opportunity today."

Thomas shook his head. "That was all his idea. I only spread the word so folks might come."

"Which they did. You did well today, Thomas."

He nodded and looked directly toward Martha. "Actually, there's something the others asked me to talk to you about. In strictest confidence, of course."

She stiffened, and the sinking feeling in the pit of her stomach warned her she might have been right to suspect Thomas would ask her to help identify possible suspects. Disappointment in Thomas, as well as the others, laced her spirit. Resolve to be true to her calling as a woman of trust stiffened her spine.

Perhaps for the first time, she understood Samuel's disdain for townspeople in general, and she even envied his ability to withdraw into a world of his own, if only for the time it took for her to realize living the life of a hermit would be as constraining as it would be empowering, especially given her duties as a midwife and healer.

She tightened her lips, poured boiling water into the mug, and stirred the contents until the root began to color the water into tea. "I'm going to see if Adelaide is awake," she murmured, and left the room without meeting his gaze.

Her steps were sure, her hands were steady, but her heart was pounding with indignation that the sheriff, along with the others, had sent Thomas—of all men—to ask her for help. Not Thomas, the mayor. Thomas, the man. The man who had once claimed her heart.

Adelaide was well on her way to healing very nicely, with Aunt Hilda hovering nearby and Daniel once again smiling, but the atmosphere in the buggy later that evening was explosive.

"I apologize."

Martha glanced at Thomas, seated only inches away from her, and let out a sigh. "And for the third time, I accept your apology."

He captured her gaze and held it. "You don't sound very sincere."

"I'm very sincere," she insisted, although her words sounded a bit shrewish, even to her own ear.

"You're angry with me."

"I'm not," she quipped, but his teasing smile snapped the last threads of her patience and self-control. "Yes, I'm angry, but more than that, I'm disappointed in you and your . . . your cronies. People here expect me to keep their confidences, and yes, once in a while I regret that when it causes undue hardship or adds fuel to malicious gossip because people misconstrue my silence for affirmation, but I deeply dislike . . . no, I resent being approached by you to ask me to break those confidences . . . especially you," she added while pausing to draw a quick breath, "because I thought you knew me better than to think I could be swayed into divulging information clearly meant to be confidential or set to . . . to spying on folks because they happen to need me."

Out of breath again, she was shocked by her uncustomary diatribe. She never lost control of her temper. Well, almost never. Her cheeks burned with embarrassment, but she was honest enough with herself to recognize anger and regret as well.

Then he grinned at her. He grinned!

She slapped at the bag on her lap. "If you say one word right now . . . one word . . ." she warned. She willed her breathing to return to normal and her heart to stop racing.

He held up one of his hands in mock surrender, but wisely held silent.

She dropped her gaze for a moment to settle her thoughts. When she looked back up at him, he had both his hands on the reins again. "I'm sorry I lost my temper."

When he looked at her, his eyes were twinkling and he had just a hint of a smile on his lips.

"And for raising my voice."

He cocked a brow.

She dug as deep as she was going to go. "And for . . . for not kow-towing to the illustrious town elders who think they can intimidate me into doing their work for them."

He nodded, but held silent.

She counted five heartbeats, then ten. When he still remained quiet, she waved at him with the back of her hand. "Go on. Speak."

"I accept your apology."

She narrowed her gaze. "You don't sound very sincere."

He shrugged his shoulders. "Maybe I'm not. Maybe, just maybe, I think you said exactly what I deserved to hear in exactly the tone of voice I anticipated, which, by the way, is precisely what I told the others you'd do when they asked me to speak with you."

Martha looked up, and her eyes widened. "You told everyone I'd lose my temper?"

He grinned again. "Just a little."

She sniffed. "And that I'd raise my voice?"

"Just a tad. They didn't believe me, of course, but they did suspect you might balk at being cooperative. I think the very word they used was *stubborn*."

"*Stubborn?*"

"I'd prefer to say highly principled and devoted to your calling, thank Providence. I also think I know you well enough to be fairly certain you'll try to ferret out the thief or thieves on your own, if only to help Reverend Hampton save the academy for the boys."

She stared at him, both awed and amazed. Guilty as charged, she blushed because he had voiced what she was going to do before she had even admitted it to herself. She had not been married to the man all these years, but he still knew the workings of her mind better than anyone ever had or could.

Perhaps it was that single issue that had frightened her, more than his wealth or his social position in the community, all those years ago when he had asked to court her. It had been disconcerting and extremely uncomfortable to have him know how she might feel or react before she even realized it herself, denying her any freedom to respond to her own impulses, to profit when she was right, or to learn from her mistakes when she was wrong without having the added burden of knowing he would have supported her whether she succeeded or failed, regardless of whether or not she had earned such total devotion.

When the buggy slowed to a halt, the door to her room was only several feet away. "I suppose you still want me to go to Clarion?" she asked, hoping he would have the good grace to be embarrassed that he had asked her to do a personal kindness for him when he knew full well what he would be asking her to do in his official role as mayor.

She had a good notion to express her disapproval by refusing his request.

He shifted in his seat. "Not for my sake. For Eleanor's," he murmured.

"I'll go. For Eleanor," she murmured, although she knew she was going to Clarion before she had asked him the question or entertained any idea of refusing his request.

And he knew it, too, confounded man that he was.

"I'll leave at first light, but there's something that needs to be taken care of while I'm gone. It won't take up much of your time. If you can wait a moment, I just need to get something . . . unless you'll be too busy with your duties as mayor," she needled.

"I'll make time."

"Good." She disembarked and went inside. Before she even lit a lamp, she knew what she would find as soon as the room came to life.

Sure enough, Bird was fast asleep on top of Victoria's pillow.

She worked quickly and returned to the buggy, where she set a bulky package on the seat next to Thomas.

Eyes wide, he looked at her with curiosity and more than a little suspicion.

She grinned as she put a small sack into his hand. "This should last until I get back, but try to find a crust of bread now and then. Fresh water every day, and don't worry if he lets himself out. He'll make a nest somewhere and be back in the cage by morning. His name is Bird, by the way. Don't ask. I don't have time for details. I need a good night's sleep if I'm going to be in Clarion in time for supper."

She grinned again, went back into her room, and closed the door.

"Martha Elizabeth Alexandra Cade!" His voice bellowed. Bird began to squawk his little heart out.

Humming softly, she secured the inside lock on her door, went to her window, and opened it. "If you two keep making that racket," she warned, "you'll wake half the town."

Thomas glowered at her. "You're testing my patience," he spat.

"I always did," she whispered, and promptly closed her window.

Chapter

EIGHTEEN

Like all gardens and fields ripe for harvesting, sickrooms had a distinctive, sadly familiar scent. Martha smelled it as soon as she entered the dim bedchamber. Instead of flowers or crops, illness and suffering blossomed with fear that permeated the very air while weeds of death gained a stranglehold on life itself.

Eleanor Dillon Landis was asleep in bed with a heavy quilt pulled up to her chin so only her face was visible, even though the room was so warm it was suffocating. Heavy drapes that covered the windows muted the busy sound of commerce on the street below and obliterated what daylight still remained. The light from two small lamps on the bureau was weak, but enough to let Martha maneuver her way into the room and edge herself between a trunk at the foot of the bed and the low bureau where bowls, linens, and a number of medicine bottles filled the space between the lamps.

She paused and lifted each bottle toward the light to read the label. By the time she finished, her worst fears about the method of treatment Dr. Park had pursued set her blood boiling and her heart began to gallop.

Dr. Park used emetics and purges, along with a sedative, that were powerful enough to put Eleanor and her unborn babe in such imminent danger that Martha feared neither one might survive unless the drugs were stopped. Immediately. Dismayed, yet heartened by her own chance to intervene and offer an alternative that might save them both, she made her way to the chair at the head of the bed and eased into the seat.

She studied the face of the young woman she had watched grow from infancy to adulthood, and her heart constricted. Eleanor's face was pale and drawn, her lips cracked and crusted with bits of dried blood. Dark circles beneath her eyes added a ghoulish appearance to her features. Limp blond hair, once a glorious mane of curls that fell to the middle of her back, now barely skimmed her shoulders.

Yet surrounded by all these signs of devastation, the promise of new life flourished in the small mound on Eleanor's stomach.

While she waited for Eleanor to stir, Martha leaned back and closed her eyes to pray. First, for Eleanor, that she might be given the gift of health, and then for the child who struggled for life. Only then did she pray for herself. For wisdom. For courage. And most of all, for patience enough to ease the anger churning in her very soul.

She let the anger build, adding fuel to her determination to battle the doctor responsible for Eleanor's deteriorating condition. Although he was only acting as he had been trained, everything Martha had learned about Eleanor's treatments, designed to guarantee delivery of a healthy, living child, was in direct contradiction to what any midwife worthy of the name would have recommended.

At the root of her anger lay two divergent views on pregnancy and birthing, philosophies that set doctors and midwives at polar opposites, with their patients' lives and futures lying in between.

"W-widow Cade?"

Though the voice she heard was weak, Martha's eyes snapped open, and she turned immediately toward her patient. "I'm here, Eleanor," she murmured. She caressed the young woman's brow and used her fingertips to lift strands of damp hair off her forehead. No fever. Good sign.

A pair of wide, deep-set blue eyes gazing up at her misted with tears. "It is you! I prayed you'd be able to come to help me, but Father hasn't written back to me yet to tell me you'd agreed to come, so I wasn't sure it was really you."

Martha chuckled. "He's writing to you today, as a matter of fact. I thought I might be delayed for a few days, but things all worked out sooner than I expected, so here I am."

Eleanor moistened her lips and stirred. She lifted one thin arm from beneath the quilt, took Martha's hand, and laid it on top of her swollen belly. "Isn't he wondrous?"

Martha smiled. "Indeed, he is. I haven't seen Dr. Park, but I talked with Micah. He tells me you hope to deliver in midwinter."

"February," she murmured. Her eyes misted with fear. "I've done everything Dr. Park has told me to do. Everything. But . . . but I'm . . . but . . ." She dissolved into gentle weeping, unable to continue.

Martha stroked the young woman's belly, concerned the baby might be smaller than normal. "But you're growing weaker. Losing weight, too, I'd venture." She gazed down at the several scabs on Eleanor's arm where Dr. Park had apparently bled her and caught a frown before it formed. She could ill afford to alarm her patient, and she needed to know much more than what Micah had told her before she could even contemplate an opinion on how best to restore Eleanor's health without putting the babe she carried at risk—if indeed there was a risk.

Eleanor sniffled and wiped away her tears. "Will you help me? I couldn't bear to lose my baby. Not again. I can't," she pleaded.

"I know how important this baby is to you," Martha crooned. "But you're important, too, especially to Micah and your father. And to your baby, you're the most important person on earth right now. I want you to remember that when I ask you some questions so you'll be completely honest with your answers. It may not be the answer you think I want to hear. You may find a question painful or embarrassing. You might not understand why the question is important, and you might wonder if you should even give me an answer because you feel loyal to Dr. Park because he's been trying to help you. But every answer you give me will help me to understand what's happened before in each of your pregnancies and what's been happening during this one so you and Micah can decide together what's right for you to do this time."

A sniffle. A brave smile. "I'll remember. And I'll try to be as honest as I can be."

"Good. Now, let's go back a bit to the first time you were teeming," Martha began. Gently, she led Eleanor through a series of questions. When she finished, she got a fresh cloth from the bureau, dampened it, and washed Eleanor's face.

"Now the second time," she prompted. Tears accompanied more of the young woman's answers this time, and she did not seem to be anything but completely forthright. Once Martha sorted the information she had already gleaned, she got Eleanor to provide more about her current condition.

By the time the young woman finished, she was near exhaustion and had to battle to keep her eyelids from staying closed.

"You've been a great help. Now rest. That's right. Take a short nap. By the time you wake up, I'll have some recommendations, and we'll have Micah join us. Then you can ask any questions you might have," Martha added, mindful that she must keep careful balance on the tightrope on which she found herself now that her worst fears about her own position here had been confirmed.

Only Eleanor and her husband had the right to choose between continuing with Dr. Park or letting Martha take over caring for Eleanor for the rest of her pregnancy—a choice that would decide the fate of their unborn child and Eleanor, as well.

Obligated by her calling to offer them both that choice, Martha eased from the chair, dropped to her knees, and bowed her head in prayer—the only weapon she had that would be powerful enough to prepare her for meeting with Eleanor and Micah and later, if they decided in Martha's favor, with Dr. Park himself.

Martha had no doubt about her recommendations. She had no doubt the decision facing this young couple was difficult. As they gathered together later that night, the only doubt that niggled at her mind and spirit was that she might fail to help them reaffirm their faith, for only faith would give them the courage they would need tonight and all the nights that would pass between now and the birth of their child.

Martha sat in the same chair as earlier. Eleanor was still in bed, and Micah sat on the bed facing her. With their hands entwined and their faces glowing with affection for one another, they looked so very young to have endured such tragedy and to be facing such uncertainty now.

"All I can give you is my honest opinion," Martha began. "Whatever decision you make about whether or not to continue with Dr. Park will be entirely your own."

"I trust you. We both trust you, don't we, Micah?"

The young man sobered. "Yes, we do."

Martha took a deep breath and quickly outlined her recommendations, which Micah challenged at every turn. She ended with one last plea. "Trust one another. Respect one another's opinion. You don't have to make your decision tonight, but I would urge you to not wait too long."

She glanced at both of them and smiled. "I've delivered hundreds of babies since Grandmother Poore passed on, and I'd like very much to deliver yours. I know how frightened you both are. With good reason. But I have every faith and hope that come February you'll be able to hold your babe in your arms—but only if you discontinue Dr. Park's treatments.

Micah paled. "All of them?"

"All of them," she repeated. "You lost your first babe very early, but don't forget that nature plays a very important role. When something is wrong, nature takes over and ends the pregnancy. It's simply nature's way of correcting itself to prevent the birth of a deformed child, for example. In the end, we must trust God to know what is best before we do, and to know that one day He will shower us with joy equal to the pain we have endured."

She paused and watched with compassion as Micah wiped away his wife's tears. She waited for Eleanor to regain her composure before continuing. "What happened the second time was an unfortunate quirk of fate. There is nothing you or Dr. Park, or I, could have done to prevent the cord from wrapping around your baby's neck as he was being born. From everything I've been able to learn, however, there is nothing that would indicate either scenario would hold true this time."

Leaning forward, she placed her hand atop Micah's and Eleanor's. "If you honestly thought Dr. Park's treatments were helping, you wouldn't have sent for me. But in the end," she cautioned, "it is your own fear and your own doubt that you must conquer. For that, you need faith. Not in me. Not in one another. Faith in God. Faith that He'll restore Eleanor so she is strong enough to deliver your child. Faith He would never send you a gift you didn't cherish, whether that gift caused tears of joy or sorrow. Faith that He will bless you with peace of mind when you make the right decision. Whether you choose to remain under Dr. Park's care or return to Trinity, where I can help you, I will support your decision because I know you turned to Him for guidance and will accept His will when the time comes for this babe to enter the world."

She rose and straightened her skirts. "I'll leave you now so you can talk this over together." Whispers accompanied the sound of her footsteps as she took her leave. She had no sooner returned to her own room when Micah knocked at her door. When she looked at him quizzically, he grinned. "I don't suppose they need a good lawyer in Trinity?"

She chuckled. "I think that's something you should discuss with Thomas."

"I will. As soon as we get there. Perhaps you could speak to him for me so he'll know what my plans are. For now, would you come back to Eleanor's room? We'd like you to pray with us."

The following morning, Martha lost no time implementing her plan to save both mother and child. While Micah waited downstairs to intercept Dr. Park, Martha tackled the room first, careful to avoid the bathing tub now sitting in front of the hearth. She tied back the drapes and opened the windows—only several inches, since the air had turned quite brisk. She left the bowls and linens on top of the bureau, but packed the medicines into a box she set out in the hallway.

She paused several times to listen, but heard no sounds from downstairs that suggested the doctor might have arrived. Satisfied that she could proceed uninterrupted for a spell, she helped Eleanor from the bed into the chair. "Now, sit still," she warned. "I want you to get used to sitting up before we attempt that bath."

With one eye on her patient, she changed the bed linens and found a fresh day dress for Eleanor in the trunk at the foot of the bed. With everything well under way, she opened her bag and perused the contents. "The hot water isn't here for your bath yet, but while we're waiting, you should get to choose the scent you'd prefer to add to the bathwater. I have some lavender here . . . and, yes, I thought so, some mint and lilac."

Eleanor winced when she cracked a smile, but giggled anyway. "Mint, I think. Do you always have bath scents in your bag? I thought you only carried remedies."

"My simples are remedies that are as different as our complaints. Sometimes, a woman just needs to be . . . pampered. I have some salve for your lips, too. It's been so dry in here, it's a wonder they aren't worse."

Thundering voices. Thundering footsteps charging up the stairs. Apparently, Dr. Park had not taken the news well. Martha froze in place, then hurried to stand next to Eleanor. She had barely turned to face the doorway when a middle-aged thundercloud of a man stormed into the room and rocked back on his heels the moment he reached the side of the bed.

Micah arrived within seconds, but remained just inside the doorway. "I think it's best if you leave, Dr. Park."

His command sounded like a plea, which the doctor promptly ignored. His dark eyes blazed with fury as he glanced around the room. His lips twitched and he sputtered a bit before he exploded, filling the room with the bitter accusations he hurled at Martha. "You!" He shook his finger at her. "You will be responsible for not one death but two! What kind of charlatan are you to prey on a weak, defenseless—"

"I am a midwife," Martha said calmly while her heart galloped in her chest.

"Same thing," he spat.

She blanched, but held her tongue.

He dismissed Martha with a snort and gazed at his former patient with surprising tenderness. "Eleanor, please. You mustn't be swayed by this . . . this woman. You're very ill. You're not strong enough—"

"Eleanor is very weak, that's true," Martha interjected to prevent Eleanor from being drawn into a battle she was too weak to wage on her own behalf. She put her hand on Eleanor's shoulder and felt the girl quaking. "Bloodletting will weaken anyone, but most especially a teeming woman. Using emetics and purges to cleanse her system very well may cause her to expel the babe. Medications to keep her sedated may, in fact, be harmful. But Eleanor isn't ill. She's teeming, a perfectly natural state for married women. With proper diet, along with moderate activity and fresh air, she'll be able to gain the strength she needs to birth her babe."

There. She put the explosive issue dividing them out in the open, fully aware that neither she nor the doctor would budge from their respective viewpoints. Doctors, by training, treated pregnancy as an illness cured only by birth, which was yet another illness that required treatment.

Midwives, on the other hand, saw the entire process, from conception through birthing, as a purely natural process that usually proceeded without the need for intervention.

She stared directly into the doctor's furious eyes and refused to blink for fear he might sense she was weak.

He glared back at her. "Your notions might be well-intentioned, but they are sorely misguided," he spat. "Your ignorance will exact a high price when you fail. Are you prepared to pay that price? Will you be able to look Eleanor and her husband in the eye when they bury yet another babe because you interfered and contradicted the advice of a trained physician?"

She refused to take the bait he dangled in front of her, and held tight rein on her temper. "I respect your formal medical education, even as I would ask that you acknowledge my own apprenticeship and training. I know when my skills are not adequate, and I send for a doctor without hesitation in those cases. This is not one of them," she said firmly.

He raised both brows, but when he attempted to speak, she cut him off. "Neither one of us has the right to argue anything here now that will distress the patient or her husband. It's time for you to leave. Quickly, if you will. It's time for Eleanor's bath."

An ominous silence enveloped the room—until Micah's voice rang out, firm and clear this time. "Dr. Park?"

The doctor exhaled, cast Martha a scowl, and turned on his heels. When he reached Micah, he poked the younger man in the chest. "I intend to speak to your father. He'll make you listen to me," he snapped, and made a noisy escape through the hall and down the steps. When the front door opened and quickly slammed shut, Martha flinched, but Micah held firm. "I can handle my father. Just tell me how soon I can take Eleanor to Trinity."

Martha let out a long breath. "Let her build up her strength for a week. I'll write down everything I want you to do," she suggested, looking down at her patient and offering her a reassuring smile.

A week from now, Thomas would be able to welcome his daughter home, although he would have the formidable task of keeping his sister at bay. Come winter, God willing, Thomas would be able to welcome his first grandchild, which would also help him to see a future for himself without Sally by his side.

Her heart trembled.

Couldn't someone, somewhere, help Victoria come home to her mother, too?

NINETEEN

She had been a coward. She had merely been practical. She had been a coward.

Martha swung from one extreme thought to the other as she returned from the apothecary, several squares from the modest town house where Eleanor and Micah waited to bid her farewell, with a new supply of simples she ordinarily purchased from Doc Beyer in her bag. If she had had any courage, she would have gone to see Dr. McMillan and talked to him about buying remedies from him, too.

"I'm a coward," she muttered, even though she had saved considerable coin by getting her supplies in Clarion. She had also gotten a new remedy for Samuel Meeks, one the druggist claimed might work wonders for the reclusive man who was losing his vision. Besides, coming to Clarion to purchase the remedies from the apothecary had given her the opportunity to visit Eleanor without revealing the true purpose of her visit to anyone else.

She stopped at an intersection and waited for a break in the parade of carriages and wagons before crossing the street.

The mid-morning sun, perched in a flawless sky of blue, was bright and warmed the day, promising a fair ride home. She wrinkled her nose, unaccustomed to the stench. Although Clarion was only a midling city, compared to Philadelphia or New York, all the trappings of city life abounded. Refuse and human waste littered the streets. Shops and homes crowded together to accommodate the burgeoning population. According to Micah, pigs roamed at will despite new laws, creating havoc now and then when they scooted under and around moving vehicles while searching for food.

She scanned the street but saw no sign of the pigs. Relieved, she hiked up the hem of her skirt and sidestepped her way across the street between a Conestoga wagon obviously heading west and a farmer's wagon loaded with squash. When she finally got to the cobblestone walk that shopkeepers had been sweeping clean when she passed by earlier, she dropped her skirt back into place and used long strides to loosen her leg muscles in anticipation of the long ride ahead.

The few precious coins she had left in her purse made it easy to avoid the temptations offered by the sundry shops along her route, but when she spied a leather-bound daybook in the window of Lynch's Stationery Store, her steps slowed. The shopkeeper was busy rearranging the display and adding more merchandise, but she kept her gaze on the daybook.

Petite, the journal was no larger than the size of her hand. The vine of flowers etched on the front cover created a delicate frame around the centered numbers, 1830. She had never owned anything quite so lovely and most certainly nothing as expensive. Actually, the little sign listing the price had fallen forward, but she did not have to see it to know the daybook was far beyond her means, although with only a few months left in the year, the price surely had been lowered.

After the shopkeeper moved the daybook and some sheet music to make room for a display of picture puzzles, she followed his every movement. When he flipped the sign for the daybook upright and set it back in front of the daybook, her hand tightened on the handle of her bag, which also held her coins.

He caught her interest and looked down at the daybook. He held it up, cocked his head, and raised his brow.

Embarrassed, she shook her head.

He paused, crumpled the sign, and held up one finger.

She moistened her lips. A single dollar was an unbelievably low price, but still more than she could afford to pay for something that was a luxury she could not justify. Without any specific use for the daybook, the purchase would be a whim, and she had been practical for far too long to change now.

She listened to her purse instead of her heart, and shook her head before turning away and hurrying on her way.

Grace was saddled. Martha's bags were strapped into place, along with a meal to eat on the way home. Anxious to arrive back in Trinity before dark, Martha waited patiently while Eleanor finished writing a letter to her father.

The rose-colored dress the younger woman wore softened her pallor, and her eyes were twinkling when she finished and handed Martha the letter. "You won't forget to give this to Father?"

Martha tucked the letter into her pocket. "I'll stop by his house before I set foot to home. Besides, your father's been caring for one of my patients, remember?"

"Oh, Bird. That's right." Eleanor chuckled, apparently still amused by the tale Martha had told her last night. "Poor Father. He's detested all winged creatures for as long as I can remember."

Martha cocked a brow. "You know why, don't you?"

A full grin. "No, but I gather you do."

The memory made Martha smile, too. "Thomas was only ten or eleven at the time. Like most boys his age, he was rambunctious, full of energy, and anxious to prove his mettle. That particular day, he and James decided to see which one of them could climb all the way to the top of that big chestnut tree behind the meetinghouse. You remember. The one that lightning struck some years back?"

A nod.

"Well, James went first, made a good third of the way up, and stopped, which wasn't like him at all. Nevertheless, your father proceeded to pass him. Halfway up, he happened upon a bird's nest and disturbed the mother bird, who was tending her young. Unfortunately, they were jays, and before your father could wriggle away, a good flock of very angry jays answered the mother's distress call and pecked his poor head something fierce."

She chuckled. "Grandmother Poore patched him up. She told me she had to snip away a good bit of his hair to clean the wounds in his scalp. Poor Thomas. He bore the brunt of his chums' cruel taunts long after his hair grew back in."

Eleanor dissolved into laughter, bringing a healthy flush to her cheeks and a vitality to her appearance. "He never told me that story. Now I know why he's not fond of birds."

Martha nodded. "We all have stories we're reluctant to share with our children until they're grown. Maybe that's a mistake," she mused as her thoughts drifted, once more, to Victoria.

Martha had plenty of her own stories, of course, but she had not shared the most difficult or most embarrassing ones with her daughter, either, and she suspected most parents had done the same. Perhaps it was nothing more than a well-intentioned effort by parents to paint themselves as more suitable models for their children to follow. Fear that any faults or misdeeds or misadventures might somehow weaken their authority might play some part as well.

The blade, however, swung both ways.

The cost of appearing more saintly than human gave parents a selective memory, if not an impossible model for the children to emulate. To be fair, adults probably blocked out experiences that if shared would humble them before their own children, when in essence, their very humanity, replete with failures, should have become a source of encouragement that the children, too, could overcome the most troubling of mistakes.

With new insight into her own relationship with Victoria, as well as Oliver, she saw the role she had played in her daughter's disappearance from a different perspective, embraced her mistakes, and quickly thought of a way to make amends when Victoria came home.

"I must be off," she murmured. "I expect to see you in Trinity next week. Micah knows exactly how to get you home, so let him worry about that. You concentrate on getting stronger, and have faith." She embraced the young woman. "I'll see you soon," she promised, and departed.

She made one stop in Clarion before she left. When she did, her purse was lighter, but her heart was far happier than when she had arrived.

Martha followed Dillon's Stream all the way home and arrived at sunset. An unusual number of men milled about, mostly along West Main Street, so she took the covered bridge at the western end of town and crossed over to the other side. She waved to the Lynn sisters, who were outside sweeping the sawdust from the new planked sidewalk in front of the confectionery, and made a mental note to stop in to see them tomorrow to see how their lozenges were coming along.

True to her word, she rode directly to Thomas's home to deliver Eleanor's letter. She was both relieved and dismayed to discover that Thomas was not home. The housekeeper, Eva Clark, was either out visiting herself or napping, so Martha simply slipped the letter under the door along with a hastily-scribbled note asking Thomas to bring Bird home to her.

Once she reached the tavern, she had to make a real effort to get past the wagons and horses overcrowding the yard to get Grace into the stable and settled down for the night. Spurred by the tempting aroma of mutton stew that laced the air, she did not bother to unpack when she got to her room. She only took the time to hang up her cape, put Eleanor's letter on the table, and wash up before joining Lydia and Annabelle in the kitchen.

"Smells delicious," she offered in a loud voice in order to be heard over the din of heated conversation in the other room.

Lydia, who was lading servings onto two trenchers while the younger woman cut several slices of bread, looked up and wiped her brow with the hem of her apron. "You're back early. Did you get everything you needed in Clarion?"

"And then some. The apothecary there is quite well supplied," Martha responded. Using the need for supplies she could only get at the apothecary's as her excuse for her trip also meant she did not have to share anything about seeing Eleanor or mention the daybook she had purchased.

She took the knife from Annabelle. "Here. Let me do that while you serve those platters. It looks like you could both use an extra pair of hands today."

Looking peaked, the girl sighed. "Yes, ma'am. It's been this busy almost all day," she complained as she lifted the trenchers and carried them to a table where hungry patrons greeted her with a cheer.

"Militia day," Lydia mumbled when Martha looked at her for an explanation.

She had forgotten all about militia day, but at least now she knew why Thomas was not at home. As a major, he would probably not return home until very late, which meant she had little hope of reclaiming Bird tonight.

Lydia stretched and rubbed the base of her spine. "Always a bad day for the back."

"And laboring women," Martha added. "Poor Genevieve Smith. She was frightened enough as it was, delivering her first. Hearing rounds of rifle shot and having the cannon balls nearly shake the house off its foundation was about the last thing she needed. I don't suppose they bothered selecting a new practice site yet."

"No," James offered as he entered the kitchen. He pecked his wife on the cheek and gave Martha a smile. "Glad you're back. As for changing the site, I wouldn't expect that to happen any time soon. They were using the site on Double Trouble Creek next to the Smith farm for lots of years before Smith ever showed up."

Martha waved her knife in the air. "But now there's the Holts' and the Winslows' and the Petersons' farms nearby, too. Not a one of them will have a hen laying eggs again for days. The cows' milk will be bad, too. You'd think they'd move the practice site just out of respect for all those nearby families. It's not like there isn't enough open land just a few miles up the creek."

James grinned. "Tradition is hard to break, but it doesn't bother me any. Militia day will always be good for my purse wherever they practice."

He narrowed his gaze. "Grace needs new shoes. Soon. You might want to talk to Jack Engels. See if he can take care of her before you go traipsing off again."

"First thing in the morning. I promise." She cut off the heel of a new loaf of bread, slathered it with butter, and took a bite. She chewed slowly, savoring the taste while her stomach growled for more. "I'm so hungry I could eat this whole loaf of bread and still have room for a plate of stew."

Lydia chuckled as she prepared a platter for Martha. "Save room for dessert. Ivy stopped earlier and left a whole tray of cookies for our oh-so-important military men. Not that they'll bother with anything sweet."

James laughed. "They prefer rum, which reminds me, I was headed for the storeroom," he said, and left the women to their work.

They chatted back and forth while Martha ate and they finished the day's work. It was nearly midnight before Martha got back to her own room. Disappointed that Thomas had not appeared with Bird, she was too exhausted to unpack, yet too anxious to begin using her daybook to take to her bed quite yet.

By candlelight, with the embers burning low in the hearth, she opened the daybook and penned a brief inscription, one she had composed and recomposed during her long ride home:

Dearest Victoria,
A child brings so many gifts—love, laughter, tears,
and sorrow—to every mother's heart. One day when you

have found your way and return home, I want you to know the many gifts you have given to me.

Mother

While she waited for the ink to dry, she leaned forward, rested her forehead on her fingertips, and briefly closed her eyes. A host of long-buried memories vied for the opportunity to be the first in her daybook. Revisiting her own moments of weakness or embarrassment was painful. Juxtaposing them with memories of raising Victoria and watching her grow to the brink of full womanhood gave Martha a more objective glimpse of her daughter's character so that her gifts were becoming clearer and more precious.

"The best place to begin is at the beginning, with my earliest memory," she murmured. The events surrounding her fall from grace years ago in the one-room schoolhouse that had later burned to the ground was still vivid in her mind, and she realized her troubles with Rosalind had really begun when Martha retaliated for some forgotten injustice by tying a dead mouse to the end of Rosalind's braid during recess.

Punishment had been sure and swift. James had shared in the punishment, too, since he had been the one to snatch the carcass away from the stable cat before it had a chance to devour it, but Martha had been the primary conspirator.

She wrote down the events as they had unfolded as honestly as she could. When she finished writing the tale, she had covered both sides of the page, with just enough room at the bottom to write her message to Victoria:

Your gift, dearest child, is your kindness, untainted by a singular moment when you failed to think of others before yourself or when you have returned a slight, however mean-spirited, with anything but a forgiving smile. Thank you for always reminding me to be kind.

Martha stared at the words until they blurred, and swiped at her tears. She closed the daybook and snuffed out the candle.

In the dark, with her heart grieving for her daughter and for all the lost opportunities of the past, she dropped to her knees and prayed she might one day be able to hold Victoria in her arms and tell her how her life had been blessed because Victoria had been her daughter.

When her prayer was done, she did not bother to light another candle, and moved about her familiar room with ease. She changed into a nightdress, brushed her hair, and crawled into bed. Even though it was dark and she could not see Victoria's bed or her pillow, she knew Bird was not there, and the room felt all the more empty with his absence, too.

She had no sooner put her head to her pillow and closed her eyes when a series of insistent knocks on her door roused her from her bed and sent her scrambling to light a candle and grab for her robe.

"I know you're in there, Martha," Thomas shouted. "Now open up this door, or I won't be held responsible for finishing off one of your . . . your patients with my bare hands!"

With a vision of Thomas standing outside with Bird safely in his cage, she chuckled to herself, slipped into her robe, belted it, and knelt down to search under the bed for her cotton slippers. "Patience, Thomas. The floorboards are cold. I need my slippers."

He pounded on the door again. "Open the door, Martha. Now!"

Her cotton slippers were nowhere in sight. She gave up her search, but took the time to light several candles and stop in front of the mirror to tie back her hair before she opened the door.

Thomas glared at her and tightened his hold on her patient—and it wasn't Bird.

Eyes wide and mouth agape, she only managed to stumble aside before he charged past her into the room with her patient in tow.

Chapter
TWENTY

M artha shoved the door closed and whirled about, just in time to see Will break free and charge straight for the door.

She crossed her arms in front of her chest and braced her feet, curious that Thomas did not give chase. Wincing with pain, he held one of his arms at the wrist and elevated his hand. His trousers were wet and caked with mud, and his frock coat was still so damp there were a number of leaves clinging to the front like wilted war decorations.

Will skidded to a halt and looked her square in the eye. His hair lay matted against his scalp. His clothes were dripping wet and clung to his skinny frame. Though he glared at her with murderous outrage, his eyes were shimmering beneath thick spiked lashes.

Two monstrous tears spilled down his mottled cheeks, red with anger and frustration. He clenched his jaw to keep his teeth from chattering. His bare feet were blue with cold.

During their standoff, several thoughts flashed through Martha's mind. Since the day had been dry and clear, she could only assume Thomas had fished the boy out of Dillon's Stream or the pond. Her curiosity about precisely what had happened was as great as her concern for the two of them, although Will surely needed attention first.

"I w-was doin' just f-fine. Till that f-friend of yours ruined everything," he spat.

"You blamed little scamp! You nearly drowned," Thomas bellowed. He flexed the fingers on his elevated hand and scowled. "Blazes, this hurts. He bit me! I tried to save his sorry little hide, and he bit me! I should have let him drown." He waved at the boy. "Next time, I will. It would serve you right for trying to ride a raft over the falls. It's a wonder you haven't died from stupidity long before now."

Will turned about to face Thomas. "I'm not as stupid as you are. I didn't lose my horse 'cause I forgot to tether him, now, did I?"

Thomas snorted. "You don't have a horse. You won't have a tongue, either, if you don't speak to me with more respect."

In spite of the gravity of the moment, Martha caught a chuckle before it escaped. "That's enough. Both of you. Keep bickering while you're soaking wet and you'll both end up in bed for a week with lung fever. How and why you both ended up on my doorstep looking like drowned rats is something we can all discuss. Civilly. After you're both dry and warm. Thomas, please build up the fire. You, young man, follow me."

After securing a heavy blanket from a trunk, she led Will into the storeroom. "Strip, young man, and wrap yourself in this blanket. Then you can come out and sit in front of the fire to get warm. Don't forget to bring your clothes with you so they can dry, too."

He eyed the opposite door that led to the tavern.

She walked through the storeroom and opened the other door. "If you want to leave, then go ahead. You can go through the kitchen and slip out the front door to be on your way. I won't stop you."

He nodded back toward her room. "What about him?"

"Mayor Dillon won't stop you, either. Right now I have to see how much damage you did to his hand and heat some water for tea." She returned to her room and shut the connecting door behind her.

In her absence, Thomas had added more wood to the fire, which was blazing back to life. At the moment, he was struggling to get out of his frock coat.

She helped him to ease out of his coat and laid it near the fire. She lit a lamp and put out her hand. "Let's see this wound of yours."

When he extended his left hand, he had a sheepish look on his face. "I can't say I remember being bitten before."

The extent of his wound surprised her. The bite was nasty, and the teeth marks were unmistakable on the tender flesh between his thumb and forefinger. The skin was bruised and badly swollen around a gash that nearly went clear through. "He really had a good grip, didn't he? The boy must have been scared to death, just like you were the day you battled with those jays. Take a seat. I'll get something for your hand."

He yanked his hand away and plopped down on the bench in front of the worktable. "It's awfully kind of you to remind me about the jays," he snapped.

"Eleanor found the story amusing," she countered while she gathered up some cloth to use for a bandage and found some jewelweed in her bag to use as a poultice. When she saw the bottle of Carolina allspice she had purchased for Samuel Meeks in Clarion, she realized she had forgotten all about it and made a mental note to take it to him tomorrow after meeting.

"You told Eleanor? How . . . how is she?"

She cocked a brow. "I left a letter for you from Eleanor at your house earlier today."

He frowned. "I haven't been home since dawn."

While she tried to think of a way to share all her news about Eleanor without unduly alarming Thomas, she set the cloth and jewelweed on the table, took several bowls from the corner cupboard, and filled one with water. On second thought, she added some wood to the cookstove and set a kettle of water to boil. "She's weak. And frightened. But looking forward to coming home in about a week," she murmured.

She sat down on the bench next to him, plunged his hand into the bowl of water, and held it there.

"A week? Are you sure? Eleanor's last letter said Dr. Park wouldn't permit her to travel."

"He wouldn't, but since she's my patient now, that's not the issue." While she cleansed his wound, she carefully recounted the details of her visit and Eleanor's decision to return home to Trinity.

"Are you sure she'll be able to make the trip? What if something happens to her or the babe?" His gaze grew troubled. "I . . . I wouldn't want her to come home . . . because of me."

Martha smiled. After she patted the wound dry and laid his hand on the table, she set the jewelweed into some warm water to soften. "She's coming home because it's best for her and for your grandchild. Micah wants to talk to you about maybe settling here permanently. Do you think there's enough call for a lawyer here in Trinity?"

His eyes began to sparkle, as if reflecting the many ideas swirling through his mind. "I don't know. Perhaps. But he wouldn't have enough clients to support a family. Not for a good while. I could help, of course, if they really want to settle here."

"Micah doesn't want charity. He made that quite clear," she cautioned.

"He discussed this with you?"

She nodded. As accustomed as she was to acting as a go-between for her patients or their loved ones, she could see Thomas found the experience unsettling. "We talked about many things, some of which are to be left confidential. Some," she added as she laid the jewelweed atop the wound, "Micah shared with me so I could talk to you about it before they came home. He didn't want to trouble Eleanor by discussing financial matters, but he didn't want to encourage her to entertain any thoughts of moving here without settling some issues with you before he brought her home."

He stiffened. "What issues?"

"Micah wants to provide for Eleanor himself. He doesn't want you to do that, but he also realizes the best place for Eleanor right now is back at home with you. He'd like for them to stay with you until the baby is born. By then, if he decides he'd like to practice law here, he'll move Eleanor and their child into a home of their own."

"He can't make that kind of living here. Not right away."

"He has an inheritance from his mother which will be enough to support them for now. Even longer while he builds his practice, although not quite in the fashion you might demand for your daughter." She wrapped a bandage around his hand while he pondered what she had said. Although she had tried to cushion her words, she could tell by the rigid set of his shoulders he had taken offense.

"I wouldn't interfere. You know that."

"I know you would try not to, but Micah doesn't. Unfortunately, his experience with his own father has been . . . difficult. Once he leaves his father's firm, he won't be able to go back. If things don't work out well for them here, he'll have to take Eleanor with him to establish his practice elsewhere. That said, I've kept my promise to Micah and to you. How you control your sister, Anne, when she gets back in December is something you'll have to handle. Now, suppose you tell me how an eight-year-old child managed to do so much harm."

"I'm not eight yet. Not till March."

She looked up and found Will standing only a few feet away, a forlorn waif swamped by the heavy blanket wrapped around him. How he had gotten back into her room without making a sound was a question she left unanswered, along with the question of how much he had overhead. She silenced Thomas with a shake of her head. "Sit by the fire to get warm. Spread out your clothes, too. I assume you have them somewhere under that blanket. And be still. You'll have your turn to speak after Mayor Dillon."

The boy shuffled to the hearth and plopped himself down on the floor so he sat with his back to them. Small hands emerged from under the blanket and set his shirt and trousers next to Thomas's frock coat. "Lost my socks and my shoes 'cause of him," he grumbled.

She put her hand on Thomas's arm to keep him from bolting off the bench. "Tell me what happened, Thomas," she urged.

He brushed a lock of hair from his forehead. "Just before dusk, I went by the pond to look for my canteen. I'd lost it somewhere along the way coming home after militia practice. I couldn't find it, so I decided to look again in the morning. That's when I met up with Stanley Pitt. He'd been to the tavern with some of the other men. He was so far into his cups, I decided to ride along with him to make sure he didn't topple off his horse and fall into the pond or the creek by his cabin."

"Which ain't got nothin' to do with how—"

"Will! Not another word," she cautioned. "Go on, Thomas."

"As I was saying," he snapped, "I took Stanley Pitt home. On my way back to town, I stopped at the top of the falls. It was well and dark by then, but I thought I heard something floating down the creek. I got closer and spied some fool poling a raft straight for the falls. I yelled, but it was too late. The raft went right over the falls. By the time I managed to ride down to the pond, I found him thrashing about—"

"I was swimmin'—"

"Drowning is more like it," Thomas argued. "The raft was torn apart, and the individual branches he used to make the contraption were too small to support his weight. Fool that I am, I waded in and managed to grab him before he drank enough of the pond to sink himself."

Thomas held up his bandaged hand. "And this is how he thanked me."

Will sighed. "Why should I thank you? It's all your fault my pack's at the bottom of the pond." He turned his head and looked at Martha over his shoulder. "It ain't like he said. I rode my raft right over them falls, too. 'Cept the blame thing busted up. I had all my stuff and my food in that pack. I kept divin' to find it, when all of a sudden I felt somethin' big grab me by my shoulder. I thought it was a bear or somethin' like that, so I gave it a big ole bite. He let go, too, squealin' like a pig with its ring caught in a fence. That's when I knew it weren't no bear. Didn't know it was the *mayor*, though. Not till he dragged me to shore and started rantin' loud as thunder when he found out his horse run off. Dumb ole thing."

Thomas gritted his teeth.

Will glowered back. "You can't say nothin' now, neither, 'cause it's my turn."

Martha caught her lower lip and stifled a laugh just begging to be set free. "Tell us why you were on the raft in the first place. And what in heaven's name ever made you think you could go over the falls? You could have been killed!"

He shrugged his shoulders. "They ain't that high. Besides, I got no horse. The only way I can get to Clarion quick is to ride down the stream."

"I see. And you were going to Clarion for . . ."

"A ship. I heard you could get a ship there."

"Don't you like it at the academy?"

He yawned and did not bother to cover his mouth. "I wanna be a sailor. I sure can't do that here. P. J. says I'm old enough to be a cabin boy. Just for now." He yawned again and curled into a ball facing the fire. "I got to get me some sleep so I can build a new raft in the morning. After I find my pack."

Thomas rose.

She urged him to sit back down again. "Let him sleep a while. I'll tuck him into bed later."

"What are you going to do with him after that?"

"Take him to Sunday meeting with me tomorrow. I can hand him over to Reverend Hampton then."

"Better think of a way to let them pick up the boy on their way to meeting. The fewer people who know about tonight, the better."

"That means someone has to ride out to the academy to let them know he's here. Are you up to the ride?"

"I don't have a horse at the moment, remember?"

"Take Grace. Maybe you'll find your mount along the way."

He sighed, grabbed his frock coat from the floor, and started for the door.

"Don't forget to watch out for Leech."

He stopped, but kept facing the door. "Fine. I'll watch out for the cat before I ride out on a slowpoke of a draft horse, soaking wet, in the middle of the night, to tell the Reverend Mr. Hampton that one of his incorrigible little monsters is safe and sound after nearly breaking his neck in a daredevil escape over the falls and then nearly biting off my hand—a tale which will cost you dearly if you breathe one word of it to anyone, especially my daughter. Then I'll ride back, hoping I find my horse, and go home, where I'll find an incorrigible feathered monster asleep on my pillow."

His words had tumbled out in a rush, apparently spending his frustration. When he turned around and glanced at the boy, his gaze softened. "Make sure he's good and warm," he murmured, and left before she could thank him.

In point of fact, a thought that had been simmering in the back of her mind began to boil into an idea so preposterous, so impossibly wild, she had no inclination to ponder the complexities of the man who had just left her.

Chapter
TWENTY-ONE

S unday meeting.
　　Martha dreaded the thought, fought the demons of fear and
worry, and let her hunger for worship keep her steps sure. She had
not attended Sunday meeting since Victoria ran off, and she was not
at all certain what she would do if her customary place had been
relegated to someone else.

　　She passed the market and rounded the bend in the road. Just
ahead, townspeople were entering the meetinghouse, where Reverend
Welsh still stood outside to welcome them. Inside, the faithful who
had arrived earlier spent their time waiting for the service to begin
by scanning those assembled to see who had not come, providing
fodder for gossip that would last until the ritual began again next
Sunday.

After a night of very little sleep, she had spent the early morning turning over one very recalcitrant guest to Reverend Hampton and keeping her promise to herself to visit with Samuel Meeks and deliver his new eyedrops. She had every excuse for being late, but dug deep for the energy to hurry her steps. Once Reverend Welsh closed the meetinghouse door, no one dared to slip inside. He was a good minister and a kindly man, but no one interrupted his service without regretting it.

When she was just yards away from the meetinghouse, he turned to close the door, saw her approaching, and waved. She ran the rest of the way. "I'm so sorry to be late," she whispered.

"'And the last shall be first.' Welcome home, Martha. We've missed you. I'm sorry we didn't have a chance to talk at the market the other day. I wanted you to know how badly Mrs. Welsh and I feel about Victoria."

"Thank you. It's good to be home." She slipped inside while he closed the door behind them and made his way through the crowd of people standing in the aisles to get to his pulpit. A sea of curious faces watched as she followed him toward the front of the meetinghouse, where members of the church vestry and town officials sat as one, leaders in the community of faith here as well as in everyday life.

Greeted by some genuine smiles of welcome, fewer frowns, and hushed whispers, she found her customary seat, on the end of the second bench next to the sheriff and his family, empty and waiting for her.

Relief she still had a place of honor at meeting did not ease the pounding of her heart for several long minutes. Winded, she drew in shallow gulps of air before joining in with the rest of the congregation as they sang the opening hymn.

Here, surrounded by the people she loved and the people she served, her famished spirit found nourishment. Here, she could find the strength, week by week, to wait for Victoria to come home and to return the whispers of gossip and scandal about Victoria's disappearance with a smile as she continued her work.

Before the echo of the final notes faded, Reverend Welsh began the service, so familiar to her she could have recited the prayers from memory. He finished his sermon nearly an hour later. His message, as well as his delivery, was not nearly as powerful or as moving as the one Reverend Hampton had given at the market, but Reverend Welsh did have a deep and abiding faith and a sincerity that precluded an unfair comparison of each man's gifts. Thus, she had no thoughts beyond his message and sang the closing hymn with gusto. Armed with joyful satisfaction, she looked forward to the impromptu reunions that lay ahead when the congregation gathered in disparate groups outside.

She also realized now that no matter how long it took, no matter how she had to prove her worth, no matter how malicious the gossip, she would reclaim her place here and meet every obstacle by taking comfort from those who welcomed her back with understanding and compassion.

When she finally stepped outside, the sun had stretched beyond a band of clouds to bathe the day with warmth. She scanned the yard, saw Thomas speaking quietly with the sheriff and several others, and thought better of approaching them now that they knew she would not help them. Dr. McMillan held court with a number of families surrounding him, but she did not see Rosalind anywhere.

Feeling a bit lost, she saw the Lynn sisters chatting with Patience Greywald and her children. She joined them immediately, if only to satisfy her growing curiosity about the contents of the baskets the two sisters carried. "A blessed morning, isn't it?" she asked before directing her gaze to Patience. "How's Charlie?"

The young woman smiled. Broadly. "Dr. McMillan truly did work a miracle. Charlie won't be able to work for some time, but he's not going to lose his hand."

Fern lifted a small package wrapped in brown paper from her basket. "Give this to Charlie, won't you? He won't have any trouble with his throat this winter, either. It's a sample of those lozenges I told you about."

Ivy glanced down at the two boys clinging to their mother's skirts.

"Some for the younguns, too." She handed a package to the youngest boy. "Now, don't forget not to chew them. Might break a tooth, you know."

Martha chuckled. "That's what's in the baskets? Lozenges?"

Fern beamed. "Hundreds of them. Lynn's Lozenges. Guaranteed to sweeten your sore throat." She leaned toward Martha and whispered, "I thought of that all by myself."

"I couldn't have said it better," Martha whispered back.

When the older boy snatched the package from his little brother and ran off, the younger one gave chase.

"I've got to go," Patience mumbled, and headed after them.

"Don't forget to let us know how you like the lozenges," Fern cried.

Ivy's bottom lip began to quiver. "I didn't mean to get the boys in trouble."

Fern sniffed. "Next time, hand one to each of the children."

"But only if you ask the parents first," Martha cautioned. "Do you want some help handing out the rest of the lozenges?"

Fern looked at Ivy and shook her head. "No, we'll be fine. You do some visiting."

As the sisters headed off together, Martha spied Alice Cornwell standing with a group of women while their husbands talked nearby and their children raced about. She was eager to see how the young woman fared, and approached the group with little trepidation since she had safely delivered all five of these women in the past.

An awkward silence replaced the animated conversation the moment Martha joined the circle of women. Alice laid her hand on her swollen stomach. "Widow Cade! It's . . . it's good to see you again."

"Thank you. You look well. Extremely well. Your time is coming soon, as I recall."

The young woman blushed. "Another six weeks. Maybe soon. Dr. McMillan says . . . that is . . . I'm sorry, but I wasn't certain you'd be back in time, and Martin . . . Martin thought it would be better if . . . if . . ."

"If you have Dr. McMillan tend to you when the time comes. I understand," Martha murmured, voicing the words Alice was clearly too embarrassed to say. Deeply disappointed, she kept her smile in place, even when the glances from the rest of the women failed to offer her the support she had hoped to find.

Letty Chase toyed with the strap on her reticule. "He's very good with the children, too. He sat up all night with Betsy after she broke her arm."

Jane Post nodded in approval. "Patience Greywald can't praise the doctor enough for saving Charlie's hand." She lowered her voice to a whisper. "Poor dear. She's teeming again, too, but Dr. McMillan assured her he would do everything he could to make sure she didn't lose this one."

Though Jane's words were softly spoken, they cut straight to Martha's heart, unleashing disappointment that sorely depleted the joy she had found today. Martha had safely delivered both of Patience's sons. A third child, a perfectly formed little girl, died several hours after birth, despite all of Martha's efforts when the child developed breathing problems. She longed to help Patience this time, too, but apparently that privilege now belonged to Dr. McMillan.

Jane sniffed. "How sad you weren't able to bring Victoria home. You must be sick with worry. It's a terrible thing for a young girl to do. I can't imagine what Victoria found so alluring about those people." She shuddered and tightened her cape around her.

Martha cringed, held a lid on her temper, and swallowed hard. "I'm very worried, but I pray the good Lord will watch over her and bring her home. I'd appreciate whatever prayers you could add to mine."

"Ladies! Ladies! We have a surprise for each of you!"

The arrival of Fern and Ivy gave Martha the perfect opportunity to escape. With no desire to diminish the little joy she had left from the worship service, she headed for the far side of the yard to speak with Reverend Hampton, only to encounter several women who surrounded Thomas.

Poor man. He looked positively dreadful, and she wondered if he had had a minute of sleep last night. Though she felt guilty, she returned his beleaguered, silent plea of help with a spirited wave.

"Good morning, all," she said as she passed by.

Jack Engels left a group of men to stop her. He nodded toward Thomas and his eyes began to twinkle. "Mayor Dillon said he'd speak to you himself, but he seems to be rather occupied."

She laughed. "Quite occupied."

"Anyway, I just wanted to apologize. I can't get to those shoes for Grace until tomorrow, but I promise that she'll be first on my list come morning."

"Grace? I thought . . . you have Grace?" Her heart began to pound. When Grace had not been in her stall this morning, Martha assumed Thomas had merely taken her home with him.

"Don't worry. I checked her out real good. She's fine. Didn't pull a muscle or anything when she threw her shoe last night. Can't say the same for the mayor, though. He took a nasty fall and cut his hand."

Martha looked over Jack's shoulder at Thomas, and her heart sank down to her knees and back again. Judging by how haggard he looked, he had probably walked all the way home from the academy, but apparently blamed the cut on his hand on the fall rather than reveal his encounter with Will. She had little doubt now that he hadn't gotten a wink of sleep, either, and it was all her fault. The echo of James's reminder to have Grace shoed rang a loud bell of guilt. "Could you bring her by when you've finished?" she asked.

"Yes, ma'am. Should be before dinner. If you're not home, I'll just settle her back in her stall for you," he promised, and left her to rejoin his companions.

She took two steps to continue toward Reverend Hampton, paused, and turned around. She reached Thomas with several long strides. "I hope you'll forgive me, ladies, but Reverend Hampton asked for a word with Mayor Dillon before he takes the boys back home."

If disappointment and anger were thorns, the glances she received from the four women would have pricked her hide from head to toe. A relieved look on Thomas's face might have been a salve that rewarded her efforts, but he almost looked reluctant to part company with Samantha Leery.

The young woman, who was as beautiful as dawn itself, glowered openly. She tossed her head, rippling the cascade of golden ringlets that fell below her shoulders. Her pale blue eyes darkened into twin thunderclouds.

Her mother, Ruth, held tight to Thomas's arm and frowned at Martha. "Won't anyone let this poor man ever have a moment to himself?"

He gently but firmly disengaged himself and offered Ruth a dazzling smile. "When duty calls, I'm afraid I have no choice but to answer. If you'll all excuse me, I'm sure Reverend Hampton is eager to return home."

He took Martha by the elbow and led her away from the group. "Jack says Grace should have been shoed weeks ago." He still had a smile on his face, but his words were surly, even though he spoke so softly she barely heard him.

"I'm sorry. James reminded me only yesterday, but with all that happened last night, I forgot," she whispered.

"Mornin', Stan. Mrs. Pitt," he cried, his voice cheerful again. He leaned his head toward her. "Like you forgot to tell me that yellow critter of yours likes to sleep on a man's pillow? Mercy! You can be one aggravating woman at times."

The fact that he could grumble and complain to her and smile a greeting to other folks at the same time annoyed her to no end. "I should have left you back there with Samantha and her mother. The least you can do is be thankful I rescued you and accept my apology."

He slowed his steps. "Forgive me if I'm less than perfect. I'm tired to the bone, and my hand aches like there's no tomorrow. Yes, I'm cranky, too, but I'm thankful for being rescued, and I accept your apology."

She frowned. "You don't sound very sincere."

He sighed. "I sincerely accept your apology, and I sincerely hope you'll stop by on your way home to collect your bird."

She chuckled. "Right after I talk to Reverend Hampton. You might as well stay, too, since you're an interested party to all this."

"Interested in what?" he asked as they neared the minister and his wife.

"In Will, of course. Good morning, Reverend. Olympia. It's good to see you again," she crooned, leaving Thomas no opportunity to argue the point.

"We're trying to round up the boys," Olympia said as she scanned the crowd behind Martha and Thomas. "There! I see P. J. The others won't be far away. I'll be right back. I think," she added with a weary smile before she hurried off.

Martha captured the minister's gaze and held it. "I wanted you to know I met with Samuel Meeks. He wants to talk to you himself, but I think he rather likes my idea. Maybe you could stop to see him on the way home. You're far more persuasive than I can ever hope to be."

He hesitated and tugged on the end of his beard. "Will won't be off punishment for a few weeks. Think Samuel can wait that long?"

"He's been waiting for far longer. He just doesn't know it. Talk to him. Let him talk to Will. It can't hurt. If Samuel agrees, Will might tolerate the punishment better knowing he has something to look forward to at the end."

Thomas looked at her, switched his gaze to the minister, then looked at her again. "Would either one of you care to explain what you're talking about?"

She grinned. "Just a little matchmaking."

His eyes widened. "Ole Samuel and Will?"

She grinned again. "It's perfect, isn't it?"

He shook his head. "Only you would think of it."

"I had a little help," she admitted. The very idea of pairing Will with the town recluse had been divine inspiration—in much the same way that she had been led to become Samuel's only friend in town and help him to accommodate the growing physical problem he had hidden from everyone else.

She knew in her heart *why* putting Samuel and Will together should work.

She trusted God to figure out *how*.

Chapter

TWENTY-TWO

Mid-November brought paler skies and weaker sunshine, but no word from Victoria.

Martha grieved for her daughter but took solace in knowing she was not alone. Rosalind's husband was still a wanted man in exile, and Aunt Hilda was still waiting for her husband to return from his thirty-year odyssey. The daybook she had started for Victoria had nearly half a dozen entries now, a source of comfort in the dark, lonely hours she spent alone.

The past weeks had been alternately difficult, challenging, rewarding, and satisfying, a rather normal state of affairs that kept her from sinking into self-pity. She had not exactly climbed the mountain of success, either, but her life had a familiar rhythm again.

Still, for every gain she had made, she had suffered a setback. The quick redemption Reverend Hampton had achieved for his wards had turned out to be short-lived. Just as Thomas had predicted, the thefts had continued, gossip had spread, and the academy boys once again became scapegoats. For every patient she treated, she lost another to Dr. McMillan. Most of the women still called for Martha when labor began, but beginning with Alice Cornwell, several had sent for the doctor instead of a midwife, an omen that did not bode well for Martha's future.

Today, like other Sunday afternoons, she joined Aunt Hilda for dinner, resuming a ritual that had lasted for nearly a decade when either of their duties allowed it. She dried the last plate, set it back into the sideboard, and closed the door. "I think that's the last," she murmured.

Aunt Hilda chuckled. "Until we dirty more dishes with dessert. You pour the tea while I get my surprise from the pie safe."

Martha poured tea into two mugs already on the table and tried to smile. Aunt Hilda was the undisputed queen when it came to making honey wine. There was not an afternurse more caring or qualified. Her crown slipped a bit at the stove, but when it came to baking, she was a complete and utter failure—so much so that she would have been dethroned and relegated to the dungeon in her own castle if folks had not been so fond of her.

When Aunt Hilda put a sugar-coated apple strudel on the table, Martha's eyes widened. "That looks too scrumptious to eat!"

"You mean it looks to good to be mine. It isn't. I stopped to see Fern and Ivy yesterday. They insisted I take this home, so I saved it for us. Not that I couldn't make it myself," she added. "But I'd have used honey instead of sugar. Hand me your plate. I'll cut you a big slice, and you'd better eat every bite. You're getting a bit thin."

"I've been busy," Martha countered.

"Delivering babies and tending to the sick is all well and good, but riding every day, searching for whoever is responsible for all that thievery, isn't your job. That's what I told Thomas before he first approached you with that idea our beloved leaders concocted. Glad you set them straight, but I'm none too pleased—"

"I know. We've talked about this before." Martha toyed with her strudel. She was almost grateful Thomas had confided in Aunt Hilda, if only to give Martha the freedom to discuss her attempt to find the culprits and put a quiet end to it all. Fortunately, Reverend Hampton's status as a minister helped to temper folks' anger and frustration. Had he not been a man of the cloth, he might very well have had to fend off angry citizens who arrived at the academy's doorstep, ready to use force to make the boys leave Trinity.

"I've visited every homestead on Reedy Creek, nearly all along Double Trouble, and half of them on Candle Creek. I haven't got an inkling so far. Maybe tomorrow will turn up something."

"How's Eleanor?"

Martha sighed and accepted the reprieve Aunt Hilda offered. "She's doing well. I promised to stop and see her today on my way home."

"And Thomas? He left the meetinghouse so quickly I never got a chance to speak with him. Then Daniel and Adelaide stopped me. That sure is one fine baby girl they showed off today."

Martha savored a big bite of strudel and chewed slowly before she answered. "Both mama and baby are doing very well, thanks to you. Did you notice how blue Glory's eyes are? Just like Adelaide's."

"You're changing the subject. I asked you about Thomas."

"I assume he's fine. I didn't speak to him, either."

"I bet Samantha did. Foolish twit. She's younger than Eleanor."

Martha chuckled and nearly choked on her tea. "Her mother has grand ideas she's been planting in that girl's head for years. You can't blame Samantha for trying to catch Thomas's eye."

Aunt Hilda sniffed. "The way she sashays up to him every time he sets foot out of the house, that man would have to be blind not to see what she's after. Not that you mind, I suppose."

"Mind? Why would I mind? Whatever Thomas and I shared years ago, it's gone. Now, let's wash up these dishes so I can be on my way. I have to stop to see Will, too."

Her aunt waved her away. "Go on. I'll take care of these. I don't imagine you'd have a mind to tell me what's happening with the boy now that he's staying with Samuel?"

Martha shrugged her shoulders. "I'm really not sure. I haven't seen him since Reverend Hampton left him there a few weeks back." She rose, stopped to give her aunt a hug, and donned her outerwear. "If there's anything astonishing to report, I'll be back," she teased. "If not, I'll see you again next Sunday."

"If not before. Melanie Palmer is ripe to deliver before then."

"If she calls for me," Martha murmured, and slipped out the door. A brisk wind greeted her outside, whipped at her cape, and stung her cheeks as she covered the short distance to Thomas's home. She bunched her shoulders to keep the cold air from blowing down her neck, and bounded up the front steps. She had her hand on the brass knocker when the door swung open and Eva Clark urged her inside.

"Come in. Come in. Before you get blown away."

Martha wiped her slippers on the mat and scooted inside. "Mercy! We'll have snow before long."

Eva closed the door. "Go on into the sitting room and get warm by the fire. Do you want me to take your cape and bonnet now or after you stop shivering?"

"I'm not staying very long. I'll keep them on."

"Eleanor will be so happy to see you. I'll just go and tell her you're here," she gushed.

While Eva climbed the ornate center staircase, Martha entered the sitting room and glanced around. She had visited Thomas and Sally in this home many times, and his parents before their deaths, but she still caught her breath at the sheer opulence that surrounded her.

Beneath her feet, a thick carpet splashed the room with jeweled color, a blend of ruby, emerald, and sapphire blue. Cushioned chairs and a matching settee sat in front of a hearth faced with green marble. A row of heavy silver candlesticks of altering height stretched across the mantel, paying homage to the portrait of Jacob Dillon. French wallpaper, with stripes of color matching the carpet, adorned the walls.

In essence, it was a room fit for royalty, if not the founding family of Trinity.

She never felt quite at home there. More out of place. Like a cornhusk doll might have felt if it had been sitting on the settee instead of the elegant china doll that adorned one of the seats.

She went directly to the fire, removed her gloves, and held her hands out to warm them. When she heard footsteps approaching, she turned around and met Eleanor as she entered the room. After a heartfelt embrace, she stepped back and let Eleanor place her hand atop the younger woman's stomach. "He's very active today. Can you tell?"

Martha waited, then felt a solid thump against the palm of her hand and pulled away. "I should say he is! Or she is," she admonished as she followed Eleanor to the settee.

"I told Micah the same thing." Eleanor giggled as she picked up the china doll, sat down with the doll on her lap, and patted the seat beside her. "I thought if I set out one of my old dolls, he might consider the possibility of a daughter this time."

Martha sat down and studied Eleanor from head to toe. "You've gained some weight. Your cheeks are rosy. I'd say you're doing very well, young lady. How are you feeling?"

"Much, much better. I still take my naps, one in the morning and one in the afternoon, just like you suggested. I'm not as strong as I'd like to be yet, but I'm very content. And very, very grateful to you," she murmured. "It's helped a great deal to be with Father, and I feel closer to Mother here at home, too."

"I'm so glad. Have you ventured out yet?"

"Micah wasn't sure I should."

Martha cocked her head. "What do you think?"

"I think I'd like to try. Maybe just a short visit with some old friends. Or a walk to the confectionery," she teased.

"Then I think you should. Don't go alone, of course. And make sure you come home before you get tired. Next Sunday," she urged as she rose, "I hope to see you at meeting."

Eleanor's smile drooped into a frown. "Must you go? Micah and Father should be home soon. They'd both love to see you."

"I'll come again during the week. I have another stop to make.

Sit. Don't get up. I can show myself out. Give Micah my best. Your father, too," she added before venturing back out the same way she had come in.

If anything, the wind had gotten stronger and the air had grown colder. She crossed through the empty plot where the meetinghouse had once stood to cut through the cemetery. When she was just beyond the old chestnut tree, she caught a glimpse of something out of the corner of her eye that made her stop to get a better look.

A blue neck scarf, caught by a gust of wind, blew up toward the overcast sky like a wayward kite struggling for the freedom of flight, then fell down to drape one of the headstones. A woman who was huddled nearby tending to a grave site was either unaware or unconcerned that she had lost her scarf.

Martha could not see the woman's face, but she knew it had to be Rosalind because the grave she tended marked the burial place of her daughter, Charlotte. Martha hesitated to intrude. Lord knew, she had wanted privacy when she visited the grave sites of her husband and young sons when her grief was still raw and blistering her heart. She also had little time to spend with Samuel and Will if she hoped to return home before dark.

She had not had an opportunity to speak with Rosalind since that day at Dr. McMillan's when she had returned his lancet. Rosalind kept to herself, rarely leaving home, and had not been to meeting since her husband had left town.

Then again, Martha had an opportunity now. Unexpected. Unplanned. Inconvenient. But perhaps a gift that gave her the chance to offer Rosalind the friendship she so desperately needed. With a prayer for courage, she retrieved the scarf and approached the woman slowly, hoping to not frighten her.

When Martha was a few headstones away, Rosalind packed up her small garden tools, stood, and brushed the dirt from her cape. She turned to leave, took one look at Martha, and clapped her hand to her chest. "You gave me a start!"

Martha closed the distance between them and handed her the neck scarf. "I'm sorry. You lost your scarf. I guess the wind blew it away while you were weeding. I found it over there hanging on Abe Chesterfield's headstone."

Rosalind tucked the scarf into her basket. "I hadn't noticed. The . . . the weeds have nearly overtaken Charlotte's plot. I didn't take care of her this summer like I should have . . . what with all that's happened."

"We've missed you at meeting."

Rosalind's gaze hardened. "I pray at home, where I don't have to tolerate hypocrites and fools who go to meeting on Sunday and spend the rest of the week gossiping."

"You have friends there, too. People who care about you and Burton."

Rosalind snorted and let loose bitter, angry words that gusted out with a fury. "Like Sheriff Myer? I'm sure the only thing he cares about is sending Burton off to the county prison, whether he's guilty or not. And he's not. He's an innocent man. A good man! But no one believes that, except for me. Webster Cabbot is Burton's friend! Or we thought he was. And now . . . and now the only place I have left to go where I know someone who believes in Burton like I do is here, a miserable, cold plot of ground where my daughter lies. But she can't talk to me or hold me or promise me someday the truth will be told and her papa can come home." She choked back a sob and put her fist to her mouth. Her chest heaved, and the basket in her hand shook as she battled for control.

Shaken, Martha attempted to reach out to comfort her.

Rosalind stepped back and squared her shoulders, but her words were plaintive now instead of angry. "Please. Leave me alone. I don't want your pity or your platitudes about God's will. Right now, I'd settle for nothing short of a miracle. That's what it's going to take to clear Burton, and I'm afraid God has no miracles to spare. Not for me. Not for Burton. Because if He had, He would have saved my Charlotte instead of letting her suffer and waste away until she was too weak to draw her next breath."

Martha shivered and pulled her cape tighter at the neck. "I can't give you a miracle, any more than I can truly understand the depth of your suffering, but I can offer you friendship. I can even promise not to tie a mouse to the end of your braid again."

Tears trickled down Rosalind's cheeks. Her hand shook when she swiped them away. Her lips shaped a tentative smile, and her gaze grew wistful. "That was so long ago."

"Would you have time for a cup of tea? I could get a good fire going—"

"No. I—I have to get back and start something for Dr. McMillan's supper. Another time. Perhaps," she murmured, and hurried away.

"Another time," Martha whispered, but she feared there would not be another time. Not unless by some miracle Burton was cleared of the charges against him. With a troubled heart, she waited and watched until Rosalind had disappeared from view before she wove her way through the rest of the cemetery, following a path that led deep into the woods. Naked trees, stripped of life and color, huddled together, pale and weak next to lush evergreens that helped to block the wind.

The ground beneath her slippers was hard and rocky, and the silence there, where no horses or wagons ever ventured, was thick, save for the sound of her ragged breathing and her footsteps. Chilled to the bone, she greeted the sight of the small cabin ahead with longing for relief from the cold and hurried her steps.

She had no idea what she would find waiting for her inside. Failure had as much a chance to be there as success. She had faith enough to be happy with a little of each, and knocked on the door using the signal Samuel insisted she use—three short taps and a long one.

Chapter

TWENTY-THREE

W hen Martha slipped inside, she entered no ordinary cabin, but an amazing replica of one any sea captain would envy as a private domain aboard ship.

Wooden shutters covered the two windows visible on the outside of the cabin, blocking any view in or out, and she was as captivated today as she had been the first day she had been invited into Samuel Meeks's home.

Gleaming mahogany on the floor reflected the coils of rope and other nautical memorabilia hanging on the wooden walls that also held shelves with half a dozen lanterns with sparkling glass globes that provided the only light in the single-room dwelling.

She approached the Franklin stove in the middle of the room that provided more than enough heat, even on the coldest of days. Two nearby chairs offered the only place to sit. Instead of a bed or cot, a thick rope hammock hung in the corner opposite a small galley. A hulk of a desk was bolted in place, just like the rest of the furniture in the room, but there was no sign of Samuel or Will, for that matter.

She removed her outer garments and laid them on a chair. Her curiosity about the contents of the several trunks stored beneath the hammock had grown stronger with each visit she made there, but Samuel had never offered to open them. She had never had the courage to ask him to, either.

She rubbed her hands together until they were warm again and took a seat in one of the chairs near the stove. She was not quite sure which prayer she hoped would be answered today. Was Will adjusting well to his temporary home? Were the eyedrops she had gotten for Samuel in Clarion working or not? Or was it too soon to tell? Where were they both? It was not exactly a good day to be traipsing about in the woods; besides, Samuel did not usually leave his home, when he left it at all, until after dark. Unless . . .

The front door flew open, cold air blew in, and she turned around to see the giant recluse amble inside. Will followed on his heels carrying an armful of kindling.

Samuel headed straight for the chair at his desk, paused, and smiled. "Close the door, mate. Make it quick. We don't want Widow Cade to catch cold."

She chuckled to herself. The first time she had seen the recluse, she had been scared speechless and gaped at him openly, almost too afraid to breathe. "I wondered where you two had gotten," she teased.

Samuel eased himself into a chair next to her while Will grumbled his way to the corner and piled the kindling in a neat stack next to the other two. "Can't see no need for all this kindlin'."

"Storm's comin', mate. You can smell it in the air."

"Can't smell nothin', not even the damn supper we're supposed to be havin'," Will complained.

"Mind your tongue in front of the lady, or you'll be gnawin' on another hunk of horseradish."

Will grimaced. "Sorry."

"Go get your ropes and plop yourself down by the fire to practice some more." Samuel leaned toward Martha. "Don't hold much hope out for this lad. Can't head off to sea till he knows his knots. Found that out when he tried to make that raft of his. It's no wonder the thing busted up when he went over the falls. Way he's goin', might take months till he learns 'em all."

Months? That was a hopeful signal that all was going well. To her amazement, Will went to one of the trunks beneath the hammock to get a handful of ropes. He laid each piece out on the floor at Samuel's feet, one at a time, until he had seven pieces, each about two feet long.

"Start with the slip knot," his mentor ordered. "Show Widow Cade what you've learned."

The boy plopped down on the floor and worked with a piece of rope. His brows knitted together until he finished the knot. He smiled and laid his work in Samuel's hand.

Instead of looking at the knot, Samuel used his thick, callused fingers to feel the twists in the rope, dashing her hopes that his vision had improved.

He nodded. "Now, that's a knot any seaman worth his salt would be proud to claim. Make another one."

Will grinned, deftly tied another slip knot, and beamed when Samuel announced it as good as the first. He laid both slip knots on the floor and grabbed another rope. "Lemme try the bowline knot."

Samuel cocked his head. "Don't be gettin' all cocky," he warned. "I just showed that to you yesterday."

"But I can do it. I know I can do it," Will argued. He toyed with the rope, shaped and reshaped the knot until his cheeks were mottled with frustration. After a fourth attempt, the length of rope was a useless, sorry twist of hemp. Will slapped it on the floor and glowered. "You didn't show me right."

"You didn't watch me right. Hand me the rope and mind your temper. Won't serve you now any more than when you're at sea and the captain's just achin' for an excuse to keelhaul somebody for entertainment."

Will handed the rope over, stood up, and moved alongside the older man's chair. While Samuel shaped the knot, he offered verbal instructions as well. "Now, pay attention. I'll show you slower this time."

Martha marveled at the interplay between the old man and the boy. She would never have described Samuel as a patient man before now. Gruff, fiercely independent, and contemptuous of most people? Decidedly. But patient? Never. She had a hard time believing what she witnessed with her own eyes.

Will was different, too. True, he still grumbled a lot, and he had a long way to go before his language was acceptable and his attitude toward his elders was respectable, but he displayed a determination now that had a positive end—one that might keep him put long enough for him to learn to trust again.

She had no idea how long it would be before Samuel lost his vision completely. He could not survive on his own for long when he did. She could not even venture to guess whether Will's fascination with Samuel would be short-lived or not. But for now, she simply accepted the pairing of the old seaman and the reforming street urchin as a gift. Perhaps, even, as a miracle-in-the-making.

While Will struggled to make a bowline knot on his own again, she chatted with Samuel. Apparently, the boy had not missed a single day with Samuel since Reverend Hampton first brought him to the cabin two and a half weeks ago.

"No word from Victoria?" Samuel asked.

She sighed. "Not yet. The mail's due again on Tuesday."

Samuel shook his head. "Makes me wonder about how my mama felt when I left. I never thought much about that before now. I was a lot younger than Victoria when I left home, though."

Will looked up and grinned.

"Older than you are," Samuel added, offering the boy a stern look.

She knew Samuel could not see the boy clearly enough to catch his facial expressions, and chuckled to herself. Even half blind and well near seventy, Samuel was still keen enough to know the boy's temperament and hold him in line.

"I was twelve when I run off to sea. Never wrote. Never went back home. Just cut the cord and let the wind blow me away."

She sucked in her breath and lowered her gaze. What would she do if Victoria did the same? What had Samuel's mother done? How had she spent the rest of her life, one day after another, never knowing the fate of her child? Had she prayed as hard as Martha did? Had she gone to her grave still broken-hearted, as Martha feared she might do?

Sadness seeped into her bones. Longing to see Victoria again tightened around her heart so she found it difficult to draw a breath because of the pain and even harder to keep tears at bay.

"But you got a home here now—and treasures, too. Lotsa treasures," Will prompted. "Can I show her? Can I?"

"I don't think Widow Cade would be much interested in what's packed away in that old trunk. Seems to me you're just lookin' for an excuse not to work the ropes."

"It's getting late. I really should go. Perhaps another time," she whispered.

When she started to get up, Will urged her back down. "It won't take more than a minute or two," he argued.

Her tears threatened to spill over. She needed to leave. Now. To be alone. To keep Samuel from knowing how much his words had hurt, even though he had not meant for that to happen. "I really do need to go. Grace needs to be fed and bedded down for the night, and I promised to be back to help serve supper, too."

Will's narrow shoulders slumped. Disappointment extinguished the excitement burning in his eyes.

She sat down again and tried to rekindle the curiosity she had always had about the contents of the trunks and failed. "Maybe you can just show me a few today. If it's all right with Mr. Meeks."

Samuel waved at the boy. "Go on. If that's what you want."

Will scampered off and carried the smallest trunk back with him. He laid it on the floor between Martha and Samuel. The lid creaked halfway open, and his eyes lit up again when he lifted a treasure from the trunk. "This here's a genuine dagger from India."

"Be careful," she warned. "That looks awfully sharp."

He scowled and laid it on the floor. "I know that." He rummaged through the trunk and pulled out an opium pipe. "He brought this all the way back from China. Strange-lookin' pipe, ain't it?"

She frowned. "Indeed."

"One more for today," Samuel ordered.

Will laid the pipe next to the dagger and studied the contents of the trunk. Finally, he turned the trunk around so Martha could see inside. "You pick somethin'. I bet I can tell you where it came from," he challenged.

She leaned forward, eager to pick something. Anything. Just to be on her way. She pointed to the gold chain lying between a piece of scrimshaw and a tin of some sort of spice. "Try that one. The chain."

He tugged at the chain and pulled it free. The moment she saw the object swinging from the end of the chain, her heart began to race and pound in her ears.

"This ain't nothin' special," he grumbled. "It's just some ole thing he found lyin' by the trash pit."

Samuel chuckled. "I tripped over that some months back. Kicked it, actually. I never would have seen it, that's for sure. Probably doesn't work so good. Bit down on it, though. Sure feels like real gold. Hard to believe somebody would just toss it away."

Nearly in shock, she took the chain from Will. Her fingers shook as they opened the gold case on the watch. When she saw the initials engraved inside the front cover, she closed the case and wrapped her hand around it. "This is something very special," she whispered. "I do believe you found no ordinary watch, Samuel. You found a miracle."

TWENTY-FOUR

D iscovering a miracle was quite different from knowing precisely
what to do with it, although Martha had little problem getting
Samuel to give her possession of Webster Cabbot's watch.

Late that same night, she laid the watch and chain on the table
near the daybook. While Bird was fast asleep on Victoria's pillow,
she finished describing another event in her life: "The end result, of
course, was that I had to admit to my teacher that I had indeed copied
my eloquent essay from a book."

She paused for only a moment, at no loss for the words she wanted
to share with Victoria:

Your gift, dearest girl, is your reverence for the truth. No matter how easy or difficult you found it to be, you always faced your own failings and spoke the truth.

"How I wish you had found the watch," she whispered, as if Victoria might hear her. While the ink dried, she toyed with the chain of the watch and let it slide between her fingers. She had several options when it came to returning the watch, but they were limited by her promise not to involve Samuel—or even Will, for that matter. Given Samuel's reputation as a gruff recluse and Will's background, even she had to agree it would be best if no one learned of their involvement.

She could take the watch to Sheriff Myer first, but that would put Webster Cabbot in an awkward position, one that would force him to explain why he had made a complaint against Burton Andrews when, in fact, Webster had merely lost his watch.

Unless he had not lost it. Maybe Burton had dropped it near the trash pit, either attempting to bury the evidence against him or losing the watch quite accidentally when he fled town. She could not very well give the watch to Burton to return. She had no idea where to find him.

She might take the watch to Rosalind, but dismissed the idea at once. Rosalind would not take it well if Martha showed up with the missing watch less than twenty-four hours after their conversation today. The woman might even get angry when Martha refused to divulge where she had gotten the watch and blame Martha in some way, even to the point of accusing Martha of having had the watch all along. Involving Reverend Welsh also seemed problematic since Cabbot was not a member of the congregation.

Leaving the watch on someone's doorstep with an anonymous note asking for the watch to be returned was the second option she rejected out of hand. She did not want anyone to think there was a thief in town who suddenly had had an attack of conscience. Not when the townspeople were already concerned about whoever was responsible for the rash of petty thievery plaguing the area. She could not afford to take that risk. If anyone ever discovered she had gotten the watch from Samuel, he might get blamed for the other robberies.

Stymied, she put the watch back into the corner cupboard for now and closed her daybook. All the options she had considered made her feel as cowardly as the day she decided to copy her essay all those years ago instead of writing it herself.

She knew, in the end, she would have to speak to Cabbot herself to right this injustice. She was just as certain Victoria would never have considered doing anything else. On that note, she decided to make an early night of it. She banked the fire in the hearth, changed into a flannel nightdress, and extinguished the candle on the table before climbing into bed.

She tugged the covers up to her chin and folded her hands in prayer. "Forgive me, Lord, for my failures this day. I thank You for the blessings I received, especially the ones I overlooked. Please keep a watchful eye on Victoria for me, and since You seem so set on putting this dilemma into my hands, I'll trust You to guide me to do what's best for all concerned. Amen."

She turned and snuggled into her pillow. "Oh, I almost forgot. You might want to think of a way I could fix Bird's wing. By spring would be fine. Amen."

Bird announced the arrival of a new day with a joyful serenade. Martha opened one eye, pulled the curtain aside, saw the dark, murky skies overhead, and burrowed back under the covers.

Samuel had been right. A storm was brewing. She immediately canceled her plans to travel the rest of Candle Creek today. In fact, she felt so toasty warm, she even entertained the idea of staying in bed for the morning. She had not really slept in late since she had returned home, and the idea was sinfully appealing.

The sound of a wagon approaching, then screeching to a halt, followed by a harsh rap at her door, ended that thought before she even had a chance to feel guilty. She got out of bed, slipped on her robe, and hurried to answer the door. The floorboards were stone cold, and she made another mental note to find those missing slippers of hers. She kept half of her body behind the door when she opened it and peered outside.

When Edward Palmer removed his hat, his hand was shaking. "It's time. Carrie and Belinda sent me to fetch you. It's time. Melanie. The baby. Can you come right away? I brought the wagon. I'll take you. It'll be faster."

"I just need to get dressed. You can wait in the tavern—"

"I'll get the wagon turned around and wait here. Just hurry. This one's comin' pretty fast."

"I will," she assured him, and closed the door. She did not bother to heat the water to bathe her face, and quickly dressed in a comfortable gown before dressing her hair in a simple knot at the nape of her neck. She grabbed her bag, took the birthing stool off the shelf, and set them just outside the door. After she slipped into her cape, she tied her bonnet into place and remembered to snatch her gloves before leaving.

When she got outside, Edward already had her bag and birthing stool in the back of the wagon. She checked the sky overhead. Dark, forbidding clouds were getting closer, but she and Edward did not have to travel far, and she was confident they could reach Melanie before the storm hit.

She climbed aboard and had barely settled onto the seat when he clicked the reins and the wagon took off. Jolted backwards, she clung to the edge of the seat to keep her balance. There was no sense telling the man to slow down. He would not listen anyway.

By the time they reached the stone cottage he had built with his own hands, she had been jostled and rocked until her bones ached. She was half afraid to check to see if any of her teeth had cracked, but her cheeks and lips were so numb with cold she could not bear the thought of opening her mouth.

Edward jumped down from his seat before the wagon finished skidding to a halt, grabbed her bag and birthing stool, and met her as she disembarked. She took her things. "I'll meet you inside," she murmured, and entered the house while he tended to the horse and wagon.

Carrie greeted her in the sitting room with an anxious smile. "I was hoping you weren't on another call. I don't think Melanie has long to go."

"How close are her forcing pains?" Martha asked as she removed her outerwear.

"Belinda says they're barely a minute apart now. We sent Edward for you when the waters broke half an hour ago. Her pains really got close after that."

A shrill scream split the air and sent Martha's heart racing. "Where are the other children?"

"Lucy took them all upstairs."

Martha grabbed her bag and the stool and nodded toward the small bedchamber behind the kitchen straight ahead that was used as a spare room as well as a birthing room. "Who else is in there?"

"Just Belinda. Everything happened so fast, we didn't have time to send for anyone else."

Edward burst through the door just as another scream shattered the calm, and stared at Martha. "Why aren't you with Melanie?"

"I'm on my way. Go upstairs. Send Lucy down. We're going to need her help. Let Mark take charge of the other children, and then get down here. We need you, too. Quickly," she urged. "Carrie, come with me."

While Edward bounded up the steps, she led Carrie to the birthing room, where Melanie lay in bed, writhing in pain. Belinda was mopping her own brow, clearly distraught. "Martha! I thought you'd never get here in time," she cried.

Melanie gritted her teeth together. "Too . . . late. Too late," she managed before unleashing a scream against unbridled pain and rode out another fierce contraction.

Martha sprang into action, wasting no thought about donning her birthing apron. She barely had time to wash her hands. While Carrie attempted to get the collapsible stool together, Martha rolled up the bed linens, starting at the bottom of the bed, and gathered them into a loose tent in the middle of Melanie's thighs. She urged her patient to bend her knees.

One touch revealed the soft down atop the baby's head, which was at the entrance of the birth canal. She climbed onto the bed and knelt between Melanie's legs. "Forget the stool. Carrie, get over here and take hold of one of Melanie's feet. Belinda! Stop mewling and hold Melanie's hand. Now then, Melanie. Let's get this babe born."

Lucy ran into the room. "Mama? Mama, are you all right?"

Martha looked over her shoulder and caught the girl's gaze. Barely thirteen, Lucy had not witnessed a birth before, but Martha had no choice but to change that right now. "Your mama is going to be fine. Come, child. Take your mama's other hand and hold on tight. Where's your father?"

The girl remained frozen in place. "He's upstairs. Jamie's cryin' and Matthew's wailin' 'cause I had to leave, then Mama screamed again, so Papa had to stay to get 'em quiet for Mark."

Melanie began to groan. Her stomach hardened. "Move, girl! Help your mama. Now! This baby isn't going to wait any longer." She looked back at her patient. "Now, Melanie. Push!"

Martha cupped the baby's head as it emerged.

"Again!"

A scream. The shoulders emerged.

"Again!"

Panting hard, Melanie gave one final effort before collapsing. Her legs were still shaking when Martha leaned back on her haunches and gazed down at the tiny miracle now lying at her knees. "You have another son. Good and sturdy lad, too," Martha murmured.

Edward charged into the room. "A son?"

The baby cried out for the first time, and Martha looked back over her shoulder. "A son. Fetch my bag so I can cut the cord. Carrie, get me some towels to wipe this baby down—and a blanket, too. He needs to see his mama."

The next half hour became a blur of activity, one so familiar, Martha scarcely had to think about what to do next. Before long, baby

Isaac was suckling at his mother's breast under his proud papa's gaze, and Lucy led the other children into the room to meet their new brother.

Martha stood in the doorway, exhausted, yet oddly exhilarated. The room that had only an hour ago been racked with anxiety and pain now radiated peace and contentment. While the scene before her was one she had witnessed countless times over the years, she was still filled with the same awe and wonder she had felt the very first time. In an instant, memories of all the long, hard journeys through bitter cold or simmering heat she had made and the sleepless nights she had endured mattered little.

She glanced down at her soiled gown. It was ruined, of course, but she would sacrifice every single gown she owned, one at a time, to be blessed with the opportunity to help birth another child.

She backed into the kitchen and eased the door closed. The moment she smelled the sausages and potatoes frying, her stomach growled. She joined Carrie at the table, and Belinda set a platter down in front of her. "Melanie only had time to peel the potatoes before she had to stop. I hope this will be enough."

"With six sausages and a mound of potatoes covering the plate? It's plenty." Famished, Martha dug in and finished every bite before fixing her tea with cream and a generous dollop of honey.

Normally full of chitchat, Carrie was strangely silent as she cut her sausage into tiny pieces. Belinda kept her gaze on her plate, but her hand twisted a napkin until it was a spiral as tight as a spring.

Martha let out a sigh. "Give it up. Whatever you two are reluctant to tell me can't be that bad."

Carrie plopped a forkful of potatoes into her mouth.

Belinda gnawed at her bottom lip. "I don't like to spread gossip."

Martha chuckled. "Since when?"

The other woman's cheeks turned pink. "Since meeting yesterday. Reverend Welsh had a stirring sermon on that very subject."

Carrie shook her head and quickly swallowed what she had in her mouth. "That was last week. Yesterday he preached about selfishness. Remember?"

Belinda opened her mouth, paused, and her blush deepened. "Oh. That's right." Her expression brightened. "Then it's been over a week. I'm doing better than I thought I was."

"Not gossiping?" Martha prompted.

"Exactly."

Martha turned to Carrie. "What about you?"

Her eyes widened. "Me? I'm not going to say anything about Mayor Dillon. Not me."

"Mayor Dillon?" Martha let out a longer, deeper sigh, wrapped her hand around her mug of tea, and looked at each of them. "Does this have anything to do with Samantha, too?"

"Not exactly," Belinda suggested.

"Oh, dash! It does, too," Carrie argued. "Samantha was all atwitter last night at the quilting. She couldn't stop talking about the gala the mayor is giving next Saturday. It's really the first time he's hosted anything since Sally died, poor dear."

"Gala? What gala?"

"The one he's giving to welcome Eleanor home. The invitations are going out today, or so Samantha said."

Martha found it odd that Eleanor had not mentioned anything about a party yesterday during their visit, and absently stirred her tea. "It's been over a year now. I don't see what the hubbub is all about. Thomas should be having people to the house. Besides, he's very excited to have Eleanor and Micah staying with him. Having a party of some sort is an easy way to let Eleanor see all her old friends."

Belinda nodded. "I'm sure that's it. I don't believe what Samantha said is true at all. And you shouldn't either, Martha," she murmured as she patted Martha's arm.

A warning bell sounded in the deep recesses of Martha's mind, but she ignored it. "Just what did Samantha say?"

Carrie frowned. "I told you not to mention it, Belinda, but you just couldn't resist, could you?"

Martha took a long sip of tea, enjoying the banter.

"I'd rather tell Martha now so she can be prepared, that's all."

Martha's spine began to tingle. "Prepared for what?" she asked as she took another sip of tea.

Belinda's gaze softened. "Samantha said the mayor is going to speak to her father this week. He's going to announce their betrothal at the party."

Martha choked on her tea. Choked. Sputtered. Coughed. Choked again. Overhead, a wicked clap of thunder shook the house and heavy rain pelted at the windows as the expected storm finally hit with a vengeance. Her throat tightened. Her heart raced, and her lungs pounded against the walls of her chest, demanding oxygen. Gasping, she finally squeaked in enough air to draw a breath. She wiped at tears and forced herself to breathe. Steady. Breathe again.

When her heartbeat returned to normal and her burning cheeks had cooled, she laughed out loud. "That's the silliest thing I ever heard you say, Belinda. I'm sorry. I don't mean to laugh, but it is ridiculous. I'm afraid you're the victim of a very cruel hoax or Samantha is going to be very embarrassed when her claims turn out to be wrong. I've known Thomas Dillon all my life, and he isn't going to ask Samantha to be his wife in this life or the next. I think we should go back with Melanie and her family now. After our prayers, I have an important errand to run. I'll stop to see Aunt Hilda and tell her Melanie needs her as an afternurse on my way."

Chapter
TWENTY-FIVE

The new planked sidewalk along West Main Street could have been a gangplank, as far as Martha was concerned. There might not be an angry sea waiting to swallow her up, but the prospect of confronting Webster Cabbot in his shop held the same allure.

After sending Aunt Hilda to Melanie Palmer, Martha had returned home, retrieved the watch, and left immediately. She had not even bothered to open the invitation to Thomas's party that Eva Clark had left for her. Many hours of reflection had convinced her she had no other choice than to return the watch to Webster. She'd probably known that the moment she discovered the watch at Samuel's, since she disliked asking anyone to solve a problem she might resolve herself.

Most especially, she disliked Webster Cabbot. A gunsmith by trade, he was as arrogant and domineering now as he had been the day he had brought his family to Trinity nearly fifteen years ago. He rarely allowed his wife, Dora, to leave their living quarters above the shop.

When they were younger, their three sons had never attended school; instead, they had taken whatever lessons they had received at home and had worked alongside their father as apprentices. Now that they were nearly grown men, she had no idea how skilled they had become at gunsmithing. They had been apt pupils, however, when it came to emulating their father's domineering nature, or perhaps it was an inherited trait they had received along with his dark looks and swarthy skin.

Webster had never joined the congregation or attended meeting or allowed his family to do so, either. He refused to vote or to attend town meetings. Quite ironically, he never participated in the militia, either, although he was more than willing to repair or replace a gun for any of the men who did.

He was about the last man in town Martha wanted to tell he had made a terrible mistake, particularly when he would have to admit very publicly he had been wrong. She did not have the right to assume responsibility for either the mistake itself or doing what it took to rectify it, and she prayed he would not disappoint her.

It was too much to hope he might act before Thursday and the monthly town meeting, but she hoped for it anyway.

After crossing Dillon's Stream via the covered bridge closest to the tavern, she walked south past the first shops. The acrid smell of burning wood behind the cooper's establishment and the pungent smell of processing leather laced the air. Pedestrians rarely gathered at this end, and she did not encounter anyone until she approached the general store and found Patience Greywald talking with Samantha's mother, Ruth Leery.

Mindful that she was not supposed to know Patience was teeming again, she inquired about her husband, instead. "Good morning, all. Has Charlie gone back to work yet?"

Patience paled. "He's not doing as well as we'd hoped, I'm afraid. Dr. McMillan is probably with Charlie now. We thought the infection had been cleared, but we're hopeful it won't be long now."

Martha had not heard anything about any complications before now and tried to keep her smile in place by changing to a happier subject. "Melanie Palmer delivered another son early this morning. They're calling him Isaac," she ventured.

Ruth nodded approvingly. "Another son? That's wonderful news. Men always prefer to have sons, don't they? I'm sure Edward is no different. At least Melanie has Lucy to help her. I know Samantha is a great blessing to me," she added. "Have you heard from Victoria?"

Martha had anticipated the question. She just had not expected to feel as if Ruth had plunged a knife into her heart. "Maybe in tomorrow's post," she murmured. "I understand the mayor is planning quite an event next Saturday."

Ruth beamed. "We're very excited, naturally. Thomas is a fine man, but of course, you know that, don't you? I do hope you'll be able to attend. Samantha is with Mrs. Ostermeyer right now, which reminds me. I must be going. I promised Samantha I would give her a chance to pick out the material for her gown by herself, but I simply must have a peek. You know how foolish and irresponsible young girls can be when left to their own devices. There's nothing like a mother's guidance, especially with something so important," she added, and quickly took her leave.

Another stab. Deeper. More hurtful. Tears welled, despite Martha's determined attempt to stop them.

"She's just excited," Patience explained. "She didn't mean to upset you. Victoria is young and impressionable, but she has a fine head on her shoulders. She'll realize her mistake and come home soon. I'm sure of it."

Martha swallowed the lump in her throat. "I pray she will, but the longer she's away, the harder it seems to be."

Patience smiled. "I know. Then to have this happen . . ."

Martha cocked her head.

"The betrothal. Thomas and Samantha. The whole town is buzz-ing. Everyone thought . . . well, after people saw you and Thomas at the market together . . . I mean, some people assumed . . ."

"Thomas is an old friend. Nothing more," Martha assured her. Apparently, Belinda's tale had not been as far-fetched as Martha had assumed. She still found it hard to believe, given her conversation with Thomas not six weeks ago, when he was still clearly missing his wife.

"Well, I'm glad," Patience said. "You have enough to contend with right now. And I have two boys at home who are probably getting in Dr. McMillan's way." She shifted her parcel from one hand to the other. "If you'll excuse me, I'd best get home."

"Give Charlie my best wishes. Tell him I'll be praying for him."

"Thank you. I will."

Unnerved, Martha turned to continue on her way when Sarah Welsh, the minister's wife, emerged from the general store. "Martha? Do you have a moment?"

"Of course."

The older woman looked drawn and haggard, despite her warm smile. "I wonder if you'd be free tomorrow night to sit with Mrs. Armstrong? She's fading, poor dear. I'm spending as much time with her as I can, but I'd really like to be home tomorrow night. It's Stuart's birthday. If you can't, then I'd understand."

Anxious to give Sarah some time for her husband, Martha did not hesitate to agree. "What time would you like me to go?"

"Seven o'clock?"

"I'll be there, and tell Reverend Welsh I wish him many blessings."

"Oh, I will. I will, dear, and thank you," she gushed before heading toward home.

Martha's spirit filled with good humor that did not fade until the moment she reached the gun shop. She took a deep breath for courage. Heartened by the delicious smells coming from the confectionery next door, she made herself a promise to stop to see the Lynn sisters and purchase a large, thoroughly decadent treat for herself. If she succeeded on her mission now, she certainly would deserve a reward; if not, she might need to drown herself in something sweet to ease her disappointment.

When she opened the door and stepped into the gun shop, the bell tinkled overhead. She glanced around the shop and waited for someone—she hoped it would be Webster—to come to the display room.

An impressive array of hand-crafted weapons, from pistols to long-barrel rifles, decorated the walls. Finely forged barrels had been shaped and shined to perfection. Most of the stocks were carved from local wood, although there was a glass display case devoted to pistols with ivory handles.

She felt like she had trespassed into private male territory, much like any man might feel upon entering the dressmaker's shop. The sound of approaching footsteps kept her from dwelling on the analogy, which reminded her of Ruth's conversation. When the door creaked open, she shivered and wrapped her fingers around the watch she had stored in her cape pocket.

Once Webster Cabbot emerged from the back workroom, he took one look at her and scowled. He closed the door behind him and folded his arms across his chest. "I don't make donations to any cause," he snapped.

Her hold on the watch tightened. "I haven't come to seek a donation. I've come to make one to the cause of justice," she responded. She laid the watch on top of the glass display case and locked her gaze with his. "I've been asked to return this to you. Apparently, you lost it out by the trash pit. I trust you'll see that Sheriff Myer drops the charges against Burton Andrews."

His dark eyes flashed with recognition when he looked at the watch, but not a glimmer of guilt shined in their depths. He snatched the watch and inspected it closely before hanging it back in place on a peg next to the door at his back. "Tell Andrews he's a bigger fool than I thought if he thinks he'll get himself cleared by hiding behind a woman's skirts or if he thinks he can hide from the law forever. I'll see Myer, all right. To give him the watch as evidence."

He narrowed his gaze and clenched his fists. "No man enters my shop, feigns friendship, and then turns thief the minute I turn my back. And no woman dare plead his case for him. Not even you," he spat.

She stiffened her spine and locked her knees to keep them from shaking. "I haven't seen Burton Andrews since long before I left for New York, and I have no idea where he is now. I have no interest in protecting him, either," she added, hoping to extinguish at least one of the sparks of anger he shot at her.

"Give me one good reason why I should believe you," he countered. "You might start by giving me the name of the person you claim found the watch."

"I can't give you that name because I gave my word I wouldn't. The reasons why are irrelevant. What matters is that you admit to a mistake and right the wrong that's been done to Burton. And his wife. You should believe me for one reason only: I give you my word what I've told you is the truth."

He snorted. "The truth? The truth is that Andrews is a thief and a coward. He stole my watch. My grandfather's watch . . . that's hung on the wall in this shop every day while I've worked for the past fifteen years and in my shop in York for ten years before that. Why do you think I left York? To get away from scoundrels like Andrews and from riffraff like what's out there at that academy, just waiting till folks let down their guard so they can steal them blind."

He snatched the watch off the peg and shook his fist at her. "Give Andrews a message for me. Tell him I wouldn't drop the charges against him if he marched down Main Street barefoot in the snow and begged me. Tell him—"

"I can't tell him anything," she protested. "I have no idea where to find him. Even if I did, I know Burton would not come home unless you admitted the whole affair was a mistake. A dreadful mistake . . . made by a man who truly regrets nearly destroying his friend's reputation, along with his marriage, because he's no better than the rest of us. We all make mistakes," she murmured. "Not all of us have the courage to admit them, but I think you do. You're a vain, self-centered man, Webster Cabbot. You rule your life and your home with an iron will. Ask anyone in town. They'll agree with me. But there isn't a soul for fifty miles who wouldn't also agree you're a righteous man. An honorable man. I know you'll do what's right. That's why I came directly to you and not Sheriff Myer. And that's why I won't speak a word about this to anyone. Ever," she vowed.

With her heart pounding, she turned about. She made a hasty retreat, so hasty she collided with Dr. McMillan as she rushed out the door. "I'm so sorry," she gushed. She held her breath while he struggled to regain his balance. "I nearly knocked you off the walk and into the street!"

His cheeks reddened. "No harm done. I was preoccupied myself," he offered, and pointed to the confectionery next door. "I had my mind dead set against it, but I found myself unable to resist since I practically had to pass by on my way home." He patted his ample stomach. "Sweets are my nemesis. I'm afraid I don't have an ounce of self-control."

She chuckled. "I've been known to skip supper and down an entire pie, instead. Cherry pie that is. Thank heavens cherries are out of season now. I was headed to the confectionery myself, actually, although I shouldn't. Lydia told me Fern and Ivy were making fritters today, and I promised myself I wouldn't buy more than one."

"Yes, well, perhaps we should go together. For moral support. I won't let you buy more than one if you help me to do the same."

"Agreed."

They entered the confectionery shop together. By the time they left, they had consumed several fritters apiece, but carried home only one.

"We don't seem to be very good as one another's conscience," he commented with a chuckle.

"No," she agreed, "but Fern and Ivy aren't much help, either."

As they walked toward the covered bridge, his expression sobered. "We do seem to be rivals, at least where some of our patients are concerned. I suppose that's to be expected."

Surprised by his candor, she caught her breath. "I suppose it is, especially when it comes to treating women and children."

He nodded. "I trained for a very long time to become a doctor. There are treatments. Modern treatments I can offer that I know surpass the old traditional ones."

She held her silence and matched her stride to his. They entered the bridge and crossed over to the other side of the street. "I wonder if I might ask your opinion about something . . . something professional."

"Opinion?" she asked, too shocked to say more.

"You know about the accident at the mill with Charlie Greywald."

"I spoke to Patience earlier. She said there had been some kind of infection."

He moistened his lips. "That's true. His hand was healing well, then last week one section of his wound became very red and swollen. I lanced it open, cleaned out the infection, and stitched it closed again."

"And today?"

He shook his head. His steps slowed. "The infection appears to be spreading. If I don't do something soon, he may lose his hand after all."

He looked so very young, so dispirited, so disheartened, she could not help but sympathize with his concern. Her admiration for him, despite their different views, rose a notch. "Try leeches. Set them along the entire wound and wherever you see bruising or red lines streaking across the flesh."

He rocked to a halt.

She backed up to be alongside him.

"Leeches? That's . . . that's medicine from the Dark Ages," he sputtered.

When she held fast, failed to take the bait and respond to his charge, he rubbed his brow. "My mentor at the university would probably have my license revoked if he heard I used leeches."

She nodded. Along with her patients, she found using leeches unnerving, even barbaric, and limited their use for circumstances that called for extraordinary measures. "On the other hand, you might be able to save Charlie from losing his hand and being crippled. Perhaps you should keep that in mind when you're weighing the issue of whether you're practicing medicine to prove yourself or to help your patients."

"Of course I want to help them," he argued. "Why else would I be here?"

"I wouldn't know the answer to that," she murmured. "If you want to try the leeches, stop by after supper. I'll have some ready for you, even though it already may be too late. You have nothing to lose by trying, but Charlie does."

Chapter
TWENTY-SIX

Dr. McMillan didn't appear until the following morning. The poor man was as pale as a winter moon. The dark circles under his eyes did not do much for his appearance, except to give silent testimony that he had spent a sleepless night coming to his decision. She handed him the jar of leeches, but decided against making any comment at all.

He stepped through the doorway into the outer yard and stopped. When he turned around, his gaze was troubled. "You won't mention my coming here?"

Still some pride left, she supposed, but his heart was in the right place. "No."

"Thank you." He drew in a long breath, nodded, and shut the door.

She did not waste time brooding about him, any more than she took pleasure in having him come to her for advice. The only thing that truly mattered was getting that infection cleared in Charlie's hand.

At the moment, she had a full plate for the day. She wanted to stop to see Jenny Ward. On the way, she could ride along the rest of Candle Creek, skirt around the lake, and travel the other side of the creek on her way home.

With only two days until the town meeting, and growing reports of stolen property outside the town limits, she had little time left if she had any hope of turning the tide of public opinion that was threatening to flood the meeting with demands the academy be closed and its boarders run out of the county, for starters.

Anxious to keep her vow to aid Reverend Hampton's worthy cause, she saddled Grace and headed out of town. The weather had turned fair for this time of year, but the sun was too weak to offer much warmth. The promise of winter bleached the glorious display of autumn color from the landscape, as if nature itself had slipped into a deep sleep. Fields lay fallow. Where livestock grazed, their breath created warm clouds that hovered close to the earth. Wispy plumes of smoke from chimneys carried the familiar smell of burning wood, inspiring visions of families tucked snug in their homes.

Everything peaceful. Everything calm.

It was hard to imagine that here, amidst such beauty, among such hardworking, God-fearing people, a thief had stolen more than sacks of grain or baskets of eggs. He had stolen the town's pride, pierced the peace of mind that came from trusting neighbor and traveler alike and having that trust rewarded by honesty and goodwill. To rectify that injustice, to reclaim the town and its people, Martha traveled on, long into the early hours of twilight.

She neared the outskirts of town at the end of the day no closer to discovering the real culprits, but duly concerned about the number of people who complained about having things stolen. At most, folks reported some chickens or some baskets of produce missing from their root cellars or meat from the smokehouse.

Every muscle in her body ached. Due to the hospitality of her friends and neighbors, she had eaten enough to keep her satisfied for days. She passed the rear of the cemetery and tugged on the reins. Rosalind was scurrying off, apparently after another visit to Charlotte's grave.

Although Rosalind had her back to Martha, Martha really had to battle with herself not to cry out and tell Rosalind her husband might be able to come home soon. Since Webster had stubbornly refused to take any action, telling Rosalind now would only make matters worse, especially if he decided to use the watch as evidence against Burton instead of to clear him.

Disappointed and disillusioned with her day, she sorely needed good news. The only place she might find it would be at Samuel's. At this hour, Will should be back at the academy, which would give her a chance to speak with Samuel openly about the boy's progress. She dismounted and walked ahead of Grace to cut through the woods to get to the path that led to Samuel's cabin.

Once she arrived, she tethered Grace to a nearby tree. "I won't be long," she promised, and rewarded Grace with a carrot before knocking on Samuel's door.

"Welcome aboard," he bellowed as she entered. "Somethin' wrong? Can't say I ever had you visit twice in the same week before."

She chuckled and took a seat in the chair alongside him. "What if I told you that you're simply irresistible?"

He snorted. "I'd say you were gettin' as blind as I am."

"Still no improvement? I was so sure the new drops would help you."

"You tried your best."

"Why don't you let me bring Dr. McMillan with me next time?"

"No doctors. Bring that up again and I'll be apt to change my mind about that lad you're so fond of," he warned.

"How's he doing? Really?"

He tugged on his beard, scattering a bunch of crumbs left behind from his supper. The glob of gravy never budged. "You tell me. You saw him here not two days ago."

She shifted in her seat. "I think you've worked wonders with Will. His language is . . . well, it's getting better."

He laughed. "That's the horseradish root. Cures all sorts of ills. You ever do anything with that watch?"

She told Samuel about Burton Andrews and recounted her visit with Webster Cabbot. "I think he'll come around. Eventually."

"There's no fool like a woman, thank God. Leave it to a man, he'll break her heart every time."

"A woman might help redeem her man," she teased.

"Thought that's what kept ministers busy. Speakin' of which, how much do you know about Reverend Hampton?"

Her pulse quickened. "Only what he's told me. Why?"

He chewed on his bottom lip. "Just wonderin'. That boy's got a back covered with scars thicker than rope. Claims his pa had a heavy hand."

She nodded, but she could not stop a chill from racing up and down her spine. "He's told me a little about his father. I guess I shouldn't be surprised. He never even called Will by his given name. He told me his name and he told you, but I don't think he's told Reverend Hampton yet. Or at least he hadn't the last time I saw him."

"Will's got a quick mind. Knows when to trust the right folks. Guess that comes from livin' on the streets for so long. Still . . ."

His voice trailed off. His fingers continued to work the end of his beard. "Guess I'm just naturally suspicious. Don't pay me any mind."

Samuel was suspicious, even distrustful, of most people, which had made pairing him with Will all the more unlikely. Because of his failing vision, if not his career at sea, where a man learned to survive by accurately judging others and trusting only those whose skills could mean the difference between life and death, Martha knew Samuel had finely tuned instincts. She trusted them now more than her own. "Is it something Will said about Reverend Hampton that troubles you?"

"It's what he doesn't say. Never talks about him or the other boys, for that matter. He gets downright defiant if I press him."

"Give him time," she urged, quite certain now that Samuel's concern just reflected his growing attachment to the boy.

"You give any thought to what you're gonna do with him later? He's gonna hit rough seas when my eyes give out completely."

"Which is why you need to see a doctor. So I don't have to worry about later, and Will doesn't have to—"

"Tarnation, woman! You must have something better to do with your time than badger a poor, defenseless, old man who can't see much past his own nose. Go on! Get yourself home and don't be comin' back here any time soon. I used to have peace and quiet till you showed up, smellin' like a field of English lavender, meddlin' where you don't belong."

She rose and pressed a kiss to his forehead. "I'll be back soon," she teased, and quickly backed away. She managed to get to the door before he bellowed at her again.

"You got so much time to waste, go bother that minister and his passel of trouble."

She shut the door. "Maybe I will," she murmured, and led Grace home.

The following day, Martha covered the rest of the homesteads along Double Trouble Creek. She did not find any potential candidates responsible for the thefts, but she found plenty of trouble brewing, as if the thief had heavily targeted the families there to make the name of the creek seem more than apropos.

Public sentiment against the academy appeared to be much stronger than she had feared, given all she'd learned in the past two days. The town meeting tomorrow evening promised to be a raucous event. She did not envy Sheriff Myer his job that night, and Thomas would have no easier time as mayor. According to James, who had many good opportunities to overhear tavern gossip, Thomas had gone to York on Monday, but everyone expected him to be back in time for the meeting.

Whether or not Webster Cabbot would even approach the sheriff by then was still a mystery to her. Even if he did, the sheriff might be too busy calming the audience to even broach the matter of Burton Andrews's innocence. Regardless, she planned to be there.

Anxious to resolve the growing doubt in her own mind about the academy, she arrived there in late afternoon. Her one and only visit to the old Rhule homestead had been in the dead of night, and she studied the property now with the advantage of daylight.

The small farmhouse appeared ramshackle, at best. Weathered, peeling clapboards begged for a fresh coat of whitewash. How the barn did not collapse was utterly amazing. Missing timbers left gaping holes in the walls, and the roof sagged low, as if it had borne one winter too many of heavy snow. There were no crops planted at this time of year, of course, but the livestock, a collection of a few mangy chickens, pigs, and one skinny cow, seemed grossly inadequate to support the number of people who now made this their home.

She dismounted and approached the farmhouse on foot. When the door opened, Olympia waved a friendly welcome and turned away for a moment. Within seconds, two boys scampered outside and ran to meet her. "Afternoon. We'll see your horse gets some water," the taller boy offered.

She could not remember his name, but she recognized his pudgy face. The other boy held back, his gaze riveted on Grace. The mare snorted and tugged at the reins.

"Be polite," she warned. She handed the reins to the younger boy. "Her name is Grace. Treat her gently. I'll only be a little while."

"Yes, ma'am. Come on, Grace. Easy, girl," he murmured, and offered his companion a funny face only a young boy could make and sauntered off.

Olympia wiped her hands on her apron and walked out to greet her guest. "Martha! What a surprise. I was just making biscuits. You'll stay for supper, won't you?"

"I'd love to, but I really can't. I need to get home in time to relieve Mrs. Welsh and stay with Mrs. Armstrong. She's doing poorly."

"Then at least come in and have some hot cider. I just set a pan on the stove. Ulysses should be back soon. He took the older boys for supplies," she offered as she led Martha into the kitchen. She moved a bowl aside and wiped the flour from the table. "Let me clean a place for you while you take off your cape."

"Please don't go to any bother—"

"It's no trouble at all. We don't get many visitors," she insisted.

By the time Martha had removed her outerwear and sat down, Olympia had two steaming mugs of cider on the table and a plate of molasses cookies set between them. Martha stirred her cider with a cinnamon stick and waited for the beverage to cool. "I hope Reverend Hampton doesn't meet up with any trouble in town."

A frown. "More thefts?"

Martha nodded. "I was hoping they'd stop. Folks are pretty upset. We're just not used to something like this happening in Trinity."

"The good Lord will set things right."

"Until He does," Martha cautioned, "I'm afraid your boys will be taking the brunt of people's anger and frustration."

"We feared as much," Olympia admitted. Her gaze grew troubled. "Ulysses has such faith in these boys, but he's not as young as he thinks he is. I don't know what he'd do if . . . if . . ."

"I wouldn't worry just yet. Sheriff Myer is working very hard to put an end to the problem. For now, the best thing we can do is pray he'll find the real culprit. In the meantime, it might be a good idea for Reverend Hampton to come to the town meeting tomorrow night, if only to convince people he's as concerned as everyone else."

"A town meeting?"

Martha sipped her cider, burned the tip of her tongue, and set the mug away from her. "Seven o'clock. At the meetinghouse. I'll be there, too, of course. I'm sure Fern and Ivy will be there." She placed her hand on Olympia's arm. "You do have friends here."

Olympia's eyes misted with tears. "Ulysses is much stronger than I am. I simply can't bear to think about all the awful things people are saying about the boys. To give up now, after we've worked so hard, just because of malicious gossip . . ."

The sound of an approaching wagon turned Olympia's frown into a smile. "That must be him now. Let me tell him you're here for a visit so the boys can unload the supplies for him." She hurried outside and returned with her husband long moments later.

Reverend Hampton removed his hat and coat and joined Martha at the table. "It's good to see you again. Olympia tells me there's trouble brewing again."

"Unfortunately, that's true."

He scratched the crown of his bald head. "I thought we'd made some progress."

"You did," Martha assured him. "We just need to calm people's fears—"

"About the academy."

She nodded. "Did you have any problems in town today?"

"Actually, we went to Sunrise. I had to make a withdrawal at the bank, so we got our supplies there. What time is the town meeting?"

"Seven o'clock," she responded as she mulled over his admission that he had gone to Sunrise for supplies. In point of fact, she could not recall a single instance when he had come to Trinity for supplies and wondered why he had not taken the opportunity to visit the town from time to time to support the local merchants there, especially when he was so anxious to dispel their concerns about the boys at the academy.

"I'll be there. We'll all be there. Might as well let the boys see what they're up against."

Visions of irate citizens clamoring for justice with their primary suspects in the same room made Martha tremble, along with visions of similar scenarios that might have developed if Reverend Hampton had brought the boys into town today for supplies. "It's bound to be rather loud, even raucous. I'm not sure you'd want the boys to see and hear all that. It might be better if you came alone. Look for me, though. I'll try to save you a seat up front."

"I should bow to your judgment," he conceded, "especially after the turnabout Boy has made, all thanks to you."

"Samuel should get the credit for that," she insisted, finding it curious he still did not refer to Will by his given name. "I stopped to see them on Sunday." She recounted her visit, leaving out only the incident about discovering the watch. "You can see the worship in his eyes when he looks at Samuel," she concluded.

Olympia set a mug of cider in front of her husband. "He rushes through his lessons at night just to have more time to practice those knots. He's even got Adam and P. J. trying to make them."

Reverend Hampton chuckled. "Hearing tales of the sea and exploring real treasure chests is like a dream come true for Boy."

"That's the dream, isn't it?" Martha whispered. "To reach into each boy's mind and heart to find something to breathe life into his dreams so he wants to learn and grow into a righteous man?"

"That's the dream. But dreams take time," he argued. "Unless I can convince the people of Trinity we are doing God's work with these boys, monitoring them even more closely than before to make sure they don't slip back into bad habits, then we won't get the time we need to help each and every one of them like we've helped Boy."

"Then we simply must get the time," she insisted. There were few men who would be ready and willing to challenge an entire community for the sake of boys no one else wanted. Reverend Hampton was one of those few, and Martha would not stand idly by to let him wage this battle alone. Even if he did seem a bit too saintly at times, he was only a man—a man who needed help.

"I'll help you. I know others who will help, too," she promised. Whatever plans she had had for tomorrow quickly evaporated. First thing in the morning, she would call on folks she knew would support the academy, if only as a balance against those who wanted the academy to close.

Chapter

TWENTY-SEVEN

E ven the best-knitted intentions could unravel.
By late Thursday afternoon, Martha's last-minute plan to encourage some of her friends and neighbors to attend the town meeting
and support the academy was nothing more than a skein of good
intentions that tangled her hopes with disappointment.

Thursday had dawned with her promise to herself and Reverend
Hampton still very real and within reach by sunset. Before she had
finished her breakfast, Jacob Ward had arrived. She had spent the
entire day with three of his children and treated them for what she
suspected was whooping cough. By the time she returned home at
dusk, the treatments had taken a toll on her, as well as on her patients.

Setting up steam tents to help clear their lungs left her feeling a
bit wilted herself. The hair framing her face had slipped free, curling

in several different directions. No matter how tight she pulled her cape on the way home, she could still smell the reek of garlic that had permeated her gown and every square inch of uncovered flesh. To make matters worse, she had stubbed her baby toe not once, but twice, in her haste to answer Jacob's knock at the door in her bare feet. She had bandaged the toe before she left, vowing to empty her entire room, if necessary, to find those missing slippers of hers.

Riding ten miles each way to the Ward homestead had been painful, and she limped back into her room now in a cranky mood. When Bird squawked for his supper, she scowled. "You'll have to wait. And stop flapping around like that! You'll break your other wing, too, and then where will you be? In more trouble than you've bargained for," she grumbled.

He scrambled to the top perch and squawked again.

She ignored him, stored her bag away, and hung up her outerwear. She took one look in the mirror, sighed, and let her shoulders slump. Barring a miracle, she was destined to show up at the town meeting, which was scheduled to begin in less than an hour, looking like an old hag and smelling just as bad, too.

She started when the connecting door to her room opened.

Lydia poked her head inside. "James set the brass tub in the storeroom for you, and I added the hot water after I saw you ride by. If you hurry, you'll have plenty of time to eat something before you go, too."

Martha was too exhausted to care that her tears trickled down her cheeks. "You're such a blessing!"

Her sister-in-law chuckled. "Tell James, will you? He's miffed at me. Just a little," she added when Martha frowned.

"Is there anything else I can do?" Martha asked.

Lydia wrinkled her nose. "Probably not. He's back to thinking about moving again. It's nearly winter. He does it every year. I should know better than to argue with him. By spring, he always changes his mind."

Martha laughed. "James is a lot like Grandfather. He always dreamed of selling the tavern and moving into a small cabin on the shores of Candle Lake, too. Don't worry. The first person who has the misfortune to offer James a fair price for the tavern will find out James will do exactly what Grandfather Poore did—run the poor soul out of the tavern without bothering to collect the man's coins for his refreshments."

"I should let him follow his dream," Lydia admitted. "As long as it stays just that—a dream. Living that far from town appeals to me about as much as eating raw fish."

James's voice bellowed from the kitchen. "Lydia? We've got hungry patrons waiting!"

"I've got to go. Now, hurry. Your water is getting cold. I'll lock the other storeroom door so you can bathe in privacy." She giggled and closed the door.

Martha quickly undressed, slipped into her robe, and snatched some lavender for her bathwater. She fed Bird and apologized. He was too busy eating to respond.

Within half an hour, she was dressed in a fresh gown and feeling quite revived. There was not much she could do with her hair. Since it would not dry in time, she had not washed it; instead, she scented her brush with lavender water, brushed it through her hair, shaped a quick knot on top of her head, and covered it with her Sunday bonnet.

The prospect of walking all the way to the town meeting with her sore foot was daunting, but she did not have time to saddle Grace again and be on time. She tested her foot, winced, and shrugged her shoulders. There was nothing she could do to avoid the long walk, but with luck, Reverend Hampton or someone else might give her a ride home. She hated to show up without the support for the academy she had promised, but there was nothing she could do about that, either. If she hurried, she might still be able to get a seat up front and save one for Reverend Hampton.

With high hopes, she limped out the door.

Getting a seat at the meeting had been a phantom hope that evaporated the moment Martha saw the crowd of people standing outside the meetinghouse because there was not room enough for them inside. She squeezed between frustrated and angry townspeople who were too busy complaining to one another to pay her much mind. She caught a glimpse of Thomas several times as he struggled to be heard above the din to call the meeting to order.

Halfway to the front, she gave up trying to get another inch closer. The crowd was packed so tightly together she probably would not be able to turn around and leave, either. Since the audience was mostly men, as usual, she could not see much past the crowd in front of her. When she looked back over her shoulder, she scanned the crowd behind her and caught a fleeting glimpse of Samuel.

Samuel? She strained her neck. There! In the far corner, Samuel stood with his back against the wall. Although he was surrounded by people, he radiated an aura of disdain that made him appear to be completely alone in the room. He caught her glance and gave an almost imperceptible nod.

"Order!" Thomas shouted. "Order! We will have order or I'll end this meeting right now."

Hoots. Groans. Jeers. They mellowed to a bearable level, but Thomas continued to glare and held silent until the citizens quieted. He stood right in front of the pulpit with Sheriff Myer at his side, along with a man she thought might be Reverend Hampton. She just could not see enough of him to be sure.

Thomas glanced around the gathering. "You will all have a chance to be heard after the sheriff reports what he's learned. Reverend Hampton has also asked to address you, which I have agreed to let him do. Then and only then will you be invited to voice your own concerns or opinions."

Deafening shouts of disapproval rang out.

"Send him and that passel of hoodlums packin'!"

"He ain't no minister of ours."

"We got no room for the likes of him and his band of thieves!"

"Order!" Thomas shouted. "Order!"

The audience eventually quieted, and the sheriff stepped forward. "As you know, I've been compiling a number of reports about the stolen property. I've investigated each and every one. Unfortunately, none of you, *none of you*," he repeated, "has been able to provide a reliable description of the person or persons responsible. None of you has offered any evidence against any specific individual, either. That doesn't make my task any easier."

He paused and looked around the crowd of people. "It doesn't do any of us a bit of good to make accusations against anyone without proof. Spreading rumors and misinformed gossip is only making matters worse."

"Close that academy and you'll see the thievin' stop real quick," a man shouted.

She recognized Barnaby Smith's voice. It sounded like he was in the back of the room.

"I don't have the authority to do that," the sheriff responded.

"Take a vote," another man suggested. "We'll give you all the authority you need."

The crowd cheered, clapped, and stomped their feet. Martha cringed. She was tempted to put her hands against her bonnet to cover her ears when she heard a familiar voice ring out. "May I? Please? Gentlemen, if I may have quiet. Please!"

Reverend Hampton's voice was calm. It was soothing. He was infinitely patient and waited until the complaints fell to just above a whisper before attempting to address the audience. "As you well know, I am the first to admit my boys' wrongdoing when it occurs, but in this case, they have become scapegoats for a pernicious thief who has maligned innocent children whom God has entrusted to my care as much as he has violated the sanctity of your homes and property. Closing the academy would not solve your problems. Closing the academy would hurt these boys because the scandal would follow us wherever we tried to resettle and unfairly taint their futures. But I do have a solution—one that would vindicate the boys as well as myself and set the thief on notice that this community will not rest until he is caught and punished."

He paused and scanned the crowd. Martha could hear grumbles

of discontent and disbelief, but apparently the audience was curious enough to hear the minister's solution that no one challenged him.

"On Saturday, we'll be leaving on a short holiday of sorts. I've accepted an invitation to visit one of my friends, the Reverend Mr. Malcolm Dewey. We'll be leaving for Denville early Saturday morning and we'll remain there until this mystery is resolved and we are welcomed back once you are all reassured none of the boys from the academy is responsible. Sheriff Myer and Mayor Dillon both know how to contact me," he added. "I pray we can return home to Trinity soon."

Both surprised and impressed by the minister's proposal, Martha immediately thought of Will and turned to gauge Samuel's reaction while Reverend Hampton answered questions from the crowd. Samuel, however, was not in the corner where she had initially seen him— or anywhere else in the back of the meetinghouse, either.

While taking the boys away for a brief spell could very well end speculation and suspicions about them, taking Will to Denville, a remote village just outside of Clarion, would also give him an opportunity to run away to sea again. Troubled, she eased her way back through the crowd, hoping Samuel might be waiting for her outside. She stood just beyond the opened door and looked around the dark yard. No sign of Samuel.

Considering his poor vision, she could not imagine how he had gotten to the town meeting in the first place. Returning home would be just as difficult, and she hurried through the yard and down East Main Street as best she could with her sore foot.

She caught up with Samuel in the cemetery. "Samuel! Wait!" she cried, and ran a bit lopsidedly to close the distance between them. Panting, she took his arm. "You shouldn't be out by yourself," she chastised.

He cocked his head. "Way you're walkin', I might say the same applies to you."

"I stubbed my toe. It's nothing. Why didn't you wait for me?"

He stiffened and removed her hand from his arm. "I've been takin'

care of myself for fifty-four years now. I'm in no need of a nursemaid."
He tapped the side of his head with one finger. "I see with this, too.
There isn't a path in or around town I haven't traveled a hundred
times at night."

"I know. I'm sorry. I just wanted to talk to you about Will."

"What about him?"

"I don't know how much you heard . . ."

"Heard it all."

"Then you know Reverend Hampton is taking the boys to Denville
on Saturday. I visited the academy yesterday. Reverend Hampton
didn't mention anything to me about this. I was wondering if Will
had said something to you."

He snorted. "The boy's been comin' regular, but he didn't say
nothin' 'bout goin' away. The past few days, he's been downright
ornery. Practically used up the last of my horseradish root, too. I knew
somethin' was eatin' at him. Now I guess I know what it is."

Martha's heart filled with hope. "He doesn't want to go, does he?"

"Maybe not."

"Could he stay with you?" she asked. "I could speak to Reverend
Hampton tomorrow. No one ever calls on you, so no one would know
Will hadn't gone with the rest."

"What if someone found out?" he countered. "If the thefts continue, then Will is right here to take all the blame. Let the boy go
with the others. If they come back—"

" 'If they come back'? What do you mean, 'if'? Of course, they'll
be back. Once the sheriff apprehends the real thief, the reputation of
the academy will be restored. I'm not worried about their coming
back. I'm worried Will might decide to run away again. There's a
port near Denville. Ships. Temptation," she gushed, unable to stop her
heart from racing with fear and apprehension.

"*Maybe* they'll come back. Maybe the boy will be with them. Maybe
not, but the boy's got to make his own choices. All I know is I'm
smelling a barrel of rotten fish. I just don't know who's packin' the
barrel, some low-down hypocrite stealin' his neighbors blind and
blamin' innocent boys or a minister with a flock of black sheep."

Martha clapped her hand to her heart. "Reverend Hampton?"

He sighed. "That's why I keep to myself. I don't trust anyone."

"Not even me?"

"Not even you, at least not all the time," he admitted. "But I'll talk to Will tomorrow and see if I can find out what's eatin' at his gut. If I learn somethin', I'll come to see you."

"No. I'll come to your cabin," she argued.

He shook his head. "I'll be in the stable about this same time tomorrow night. If I'm not there, then you know I didn't learn anything new." He paused and tapped the rim of her bonnet. "In the meantime, you might try to do somethin' about that garlic I'm smellin'." Chuckling, he ambled away, leaving her alone with only her fears and doubts for company.

As much as she believed in Reverend Hampton and accepted his decision to leave Trinity for a short spell until the real culprits were caught, she had the troublesome feeling he might not return at all. The very notion was irrational and completely baseless, but she could no sooner deny what she felt than prove it wrong.

Convinced she was merely so unnerved by the continued thefts and so worried about Will that she was becoming as much of a skeptic as Samuel, she started for home.

Chapter

TWENTY-EIGHT

The appointed time on Friday night came and went, but Samuel never appeared. Early Saturday morning, Lydia knocked on Martha's door and poked her head inside. "Reverend Hampton is outside with his boys waiting to see you. They're leaving for Denville."

Martha followed her sister-in-law through to the kitchen and then went out the main tavern door. The air outside was cold, but the skies were clear and the sun shone brightly on the canvas covering the Conestoga wagon. Reverend Hampton was at the reins with two of the older boys sitting alongside him, freshly scrubbed and dressed as if they were going to Sunday meeting.

Sober, but looking optimistic, Reverend Hampton smiled. "We wanted to bid you a temporary farewell and to thank you for all your kindnesses."

"You have a good day to travel. I pray you'll all be able to come back very soon. Godspeed," she responded. She braced against the cold and wrapped her arms against her waist.

He tightened his hold on the reins. "We appreciate your prayers most of all. Olympia is in the back with the rest of the boys. She'd appreciate a word with you."

Martha found the minister's wife seated on a crate. Behind her, the remaining five boys sat amidst the supplies they were taking with them. Will had his back to her, but the other four boys met her gaze. Olympia offered a brave smile, and her tear-stained cheeks were pale as she twisted a handkerchief in her hands. "I do hope we can come home before winter sets in," she murmured. "I don't know what Ulysses will do if they don't catch the person responsible."

Martha covered her hands with one of her own and gave a reassuring squeeze. "I'm sure it won't be long. Is there anything I can do for you while you're away?"

Olympia leaned forward. "Would you mind stopping by the house while I'm gone? John Wilson is tending the livestock for Ulysses, but I'd feel better if you could check on the house itself from time to time and make sure . . . We've left so much behind . . . You wouldn't need a key. The front lock is broken."

"Of course, but I'm sure everything will be just as you've left it."

"Thank you."

When the wagon started forward, Olympia grabbed the edge of the crate and Martha stepped back. "Looks like we're on our way. Perhaps we'll see you soon."

"Very soon," Martha promised. She returned Olympia's wave before the wagon disappeared into the covered bridge. Disappointed Will had not turned around to say good-bye, she hurried back into the tavern. Convinced by Olympia's parting words that Reverend Hampton would surely be returning to Trinity as soon as circumstances allowed, she dismissed her reservations that he might not return at all as completely unfounded.

From the front window, she watched the wagon exit from the bridge, turn, and head directly down West Main Street. As the wagon passed by the homes and businesses, townspeople emerged. Some waved good-bye. Others stood stone-faced, observing the wagon carrying the town's nemeses away with no small measure of contempt as a fare-thee-well. At the confectionery, the Lynn sisters hailed down the wagon and handed baskets of sweet treats to Olympia.

Once the wagon left the town proper and disappeared from view entirely, Martha returned to her room. Bird was in top form, serenading his heart out while she tidied up. She spent half an hour searching for her missing chamber slippers before giving up all hope of ever finding them. Her bruised toe was healing nicely, but she had no desire to reinjure it or spend the winter walking on cold floorboards.

She donned her cape and bonnet, checked her reticule to make sure she had a fresh handkerchief, and returned to the kitchen, where Lydia was peeling potatoes. "I'm going to the general store. Do you need anything?" she asked.

Lydia paused and held her knife in midair. "I can't think of anything. What takes you there?"

"A new pair of chamber slippers. Mine have all but disappeared from the face of the earth."

Lydia frowned. "I haven't seen them. Maybe you left them somewhere along your journey."

"No. I distinctly remember wearing them once or twice after I came home, but that's neither here nor there. If anyone comes for me, tell them I won't be long," she offered before heading back outside. She walked briskly, with only a mild aching in her foot now. She arrived at the general store, where several elderly male patrons were gathered around the cookstove, smoking pipes and discussing the minister's departure earlier.

With her reticule in hand, she approached the display case in the rear of the shop. Just as she had remembered, a pair of chamber slippers was nestled next to a pair of shiny black satin dancing slippers and sundry female notions. When Wesley Sweet finally responded to the bell that announced her arrival and emerged from the back storeroom, he acknowledged her with a smile.

"Good mornin', Widow Cade. Haven't seen you in here since you got back." He eyed the case and grinned. "What'll it be today? Got your eyes on those dancing slippers?"

She chuckled. "Not exactly. It seems I've misplaced my chamber slippers." She pointed to the pale blue slippers. "I wonder if I might see those?"

He removed them from the case and set them on top. "Straight from Philadelphia. Soft as a lamb's ear and lined with wool, too. You want to try them on? I'll get a chair—"

"That won't be necessary," she insisted. After slipping her hand inside and gauging that they would fit well enough, she nodded. "They're fine. How much do they cost?"

The young man hesitated. He was tall and finely built, with taut muscles, and she could almost see his mind at work, carefully calculating his profits. "One dollar."

She raised a brow. "That's a bit steep, isn't it?"

He pursed his lips. "Eighty cents. That's the best I can do."

She sighed. "Eighty cents. Check the books, will you? I think I have enough on account to cover them," she suggested, although she was certain she had much more than that. Before she had left to follow Victoria, she had sent over a reward she had received, a barrel of flour and a large crock of butter, to be put on her account, and she had not made any purchases since then.

He turned and went directly to his desk. When he returned, he confirmed her thoughts. "You have two dollars on account. Minus the slippers, that would leave you with one dollar and twenty cents. Would you like me to wrap up the slippers for you?"

"I would."

"Anything else today?" He glanced down at the case again. "We just got a shipment of fine Belgian lace and some hair combs. Just in time, with Uncle Thomas's shindig next week," he suggested. "Guess you heard about that."

"Indeed," she murmured, wondering what his mother, Thomas's sister, would say when she heard about the betrothal. "Just the slippers for today."

While he took the slippers to wrap them, she heard the bell tinkle again. She turned and saw Rosalind enter the store. She walked directly toward Martha, but her troubled expression did not raise any hopes that Webster Cabbot had dropped the charges against Burton Andrews.

"I wonder if we might talk. Privately," she whispered.

Martha took her package and nodded toward the door. "I was just leaving." Curious as well as concerned, she followed Rosalind outside.

Instead of pausing to explain, Rosalind simply said, "Please. Come home with me. I can't discuss this here, where someone might overhear us."

Fearful that Rosalind had somehow learned about the discovery of the watch and Martha's role in returning it to Webster Cabbot, however impossible that might be, Martha did not relish explaining what she had done or why, or offering Rosalind any rationale for not coming to her at once so she could clear her husband. Martha was still confident she had done the right thing by going to Cabbot directly. Whether or not he would reward that confidence was still an issue that had Martha praying about it daily.

Once they reached Dr. McMillan's house, Rosalind ushered Martha into the kitchen and bolted the front door closed. "It's Dr. McMillan. He's very ill," she gushed in a whisper.

Martha was so surprised she could scarcely find her own voice. "Dr. McMillan? Ill? What's wrong?"

"I don't know. He's been upstairs for several days now. He won't come out of his bedchamber, not even to eat. I leave his trays at his door with clear broth and tea, just as he asked, but he barely touches them. Beyond emptying his chamber pot, I just don't know what else I can do for him. I thought maybe you could . . . well, maybe you can talk to him. Find out what's wrong and make sure he's all right."

Relief that she had misjudged the purpose for Rosalind's invitation to talk was short-lived. "Does he know you came for me?"

Rosalind's eyes widened. "No."

"I don't normally treat men. It's not entirely proper," Martha ventured.

"But there is no one else," Rosalind argued. "I'm very worried about him. He wouldn't even answer my knock this morning, and he hasn't touched his tray and he could be very ill. If not, I know he'll be upset with me for fetching you, especially if this isn't something serious, but what else could I do? I can't just let him lay in there, not knowing for sure—"

"I'll try," Martha offered. She was as concerned about Rosalind's frazzled state as she was about Dr. McMillan, although she was reluctant to step over the boundary that separated her calling from that of the physician. She removed her outerwear and laid everything on a chair next to the table, along with her package. "Where's his bedchamber?"

"At the top of the stairs. The room is all the way at the front of the house."

"At the very least, I'll see if he will take some tea. Can you heat some fresh water?"

"Right away. Is there anything else?"

"No. I'll have to see him first." Martha left the kitchen and mounted the stairs. She would not be able to explain away her visit as just a neighborly call, not if she appeared at his bedchamber door, and there was little she could do to protect Rosalind. Right or wrong, Rosalind had every reason to be concerned, a point Martha intended to stress to the doctor if he became upset with either one of them.

When she reached the door to his bedchamber, she took a deep breath, knocked on his door, and called his name.

No response.

She tried again. Harder. Louder.

Still, no response.

Growing more alarmed with every thud of her heartbeat, she turned the knob and eased the door open. The room was too dark to see much of anything beyond the muted shadows of the figure abed. The distinctive scent of illness was strong, but it was the sound of his labored breathing that shoved aside her reticence and pulled her into the room.

"Dr. McMillan? It's Martha Cade," she offered as she entered.

He groaned. "I'm sick. I can't . . . can't help you. Not . . . today."

"I'm here to help you," she countered, and tied back the drapes covering both the front and side windows. Daylight flooded the sparsely furnished room. There was little furniture beyond the bed, a single dresser, and a chair.

The young doctor covered his eyes and burrowed his face against his pillow before she had a chance to really see him. "Go away. I'm a doctor. I can treat myself. I don't need a . . . a *midwife*," he spat. His vehement protest set off a coughing spell that racked his body.

She approached the bed and put her hand on his shoulder. "Sometimes it helps to get a second opinion. Just tell me what's wrong. Maybe I can help."

When he dropped his arm away from his face and turned toward her, she caught her breath and held it. Of all the illnesses she might have envisioned, she would never in the space of two lifetimes have suspected this. When she leaned closer, he pulled back against his pillow.

"Take a good long look, if you must," he murmured. "Then leave me in peace."

Chapter
TWENTY-NINE

Martha leaned closer, but even with a clearer view, her original diagnosis stood firm. A swarm of angry red blisters covered his entire face as well as his hands. His eyes were swollen shut, and even his eyelids bore the telltale blisters. Some were quite fresh; others had cracked open and dried into crusty scabs.

Though she had treated few cases like this in adults, she had no doubt about the illness that was ravaging his body. "You have the chicken pox," she exclaimed.

"I do *not*," he argued. "I had them as a child. This is . . . this is just a severe case of impetigo. Nothing more. Now, if you'll just leave . . ." He wheezed again and again, unable to argue further.

"You may or may not have had the chicken pox as a child, but you certainly have them now. How long have you been coughing and wheezing like that?" she asked, fearful he had developed lung congestion as a complication.

"Since yesterday. It's nothing serious," he assured her. "Now, if you'd be kind enough to get out of my chamber—"

"What medications are you taking?"

He turned away and presented her with his back before scratching at his arms. "They're on the dresser, not that it's any of your concern."

She checked the three bottles on the dresser. She could read the names of each medication, but she had not heard of any of them before and had no idea whether or not they would be effective against chicken pox. She did, however, know precisely what herbs would help to relieve the itching and soothe his skin, although there was no herb to ease the sting in his pride.

Of all the things for a young doctor trying to establish himself in a new community as a competent physician to contract, chicken pox was probably the worst. It was a miserable childhood disease that was far more serious in adults and quite embarrassing for a man to endure.

"What about the congestion in your lungs?" she asked.

He sighed. "Too tired. Later," he murmured, and drifted off to sleep.

She laid her hand on his brow. His forehead was hot. Too hot. "Later may be too late," she whispered, and tiptoed out of the room.

Downstairs, she met Rosalind's worried look with a troubled look of her own. "He has the chicken pox. A right good case, too. As uncomfortable as he is right now, that's not my major concern. He's developed complications. His lungs are very congested, and his fever is raging. We need to make it easier for him to breathe, so we'll need lots of water. Both hot and cold. I need to make poultices to help ease the itching, too, which means I need to get several herbs from home."

"Will he . . . will he be all right?"

Martha donned her cape and bonnet and grabbed her package from the general store. "I expect he'll recover quite well, but he'll need lots of care for the next few days. I'll tell Lydia I've been called to a patient, but that's all. We'd do well to keep this to ourselves. Once

Dr. McMillan recovers, he'll forgive us both, eventually, but not if we breathe a word of this to anyone."

Rosalind's eyes widened, and she instinctively scratched at her arm. "It's contagious. I'm going to get the pox!"

Martha frowned. "It's unusual to get them twice. You've had them before as a child, I'm sure."

To her amazement, Rosalind shook her head. "No, I never did. My brothers all did, but . . . oh, no," she whimpered. She dropped into a chair and held her head with her hands. "Not the chicken pox. I can't. It's too . . . too . . ."

"Embarrassing?" Martha prompted.

Rosalind nodded.

"Then perhaps you can understand why Dr. McMillan was loath to diagnose chicken pox on himself or to let you see him. You'd recognize the blisters at once. There's still a good chance you won't contract the disease, but little we can do about it now. Get the water started. Find some cloth in his office I can use for poultices when you're done. Now, Rosalind. We've got no time for self-pity. He needs both of us," she urged in a stern voice when the woman seemed to be ignoring everything Martha had to say.

Rosalind wiped her face with her hands and rose from her chair. "Of course. I'm sorry."

Once Rosalind was bustling around the kitchen, Martha hurried out the door and toward home. If she truly meant to keep the nature of the doctor's illness and her intervention secret, she would have to stay at his home until he was well on his way to recovery so no one would see her coming and going. While she walked, she made a mental list of the herbs she would need and the clothing she would have to pack. She did not want to ask Lydia and James to watch Bird again, so he would simply have to come along, too.

Why the good Lord had put her in this awkward position was a mystery—a gift she did not accept gracefully. The young doctor was not her responsibility. He was her competitor, a threat to her place in the community, yet time and time again, she seemed destined to be almost his mentor, guiding him along his journey to becoming a competent, experienced physician.

Now she actually had to step beyond the well-recognized boundaries separating her work from that of any doctor, which was sure to cause gossip if anyone learned she was treating a grown man. Add to this mix of trouble one very reluctant patient who had little respect for her or faith in her abilities, and she had one big problem on her hands.

"Why me?" she grumbled as she entered her room. In her heart, the question echoed again and again, but no answer came whispering through her mind. Only the question, again and again.

Why me?

Late Friday night, Martha kept vigil at the doctor's bedside. Low burning embers in the hearth provided light, gentle enough to not disturb her patient's sleep yet strong enough for her to observe him.

Had she been tending one of her usual patients, either a woman or a child, she would have been wearing her nightdress and robe, along with her new blue chamber slippers. For propriety's sake, she still wore her day dress, but she could not resist wearing her chamber slippers anyway.

The room carried the heavy scent of the Labrador tea she had used as a poultice on his trunk and limbs to relieve the itching. The doctor had been asleep for several hours now, thanks to several doses of catnip tea, which also helped to alleviate the congestion in his lungs. His fever had spiked in late afternoon, but the cool poultices had helped to bring it down again.

All in all, she was quite satisfied. Rosalind had proven her worth as a capable and compassionate assistant, which only made Martha feel worse for harboring her secret about the watch. Her treatments had begun to take effect, just as she had hoped. The doctor had been too sick to offer much physical resistance to her role as his healer, but he was not too ill to be rather vocal in his mockery of her methods.

Dr. McMillan was hands down her most ornery patient, even considering all the children she had treated over the years. Not for the first time in her years as a healer, she was quite eager to leave the treatment of men to doctors.

Bone weary, she still kept propriety in mind and sagged against the back of the chair instead of crawling into the cot Rosalind had insisted on bringing into the room. She folded her hands on her lap and sighed. Worry for Victoria weighed most heavily on her heart at night while the rest of the world was sleeping.

Nearly five months had passed now, with not a single letter to tell her where Victoria had gone or when she might be coming home. Was she actually performing onstage with that theater troupe? The very thought made Martha shiver. More likely, Victoria had taken up her pen, but she had never expressed any interest in writing plays. Was she in London, or had she gone to Charleston? Did she lay awake at night thinking of home, or was she too enamored with her new-found freedom to care one whit about the mother she had left behind?

Why me?

The question loomed in Martha's mind again.

"Why me?" she murmured. "Why me?"

And in the stillness of the night, in the depths of her pain, in the hollow of her heart, she searched, but found no answer.

"W-water. Please."

Startled out of her reverie, she turned toward her patient.

Dr. McMillan moistened his cracked lips and looked at her through slits of blistered flesh. "Please."

She rose, went to the dresser, poured a glass of cooled catnip tea, and returned to him. She helped him to lift up his head and offered him the drink. He barely took more than a few awkward sips before he closed his eyes, and she let his head sink back against his pillow.

"Feeling any better?" she asked as she patted his chin dry with a fresh cloth.

"I feel . . . like a mummy," he responded.

She chuckled. "As a matter of fact, you do resemble one. The poultices should help with the itching, though."

He let out a long breath. "Do I taste mint?"

"That's the catnip tea."

He cracked open one eye. "Did you say catnip?"

She grinned. "Grandmother Poore always swore by it. Cures all kinds of ailments like fever, lung congestion, and coughs, just to name a few you just happen to have."

He slammed his eye shut. "Dare I ask what that . . . that smell is coming from the poultices? No, never mind. Don't tell me. I don't want to know. I suppose you find all this rather amusing, don't you?"

She cocked her head. Pride stiffened her backbone. "Illness is never amusing."

He chuckled, coughed a bit, and sighed. "Actually, I find this all highly amusing," he murmured.

She glared at him and huffed. "Pray tell me! Is it because you're at the complete mercy of a lowly midwife? Or is it entertaining for you to have the woman you believe to be so ignorant and incompetent as the person helping you now? In either case, I should leave you to suffer your own incompetence! Impetigo, indeed! Where did you receive your training?"

He laughed again. "So you have a temper, too," he teased, and scratched at his face.

She knocked his hand away. "Temper enough. Especially when my patient mocks me. I have a good mind to go to meeting on Sunday and ask the entire congregation to pray for the good Dr. McMillan, who will no doubt bear any number of scars because he won't stop picking at his scabs."

"They itch!" he whined.

"They're supposed to itch. They're chicken pox, you fool. Now, lie still and don't scratch at your face again. I can make another poultice for your face. That should help, which is what I tried to do earlier, when you rejected the idea."

He cracked one eye open again. "I have medicine on the dresser you seem to enjoy ignoring. I can barely breathe as it is, and I'm afraid you'll suffocate me if you cover my face with a poultice."

"Don't tempt me," she snapped. "Either let me use the poultice or suffer in silence."

He opened the other eye and stared at her.

She stared back.

Stalemate.

He twitched one cheek, then the other. He balled both hands into fists and stiffened his arms.

"Suffering enough yet?" she taunted.

He squared his jaw. "Get the poultice before I tear the skin off my face," he gritted through clenched teeth.

She accepted his surrender, grinned, and prepared several narrow strips of cloth lined with Labrador tea leaves. Gently, she arranged the poultices across his brow and eyelids and the bridge of his nose, as well as his cheeks. "Try not to move," she cautioned.

He chortled. "Move? I'm trussed up like a Christmas goose."

"Precisely. Kindly remember that before you whine and complain about my treatment. I haven't abandoned a patient. Ever. But there's always a first time, and you're in no position to stop me if I choose to leave you here."

"You don't have to be so grumpy," he countered. "I'm sick. I have an excuse, but you're supposed to be compassionate and caring and gentle and—"

"And I'm not?" she asked, highly insulted that he did not recognize she had had almost as little sleep as he had.

He yawned. "Indeed you are. In fact, you're not at all what I expected. That's what I find so amusing—my ability to be wrong as often as I am," he murmured, and drifted off to sleep, leaving her with only her conscience to measure the full impact of his words.

Chapter
THIRTY

By Tuesday morning, the doctor was remarkably improved, although he would not be able to resume his practice for several weeks. "I'll stay until nightfall, then I'll be going home," she informed him.

He nodded. "I think I slept through most of Sunday and yesterday. Did you attend meeting?"

She fluffed the pillows behind his back and set his breakfast tray in front of him. "No. I stayed here with you, listening to an endless litany of arguments why my treatments reminded you of ancient remedies long abandoned by your learned teachers and colleagues at the university."

His brows raised in surprise before he tackled the bowl of steaming oatmeal instead of responding to her complaint. "Funny. I expected you to go to meeting, but then nothing has been very normal since I took ill. I actually thought I heard a bird singing every morning, which is impossible with winter breathing down our necks. Must have been the fever," he suggested between spoonfuls.

"That was Bird. He's a . . . a patient of sorts. I brought him with me."

He swallowed a mouthful of oatmeal. "You have a bird for a patient? Here?"

She sat down on the chair and nibbled at a piece of toast she took off his tray. "I have him in the next chamber. He was a rather unusual reward I received when I first returned from my long journey."

He dropped his gaze. "Reward? I'm ashamed to admit I haven't given your reward any thought. I'm not certain what fee you charge, but whatever it is, I'll settle with you as soon as I get back on my feet."

An idea popped into her head, and she latched onto it before it burst into nothingness. "I do have a fee in mind. Several, in fact. First, Doc Beyer used to let me take some wild hydrangea and some buttonbush from the front walk. I'd like you to extend the same courtesy. Second, well . . . I'd better just show you."

She hurried to the chamber she had used since her arrival, returned with the cage, and set it onto the seat of her chair.

Dr. McMillan tried another spoonful of oatmeal, apparently uninterested.

When she cleared her throat, he looked up at her, and she pointed to Bird. "See his wing? Apparently, it healed wrong after being broken. I don't know anything about setting broken bones and even less about birds and their wings. Do you think there's something you could do to help him? I hate to think he'll spend the rest of his life in a cage. If you could fix his wing, I could set him free in the spring."

He choked down his oatmeal and stared at her. "You're serious? You want me to treat your . . . your bird as payment of your reward?"

"If you would, yes," she responded.

He laid down his spoon and shook his head. "I don't believe this. You're actually serious. You really do want me to treat your bird! I'm a doctor, not a veterinarian," he argued. "I treat people!"

Rosalind burst into the room before Martha could properly respond. "I'm sorry. I know you're not treating patients, Doctor, but Billy Frankel is downstairs with his father. The boy's arm is broken. I didn't know where to send them."

The doctor sat up straighter. "You're sure it's broken? It's not merely a bad sprain?"

She shook her head. "It's broken. I could see that with my own eyes, even though the skin isn't broken. What do you want me to tell them? The poor boy's in a great deal of pain. I don't think taking him all the way to Clarion is a good idea."

"Where is the break? What part of his arm?"

She pointed to her forearm, halfway between her wrist and her elbow. "Here."

Dr. McMillan lowered his gaze for a moment. When he finally lifted his eyes, he sought Martha's gaze and held it. "Tell Mr. Frankel I'm far too weak with my illness to set the boy's arm but that Widow Cade will be able to help him."

Martha practically leaped out of her chair. "I'm a midwife, not a doctor. I deliver babies and treat minor ailments. I haven't a clue about how to set a broken bone."

"You're reasonably intelligent and strong, but more importantly, you have a steady hand and a gentle touch. I'll tell you exactly what to do. It's not really that complicated when it's a simple break, which it is, from what I've been told. If it's not, whatever you do will be better than letting the bone heal as it is so the boy's arm is as useless to him as that bird's wing."

He looked directly at Rosalind and ordered her downstairs. "Get the treatment room ready. You know what I usually use. Set out a splint, wrappings, and a suitable piece of cloth for a sling."

Rosalind quickly disappeared, leaving Martha alone to argue her case against this ridiculous idea. Before she could proffer a single objection, the young doctor grabbed her arm. "Roll up your sleeve.

I'll show you what to do and how to do it. Watch closely and don't argue with me. There's a little boy downstairs who needs you."

She could scarcely breathe. Her heart galloped in her chest. "You're serious? You really want me to set his arm?"

He tightened his hold. "You're the boy's only hope."

She hesitated, torn between the fear that she might fail and the even greater fear that she might succeed, and rolled up her sleeve. "Show me what to do. While you're at it, you might want to think about how I'm going to explain my presence here."

He shrugged his shoulders. "Tell them what you may. I'll deal with whatever you decide. The boy's more important right now than my pride."

His words called a truce to the battle they had waged between them. For better or worse, she could no longer continue to fear losing her patients to a man who would put his patient before his own reputation. Though they would invariably lock horns over the proper care to be given to teeming women or over appropriate interventions during labor and delivery, he had already proven his willingness to accept her as a healer, competent enough in her own right to stand in his stead for the welfare of his patient.

She accepted the lesson as a most unexpected gift, one she would sincerely have regretted had she rejected His call to care for the young doctor, who would one day be a very fine physician for the people of Trinity.

"You're a brave lad, Billy Frankel," Martha crooned. She positioned the sling and slid his splinted arm in place. She looked up at his father, Theodore, and smiled, even though her heart was still racing and her body was drenched in sweat. "Dr. McMillan would like to see him in a few weeks. Make sure you tell Anne to steep the boneset until it's quite strong and give the boy some to help alleviate the pain."

"We're obliged to you for helpin'."

"I'm just glad I was here visiting Rosalind when you arrived." She prayed her little lie would be forgiven.

"How long do you think the doctor will be recuperating?"

She moistened her lips. "Another ten days at most. Lung congestion is always serious, especially with the cold weather setting in. He's got to rebuild his strength before he travels about to call on his patients," she said.

While only partially true, her little lies were well intentioned and close enough to the truth to not be judged as sinful. She hoped. Besides, it would serve no purpose to put the young doctor at the center of a round of jokes bound to undermine his credibility because he had had the misfortune to contract a childhood disease.

Theodore shifted from one foot to the other, and a blush colored his cheeks. "About the fee . . . I don't have hard coin, but I slaughtered a few hogs some weeks back and have some fine hams in the smokehouse . . . if you think . . . that is . . ."

"That would be fine," she agreed, even though she was not quite certain of the fee involved.

He brightened. "You want me to deliver the hams here or at the tavern?"

"Bring Dr. McMillan one right here when you bring Billy back. It's his office. I used his supplies. And he'll be checking Billy until that arm heals," she explained when Theodore seemed a bit surprised.

"Yes, ma'am. Let's go, son. Your mama is home worryin' herself about you."

"Easy," Martha cautioned as the boy scampered off the table. She ushered them to the door with no small measure of relief. Once they departed, she closed the door, sagged against it, and offered a silent prayer of gratitude that He had guided her through the entire ordeal.

Rosalind entered the kitchen, took one look at Martha, and went right to the stove. "You look like you need some tea."

Martha wiped her brow and noticed that her hand was still trembling. "Half a pot, at least."

Rosalind put some water on to boil, set two mugs on the table, and measured out tea for the pot. "I gather you managed to set Billy's arm?"

Martha nodded. "Dr. McMillan was right. It's not a complicated procedure, but it's not something I'd care to do again."

Rosalind chuckled. "To be honest, I think that's how he feels when he's called to deliver a baby. That night with Adelaide? He was very nervous. When you arrived, I think he was actually relieved."

"Really?" Martha joined Rosalind at the table while they waited for the water to come to a boil. "He seemed perturbed, even hostile. You weren't very happy to see me, either, as I recall," she ventured.

Rosalind bowed her head. "I'm ashamed to admit I wasn't. I apologize. I wasn't very cordial at the cemetery, either," she murmured.

"You've been having a difficult time. We all know that," Martha suggested to ease her friend's distress.

"That's no excuse," she countered. When she looked up at Martha again, tears misted her eyes. "I should have had more faith in Burton, more faith in my friends . . . more *faith*." Her bottom lip trembled. "I've made a proper mess of things. Now . . . now I'm not sure what to do or say. . . ."

"Now?" Martha repeated. Her pulse began to race.

Rosalind dabbed at her eyes with the hem of her apron. "Sheriff Myer came by early this morning. Webster's dropped the charges against Burton. He claims he found the watch lodged between the floorboards. It must have fallen off that peg on the wall in his shop. It was all a mistake," she whispered.

Martha did not have to feign surprise, although it was Cabbot's timing, not his actions, that widened her eyes. "That's wonderful news! So wonderful, I'd expect you to be grinning from ear to ear instead of weeping."

Rosalind's smile was tepid. "I'm happy, and I'm relieved, of course, and I know Burton will be, too, when I write to him, but . . . but . . ." Her hands shook as she twisted the corner of her apron. "I don't think he'll will be very proud of how I behaved while he was gone. If I'm not proud of myself, why should he be? I acted like he was guilty and shut myself off from everyone, letting my loneliness and my shame turn me into a bitter, angry woman."

Martha moistened her lips. "Quite true. You did."

Rosalind flinched, but Martha smiled and covered her friend's hands with one of her own. "There's not a woman in Trinity who wouldn't admit she might have done the same. Not if she's honest with herself. But Burton should share the burden of this awful experience, too. He ran off instead of staying to defend himself. He left you to do that for him, and I suspect some of your anger is directed at him. Rightfully so."

"Still," she continued, "right prevailed in the end. For that, you should both be grateful. I'm sure it wasn't easy for Webster to admit his mistake. No one, not Burton, not even Webster, will find it easy to put this matter aside easily, but you can and you must."

Rosalind wrapped her hands around Martha's. "I'm not as strong as you are. People will be gossiping again, asking questions about what happened or where Burton has gone. I won't know what to say."

Martha chuckled. "You're stronger than you think. Just hold your head high and smile if anyone asks you details that are none of their concern. It might help to see the past few months, as difficult as they've been, as a gift. An opportunity to test your faith in God as well as your husband and your friends."

Rosalind's eyes widened and filled with new tears. "But I failed them all," she gushed. "I failed everyone, especially God. I stopped going to meeting. I couldn't even pray anymore without becoming angrier. Why would God reward me with Burton's vindication? Why did I deserve this . . . this miracle?"

"Because He loves you. Because He wanted to give you another opportunity to see that He loves you even when you turn from Him, so that in the future, when your faith is tested again, you will remember what happened this time and turn to Him, not away from Him. Pray for forgiveness, Rosalind, but know He has forgiven you already and welcomes you back into His arms because you are His creation. If you do, finding peace with your husband and your friends will come to you as well."

Rosalind dropped her gaze. "I'm not sure I can do that. I'm too ashamed."

"Would you prefer to spend the rest of your life as unhappy as you've been the past few months?"

"No, but—"

"Pray, Rosalind. He'll listen. We'll pray together," she suggested. "Between the two of us, we'll find the right words. When we do, perhaps you might be able to help me ask Him for some help, too."

Rosalind sniffled. "For you? Or for Victoria?"

"Both of us. For starters," she responded. "Somehow, I must find the words to ask for forgiveness for myself for not having faith enough that He would help me keep my calling and make room for Dr. McMillan, too," she whispered. "It took a simple case of chicken pox and a little boy with a broken arm to remind me how weak my own faith has become," she admitted.

When the bell at Dr. McMillan's bedside starting ringing again, she chuckled. "Lord, spare me from sick men! I'd rather deliver ten babes before I took another man for a patient. Pour the tea," she suggested as she rose from her seat. "Let me see what he wants now, then we'll spend some time together. Just remind me to add a prayer that Dr. McMillan lives long enough and with good health to spare me from ever treating him again."

Chapter
THIRTY-ONE

B y late Saturday afternoon, only hours before the gala was to begin, Martha admitted defeat.

Much to her chagrin, she had no reprieve. Not a single valid excuse
to offer that would spare her the ordeal of attending the gala tonight.
Not that rumors of Thomas's impending betrothal bothered her. Not
a bit.

"Drat!" she exclaimed. She set aside the daybook for Victoria, unable to concentrate enough to make another entry today. She was all
alone in her room. Not even Bird was there to listen if she spoke
aloud. He was staying with Dr. McMillan. Much to her surprise, the
doctor had taken an interest in figuring out a way to fix Bird's wing
and insisted on keeping the bird with him until he did.

"Thomas Dillon can marry whomever he likes," she grumbled, and laid her russet gown on the table to press out the wrinkles. She put the iron on the stove to heat and slipped again on her way back to the table. The wool socks she wore kept her feet warm, but they were a poor and apparently dangerous substitute for her new chamber slippers, which she had forgotten and left behind at Dr. McMillan's in her haste to return home.

She made another mental note to stop at his house after meeting tomorrow to collect her slippers and walked more slowly in her stockinged feet to keep from taking a nasty spill.

The rumor about Thomas's announcement tonight had overshadowed the evening's original purpose, to allow Eleanor to see all her friends again. As the day approached, Martha had had ample opportunity to examine her feelings for Thomas. Even now, she remained confused. She had loved him once before. Did she love him now?

"Certainly not," she grumbled as she tested the iron and proceeded to attack the bodice of the gown first. Whether she had any affection for him, beyond friendship, was beyond the point. As his friend, she worried that he was making a terrible mistake by asking Samantha to be his wife.

The girl was beautiful enough to turn any man's head, but she was also younger than his own daughter! Martha also knew Samantha and her mother well enough to know the twit would not have given Thomas a second look if he had been a yeoman farmer like Alexander Pratt, who had been in love with Samantha since childhood but had found his plea for courtship soundly rejected not once but three times. She had also spurned the interest of Matthew Lansdown, a middle-aged, well-heeled shopkeeper in Sunrise who visited his sister in Trinity each month.

Lansdown had money but no status. No power in his community. As mayor and heir to the Dillon fortune, Thomas Dillon had everything Samantha apparently found attractive, along with roguish good looks. Whether she loved Thomas was altogether possible, but not likely. Given the attention of someone wealthier and more powerful, Samantha would no doubt leave Thomas standing alone to pledge his vows.

Martha moved the iron too quickly and pressed a wrinkle into the fabric. She scowled. Thomas was going to make an utter fool of himself tonight. From all accounts in tavern gossip, he had been acting like a lovesick schoolboy. Unless Martha was wrong, he was going to saddle himself with a wife who was going to make his life utterly and completely miserable in the long run, but probably very satisfying in the short.

Witnessing his announcement tonight with a happy smile would only make it harder later, when she might have to tell him why she had not warned him he was making one of the biggest mistakes of his life.

Annoyed that he could be so blind and so foolish, she pressed the wrinkles out of the gown's skirts with a vengeance. She dressed slowly, still half hoping someone would call for her help. Babies usually picked the most inopportune times to enter the world. Why not tonight? Why not now?

She checked her appearance in the mirror, donned her outerwear, and pasted a smile on her face. When she opened the door to leave, Samuel rushed in past her and nearly knocked her off balance.

Panting, he held his side with one hand and his forehead with the other. Blood trickled between his fingers and down the bridge of his nose.

"Get your bag. Quick!" he ordered.

"Mercy, Samuel! What did you do to yourself?"

"I lost an argument with a tree branch. Don't fuss with me," he argued when she tried to pry his fingers away from the wound. "Will's at my cabin. He's bad off, far as I could tell. I didn't want to move him. Get your bag of simples! You need to see him. Now."

She handed him a clean cloth to press against his forehead and grabbed her bag. "What's he doing back here? How did he get here?"

He shrugged his shoulders. "He's ramblin' 'bout my treasures and other nonsense. I couldn't get much outta him that made any sense.

Maybe you can," he suggested. He tugged something out of his pocket and handed it to her. "Found this in his pocket."

She recognized one of her old bedroom slippers despite the fact that it was covered with dirt and leaves. A chill raced down her spine, but she had no time to ponder why or how Will had one of her slippers. "Hold that cloth tight against your forehead and take my arm," she ordered.

Of all the reprieves she might have gotten, this one probably inspired the most guilt. "Tell me what you could see was wrong with him while we walk."

When Martha entered Samuel's cabin, she found Will lying on a makeshift mattress of old blankets on the floor in front of the Franklin stove. The boy was completely oblivious to their arrival and in far worse shape than she had hoped.

She tugged off her bonnet and cape and studied him while Samuel found his way to his chair and plopped down. The boy had tossed off the blanket on top of him, so she could see his tattered and torn clothes. His face was bruised and badly scratched, as if he had battled his way through a forest of thorned thickets. His hands were covered with caked mud. His knees, scraped and bleeding, were visible through the rips in his trousers.

The skin on his forehead was cold and clammy to the touch. His breathing was labored and irregular and far too soft. "Will? It's Widow Cade. Don't fret. I'm here with you now, too."

His eyelids fluttered briefly, then stilled. She ran her hands over his lean body. She detected no broken bones, but she suspected he was bruised from head to toe. She looked up at Samuel. "Add more wood to the stove. He's still very cold, and he's in shock. I'll need more blankets, too. Once I get him warm, I can undress him and wash him up. For now, I can tackle his face and hands."

While Samuel worked to fulfill her requests, she set water on to heat. "I'll need some clean cloths and some soap."

Samuel pointed behind her. "In the bottom of the cupboard."

She secured the cloth and soap. While she waited for the water to heat, she removed Will's wet shoes and socks and rubbed his feet until they were no longer blue. She took the blankets from Samuel and tucked them around the boy until only his face was visible.

Still frighteningly still and silent, he offered no resistance. When the water was hot, she bathed his face as gently as she could and still work away the crusted filth. He groaned several times, but never regained full consciousness.

When she finished, her horror at his condition deepened. Dark bruises beneath each of his eyes, as well as one on his left temple, left no doubt the boy had been beaten. Recently, judging by the dark purple and red coloration of the bruises.

Anger churned in her stomach, but her hands were steady as she prepared several poultices for his face. "He's been beaten, Samuel," she murmured. "These bruises aren't from a fall or from running through the woods to get here."

Samuel scowled. "I feared as much. Couldn't see well enough to be sure."

She washed the boy's hands, one at a time, and placed them back under the blanket. "His knuckles are scraped raw."

"No doubt the lad tried to protect himself. He's a good scrapper for his size. Musta ganged up on him."

The image of the other boys attacking Will made her shiver with outrage. "But why? Why would the other boys attack him? And why wouldn't Reverend Hampton stop them?"

Samuel shook his head. "We're gonna have to wait for Will to give us those answers." He slapped his knee. "If I had two good eyes, I'd ride straight to Denville and get those answers for myself. I knew somethin' was wrong! I shudda listened to my gut. I shudda listened to you and let the boy stay here with me."

"There's nothing either one of us could have known that would have predicted this would happen," she assured him. Her words, however, rang hollow, and she wished she had forced the issue with Samuel and convinced Reverend Hampton to let Will remain behind.

"Mama? Mama? Help me, Mama!" Will thrashed about and whimpered while tugging at the poultices on his face.

"Sh-h-h," Martha crooned. "You're safe now, Will. Samuel is here with me. He'll protect you, too."

Instead of being a comfort, her words only made the boy more agitated. "No. Can't stay. Gotta go. Can't stay," he pleaded. He opened his eyes as wide as the swollen flesh would allow. "I tried to stop them. I tried," he cried. "They're comin'. They're all comin' back here!"

"Who's coming back, Will? Who do you think is going to hurt you?"

He turned his head and faced the fire as sobs racked his entire body. She stroked his back until he quieted. "All of 'em. They're gonna come back." He yawned and curled into a ball. "Fire. Big fire," he whispered, and fell asleep.

Confused, she looked up at Samuel. "Did he say 'fire'?"

"That's what I thought I heard. Don't make no sense to me. The boy's probably outta his head. He don't know what he's sayin'."

She chewed on her lower lip. "I suppose. Earlier, you said he kept rambling about your treasures. What exactly did he say?"

"Not much. He's always been fascinated by 'em. You know that."

"Yes, I remember." In fact, Will had been fascinated by everything and anything connected to Samuel. Olympia had even mentioned how Will had been teaching knots he had learned to some of the other boys, which meant Will had probably talked about the treasured mementos Samuel had accumulated during his years at sea, too. Try as she might, she could not connect those treasures to Will's injuries or a fire of some sort, and concentrated, instead, on washing the rest of his body while he slept.

By the time she finished, his clothes were piled up, ready to be discarded in the trash pit. He was sleeping comfortably now, snug in a cocoon of blankets. "Let's see to that gash on your forehead," she told Samuel.

He snorted. "I've had worse. Dozens of times. It'll heal."

"I'm sure you did and it will, but I'd feel better if you'd let me take a look and put something on it."

"I know you were just born to meddle. Can't help it. Comes with bein' female," he complained.

"And you're an incurable curmudgeon," she teased. She rose from Will's side and lifted Samuel's hand away from the cloth he held to his forehead. When she tried to remove the cloth, dried blood held it fast. "Let me soak it a little," she suggested.

He ripped the cloth away before she could stop him and opened up the gash again. Fresh blood oozed to the top of his right brow. "That helped," she quipped. "You've opened the wound again."

"Best way to clean it out," he argued.

She cocked a brow. "According to whom?"

"Just do what you're gonna do and leave me in peace."

"That's exactly what I had in mind," she snapped as she inspected the wound. From the bruising around the small gash, she suspected he had smacked headlong into a fair-sized branch. "You probably knocked the tree down," she remarked as she washed his forehead.

"Got a right mind to do just that. Tomorrow. If I can find the danged thing again."

She chuckled, made a poultice, and tied a strip of cotton around his head to hold the bandage in place. "That should do it. I'll change it again in the morning."

"What about Will?" he asked.

She hesitated. Taking him outside tonight in the cold might not be wise, but tomorrow would hardly be better. With his poor vision, Samuel would not be up to caring for the boy, so she had little choice but to take the boy home with her. "If you could carry him, I'd like to take him back to the tavern. That way, if I get called away, Lydia can keep an eye on him for me. Once he's feeling better, I'm sure he'd want to be here with you," she added.

Samuel clenched his fists. "You won't send him back to Reverend Hampton?"

"No. Not until I find out from Will exactly what happened. I doubt Reverend Hampton knows what the other boys did. Even so, he won't be bringing them all back to Trinity for another few weeks. Will can use the time to fully mend."

Samuel rose from his seat. "I'll talk to Reverend Hampton first before you give Will back to him. Pack your bag. I'll get the boy ready."

Within moments, Will was cradled in Samuel's arms, still asleep and unaware he was being moved. Martha tugged the blankets tighter around his bare feet and tucked the end of the blanket between his knees and the crook of Samuel's arm. As they approached the door, Martha heard an ominous sound that raised the hackles on the back of her neck. She paused, heard it again, and grabbed a firmer hold on Samuel's arm.

"Did you hear it, too?" he asked.

She swallowed hard. "I heard it. We'd better hurry."

She opened the door, saw the brilliant orange glow that lit the night sky, heard that awful sound again, and felt her entire body go numb. "It's the fire bell," she croaked, unable to stem the rising fear that she also knew exactly which building in Trinity was on fire.

THIRTY-TWO

Martha stood in the doorway of Samuel's cabin, transfixed by fear as an image of more horrendous proportions formed in her mind. The bits and pieces of Will's ramblings fell into place next to the images of all of her interactions with Reverend Hampton.

Her mind raced back and forth through the recent past and collected snippets of her impressions of Reverend Hampton and his proclaimed intentions to minister to a motley crew of orphaned street urchins.

Boys. Treasure. Thefts. Fire. Was Reverend Hampton truly a minister? Or a Pied Piper, luring lost children into his lair, where he had transformed them into a ring of thieves? Was the fire an accident? Or a diversion?

She trembled as the truth dawned. With wisdom born too late to matter much now, she realized she had dismissed a healthy skepticism of the stranger who had used a collar and a gift for preaching to slip past her defenses. She no longer dismissed his attitude toward the boys who managed to escape and run away, any more than she could justify his trips to surrounding towns for supplies instead of coming to Trinity. His reluctance to place Will under Samuel's tutelage now took on ominous undertones. ·

"Hurry, Samuel! We haven't got a moment to lose," she urged. She feared she might be wrong, but she dreaded the greater possibility that she was right even more. After he got Will outside, she went back into the cabin, stuffed her slipper into her bag, and dragged the trunk with Samuel's treasures outside. "We need to hide this. Quickly. Where?"

Samuel looked down at her for several long moments before his clouded gaze brightened, as if he had the same thoughts that troubled her. "In the outhouse."

She set down her bag, dragged the trunk to the rear of the cabin, and stored it inside an outhouse that looked far too decrepit to be standing on its own. When she made her way back to Samuel, he nodded toward the path ahead. "I can take it slow and easy. Go on. Warn the others. I won't let no harm come to the boy."

She grabbed her bag and lifted her skirts with her other hand. "Take him to Dr. McMillan's and tell Rosalind to put Will in the guest chamber upstairs. I'll meet you there later," she cried before she raced toward the fire in the distance.

A host of emotions pounded through her veins with every beat of her galloping heart. Anger, betrayal, and outrage dueled with her fears while pride in Will's attempts to foil the nefarious plot against the people of Trinity kept her running long after the stitch in her side would have sent her to her knees. The blurry faces of the people she had trusted, in blind faith, jeered at her through her fears, but she had no time to waste on self-recrimination.

Not now.

Not when her home might be burning to the ground.

Once she reached the cemetery, her worst fears were confirmed.

The tavern was on fire. She paused to catch her breath and stared at the conflagration consuming the tavern her grandfather had built some sixty years ago. She could hear the shouts and cries of her friends and neighbors as they joined together to fight the fire set by either Reverend Hampton or one of the boys while the rest ransacked abandoned homes.

"James! Lydia!" she cried, and tossed her bag aside, praying her family, as well as the patrons in the tavern, had escaped. Concerned that the fire also posed a real threat to Grace and the other horses in the stable, she ran at full speed through the cemetery. When she reached East Main Street, the smoke was heavy enough to sting her eyes and ashes blew in her face. Straight ahead, men who were still dressed in formal clothes had formed a fire brigade and passed buckets of water up from Dillon's Stream. Some of the women, their fancy gowns now ruined, stood in groups holding children back a safe distance, while others were down at the banks of the stream filling buckets with water and passing them up to the men.

She ran up to Fern and Ivy, who were watching several small children. "James and Lydia? Are they safe?"

"Thank mercy! No one was certain you got out alive. James is frantic, but he got everyone else out and cleared the stables, too," Fern gushed.

"So is Lydia," Ivy added. "They're at Dr. McMillan's office, but they're not hurt. Only shaken," she assured her.

Martha closed her eyes and said a quick prayer of thanksgiving before panic struck again. "The diaries! I've got to get the diaries!"

When Ivy reached out to keep her from getting any closer, Martha shrugged free. "Tell James and Lydia I'm all right. Where's Sheriff Myer? Or Thomas?"

"Up ahead, but don't worry about the diaries," Fern admonished.

"Fern, please take the children home with you and lock your doors. Ivy, tell the other women to do the same. Find the sheriff and tell him, too. I don't have time to explain," she shouted before running toward the tavern. She prayed Ivy or the sheriff or Thomas or someone would warn the townspeople their unguarded homes were being robbed, even as she ran forward to save her precious diaries.

The smoke became a thick fog that made it hard for her to see or breathe. The heat from the fire was so strong she thought the sun itself had fallen from the sky and landed on top of the tavern. Flames licked through the roof of the building like orange fingers clawing at the sky. She cupped her hand over her mouth and rushed past the men fighting a losing battle with the blaze to the back of the tavern, ignoring the men who screamed at her to stop.

Her room was fully ablaze. The door was open, just far enough that she could see there was still time to save her diaries. Choking, she ran into her room and grabbed her diary as well as the daybook for Victoria. The covers were singed and hot to the touch, even with her gloves on, but she tossed them into a basket of sorts she created with the folds of her skirts. Her eyes were tearing so badly she could barely see. She got to the other side of the room only seconds before a large timber fell precisely where she had been standing. Sobbing in frustration, she finally found the smoldering box containing her grandmother's diary.

Without thinking beyond the possibility that the precious papers inside were still salvageable, she kicked the box to the door and outside. Struggling for fresh air, she lunged for the door, but not before burning bundles of her herbs fell like a wreath and encircled her bonnet.

Fighting to free herself, she dropped her diary and Victoria's daybook. She could feel the flames burning through her gloves as she dropped to her knees to search for her books. First one. Then the other. She shoved them outside and blindly crawled after them until a pair of strong arms lifted her off her hands and knees.

Thomas bellowed as he carried her to the back of the wagon yard. "You damn fool! You could have been killed!"

She wriggled free and dropped to her feet with a thud that shook her bones. Struggling to remove her smoldering gloves, she shouted back at him. "My diaries! I shoved them outside. I have to find them!"

When she started back toward the tavern, or what was left of it, he braced a hand on each of her shoulders. "For heaven's sake, stay here. I'll find them."

"I can't lose them. Not now! Let me—"

"Stay here! I'll get them." He tightened his hold. "The longer we argue, the greater the chance they'll be reduced to ashes," he warned.

She slumped her shoulders. "Just be careful. There are three, all told."

He left her standing there. When he returned moments later with her diary and the box with her grandmother's papers, he laid them at her feet. "The other book was on fire. I'm sorry," he murmured.

"Victoria's daybook," she whispered. Gone. Forever. Her disappointment was profound, but she still had room for some optimism. The fire might have claimed the daybook, but not the memories it contained or the wisdom she had found by making each entry. She could only pray Victoria would one day come home so they could share the memories together and create new ones.

With her most irreplaceable possessions at her feet, she quickly explained her suspicions about the academy to Thomas. "Tell the others before it's too late. Before . . . before . . ." The world around her began to swirl, and she caught his arm to keep from falling. The last thing she remembered before a wall of heavy silence fell and a curtain of darkness blanketed her world was the sound of the tavern roof caving in and the sight of her home being thoroughly consumed by flames.

The pain that pulled Martha from her sleep was centered in her fingertips. When she opened her eyes, she found a familiar pair of dark eyes staring back at her.

Will grinned. "Thought you mighta died."

She moistened her lips. "I might have said the same to you when Samuel brought me back to his cabin to care for you," she croaked.

Was that raspy sound really her voice?

When she tried to sit up, Will urged her back down with a gentle shove. "Dr. McMillan said you gotta lie still. Just till he comes to check you. I'll tell him you're awake."

When he turned to leave, she pulled him back. Wincing, she dropped her hold and noticed the bandages on her hand. Both hands, she realized, when she tugged her other hand free from beneath the covers. "Wait. Tell me what . . . what day is it?"

He eyed her suspiciously. "Monday. Why?"

"Monday?" Had she really slept for two days?

He nodded and dropped his gaze. "Guess I got here too late."

"Too late to warn us?" she asked, hoping to confirm her assumption that Will had refused to participate in looting the town.

He nodded again.

"Then I was right," she murmured, although being right brought her little joy or satisfaction. "Did they take much of value?"

"Lotsa stuff." When he lifted his gaze, his eyes lit with subdued excitement. "Didn't get the treasures, though. Samuel told me where you hid them."

"Did they catch anyone?"

He shook his head. "Naw. Reverend Hampton had a couple of rafts waitin' just south of town. Floated right down Dillon's Stream to Clarion, then probably had everything in the ship before anyone suspected much of anything."

She let out a long sigh. Being right about Reverend Hampton's evil intentions, albeit belatedly, offered little consolation now. She was still confused about Olympia's role in the whole affair, but she did not have the energy right now to consider why a woman would be so devoted to her husband she would follow him in a life mired in sin and deceit. In point of fact, she had encountered more than a few women who put their own lives, if not their souls, in danger in order to please their spouses. Perhaps Olympia Hampton was just one of those women, instead of a wicked woman who took pleasure in her husband's evil endeavors. She liked to think so, anyway.

Martha's mind was nearly numb now and clogged with too many

other troubling thoughts, save one that branded her guilty at being caught in Reverend Hampton's net. "I guess you weren't the only one who was too late."

"Sheriff Myer came for me this morning, but Dr. McMillan sent him away. He'll be back, though." He cocked his head. "Think you might talk to him for me? I got here late, but I tried. I really tried to help."

"You were very brave and loyal, in the end, but you do have some explaining to do," she insisted. "Once the sheriff knows how hard you tried, I'm certain he'll let you stay."

"With Samuel?" he asked, his expression hopeful.

"I don't know," she admitted. "You also owe me a pair of new slippers, young man. I expect you to work off the debt."

He blushed, and the color in his cheeks added an odd look to his already bruised features. "Reverend Hampton said I had to prove I could sneak into somebody's house and steal somethin' without gettin' caught. I knew you wouldn't do nothin' if you caught me," he murmured before his lips shaped an irascible grin.

"Oh, you did, did you? Pray tell, why wouldn't I do anything if I caught you stealing?"

He squared his shoulders. " 'Cause you'd believe me when I told you I was only stealin' 'cause he said I had to."

When Dr. McMillan entered the room, Will took a step back from Martha's bed.

"I thought I heard voices," the doctor said. He looked at Will and frowned. "Didn't I ask you to tell me when Widow Cade woke up?"

Will rolled his eyes. "She just did. We had somethin' important to discuss first."

"Sir. We had something important to discuss first, *sir*."

Will rolled his eyes again. "We had somethin' important to discuss first, sir."

"That's better. Now, head downstairs. Slowly. Mrs. Andrews has some supper waiting. Eat first. Then I want you to head out to the stable and clean Grace's stall. I need to change the dressings on Widow Cade's hands."

Will eased out of the room, and Dr. McMillan shut the door. Although his color was good, he still bore a few scabs on his cheeks and several scars were visible. "I still can't believe how quickly children can heal. Stubborn women take much longer," he admonished.

She ignored his taunt and studied her burns after he removed the bandages. Quite miraculously, the damage done by the fire was not as extensive as she had feared, although she had a number of angry blisters on the palms of both hands and several fingers. "I thought this would be worse," she admitted as she flexed her fingers.

"The miracle of modern medicine," he explained. He covered her hands with a pale yellow ointment and wrapped them again. "I won't bore you with the details about the ingredients, but this ointment is relatively new. Heals burns much faster than butter, which is what I suspect you'd have used."

She sniffed. "Actually, I prefer lily-of-the-valley."

"An antiquated home remedy, but not entirely without merit," he admitted.

"I assume this . . . this ointment is rather expensive," she ventured, reluctant to admit his treatment was probably superior to anything she might have used.

"Very. As a matter of fact, it's far too expensive for your purse."

She laughed sardonically. "My reticule, no doubt, is long reduced to ashes, along with my simples and . . . and my birthing stool," she murmured. Tears misted her eyes. She had completely forgotten about the collapsible stool Grandmother Poore had brought with her all the way from Maine.

"I have your stool downstairs, along with your treatment bag, which Samuel left here," he assured her. "Your sister-in-law saved your birthing stool from the fire for you. It's an interesting design. Somewhat archaic for today's use—"

"Archaic?" She pulled her hands free and narrowed her gaze.

He held up his hands and grinned at her. "I was only teasing."

"I don't find you amusing at all. Fairly competent and earnest. Even decent. But you have a lot to learn, young man. Or unlearn," she added.

He raised one brow. "I have plenty of room here. You could convert one of the treatment rooms into an office. I don't suppose you'd consider the offer, in exchange, perhaps, for sharing some of your treatments and showing me how they work?"

Her eyes widened, but she rejected his offer without giving it more than a heartbeat of thought. "Certainly not! I have my own duties, which keep me quite busy, and my own methods, which have been passed down to the women in my family for generations. I'll not squander that knowledge by sharing it with someone bound and determined to put me out to pasture like a . . . like a broken-down mule too decrepit to earn his keep."

She ignored the disappointment that laced his entire expression. There was no way, in this lifetime or any other, that she would help him learn enough to replace her. Never. He would simply have to muddle through on his own. After all, he had a wall full of diplomas and university training. Let that suffice.

Amen.

Chapter
THIRTY-THREE

Shock and grief numbed Martha's soul and tempered her anger so that only despair remained.

With James and Lydia by her side, Martha stood in front of the charred shell that once had been Poore's Tavern. Only the front wall remained. Through the doorway, she could see clear past the rubble to the scorched stable and the wagon yard, now littered with debris.

"It's a total loss," James whispered. His voice was still hoarse from fighting the fire. "Everything we owned is gone, except for the horse and wagon and the land."

She swallowed hard and fussed with the skirts of her gown. "What are you going to do?" she asked, wondering if he would use this disaster as an opportunity to fulfill his dream and settle along Candle Lake.

His shoulders sagged, and he clasped Lydia's hand. "I'm too old to start over. Even if I did have the funds to rebuild, I'm not sure I want to."

"We're going to Sunrise to say with Clara for a spell," Lydia murmured. "Come with us, Martha. At least until we decide what's best."

Martha dropped her gaze. Leaving Trinity and living with her niece was not an option that appealed to her. "I need to stay here."

"Where?" Lydia asked.

Martha swiped at her tears with her bandaged hands and stared at the destruction before her. Accepting Dr. McMillan's offer to remain at his home was another option she dismissed. Again. Aunt Hilda would probably welcome Martha into her small home, but she hesitated to impose on someone so elderly. "I don't know. I'll talk to Fern and Ivy. They might let me stay with them until . . . until you decide whether or not you're going to rebuild the tavern."

"And if we don't?" James asked.

"Then I'll think of something more permanent."

When he looked at her, his gaze was troubled. "You're always welcome, wherever we settle. You know that."

She smiled. "Thank you, James. I do. But my work is here. My life is here. I can't simply abandon all the people who depend on me, and I can't leave Trinity, especially not now. What if Victoria comes home? How will she know where to find me?"

Fear raised her voice to a shrill pitch. "I can't go. Not without Victoria."

He put his arm around her shoulders and pulled her close. "Victoria knows you'd be with family, and folks here would know where to send her to find you."

She pulled away and squared her shoulders. "No. I'm staying here. When . . . when did you plan to leave?"

"First thing in the morning. Sleep on it, Martha. You can still change your mind and leave with us. We want you to come," Lydia urged.

Martha took in a deep breath, swallowed the lump in her throat, and smiled through her tears. "I'd like to see you off. Right now, I think I should go to see Fern and Ivy."

Lydia nodded. "We're still staying with Reverend Welsh. If you change your mind today . . ."

"I'll see you in the morning," Martha responded. "Don't worry. I'm sure God has His own plan in mind. For all of us." She turned and walked away. Her steps were a bit unsteady. Her mind was awash with a thousand questions about her future, and her spirit was too burdened with disappointment to hand her troubles over to Him.

She had rebuilt her life more than once. She would simply do it again. With grit and hard work, she would dig out of the ruins of her life and start over. One step at a time.

As she walked down West Main Street toward the confectionery, townspeople stopped to wave across the way. Their expressions were sober and sympathetic, but their concern did little to assuage her grief or mitigate the guilt she carried for having staunchly defended the academy.

She entered the confectionery, but barely managed to take more than a few steps inside the door when she had to stop immediately or run smack into the packages Thomas held in front of him.

Fortunately, he managed to avoid disaster with a quick sidestep.

She clapped her hand to her chest and felt her heart pounding beneath her fingertips. "I'm so sorry," she gushed. Her cheeks grew hot, and she did not have to look in a mirror to know they were probably cherry-red.

He chuckled and held the packages off to the side. "Not as sorry as I would have been when I had to go home and explain to my daughter how I managed to drop the very last strudel and she had to settle for something else."

Despite the jovial words he used, his gaze was uncommonly clouded with trouble. He usually kept such things hidden from the rest of the world. She had not seen him at all since he rescued her treasured diaries from the fire and sensed he was suffering a private tragedy of his own. "I'm . . . I'm sorry the fire ruined your party. I don't remember everything from the other night, but I hope I remembered to thank you properly for saving my diaries."

"Indeed, you did, but I was more concerned you might have sustained injuries far worse than did your diaries. As for the party..." He cleared his throat. "I'm tempted to think the fire was actually a blessing that eventually saved me from making a terrible mistake." He looked at her and shook her head. "You're probably the only woman alive who might not berate me for being insensitive by finding some sort of blessing for myself in a tragedy that spelled disaster for her and her family."

She moistened her lips and swallowed hard. "I'm not sure I can grant you that," she managed. "At least not right now, when I've yet to find a place to live. I take it you've decided against marrying Samantha?"

His cheeks actually reddened, and his smile was decidedly sheepish. "Actually... well, the truth is that Samantha decided I was a lout for suggesting she help the other women in the fire line and changed her mind about accepting my proposal. That was the first time I realized what a selfish child she is, even though Eleanor never seemed to miss an opportunity to tell me so often before that night."

Martha caught her lower lip to keep it from smiling back at him. "She's beautiful enough to turn any man's head, Thomas. Don't be too hard on yourself. At least the fire broke out before you had a chance to formally announce your betrothal," she murmured, remembering a different time and a different place when it was she who had refused his suit.

When he gave her a smile that hinted he might be sharing her private thoughts, she smiled back. "The rumors about your impending betrothal now can remain just that. Rumors. Eventually, they'll die down. They always do."

He gazed at her with such tenderness and yearning, she found it difficult to breathe or to think about the bonds they had shared— bonds that still beckoned and tempted her beyond all reason. Fortunately, the sound of approaching footsteps broke the spell, and Thomas quickly took his leave before Fern and Ivy entered the room through the kitchen door.

They ushered her straight to the kitchen and doted on her like a pair of mother hens.

"You poor, poor dear. Come. Sit down," Ivy clucked.

Martha took a seat at the table.

"You need a chocolate tart," Fern said, setting one in front of her.

Martha held up her hands and wanted to cry. "I don't think I can manage."

Fern held up her hand. "Wait. This should help." She cut the tart into small pieces and handed Martha a spoon.

The first spoonful was heavenly. So was the last.

"Have another," Fern urged. "Chocolate again or apple?"

"Apple this time."

She polished that one off, too. "I came to ask for a favor, not eat my way through your shop," she confessed.

The two sisters answered simultaneously.

"Anything."

"We'll help you, of course."

Martha licked the last bit of sugar from her lips. "I need a place to stay. Just temporarily, until James decides whether or not to rebuild the tavern. If he does, then it may be months before the new one is finished, especially with winter here. If he doesn't, then—"

"We have two extra rooms. You can choose whichever one you like best," Fern assured her.

Ivy nodded approvingly. "And all the sweets you want, too."

Martha felt her heart constrict. "I'd try not to bother you, but I do get calls in the middle of the night."

"We wouldn't mind, would we, Fern?"

"Not in the least."

"I'll be away quite a bit, too, for deliveries. If Victoria should come back and find the tavern in ruins . . ."

Fern winked. "Then we'll just keep her right here until you get back."

Martha's throat tightened as she fought off tears. "I don't know how to thank you. If it's all right, I'd like to move in tomorrow after James and Lydia leave. I'll . . . I'll give you a share of my rewards, just like I did with James."

Ivy sniffed. "Nonsense. With all you've lost, you'll need every bit you earn. Come. I'll show you the rooms. Fern, see if you can't find some undergarments and gowns in the attic that would fit Martha." She looked at Martha's bedraggled gown and giggled. "This one's a mess."

Martha looked down at her skirts and would have chuckled, too, if she had not been on the verge of tears already. She followed the sisters upstairs. At least now she had a place to stay. It was not much, compared to what she'd had just a week before, but it was a beginning.

Martha crawled into bed, thought about saying her prayers, and snuggled under the covers. The disappointment that had been simmering all day and fueled her determination to remain in Trinity grew into flames of anger that kept her from praying.

She closed her eyes and pursed her lips, but the throbbing in her hands did not lessen, either. "Forgive me for not praying tonight," she whispered. "I'm not in the mood. And this is one gift You could have spared me, if You don't mind my saying so."

Tears welled. Unbidden. Unwelcome. "I'll fix this myself."

Will you?

Startled, she held very still. "Of course I will. I always do," she snapped. Horrified because she had spoken so sharply, on the unlikely chance the voice she heard in her mind was not her conscience but the voice of God, she let out a sigh. The notion that God would speak to her was almost blasphemous, and she hoped this odd soliloquy would be forgiven. "I'm not able to think straight right now. I'm upset."

And angry?

"Yes, I'm angry," she admitted, hoping to quiet her conscience so she could get some sleep. "Haven't I suffered enough? Look at my hands. They're useless now and will be for weeks. I'm so helpless I can't even dress myself, not that I have a single gown of my own left that isn't ripped or charred. Not that You care."

Very angry.

"Very. I've lost my daughter, who is traipsing around somewhere all alone. I've lost my home. My brother is leaving in the morning, so I'll be left here all alone with no family. But I'll manage on my own, thank You very much. I will," she insisted.

With her room at the Lynn sisters', she would still be in Trinity if Victoria came home, and her patients would be able to find her quite easily. The fact that she might eat herself into sweet oblivion by living at the confectionery was only a minor problem compared to the troubles she would face by accepting Dr. McMillan's outlandish proposal.

Help him.

Her eyes snapped open, and she stared at the darkness that surrounded her. Her heart began to gallop in her chest. "Help Dr. McMillan? That's absolutely ridiculous. Out of the question," she muttered. "I'm a midwife. He's a doctor. Trying to work together would be like mixing oil and water. You can't expect me to spend my time teaching him to be a better physician all by myself any more than You can make me believe this . . . this disaster can be turned into some kind of miracle."

Like changing water into wine?

"Precisely," she grumbled. "But . . . but I can't help him. I won't. This is asking too much. I must be delirious," she whimpered, certain she must be desperately ill to be hearing voices. She tugged off one of her bandages and felt her forehead. She could not detect any sign of fever, and slammed her eyes shut. She tossed and turned, but found no peace. No rest. No sleep. No assurances, either, as she battled her deepest fears. As her conversation with Rosalind just the other day replayed in her mind, she realized, among other things, she was a hypocrite of the first order if she did not follow her own advice and accept His will instead of forcing her own.

"Pray. I need to pray." She crawled out of bed and dropped to her knees. Sobbing, she emptied her heart and let her faith wash over her anger and disappointment. When she was done, when she was too limp to kneel without leaning against the side of the bed for support, she bowed her head and surrendered her will to His. "I can't do this alone," she whispered.

I am with you. Always.

Peace. Sweet, healing peace invaded her very spirit, extinguishing all fear and doubt, as well as anger. She sniffled and wiped the tears from her face. When she crawled back into bed, she fell asleep almost immediately.

Half the town turned out to bid James and Lydia farewell the following morning. Men, women, and children gathered on the planked sidewalk along West Main Street, waving and calling out good wishes as James and Lydia rode slowly by the homes and businesses. The back of the wagon nearly overflowed with trunks of donated clothing and barrels and baskets of foodstuffs.

Martha walked alongside the wagon with the memory of their private farewell tucked next to her heart. Still, the prospect of seeing them disappear from view lay heavy on her spirit. James slowed the wagon to a halt when Webster Cabbot stepped out from the crowd and approached them. He handed James a pair of ivory-handled pistols. "Don't expect you'll have much use for these yourself, but they'll bring a good value at trade. Enough to help you get started again."

James swallowed a visible lump in his throat. "I'm obliged to you, Webster," he managed, and set the pistols behind him.

Cabbot nodded, then looked directly at Martha. "I gave a pair to young Sweet at the general store to credit to your account," he informed her, turned, and strode back into his shop.

Stunned, Martha barely had the wherewithal to follow along when James started the wagon forward again.

"We'll get that rubble cleared away in no time," one man shouted.

James smiled in reply.

Lydia moved closer to her husband. Weeping openly, she kept her gaze on the roadway ahead.

Each step Martha took was harder than the last. With fresh tears of her own threatening, she was anxious to bring this town-wide farewell to an end before she broke down in front of anyone. If her friends and neighbors learned she was planning to be a mentor, of sorts, to Dr. McMillan, folks would suspect she had become distracted. Blubbering in front of them now would only make that suspicion seem more likely.

When Wesley Sweet ran out of the general store and hailed down the wagon, she nearly cried out in frustration. Why couldn't everyone just let James and Lydia leave?

Panting, he held on to the horse's bridle. "Sorry. Don't mean to hold you up, but I just found this." He held out a letter. "It was stuck to one for . . . well, that doesn't matter. What's important is that I found it in time. No charge. It's my fault it's been held up."

Martha took the letter and handed it to James.

Wesley opened his mouth to speak, but James spoke first as he handed her back the letter. "It's not my letter. It's yours, Martha. It's addressed to you. Best open it before we leave."

She stared at the familiar scrawl and her heart skipped a beat. With her hands still bandaged, she was afraid to try to open it for fear of ripping the letter. She handed it back to James, almost too excited to breathe. "Open it for me. Hurry!"

He unsealed the letter, and she grabbed it back. She read the short missive twice before a flood of tears made it impossible to see a single precious word.

"It's from Victoria. She's coming home. She's coming home!" she cried before she dissolved into tears. Her knees grew weak, but strong arms suddenly appeared and held her upright—arms with a strength and familiarity that echoed from long ago.

She wiped her tears away and looked up. Thomas's gentle gaze locked with her own. His eyes glistened with an unspoken but heart-felt promise that the future held long-awaited fulfillment and love, if each of them had the will and the courage to fight for it.

Overwhelmed, she reached up and cupped the side of his face. "She's coming home, Thomas. She's coming home," she whispered.

As the echo of her announcement rippled through the crowd, a round of applause began slowly, then built into a crescendo replete with whistles and cheers for a daughter of Trinity who was finally coming home.

Overwhelmed, Martha let herself relax in Thomas's strong embrace, but she offered to Him all the accolades from the crowd for the wonderful news of Victoria's impending homecoming—and for leading her through life's greatest troubles, for knowing the deepest secrets of her heart as well as her faults, and for loving her. Still.

Author's Note

Modern midwifery has made significant advances since the nineteenth century. Readers who are interested in modern midwifery techniques and their advantages are encouraged to refer to contemporary literature for information and advice rather than applying any historical midwifery practices explored in this novel. They are also advised to contact their physicians and modern-day midwives. Any decisions readers make regarding pregnancy and labor/delivery should be based on sound, professional, up-to-date information.

The interest in alternative medicine, which includes herbal supplements and/or treatments, has grown enormously in the past few decades. The treatments used in this novel are historically accurate, but they are not suggested for modern use; instead, readers should combine research of contemporary herbal medications with standard medical advice from their physicians and other trained health-care providers.

I hope *A Place Called Trinity* will place midwifery and herbal treatments in historical perspective. Not only can this help explain the evolution of modern medical practice and treatments, but it can help to document the active participation of our foremothers—women who safely guided our ancestors into this world and comforted and treated them when they became ill.

God bless.

READING GROUP GUIDE

1. Though *A Place Called Trinity* is set in 1833, did you find any modern echoes in the way the characters behaved? What are some examples?

2. How did you feel about Martha's desire to have her daughter follow in her footsteps and become a midwife?

3. Did you understand why Martha's daughter would leave home?

4. *A Place Called Trinity* often illustrates the clash between "modern" medicine and traditional medicine. Do you feel that clash still exists today? How?

5. How did Martha's faith help her through her trials?

6. When did you feel Martha's faith in God waiver the most? Under the same circumstances, how would you react?

7. Did you feel Martha had to choose between her career and her family? Do women still have to face or confront these same issues today? How is it different?

8. Why do you think Martha Cade never remarried?

For more reading group suggestions visit
www.stmartins.com

Get a
Griffin St. Martin's Griffin

Return to Trinity...

Midwife Martha Cade may be reunited with her estranged daughter, but now she must walk the fine line between guiding her into adulthood and letting her grow up on her own.

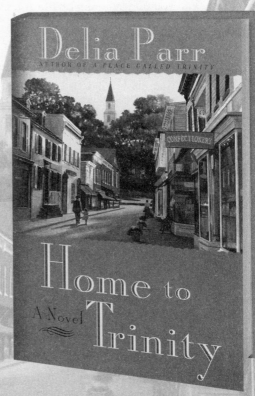

"There is a freshness to [Parr's] writing, almost an innocence...[it] will bring comfort to its readers and leave them deeply satisfied."

—John Medlicott, author of *The Gardens of Covington*